FIGHTING FOR YOU

FIGHTING FOR YOU

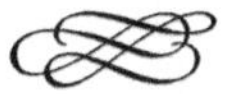

MONICA MURPHY

PLAYLIST

"SOMETHING FOR NOTHING" -
Cautious Clay
"Fire for You" - Cannons
"Feel It All Around" - Washed Out
"suburban wonderland" - BETWEEN FRIENDS
"You & Me" - Marc E. Bassy, G-Eazy
"Pursuit of Happiness" - Kid Cudi, MGMT, Ratatat
"Dissolve" - Absofacto
"Easily" - Bruno Major
"Saved" - Khalid
"Therefore I Am" - Billie Eilish

Find the rest of the **FIGHTING FOR YOU** Spotify playlist
here:
https://bit.ly/FFYplaylist

THE PAST

DIEGO

"Hey loser." My big brother Mateo nudges me hard in the ribs, sending me stumbling forward. Lucky enough, I catch myself before I fall. "I dare you to go tell Marty he's a homo."

All of Mateo's friends crack up the moment he makes the dare, and he laughs too, the loudest one of all.

I frown, glancing over at where my cousin Marty is playing with all of our girl cousins. He's laughing and having a good time, and I don't want to go over there and call him a homo. He might tell. And my Aunt Lisa—his mama—she can be mean.

Besides, who cares if he's gay? It doesn't matter to me.

It's my brother's birthday party. He just turned fifteen, and most of our family is here to celebrate, along with his friends. Mateo complained about having a party with the family, calling it kid stuff, but Mom wouldn't hear of it. She's always looking for an excuse for the family to get together.

Mateo was mad that he didn't have a choice. It didn't matter that Mom let him have as many friends over as he wanted. It didn't matter that she bought him two video games that he wanted instead of just one. He didn't get his way, so he'd show her.

He and his friends have been stealing beers out of the ice chest all afternoon, sneaking off and drinking them in his room. I can smell the beer on his breath right now, and I would never say it out loud, but knowing he's a little drunk scares me.

Alcohol makes my big brother meaner. And he's already mean enough.

All of the adults at the party are oblivious to Mateo and his friends stealing the beers. Mom's having too much fun hanging out with her sister. They're drinking and laughing, having a good time. It makes me happy to see her like that. She's always so sad, or mad. Angry with Mateo.

Angry with me.

"Please tell me you're not a little chicken shit," Mateo snarls and I jerk my gaze to his, staring at him.

He stares back, until I'm the one who looks away first. I'm always the one who does that.

Marty is my age. We're eleven, and in the fifth grade. And while Marty has never come right out and said it, we're all pretty sure...

He's gay.

"Are you going to tell him he's a homo or not?" Mateo asks, his rough voice jolting me out of my thoughts.

I glare at him, realizing quickly all of his friends draw in closer, until they've formed a tight circle around me. It's me against them.

And I'm going to lose.

"Why don't you do it?" I toss at my brother, stalling for time. My stomach hurts. I don't like calling people names, or causing problems, especially at family parties. But Mateo has been pushing me a lot lately. Daring me to say things. Do things. I stole a soda from the grocery store for him last week. He said he would beat me up if I didn't, and I thought if I could catch a break for at least a couple of days, it was worth it to steal.

I was scared the whole time I snuck that Pepsi in my jacket, afraid I'd get caught, but I didn't.

"I dared you first, asshole. Think of it as your birthday gift to me." Mateo smiles, his eyes dark and a shiver moves through me. He looks hard. Almost...

Evil.

"Go. Do it." He grips my shoulders and forcefully turns me around. His friends part without a word and Mateo shoves me. Hard. "And since you're being such a pussy about it, now you get to tell him he likes to suck dick."

I frown, glancing over my shoulder at the boy I idolize more than anyone else in this world. I don't want him mad at me. I hate it when he's like this.

I just want him to like me.

"Go on." Mateo waves his hands, like he's shooing a pesky animal away. "I triple dog dare you, you little pussy ass."

His words, and his friends' laughter, spur me on. Determination sets in my shoulders and I stalk over to where Marty is with the girls. He's telling them a story, his words and gestures exaggerated and they're all laughing at him, and he's laughing too. I catch a little bit of what he's saying, and I think it's funny. I even smile.

But then I remember what my brother said, and my smile fades. If Marty really is gay, then that means he likes to suck dick, and that's disgusting.

Marty notices me standing near them and he smiles, waving his hand. "Diego! Come here!"

"No," I tell him defiantly, my voice hard.

I sound exactly like my brother, and the realization makes me stand a little taller.

Marty frowns. "What's wrong with you?"

We've always been close. Like I said, we're the same age. We've been in the same classes together at school. We used to have the same friend group, but as we get older, we've drifted apart. I don't think I want to hang out with him anymore if he's gay. Mateo's told me that before. He said if I spend too much time with Marty, I might end up gay like him.

I don't want to be like Marty. I want to be like Mateo.

"Diego," Marty says. He's still laughing. He has no idea what's about to happen. "Let's go get some cake."

"No way. I can't hang out with you anymore. You like to suck dicks," I tell him, freezing the moment the words leave me.

Marty's mouth pops open, his brown eyes going wide with shock. He's shorter than me, and super skinny. My mom says my Aunt Lisa needs to fatten him up.

"What did you just say?" Marty asks when he finds his voice. It's trembling.

He's trembling.

"You like to suck dick. Because you're gay." I spit the last word out like it's a curse. "Have fun sucking dicks!"

Before I can apologize or stare at Marty's crumpled face any longer, I turn and run to my brother and his friends. My chest is tight. My eyes sting. That was…

That was awful.

"You did it! We could hear you all the way over here!" Mateo says when I rejoin them. He holds his hand up for a high five and I slap my palm to his, pleasure coursing through me at his obvious approval. His friends all give me high fives too, and I'm standing in the center of them once more, though this time I'm not scared.

I finally feel like I belong.

"Didn't think you had it in you," Mateo says, his hand clamping around my shoulder. I tense up for a moment, like I always do, but I realize he's giving me a friendly shake instead of a mean shove. "Good job, little man. Keep that shit up."

That's all it takes, I realize, to earn my brother's approval. I act like him, and he likes me. And that's all I want.

Is for my big brother to like me.

THAT NIGHT...

JOCELYN

"Come on."

His voice is urgent, with a hint of demanding in it. That's how he's been operating lately, and most of the time I don't mind.

Like now.

I take his offered hand and he links our fingers together, whisking me out of Tony's house through the back door and into the still warm night.

"Where are we going?" We're wandering through Tony's large back yard, passing people we know. I nod and smile, but don't really say anything. I'm too keyed up, too excited. The football team won tonight, which means my boyfriend is in a great mood. His good moods are hard to come by lately, and I'd give anything to keep him happy tonight.

Anything.

"I think his back yard is as big as my entire neighborhood," Diego mutters, and I silently agree.

Tony Sorrento's house is a freaking mansion that sits directly on the lake. My father's a lawyer, so we're pretty well-to-do, but our house isn't nearly as opulent as this one.

There are so many rooms, I get lost every time I go in there. And it's only Tony and his mother who live there.

What's sad is, most of the time, Tony is completely alone. His parents divorced a few years ago, and his dad moved out. He lives in San Francisco now. Or Los Angeles—I can never remember. His mother is never around. She's constantly going out of town. I think that's why Tony has so many parties.

He's lonely.

"Let's check out Tony's guesthouse." The wicked grin Diego flashes at me from over his shoulder makes my stomach bottom out. And not in a bad way.

In a very, very good way.

"Diego." I come to a stop and so does he, a questioning look on his too handsome face. "Are you suggesting what I think you're suggesting?"

He nods, hope and expectation written all over him. "When do you have to be home?"

I grab my phone out of the back pocket of my denim shorts and check the time. "Midnight. We have maybe an hour before you need to take me there."

"Thank God you don't live too far from here. We can get a lot done in an hour." He waggles his dark brows at me, making me giggle, and then he smothers my laughter with a heated kiss.

We only come up for air when we hear voices nearby, and then Diego's leading me toward the lakeshore, where the tiny one-room cabin/guesthouse sits. It's owned by the Sorrento family, and it sits unoccupied most of the time.

"I called dibs on this place," Diego tells me when we stop in front of the closed door. He rises up on tiptoe and feels around the top of the doorframe, a triumphant "aha" leaving him when he shows me the key he discovered. "Someone else always gets it first. But tonight, it's ours."

I'm a little skeeved out that the guys call dibs on this cabin so they can mess around with girls privately, but I can't complain. Diego and I only recently started having sex. We've done plenty of other things, but mostly in a car. Or sometimes even outside. It's hard to find somewhere to be together, completely alone. Forget about getting comfortable, or even taking off all of our clothes. It's always hurried between us, with that nagging worry we might get caught.

His house is small and he lives in one of the older neighborhoods in the area. I think he might be ashamed of it, which is why we don't spend a lot of time there. I've only been there a handful of times, even though I get along great with his slightly overbearing mother.

And my house? It's never empty. Mom is always there. Or one of my siblings. I get no alone time.

None.

Excitement ripples over my skin when Diego opens the cabin door and we walk inside. There's a couch and a bed. That's it. Oh and there's an end table next to the couch with a lamp on it. Diego lets go of my hand and walks over to the table, switching on the lamp and illuminating the room in a pale-yellow glow.

"Not bad," he says as he glances around the space. He rests his hands on his hips, his gaze meeting mine. "What do you think?"

"It's small." But it looks clean. "Do you think they wash the sheets?"

"Probably. The asshole has servants at his every beck and call." Diego pulls me back into his arms, holding me close. So close, I can feel every inch of him. And he can feel every inch of me. "Who cares?"

"I kind of do," I say, just as he leans in and presses his full mouth against my neck, making me forget all my worries at the first touch of his lips. I close my eyes as he continues to kiss me, immediately lost in the path his mouth takes on my skin. "Don't—don't you care?"

"I only care about you," he murmurs against my throat, making me shiver. "If you're not comfortable with the bed, we can take this to the couch."

I open my eyes, gazing at the leather couch nearby. "Uh, no."

He laughs and pulls away from me, keeping my hand in his. "Then let's go to the bed."

I let him lead me there, and we both fall onto the mattress, reaching for each other, our mouths seeking. Finding.

Locking.

We kiss for what feels like forever, and again, I lose myself in him. His taste, the stroke of his tongue, the things he whispers to me. How good I make him feel. How much he misses me. How much he *needs* me.

His words are heady. Sometimes even overwhelming. He wants so much. *Needs* so much. Sometimes, like tonight, he calls me his angel. His savior.

I don't know if I can save him, but I want to try.

We've been arguing lately, but kissing seems to make us forget why we were mad at each other in the first place. His hands start to wander and I lean into his touch, too nervous still to ask for what I want. His fingers drift across my stomach and I imagine those fingers in other places. The throb starts low, steadily insistent and when he reaches for the snap of my shorts, I settle my hand over his, stopping him.

"Not yet," I whisper, afraid he might get ahead of himself and it'll be over before we even truly started.

He doesn't protest or act mad, which he does sometimes. Instead, he reaches for my shirt, and I help him pull it off of me. He gets on his knees, rising above me on the mattress, his gaze scorching as he drinks me in.

"Fucking beautiful," he breathes, the look on his face, the reverence in his voice making me ache.

He loves me. So much.

I reach between my breasts and undo the snap, the bra cups springing away from my skin. He leans in, gently pushing them away, his fingers brushing against my skin, making me gasp. Without warning his mouth is on me, his lips wrapped around a nipple, drawing it deep into his mouth. The ache intensifies, making me squirm, and when he moves to my other breast, I sink my fingers into his thick hair, holding him to me.

I wouldn't mind if he did this for the entire hour. Kissing me all over. He's pretty good at it. He's gone down on me a few times, and the first time was kind of awkward, but it's gotten better. To the point where I almost prefer it to actual sex.

He has a really talented tongue.

I watch as Diego whips his shirt off, ruffling his hair when he jerks the shirt over his head almost violently. His chest rises and falls at a rapid pace, as if he just ran clear across the football field. He rubs his hand across the front of his shorts, a wince on his face when he touches his erection.

It's fascinating, how he handles himself. Almost…roughly. He catches me watching, his lips forming into that arrogant smirk he wears so often. The one that masks all the insecurity and pain that he carries within him.

Diego is all bravado. Deep down, he's a scared little boy who's afraid he'll never measure up.

"You like watching?"

Maybe I should be embarrassed he asked that question, but I'm not. "Yes," I say truthfully.

"Want me to get naked so you can really see something?"

I nod, my heart rate speeding up. We have the time and I'm curious to see him in all his naked glory.

Without hesitation he hops off the bed, shedding the rest of his clothes in seconds. Until he's magnificently naked, crawling back onto the bed, rising on his knees once again. I spread my legs, accommodating him as he scoots closer, and his hand automatically goes to his erection, long fingers gripping the base.

"This is all for you," he says, his voice full of promise as he starts to stroke.

I have no other boy to compare him to, but I'm fairly certain he doesn't lack in the penis department. He's long. The first time we did it, it hurt. And he was sloppy. He pumped inside me maybe twice—or was it three times?—and then he came.

All in all, it was a complete disappointment. Not that I would ever tell him that.

It's gotten better between us lately. Sad that our actual relationship is suffering a little bit, but the sex is good. Maybe we're using it as a band-aid. I don't know. I love him. I want to show him that I love him, but sometimes, he makes it really difficult.

This time when he reaches for the snap on my denim shorts, I don't stop him. I help him get rid of them, though I leave my panties on. He strokes me there, over the thin fabric, touching me with purpose.

"Soaked," he murmurs, sounding pleased, his fingers sneaking beneath my panties, touching my bare flesh. "Fuck, Jos, I don't know how much longer I can wait."

I want to ask him to go down on me, but the words don't come. Instead, I arch into his hand, lifting my hips, a little whimper sounding when he touches me in a particular spot. I haven't orgasmed yet when we've had actual sex, and I want to so badly. I've realized quickly I need lots of foreplay, and sometimes Diego is patient.

And sometimes, he's not.

He continues stroking me, his thumb slipping over my clit, back and forth. Circling it. I push my panties down past my hips, and he helps me until I'm kicking them off, and now we're both completely naked. He returns his attention to my breasts, sucking my nipples, licking his way down my stomach.

Oh God. His mouth is getting closer to where I want him. My breath catches in my throat when his face is right there, and when he licks me, a ragged groan leaves me.

"You like that," he says, just before he licks me again.

"I love it," I say on a sigh, a wave of pleasure washing over me when he slips his finger inside my body. His mouth on me plus his fingers inside me? I'm already close to coming. It didn't take much time tonight, and I hope he keeps it up. If he stops now, I'm going to—

Diego stops, lifting his head to look at me. His lips are glossy with my juices and he runs his tongue across his upper lip, as if he's savoring the taste of me. "Want me to keep going?"

I want to kill him. Why would he stop now? I was so close. "Yes," I say through gritted teeth and he laughs.

Like he knows exactly what he's doing, though I don't know if he's that smart. I'm not insulting him. We're only seventeen. We still kind of don't know what we're doing in the sex department.

He experiments on me. Licking faster. Slower. Circling his tongue around my clit, pressing his tongue flat against my flesh. He adds another finger. Sucks my clit between his lips, and it feels so overwhelmingly good. I finally find the courage to give him direction, and he takes it.

"Faster," I whisper and he speeds up.

"Oh, right there," and he listens, staying at that one spot, lavishing all of his attention where I want it.

"Right—please. Oh *God.*" I'm overcome. As in, I'm coming. Sounds are leaving me, but they're not quite words. I'm not making any sense. And it's okay. I'm moaning. Thrashing about, and Diego grabs hold of my hips, keeping me in place as he continues to torture me with his mouth.

"Fuck," he breathes when he finally moves away from my body, his dark eyes hooded, his lips parted as he gazes at me as if I'm the prettiest girl he's ever seen. "You need to come like that more often."

I need to come more often in general, but I don't say that. Our satisfying sexual encounters lately have been a little one-sided. But not tonight.

Tonight I'm satiated. I feel downright lazy. Sleepy even. I watch as he positions himself in front of me, his erection in one hand as he leans over and props his other hand on the mattress beside my head. He brushes the tip against me, slowly dragging it between my folds and I tense up, my eyes going wide.

"Do you have a condom?"

His expression is pained. "Fuck. I forgot."

I reach out, resting my hands on his shoulders to push him away. "You need to get one."

"You need to get on the pill," he throws back at me, sounding the slightest bit irritated.

This is one of the things we argue about. He hates condoms. I don't know where to go to get on the pill. I can't ask my mom. She'll freak. Plus, our town is so small. If I show up at our doctor's office, I'm almost guaranteed to see someone I know. Or someone my mom or dad knows. And we don't have a Planned Parenthood around here.

I don't know what to do.

"I will get on the pill, but that doesn't mean we won't use condoms still," I remind him. I don't want to get pregnant.

That would ruin everything.

He thrusts against my core nice and slow, slipping inside my body only a little, and he groans. "Just—let me do this. Only for a few minutes. I'll pull out. Promise."

He pushes deeper, and I silently agree it does feel good. Diego inside of me with nothing between us. Just skin on skin. His flesh in mine. He starts to move, and I move with him. Surprisingly, we find our rhythm quickly, and I wrap my arms around his neck, pulling him down so he has no choice but to kiss me.

Our tongues tangle and our heated breaths mingle. He grunts with every thrust, pushing me farther up the mattress, a little bit at a time, and then he's suddenly moving in earnest.

Fast. Hard. He lifts his body away from mine, his hands shifting to my hips as he drives inside of me. Again and again.

"Oh shit, you feel so fucking good—" Diego's head hangs back, his eyes sliding closed just when mine pop open. He's coming.

"Diego!" My sharp voice snaps him back to reality and he reaches between us, pulling himself out of me, and I feel a little dribble on my skin. Not enough though.

Not nearly enough.

Without a word he flops over to lie beside me, both of us panting, trying to catch our breath. I stare at the ceiling, hating the fear that slowly creeps over me, like a low moving fog, until I'm completely engulfed and it's all I can think about.

He came inside of me. And I'm not on the pill. What if…

What if?

THE FIGHT

DIEGO

I spot Jocelyn in the hallway, standing at her open locker. She's been avoiding me all damn day at school, and I'm sick of it. Shit has gone sideways between us for weeks. Over a month. Maybe longer. Our relationship is this close to being over, I can feel it. And I know I'm not making things better by hanging out with Cami Lockhart. Cheer captain. Hot piece of ass. Tempting, though I haven't tapped it yet.

I won't cheat on my girlfriend, no matter how bad our relationship is.

But at least Cami is showing me some attention. More than my own girlfriend, that's for damn sure. Jocelyn is always busy. Too busy for me. Volleyball practice. Volleyball games and tournaments. Homework. Her friends. Her family. I come dead last in that lineup, and all I've ever wanted was to be first.

I'm dead last everywhere. Mom loves me, but she worries about my brother Mateo more. Dad left us a long time ago. I have my friends, but that's different.

I thought Jocelyn loved me, but I don't know. Lately, she has a funny way of showing it.

Determination filling me, I make my way over to her locker, ready to have it out, once and for all. We were nominated for homecoming queen and king a few days ago, and of course, we're going to pair up together, but it's like she can barely look at me lately. This is supposed to be a big moment for us, but she acts like it's the last thing she wants.

I don't get it.

"Jos."

My voice, my nearness startles her and she slams her locker extra hard, turning on her heel and walking away from me. I run to catch up, grabbing hold of her arm and stopping her.

She jerks her arm out of my hold, her blue eyes extra big and full of...what the hell? Is that fear? She looks fucking terrified.

Why?

"I can't do this right now," she tells me and I shake my head, cutting her off.

"You can't avoid me forever," I tell her, my voice firm. "Come on, babe. Why are you treating me like this? Talk to me."

She takes a step back, as if being close to me is freaking her out. The bell is going to ring any minute, signaling that lunch is over, and these halls are going to fill with people. I do not want to have this conversation with an audience, that's for damn sure.

"Are you fucking around with Cami Lockhart?" she suddenly asks, startling me.

I blink at her, absorbing her words. The rumors have been going around for a week, maybe two, but I ignored them. So what if Cami and I were hanging out at parties together? It meant nothing. She flirts, but the girl flirts with *everyone.*

Didn't help that my best friend and I got into an argument at Tony's house after a game. It was more than an argument, it was a fight, and it was partially caused by me hanging out with Cami. I know it. She's Jake's ex, and while he doesn't give a shit about her, he gives a shit about me, and he doesn't want me hanging out with a girl who's toxic.

Maybe I'm the toxic one in this situation.

"Well, tell me. Are you fucking her or not?" Jocelyn snaps, her expression full of disgust.

Figures. Just like everyone else in my life, she assumes the worst of me. I've been dealing with this for a while, thanks to my brother. Of course, I emulated him for years, so teachers automatically assume I'm a shitty student like Mateo.

Guess what? I'm not. I'm a good football player too. I have a job every summer, and I save my money. I have a girlfriend and I'm madly in love with her. Don't know how she feels about me though.

Actually, I *do* know how she feels. She doesn't trust me. She thinks I'm fucking Cami on the low, which is…unbelievable.

"What if I was?" I ask Jocelyn, my voice taunting. The words come out of me as if I have no control over them.

Jocelyn's eyes immediately fill with tears and she comes for me, smacking my chest with her fists. There is so much anguish in her face, in her eyes, and I hate that I caused that. "You bastard," she hisses.

Just before she turns and runs.

I chase after her, calling her name but she ignores me. The bell rings and as predicted, the halls fill with students. People I know, waving at me, saying hello, giving me odd looks as Jocelyn rushes past them and they know I'm in pursuit.

We're causing a scene. Again.

I corner her in the girls' bathroom near the band room. There are a few girls inside, all of them staring at me with wide eyes when I enter their domain.

"Get the fuck out," I snarl and they leave without protest.

Locking the door, I turn to face Jocelyn once more. She's got her back to the wall, standing on the other side of the sinks, tears streaking down her face.

"I don't want to be with you anymore," she says, her shaky words making my heart shatter into a billion pieces. "We're done, Diego."

"One rumor and that's it? You're giving up on us?" I ask her, incredulous.

"It's not just one rumor. It's multiple rumors! It's the way you act around me! You don't care about me anymore. Did you ever? Or were you just using me because you wanted an easy fuck?"

I flinch at her words. Jocelyn doesn't cuss much, so it's a shock to keep hearing her say fuck. "I love you, that's why I want to fuck you!" I'm yelling at the top of my lungs, because that's what we do in my house. We yell and shout and curse. Mom says we love hard and we fight harder, and while I agree with her about the fight harder statement, I'm not so sure about the love hard part.

Yes, my mom and I have a good relationship. Me and Mateo though? My brother has terrorized me for most of my life.

Jocelyn flinches at my choice of words, and she covers her face with her hands, crying into them. "Go away."

I don't know why she's so willing to toss aside our relationship, all over a couple of false rumors about Cami and I? I decide to change tactics. "Come on, Jos. It's me. I would never cheat on you with Cami—"

"Everyone sees you with her." She drops her hands, glaring at me. "I keep getting reports back from friends.

From people who aren't my friends. You hang out with her after every single game."

"At least someone hangs out with me. You're too busy," I throw back at her.

"See!" She jabs her index finger in my direction. "This is why we shouldn't be together anymore. We don't work, D. It hasn't worked for a long time."

"What about homecom—"

"I don't give a shit about homecoming!" she screeches, sounding damn near hysterical. "God, I don't know what I'm going to do."

She covers her face with her hands once more, her shoulders shaking, and I feel helpless. Slowly I approach her, until I'm standing directly in front of her. I wish I could take her pain away. I wish I could make this better. If she'd only listen to me. "Jos. What's going on? What are you talking about?"

Jocelyn lowers her hands, sucking in a shaky breath before she blurts, "I'm—I'm p-p-pregnant."

I stare at her in disbelief. No. No fucking way. "I don't believe you."

She starts to laugh, though nothing I said was funny. "Of course, you would say that. God, you're such a prick."

I shake my head, backing away from her. "Come on, you're mistaken. There's no way—"

"I am." Her voice is filled with determination. "You can go ahead and believe whatever you want, but I'm pregnant with your baby. Not that you give a shit."

I don't want to believe her, because a baby could ruin everything I've worked for. Mom will shit. Mateo will laugh his ass off. My friends will freak the fuck out.

No. She can't be.

"Jocelyn..."

"Don't talk to me. I don't even want you to look at me." She stalks past me before I can say another word, pushing her way out of the bathroom. The door slams behind her, and I glance toward the mirrors, noting the shock in my eyes.

Yeah. No. I don't believe her.

I can't be a father. Not yet.

I'm only seventeen.

THE AFTERMATH...

JOCELYN

I stare at my reflection in the full-length mirror hanging on my wall, looking for a sign. Something on my face, in my stance, within my body, that tells me I'm different. Because I am. Everything in my life has drastically changed in the last month. It all started when I found out my boyfriend Diego, the supposed love of my life, was cheating on me.

Yes, my heart broke, but more than anything? I was mad. *Furious.* I've heard whispered rumors for a while about Diego's flirting, but I blew it off. So he's flirtatious, so what? I know he is, but I always believed it was completely harmless behavior.

But when he goes to a party with Cami and flaunts the fact that they're all over each other—of course I'm going to hear about it.

And lose it.

We broke up, right after we got nominated for homecoming court. It was pure torture, having to stand beside him, and then not make it to the finals. Nope, that honor went to him and Cami.

Thank God, they didn't actually win.

That was nothing though. The final layer of frosting on my shit cake?

I'm pregnant.

I blink at my reflection, slowly shaking my head. But I just look like…me. Same ol' Jocelyn.

I turn to the side, smoothing my hand over the front of my shirt, over my stomach. It's flat. Yet there's life growing inside of me. A baby who's about as big as a grain of rice—according to the internet. Hard to believe.

Worse? I don't know what to do.

I thought about keeping it a secret at school, but what's the point? They're all going to find out eventually. I told a few people I was pregnant with Diego's baby, sprinkling the truth like little bombs here and there, detonating nothing because everyone's either actually keeping my secret, or no one cares.

The last part hurts, and I know that sounds messed up, but it's true.

Diego has been no support whatsoever, not that I expected him to be. He probably sits around and laughs about me with his new girlfriend, Cami *the worst human being in the world* Lockhart.

God, I hate him. I hate her too.

I shove all thoughts of Diego and Cami firmly out of my brain. Forget them. I have more important things to focus on. Like the fact that I'm responsible for another human being's life. I'm going to be a mother.

A mom.

I'm seventeen. I'll be eighteen when the baby is born.

Only eighteen.

A shiver moves through me and I collapse on top of my bed, burying my face in my pillow.

I've cried enough to fill a bucket full of tears. I've wailed and lamented at how unfair life is. Then I remember I'm the idiot who told Diego he didn't have to use a condom that one time, and I cry all over again because I've got no one to blame but myself.

At one point I even told myself I asked for it. I deserved to get pregnant, like it's some sort of punishment. But now…

Now I'm going to be strong and deal with it. I have to. This isn't the end of the world. I'm going to survive. Maybe my dreams will have to be put on hold somewhat. Or just— rearranged. Postponed. But I can make this work. I can be a mom and go to college. I can take care of myself and someone else. I'm the oldest of three, and I've been the responsible one my entire life.

I can do this. I'll need a little help, I'll need my poor, distraught parents to come around, but I've got this.

Rising to my feet, I go to the mirror once more, and stare at my reflection. I look myself square in the eye, my lips curling in the faintest smile, but it feels phony, so I let it fade.

"You've got this," I whisper to myself, ignoring my too wide eyes and my trembling lips.

And I swear that no matter what, I'll keep telling myself it's true.

CHAPTER 1

JOCELYN

I'm sitting in Mrs. Adney's office for the first time in my high school career. My mom is with me, and the reassuring smile she flashes in my direction, every once in a while, as we wait for the vice principal to return does little to calm my nerves.

Everything is changing. All because of one stupid mistake. One careless decision altered the course of my life and I don't know how to change it.

Well. I *do* know how. I just don't want to make that my choice. And that's the beauty of it, right? A girl in my situation might want to abort her baby, and that's her right, but I don't want to.

And that's my right too.

"Sorry about that." Mrs. Adney bustles into her office, settling behind her cluttered desk onto her groaning chair. She called us into her office almost ten minutes ago, then immediately had to leave to go take care of a "situation" on campus.

"It's all right," Mom says, her barely there smile appearing almost brittle. My news pushed her straight over the edge and I don't think she knows what to do about it.

About me.

"What did you want to talk about?" Mrs. Adney's expression is impassive. Blank as a fresh piece of paper. But come on. She has to have heard the rumors. They've been spreading around campus for weeks. Over a month.

It's November. Volleyball season is over—my last year playing since I'm a senior. We made it to the semi-finals before we got beat, and I cried and cried. All the other seniors did too, but not as much as me. It was probably hormones.

Being pregnant is weird.

I told my parents about my little situation a few weeks ago, and after much arguing, crying and carrying on by all three of us, Mom finally said she was calling Mrs. Adney. Like my vice principal has the magic solution.

The woman runs around putting out fires all day. Though I don't think she's going to have an answer to make my predicament any easier.

"I appreciate you taking the time out of your busy day, Mrs. Adney." Mom smiles, the brittleness disappearing some. My mother has impeccable manners. She's polite. My entire family is polite.

I'm sure that's why what I've done is so shocking. Good girls like me don't get pregnant. They go to school, date good boys, do good things and get good grades, and then they get into a good college.

I sort of went off the good path. Probably getting together with Diego was my first mistake.

"Please, call me Diane." Mrs. Adney's gaze slides over to me. "Your daughter is a delight. It's always bittersweet, losing our seniors. Especially the good ones."

I've heard that my entire life. *A pleasure to have in class. An excellent student. Quiet. Respectful. Oh so smart.*

All those compliments can be tossed out the window now. I'm the bad girl. The dumb one who got knocked up by her cheating boyfriend, who then proceeded to dump me rather publicly. Oh, and at one point he even implied I was *lying* about the pregnancy.

He's a great guy, huh?

Fucker.

"Well, that's why we're here." Mom sounds hesitant. This confession will be her first to someone outside the family, and I know she's having trouble with it. She needs to spit it out quick, like ripping off a Band-Aid. "Something's—come up. With Jocelyn."

The look of concern on Adney's face is instant. "What is it?"

Mom hems and haws until I can't take it anymore.

"I'm pregnant." The words fly out of my mouth easily. Helps that I've been telling a few people at school. They've all kept their mouths shut. Even Marty Torres, my ex's cousin.

Though Marty hates his cousin so he's totally taken my side.

Adney doesn't even blink. "I see. I suppose you want to talk about transferring to online schooling? We have an excellent program—"

"No, I don't," I say, interrupting her. "If I transfer to online only, then I'll be considered graduating from a continuation school, correct?"

"Well, yes," Mrs. Adney says, clearing her throat. "But it's more understandable, when a student is in your—situation."

I'm reminded of AP English my sophomore year, when we read *The Scarlet Letter.* I have become Hester Prynne.

"I want to go to college—a state university, not community college." Mom starts to speak, but I talk right over her.

"It's been my goal since I graduated eighth grade to go to San Diego State."

I've been working toward that goal for the last three years. Made a vision board and everything. When I peed on that stupid stick and it came up with two pink lines, I started to cry. Not just because I was pregnant, but also because I ruined my future plans. There will be no San Diego State for me. I can't go to school with a baby, that far away from my family and friends. I need help.

After a few days of debilitating depression and constant weeping, I set my goals closer to home.

"That's impossible now, Jocelyn," Mom says, her voice soft.

"I know." I turn to look at my mother, spotting the concern and worry in her gaze. I look just like her, minus my eye color. Mine are blue; hers are brown. I love her fiercely. Even when she's looking at me like I'm broken and she knows there's no way she can fix me.

"I only brought it up because when faced with this type of situation before, the student usually opts to go to school online," Mrs. Adney explains, her tone gentle. "They believed it was best they remain off-campus."

"You want to hide me?" I ask her point blank.

Mrs. Adney blinks rapidly, but that's her only outward reaction to my question. "Absolutely not. You are more than welcome to finish your school year on campus."

I lift my chin. "I think that's what I'm going to do then."

"Jocelyn." I glance over at my mother once more. She's studying me as if I've sprouted a second head and she's absolutely horrified. "You should reconsider your decision, don't you think?"

"You don't need to make any decisions until…how far along are you?" Mrs. Adney asks.

"Around eight weeks. Maybe nine. Ten?" I answer, a little

unsure. My hand automatically goes to my stomach, resting there. I'm not showing. Not at all. Everything feels the same. I've not really experienced morning sickness either, though certain smells get to me.

Pancake syrup? Gross.

Lunch meat? Please don't make me eat it.

Raw chicken? Hurl.

Otherwise, I just feel like myself.

Oh, minus the exhaustion. I live for naps lately.

"You won't really show for a couple of months still, and we'll be in full-blown sweater weather by then. You can hide your belly easily." Mrs. Adney hesitates for only a moment before she adds, "If you want to."

I've discovered there is a lot of shame in being a pregnant teenager. Everyone wants to keep it hush hush, and they treat you like someone with a contagious disease. Some of my friends are avoiding me at all costs, and that…

Hurts.

"I don't care who knows I'm pregnant, or if they see my belly." I shrug, feigning nonchalance. The idea of waddling around campus in my eighth month of pregnancy is terrifying. What if I get really fat? No boys will look at me.

No boys will look at me now, so I guess I'll be used to it by the time I'm ready to burst.

Mom's shaky hand settles on my knee. "Are you sure?" Her question is a whisper.

I shrug, not looking at her. I can't, or I might start crying all over again. "I have nothing to hide."

A choked sound escapes her and I glance in her direction for only a second. She appears ready to crumple. Mrs. Adney looks as if she's almost…

Impressed.

"We'll stand by you, no matter what your choice is. And if it gets harder to be on campus, or the workload proves difficult, please don't hesitate to contact me. We can go ahead and enroll you full-time online or even a couple of courses, whatever your decision may be." Mrs Adney rises to her feet, an indication this conversation is over.

Which is fine with me, because I'm starting to realize it was sort of pointless to meet with her anyway.

Within minutes Mom and I are ushered out of Adney's office and we're exiting the administration building. I take a deep, fortifying breath of the crisp fall air, a shiver stealing over me. It's after school, there aren't too many people around, and I'm dying to be alone in my car with my thoughts. Thank God, Mom met me here so I don't have to ride home with her. The last thing I want is to hear her go on and on about 'my situation,' as she calls it.

"Well, that didn't go as planned," she says wryly.

"I've been giving it a lot of thought, and it came to me last night that I don't want to go to school online. I'll miss all of my friends. And graduating from a continuation school will only hurt my chances to get into a good college," I explain as I walk with her to the visitor parking lot where her car is.

"It's just—" Mom stops and I do too. "They're all going to talk about you."

"They're already talking about me," I say, not really caring. Only because I've become used to it. The gossip. The stares. The whispers behind my back.

It sucks, but what can I do?

"And you'll see Diego," she continues.

"I see him already." Seeing his face in class or in the halls is slowly killing me inside, but I deal with it. He won't even look at me, and I return the favor, clinging to the knowledge of just how badly he did me wrong. Remembering what he did to me justifies my hatred toward him.

Hatred toward the father of my unborn child.

Yeah, that is so…depressing.

"And doesn't it hurt you, having to see him? Is he still with that—*girl?*" Mom's face screws up when she says the last word, and I appreciate her disgust toward a certain person named Cami Lockhart.

I hate her too.

"I don't know. I've heard rumors about them," I say with a shrug.

"Like what?"

"Like they might've already split up." I don't know if what I've heard is the truth. They weren't together very long if the rumors are true, because I've been hearing them for a while. I don't see them together on campus, but that doesn't mean anything.

I never saw them together on campus when he was cheating on me with her, so they could still be messing around in secret.

"Oh really? That's *interesting*. And what is Diego doing right now?" Mom's lips grow tight.

She didn't like him much when we dated, and it made her crazy that we were together for so long. She hated how serious we became. He is the complete opposite of me, of us. My family is quiet and subdued and…I don't know. Normal? Boring? No one ever really argues or causes problems. Us kids do as we're told. Mom and Dad aren't yelling at us on a constant basis.

His family is loud and boisterous and his mother is just— there are no words to describe her, though I did appreciate how much she loved and protected me. Always reminding Diego I was the perfect girl for him.

Guess that prediction didn't come true.

Mom and Dad didn't like Diego's mother. They found her too loud, too rude. Too—everything. They thought the same about Diego. *He'll bring you nothing but trouble* is what my mother said when I first started seeing him. When I asked her exactly why she thought that, she didn't have a good answer.

The gleam in his eyes is what she finally came up with.

Her constant nagging on me, telling me I shouldn't be with him, only drove me away from her. Who can resist a bad boy? In my parents' eyes, Diego was that and more.

Whatever Mom. Looks like you were right.

"What do you mean, what is Diego doing right now? He's going to school, like the rest of us," I tell her. "The football team is still in the playoffs."

"So his life goes on perfectly normal, while your entire world is completely rocked." Mom shakes her head, her disappointment—and disgust—clear.

"The curse of being female, I suppose," I tell her, my voice light, my thoughts chaotic. The burden of a baby is on the female only because of biology. Not like Diego can get pregnant. But he suffers no consequences while I walk around campus with an imaginary red A on my chest like my new idol, Hester Prynne.

"Are you going to be okay driving home by yourself? You can ride home with me. I'll bring you to school tomorrow," she offers.

"No, I'm okay." I shake my head and pull her in for a quick hug, clinging a little too long when I smell her familiar, comforting scent. Holding onto her makes fresh tears spring to my eyes and I push away before I start full-blown crying. I don't want her to see me like that. She'll start crying too. "I can drive home. I'll see you in a bit."

"Drive carefully!" she calls as she unlocks her car and opens the driver's side door, sliding inside.

I watch her back the car up and pull out of the spot before I turn and head for the student parking lot. There is truly no one around. Basketball is practicing inside, as is the wrestling team. The football team might be on the field, but that's on the other side of campus, so no worries of running into Diego.

Thank goodness.

Music is coming from the cheer room as I walk past it, and the flicker of relief knowing I won't run into Cami either is reassuring. She avoids me, and I avoid her, but she's been known to be confrontational. I'm surprised she hasn't said something shitty to me yet.

That moment is coming, I'm sure.

I'm passing by the gym when a door swings open, and I hear a familiar voice. I start walking faster, my sixth sense kicking in, fear wrapping all around me at the possibility of who that might be.

No. Life doesn't work like that. It can't be him. He wouldn't be in the gym.

I'm almost to the parking lot, and my car is in sight. I pick up speed, my heart dropping when I hear pounding footsteps coming from behind me. Like someone is following me. I don't bother looking over my shoulder.

Without hesitation, I break out into a run.

When I'm close to my car, I feel fingers wrap around my upper arm, halting me from making my escape. Out of breath, I turn, knowing who it is before I even see his face. I recognize his scent. His touch. His freaking *aura*.

"What do you want?" I ask, my voice hostile, my entire body tense. And why isn't he at football practice?

Diego's grip lessens on my arm, but he still doesn't let me go. My gaze drops to his hand, my lip curling in disgust. I don't want him touching me.

His fingers spring away from me and he takes a step backward, giving me much-needed space. "You won't answer my calls."

He's actually tried to call me? What does he want? "I blocked your number." I blocked him everywhere I could. I didn't want to see him or have a constant reminder of him on social media.

His expression turns incredulous, as if he can't believe I would actually block his ass. His ego is enormous, though most of it is a front. Though I have to admit, my ex-boyfriend is very attractive. Dark hair, dark eyes, tall and broad. He used to have an easy smile but over the last six months or so, he's become angrier. Those smiles don't come as quick as they used to.

And now they'll eventually belong to someone else.

"Why the hell would you block me?" He sounds genuinely confused.

Why are men so stupid?

"Because I don't want anything to do with you anymore, Diego." I say the words slowly, and they drip with anger. I haven't talked to him face to face in weeks, and now he acts like it's no big deal that we're having a conversation.

Clearly, he's delusional.

"But—"

"No buts. No arguments. Nothing you can say will change my mind." I sound like I've got this conversation—and my entire life—under control, but inside, I'm shaking. "Everything you've done since I told you I was pregnant proves to me how you feel about this—about *me*—and I get it. Go back to Cami."

I start to walk away, but he grabs me yet again, and I violently jerk my arm out of his hold, glaring at him.

"I'm not with her," he says, his voice turning plaintive. "I haven't been for a while."

"How unfortunate. I'm sure you'll find someone else." I start walking.

So does he, keeping pace right beside me.

"I don't want anyone else," he says.

Keeping my gaze straight ahead, I pick up speed, grateful

my car is nearby. "Have fun spending the rest of your senior year all alone. No one will want to get with the guy who knocked up his girlfriend."

"Come on, Jocelyn," he says, sounding frustrated.

"Fuck off, Diego." I raise my hand up in the air and give him the finger, just as I'm about to get into my car.

"The reason I don't want anyone else," he hesitates and like a fool, I glance over my shoulder, my fingers still curled around the car door handle, "is because I'm—still in love with you."

My heart trips over itself, then starts pounding out of control.

How—

Why—

Who the hell does he think he is?

Whirling around, I march up to him, ignoring the fact that I'm only about five-foot-seven to his six-foot. I'm not short, but standing next to him, he makes me feel like I am.

At the moment, though, I'm on him as if we're equals in height and strength, drilling my index finger into his chest as if I want to puncture his heart.

Which I sort of do.

"Fuck you and your *love*. It's meaningless. You put me through straight hell the last six months of our relationship, and now you claim you still *love* me? After you accuse me of getting pregnant to get you back?" Yes, that's one rumor I heard, though I've never mentioned it to him before. Not like we're talking on a regular basis.

"What are you talking about?" He sounds completely dumbfounded. Shocked.

I ignore his question. "It's bullshit, Diego. All of it. You. Me. *Us*. I don't need you anymore. I never really did." I poke him one more time in the chest, just for good measure, before I turn on my heel and go to my car.

He doesn't say another word. I climb into my old lime green VW bug and start the engine, my gaze going to him automatically. Like I can't help myself.

Diego stands where I left him, his eyes on me, his expression sad, his hand on his chest where I poked him.

I hope it hurts.

Though it won't even come close to the pain he's caused me.

CHAPTER 2

DIEGO

I enter my house to the sound of arguing.

Nothing new there. This time it's Mom and my older brother, Mateo. They're screaming in rapid fire Spanish, my mother calling him every name in the book and Mateo constantly telling her she's *disparatado.*

Meaning she's lost her damn mind.

That's her trigger. You can call her names, you can give her a list of all the shitty things she does, but don't call her crazy. She loses it every single time, proving to us all yet again that she is, indeed, crazy.

She's just very—passionate. About a lot of things.

I enter the kitchen and go straight for the fridge, walking in between my yelling mother and brother as if they don't exist. They treat me the same way, keeping up their argument, not blinking an eye as I pass by them yet again with a Gatorade and a bag of chips in my hands, heading for my bedroom.

It's like I'm a ghost in my own house.

"Dinner is soon," Mom says to me, acknowledging my

existence while she glares at Mateo. "Don't fill yourself with junk food."

I ignore her as I exit the kitchen, and they start yelling at each other all over again.

Once I'm inside, I shut and lock the door, then set my predinner snack on my desk. Grabbing my earbuds from my backpack, I push each one into my ears and then pick up my cracked phone, thumbing through my best friend's Jake's playlists on Spotify until I find the one I want to listen to. It's called:

Fucked Up Workout.

I hit shuffle and the angry clash of guitars fills my ears. Slipping my phone into my sweatpants' pocket, I bring my snack along with me and collapse on top of my bed, propped against the pillows. I twist off the Gatorade lid and take a long drink, wishing it was laced with alcohol. I munch on the stale potato chips and look at the expiration date on the bag to see it's two weeks past.

I eat them anyway.

Filling up the hole growing inside of me with junk food doesn't help. I am hollow. Weightless. Fucking lost. Seeing Jocelyn earlier, talking to her, brought all those overwhelming emotions to the surface, making me say stupid things.

Like I'm still in love with her.

Not that it isn't true, but fuck. Why admit it when she's still so angry with me? And she has every right to be mad. I've messed everything up to the point of it—us—being utterly destroyed. I have no one to blame for our demise except me. I'm the one who ruined it all.

Frustration filling me, I turn up the music as loud as it can go, drowning out the yelling still coming from the kitchen. Drowning out my thoughts. I don't want to think about Jocelyn and a baby and what that'll mean for me. She's pushed me out of her life so far, maybe I should be relieved. It means she doesn't want me in our baby's life.

She doesn't want me in *her* life.

Anger makes my chest tight and I curl my hand into a fist, punching the mattress. It gives me no satisfaction. I'd rather hit a wall. Last time I did that, though, Mom lost her fucking mind and made me patch the hole up, standing over me and yelling at me the entire time.

The song ends and just before the next one begins, I hear incessant pounding on my door. I rip one of my ear buds out. "Who is it?"

"Me, fuckhead," Mateo says from the other side of the door.

I jump off my bed and go to the door, unlocking it just as Mateo pushes his way inside. "What do you want?" I practically snarl at him.

My brother and I? We don't really get along. He's three years older than me and when we were little, he always picked on me. Beat me up. Made fun of me in front of his friends. All I wanted was for him to like me.

All he wanted was for me to disappear.

"You got any cash?" Mateo has a hard time keeping a job. He didn't go to college after he graduated high school. He didn't apply anywhere, not even community college. He told Mom college wasn't for him. He was sick of school and claimed to anyone who was listening that he was going to find a full-time job somewhere and become successful. Maybe even open his own business someday.

Yeah. That hasn't happened. Knowing Mateo and his lack of motivation, it probably never will.

"No, I don't." The lie falls from my lips easily. I work full-time at a resort on the lake in the summer and save up all my money. Funny thing is, Mateo is the one who helped me get the job the summer after my sophomore year. He was already working there and convinced the dock manager to hire me. A month after that, he got fired for getting caught smoking a joint on the job.

I've worked on the dock the past three summers. They love me. And I may smoke joints on occasion, but never on the clock.

I'm not a complete dumbass.

"Liar," Mateo says as he glances around my room, looking for a spot where I might hide my money, I guess. "Come on. Twenty bucks for your big bro? I'll pay you back."

You know how many times I've heard that before? Too many to count. I'd be rich as hell if he finally paid back all the money he's "borrowed" from me over the years.

"Sorry, bro. No can do." I send him a measured look and he glares back, his face still red from the argument with our mother.

"You're just like her, you know. Acting like you're perfect and better than me, when we all know how fucked up you really are, deep inside." Mateo takes a step closer to me, but I don't back away. "Does she know your little secret yet?"

My stomach twists. Does my brother know my little secret?

"I'm guessing you haven't told her," Mateo continues.

I remain silent.

"About Jocelyn? How she's pregnant? With your baby?" Mateo laughs, the asshole. How the hell did he find out? He still hangs out with high schoolers despite the fact that he's almost twenty-one, so I assume someone must've told him. "The poor girl."

My lips grow tighter, but otherwise, I don't react. Don't speak. Saying something is admitting it.

Remaining quiet is probably admitting it too.

"Though I guess we can't call her a poor girl. Your ex is rich, with her fancy house on the mountain and her bigshot lawyer daddy." Mateo shakes his head. "I'm guessing they'll hit you with a custody agreement and you'll have to pay child support, which means your days of playing ball with your friends are gone. There goes your chance to get out of here. You're stuck. Just like me."

His words are worse than any blows he could've delivered. He knows my goals. My dreams. How badly I want out of this town. How much I want to go to college. My grades are decent. I scored well on the SAT, which was a shock. And I'm an excellent football player. I've talked to coaches from a few colleges, and Coach Callahan has encouraged me to chase after a scholarship, which I've been trying to do. I've turned in my applications already, and my fingers are crossed I get in somewhere. Even Fresno State would be good, though it's not far.

Far enough in my eyes.

"You saving your money for an abortion then?" Mateo asks, knocking me from my thoughts. "Twenty dollars isn't going to make or break you."

"Get out," I tell him, hating that he knows just how to get to me.

"Give me twenty bucks or I'm telling Mom that you're going to be a daddy," he taunts, sounding like he's thirteen and I'm ten and he's bullying the shit out of me.

We stare at each other like we're in a showdown. Isn't he too old for this shit? Threatening to tell Mom like I just spilled my orange juice all over the table after Mom told me to watch out?

"Go ahead and tell her," I say, my voice tight. All bravado on the outside when deep down, I'm quaking.

Mateo gives first. "No way am I talking to that bitch right now. It's your lucky day. The both of you can go to hell."

He storms out of my room, slamming the door so hard

the window rattles. The moment he's gone, I collapse on my bed, staring at the ceiling.

I need to tell Mom about Jocelyn and the baby before Mateo does. Or someone else. She'll be so pissed if she doesn't hear it from me first.

But how do I tell her? How do I swallow my pride and my fear and admit I got my girlfriend pregnant? Oh, and supposedly I cheated on her and left her at pretty much the exact moment she found out about the baby? Mom has already heard the rumors about me and Cami. Hell, when people started saying we were seeing each other, I legit started hanging out with her. May as well live up to everyone's expectations of me, right?

I was fucking stupid for doing that. Mom hated Cami on sight, and openly expressed her disapproval. She adores Jocelyn.

Everyone adores Jocelyn.

Even me.

CHAPTER 3

JOCELYN

I'm at the playoff game because I like to torture myself watching Diego out on the field playing his heart out. I know this game means everything to him. It's his senior year, and they've come so far. He wants to go all the way and win the state championship, and I think they have a good chance.

If I didn't come tonight, it would look weird, and besides, I want to appear above it all. *Everyone* is at this game. We've had home field advantage since playoffs started, and people from the community have shown up in droves. It's freezing cold outside, so I'm layered up, sitting on a thick blanket so the cold metal bleacher won't seep into my butt, and I can see my breath every time I exhale, but I don't care. No one does. We're all yelling and screaming, cheering on the team as they continue to dominate.

My best friends Marley and Samantha sit on either side of me, both of them bouncing up and down with every solid play our team makes, expressing their displeasure loudly when the opposing team has the ball.

We've known each other since we were little and got

closer when we all played for a traveling volleyball team during middle school. I'm still close with both of them, though I sort of forgot about all of my friends when Diego and I were together.

And some of those friends forgot about me too. Luckily, Sam and Marley brought me back into their friend group, something I really need right now.

I have to savor this while I can. My life is about to change in the most momentous way possible, and I still don't know how to feel about it. It's like I'm numb. Maybe I'm in shock. I'm a little resentful too. My friends are able to enjoy and savor these high school moments, and while I'm at this game and trying to enjoy it, all I can focus on is this is it. I'm going to start showing soon. And then everyone will want to stay away from me because I'm the pregnant girl.

This was my choice, but at this very moment, I sort of hate myself for it.

"Jake is so good," Marley says, after yet another pass is completed. No mention of who completed it.

That would be Diego.

"I hear he's going to Stanford," Sam says.

"Nope." Marley shakes her head. "USC."

Sam's eyes go wide. "No kidding? I just applied there too. And UCLA. Berkeley. Stanford. San Diego State."

My heart cracks at her last mention. Sam is really smart. She'll probably get accepted into every one of those colleges, while I'll have to stay close to home.

"He already said yes to USC," Marley tells us, tucking a strand of long, brown hair behind her ear. "He's in my English class, and Skein was asking about it the other day. I swear, Jake almost seemed embarrassed when we all started clapping for him."

"Good for Jake," I murmur, my gaze going to him, then Diego. We haven't talked since our interaction in the parking lot, and that was almost two weeks ago. Now we're actively avoiding each other on campus. We don't even make accidental eye contact anymore.

It's the Friday before Thanksgiving, meaning we have all next week off of school, and I'm looking forward to the break. Though we're driving to Oregon to see my dad's family to spend the holiday with them, and I'm not looking forward to it.

I actually don't want to go. My father asked that I not bring up my pregnancy to anyone else in the family while we're there, especially my grandparents. How am I supposed to do that? It's not as if I'm consumed with all things baby, but being pregnant is a part of my life now.

It's like I'm my father's—my entire family's—secret shame.

Which I suppose I am.

Diego's standing on the sidelines, his dark hair a mess, that permanent scowl on his handsome face. I can see it from up here at the top of the stands. He never looks happy anymore.

Despite my anger toward him, seeing him like this makes me sad. I know I should revel in his bad mood and hope that I'm the cause of it, but I don't. I still—God, I hate admitting this—care about him. He's the father of my baby. I'm forever tied to him.

Now, though, we pretend neither of us exists.

"Coaches from Fresno State have been here talking to Caleb," Marley says, her gaze softening. She's had a crush on him for years, and he knows it. Caleb is the biggest player in our class—possibly in the entire school. "I think they're talking to Diego, too."

He's wanted out of here for years. Away from his family. Away from this town. We used to talk about us going to San Diego together, though they don't have a great football team.

But he swore he wanted to follow me, no matter where I went, and like the lovesick fool I was, I believed him.

That should've been my first clue what he told me was utter crap.

"Marley," Sam says, her tone accusing, her head jerking in my direction. "Don't mention him in front of Jocelyn."

"You can say his name. I'm not going to have a meltdown," I say, trying my best to sound bored. Like he doesn't affect me.

But I'm dying to hear what else Marley has to say about him.

They both send me skeptical looks, but thankfully Marley keeps talking.

"I think a lot of the boys from our team are going to end up there. Diego. Tony. Caleb." Marley tacks on a dreamy sigh when she mentions her not so secret crush yet again. "Maybe I should apply to Fresno State."

I nudge her in the ribs, making her jump. "You always tell us how you don't want to go there. Do not follow after Caleb by applying to Fresno State. Your dream school is UC Irvine, remember?"

Marley glares, but otherwise doesn't argue with me. Probably because, deep down, she knows I'm right. Why should she sacrifice her dream school for a chance to catch a glimpse of Caleb on campus? Because that's all she'll get.

I like Caleb, but he isn't interested in anyone but himself.

"Are you applying to San Diego State, Jos?" Sam asks me.

I slowly shake my head, fixing my gaze on the field below. "I can't. It's too far."

My best friends are quiet for a moment, and I'm sure they're wondering how to broach this subject next. It's a sensitive one for me. One we haven't talked about since I discovered I'm pregnant. November is when you apply for colleges, and I'm going to submit my one application. If I don't get into Fresno State, then I'll go to community college. I can't stray too far. I need my family's help with the baby.

I suppose I could apply to UC Merced, since it's close by too, but I don't know. I've never thought about going to that school before. I've never thought about going to any other school besides San Diego. Everywhere I apply now feels like I'm settling.

And is that the way I'm going to feel about a lot of my life choices? Maybe even...all of them? I have to settle for this because of what I've done? What *we've* done?

I hope not.

"Are you going to try for college at all?" Marley finally asks.

I meet her gaze. "I applied to Fresno State. It's close, and I can still live at home and go to school. Mom told me she can watch the baby while I'm in class."

Marley smiles. "I'm so glad you're going to try and stay in school. It's been your dream, to go to college."

It has, but as a true college student. One who'd join a sorority or a bunch of clubs. One who'd live on campus in the dorms and make loads of new friends. Go to parties and get drunk and hang out with my cute boyfriend. That all sounded perfect. Like I would be living the dream.

My dream has gone up in smoke, and I can only blame myself because I chose to keep the baby. The idea of destroying the baby that's a part of me, that's a part of Diego —even though I'm furious at him and don't want anything to do with him—I couldn't do it. We aren't a particularly religious family, though we went to church a lot when I was much younger. Over the years, though, we eventually stopped.

It wasn't the voice of God stopping me from getting an abortion. It was me. Myself. I couldn't do it.

The crowd erupts around us, jolting me back to the

present and I realize we just scored another touchdown. This one was caught by Tony, and my heart pangs when I watch the boys from our team run toward him in celebration. Including Diego.

I remember when I'd accompany Diego to one of Tony's aftergame parties. I'd stand with him and listen as he told everyone stories about the game. But the start of this year, I couldn't go to very many of the parties. I was busy with volleyball. So Diego went by himself to most of them, texting me throughout the night and letting me know he missed me.

He eventually stopped texting. Probably when he started hanging out with Cami.

My gaze automatically goes to the sidelines where the cheer team is. They're not wearing their usual uniforms. It's too cold, so they're clad in cold weather gear, but they still look cute with the giant white bows in their hair and their shiny metallic blue poms clutched in their hands. Cami stands front and center, beaming up at the crowd as she leads her team in yet another chant. She's pretty, I can give her that, but her ugly black soul makes her hideous to me.

I hate that she stole Diego from me. I hate that he went to her so willingly, despite knowing she's such a snake. I hate that in my desperation to keep my boyfriend's attention to make him happy, I let him have sex with me without a condom. We were both too caught up in the moment, but I should've been more responsible.

Then again, he should've been too.

The opposing team comes out onto the field and the cheer team launches into a familiar cheer. We all say the simple words along with them, everyone in the stands yelling at the top of their lungs.

This is Badger country! This is Badger country!

Nothing gets our teams more fired up than when they hear this, the volleyball team included. It fills me with adrenaline and makes me want to play better and make everyone watching us cheer us on even more.

It makes me want to win. I know the football team feels the same way. We're staking a claim on our field, and we never want to lose at home.

This is our territory.

Somehow, some way, the Badgers intercept the ball. The crowd goes wild. Members of the cheer team are jumping up and down and screaming hysterically. The band is playing a raucous fight song, and I leap to my feet, as do Sam and Marley. I watch as the offense jogs back out on the field, my gaze seeking out and finding Diego.

I glance at the scoreboard. We're up by a touchdown and a field goal. We could win this. And then they'll go off to the final league playoff game. Which I'll miss, thanks to me being in Oregon for Thanksgiving.

I don't want to go.

Marley clutches my arm, her grip tight. "Oh my God, they might win!"

"This is amazing," Sam breathes, her focus on the field. Samantha is totally into sports. She played volleyball with me and also runs track. She's super athletic and could probably kick anyone's ass, she's that strong. Sometimes I think guys are intimidated by her. She's smart, strong, and confident.

That sends a lot of boys scrambling.

We don't bother talking as we watch the team move the ball down the field. They make it look so easy, especially Jake Callahan. He's going on to greatness, of that I have no doubt.

Jake launches the ball, and my gaze automatically goes to Diego. The throw is meant for him and I'm breathless when the ball lands perfectly in Diego's hands. He keeps running, outdistancing the players from the other team who are trying to tackle him.

He runs it all the way into the endzone.

The crowd erupts in cheers, once again. This is it. The game is pretty much over, considering we only have about twenty seconds left on the clock. We're going on to the final playoff game. I'm sure the team is so excited.

I'm sure Diego is too.

CHAPTER 4

DIEGO

e won.

This is the best moment of my life. We're going on to the final league championship game, and if we win that game, we'll go onto state. The ultimate goal. The biggest dream for high school sports. And if we do win next week's game, and play for the state championship? I could cinch my chances of becoming a member of the Fresno State Bulldogs football team for college.

First, I gotta get accepted. Fingers crossed.

But I can't worry about that now. Instead, I look around at my teammates as we all crouch on the field, surrounding our coach, the NFL football legend himself, Drew Callahan. Jake stands next to him, his hands on his hips, his smile so bright he could blind us. Trust me, that motherfucker rarely smiles, so it's a sight to see.

"Don't get too cocky," Drew warns all of us, though he's smiling. He knows how we are. "We still have one more team to conquer before we go onto state. And they're tough. The toughest in the league."

"We're fucking tougher!" someone yells, making us all laugh.

Coach scowls. "Watch your mouth. Save the language for the locker room."

We go quiet.

"Jake, there was something you wanted to say." His father, our coach, nods at him.

Jake takes a few steps forward and stands up straighter, his gaze searching as he studies all of us kneeling before him. Like he's the king and we're his subjects. Normally this sort of thought process would piss me off, but right now, I'm all for it. Jake is our leader. He played like a master tonight, and I benefited from it, catching almost every pass he threw my way.

He's the man, and right now, he should revel in it.

"You guys played an outstanding game tonight," he says. "I couldn't do what I do without your support, without your expertise. I know we hit a few rough spots early in the season."

Jake's gaze finds mine, and I incline my head in acknowledgement. We weren't getting along. Shit was going sideways in my life, and I acted like a dick, hurting everyone around me. Even those I cared about the most.

Like Jocelyn, the girl I love. And Jake, my best friend.

"But we rallied around each other and pushed that shi—stuff behind us. Now we've got ourselves into a rhythm, and it's working. We've got each other's backs." We roar a "yeah" in answer and Jake grins. "And nothing is going to stop us from winning next week. Am I right? Nothing!"

We yell and scream, then jump to our feet, ready to break free and talk to our family and friends who are waiting for us. Coach Callahan always makes us stay directly after the game for a little speech. I used to hate it. I just wanted to get out of there. Go see my girlfriend and listen to her tell me how great I played. She'd go on and on and I'd act like it was no big deal, but her words always touched me deep. Always made me feel like I was special. Jocelyn was the only one who could do that.

No one waits for me now, so what's the point?

We've just been cut loose, and I watch as Jake goes jogging past me, heading right for his girlfriend, Hannah, who's waiting for him. I spot Hannah in the distance—she's hard to miss, with her vibrant reddish gold hair—and I remember all the shitty things I said about her when she and Jake were first getting together.

I was a complete asshole to her. To Jake. Pissed that some chick was stealing my best friend from me. How stupid was that? I need to apologize to her.

Someday soon, I'm going to do it.

Tony ambles up so he's walking beside me, giving me a shove. I shove him back, and we grin at each other.

"Nice game tonight," he tells me, his expression somber.

Guy shows no emotion. I'm surprised he's complimenting me. "Thanks. Same to you."

"Thanks." He sends me a look. "Jos is right over there."

I check out where he's indicating with a nod of his head before I return my now confused gaze to his. "So?"

"She's not waiting for you?" Tony lifts his dark brows.

What the fuck? "Bro, you know we split up."

Tony slowly shakes his head. "Girl is pregnant with *your kid*. Maybe she's had a change of heart."

"Doubt that, but okay." I shrug, fighting the melancholy that wants to grab me in its clutches and not let go.

I feel like shit over—everything. Somehow, my mother still doesn't know Jocelyn is pregnant. I don't know why Mateo is choosing to remain quiet, when his favorite thing is to abuse my ass on the daily, but he is. He's got his own problems he's dealing with. Like how he owes some dealer a bunch of money.

How he found my secret stash and stole some of my cash.

How we got into a blistering fight out in the back yard a couple of days ago. He swung and caught my jaw. I drove my fist into his rib cage. Mom caught us, demanding to know what we were arguing about, but we both remained mum.

I kept his secret quiet, and he did the same for me.

Is it really helping though? No. My life is fucked.

Fucked.

And I'm just cruising along, acting like everything's cool.

It's not.

We're quiet as we continue walking, and I can tell Tony is struggling. He's got something to say.

"Aren't you two going to try and work it out?" he finally asks me.

I come to a stop. So does Tony. We face each other, and while my normal reaction is to get mad and tell him to fuck off and mind his own business, I realize I'm just…

Tired.

"I don't really want to talk about Jocelyn right now," I tell him, which is the honest to God truth. "I'd rather focus on the win tonight."

Tony blinks. I think I've shocked him, and that doesn't happen very often. "Yeah. Sure. I get it. Probably shouldn't have brought her up."

"It's okay. I know you're all curious." I haven't really talked about Jocelyn and our situation with any of my friends. Not even Jake. What are they going to say? The one time I mentioned it to Caleb, he said I should convince her to get an abortion.

"Taken care of just like that." The asshole snapped his fingers.

Yeah. No. Not going to happen. I mentioned it to Jocelyn

—a week after I first accused her of lying because I couldn't wrap my head around what she said to me—and she basically told me to go fuck myself.

I really didn't believe she was pregnant at first. I thought she was just freaking out. Wanting me back. That's what Cami said.

Everything inside me sinks when I think of Cami. What people said about me. About her. How we were together behind Jocelyn's back. When you hear something enough, you tend to believe it.

When you're told something enough, you tend to do it. That was me.

With Cami.

Never admitted it to anyone, but I wondered at first if Jocelyn was keeping the baby out of spite. To get back at me for supposedly cheating on her with Cami. But the more I thought about it, the more I realized that would be a really stupid way to get back at me.

And Jocelyn isn't stupid. She's not one of those vengeful girls either. She wouldn't do something just to spite my dumbass.

She must really want this baby.

"You never talk about it," Tony says, once we resume walking. "The baby. Jocelyn. The breakup."

My gaze snags on Jocelyn standing almost directly behind Tony's girlfriend, Sophie, and my steps slow. I feel like I'm a dead man walking. Jocelyn will catch sight of me and either blow me completely off or say something shitty.

Wait, no. Jos wouldn't say something shitty. That's more Cami's style.

I whip my head around, searching for Cami. No way do I want her coming near me tonight. That bitch starts trouble no matter where she goes or who she talks to, and when I finally spot her, I almost want to laugh.

She's with Wyatt, and one of the girls from the cheer team is taking photos of them together. He's a junior. Decent guy. Actually, a really nice guy, so I have no idea what he's doing with her. She'll chew him up and spit him out and he'll be left bleeding for days.

Dramatic but fucking true, mark my words.

"I don't know what to say," I finally admit.

"You gonna help her with the baby?" Tony asks.

I shrug. "I dunno."

"Gonna pay child support?"

I'm seventeen. Those words do not compute. "Will she make me?"

"She might. The baby is yours." He sends me a look. "Right?"

"It's definitely mine," I say fiercely, tamping down the anger that wants to erupt. Jocelyn was my first. I was hers, too.

"Just making sure. Weirder things have happened." He claps me on the back, giving me a gentle shove. "Like I said, good game tonight. See you at my house later. And don't worry. You've got this."

He leaves me where I stand, heading for his girlfriend. Her entire face lights up when he draws near and he pulls her into his arms, whirling her around before he kisses her.

Seeing them together leaves me shattered. Jealous. Everyone's got someone. Well, except for Caleb, and he doesn't mind because he's currently surrounded by his fan club. They're all jostling for a chance to get a photo with him, and it's kind of pathetic, how they slobber all over him yet he doesn't care about them whatsoever.

Caleb loves every minute of it though.

I keep my gaze on Caleb and his adoring ladies, wondering if my mom and brother came to watch the game like they promised they would, when I feel someone tap me on my shoulder. I turn to find Jocelyn standing in front of me. All by herself. Her expression is solemn, and she looks…

Beautiful.

Her hair is down, and she's got a beanie tugged down low on her head, practically covering her eyebrows. Her face looks fuller and her eyes are sparkly. She's wearing so many layers I have no idea if she's got a baby belly yet, and my gaze automatically goes there, checking.

I can't tell. And I sort of want to know.

"Good game," she says, her voice scratchy, like it took a lot for her to say that. I bet it did.

"Thanks." I can't believe she's here. Standing in front of me. That she willingly just spoke to me after that blow up we had in the parking lot a couple of weeks ago. We haven't spoken since. About anything.

And there are things that need to be said between us.

"I can't believe we won," I tell her, because it's the truth.

"You caught the winning touchdown." A glimmer of a smile touches her lips, and seeing it gives me so much hope. Too much. "That's pretty major."

"Think someone got a photo of it?" I ask hopefully.

"Probably. Ask around. Someone from yearbook maybe? I'm sure someone caught your moment of glory," she says.

I immediately regret asking that question. I sound like an egotistical ass. Typical. "Yeah. Maybe." I let my gaze roam over her body, lingering on her stomach yet again. She's wearing a thick school hoodie and joggers. Her body basically looks the same. "Ah, you feeling okay lately?"

"I am."

That's all she gives me.

"You know what you're having yet?"

"No."

"Going to find out?"

"Yes."

"Jos." I let my irritation show at her short answers.

"What?" Her eyes are wide, her expression innocent.

But she knows. She's torturing me, and I'm sure she's enjoying it.

I deserve it for what I put her through when we broke up.

"You're mad at me, and I get it, but there's so much more going on than you know." It's my turn to clear my throat, and I become uncomfortable. "I'd like to—help you in any way I can. If you're cool with it."

"Help how?" She lifts a brow, studying me.

"I don't know." I shrug, feeling inept. I am completely out of my element right now. "If you need someone to take care of—things."

"What things?"

I think she's trying to torture me. "You need money?"

"Not right now." She glances around, as if sensing there might be prying eyes and ears. I'm sure there are. It's not smart, having this conversation in front of everyone out on the football field. "We can talk about this some other time."

"You going to Tony's?" The words leave me before I can second guess myself.

"I wasn't planning on it."

"You should go." I say with all the confidence I can muster. I'd beg her, but she'd tell me to get lost if I did that. "We could hang out."

"I don't think that's a good idea, Diego," she says, her voice soft, her gaze cutting away from mine briefly. "We're not together anymore. Remember?"

We stare at each other, and the longer we do, the more painful it is. My head is roaring. My heart is cracking. Sadness and frustration and even a hint of anger runs through my veins, boiling my blood. This isn't...

It wasn't supposed to happen like this.

"We're going to have a baby, Jos," I finally say to her.

"Oh, I know." Her gaze returns to mine, full of fire, and I think I touched a nerve. "Trust me. I've been dealing with it every single minute since I found out, while you've been out living your same life, oblivious to everything."

If she only knew the shit I've been going through. "I'm not oblivious."

"You so are. Asking me to go to Tony's party, like I can stay up half the night and drink beer with the rest of you. I can't drink, Diego. I can't party. I can barely keep my eyes open past ten o'clock, I'm so exhausted all the time," she says irritably.

Concern smacks me in the chest, and I take a step toward her. "Are you all—"

"I'm fine," she snaps, taking a step backward, wrapping her arms around herself. "It's just one of the side effects of being pregnant."

See, I had no idea having a baby made a woman this tired this early in the game. Maybe she's right.

Maybe I am oblivious.

"We should talk. And we can talk at Tony's, okay? We can hole up in one of the bazillion rooms he's got in that house and you can tell me everything that's going on with you. What do you think?" I sound like I'm pleading. Begging. Old Diego would never go for this. I'd rather shoot myself in the nuts than beg a girl to spend time with me.

Now, I'm not above anything. I'll do what it takes to get this girl—especially this girl—to talk to me again. To tell me what's going on in her life. To explain to me where we went wrong, and why we can never make it right.

That's the biggest question I have. I can't make this right, and I don't know why.

Well. I know why. She thinks I cheated on her.

But what if everything they said about me is a lie? If I told her that, she wouldn't believe me.

I know she wouldn't.

Jocelyn slowly shakes her head, not one ounce of regret in her gaze. "I can't. Maybe another time."

Before I can say anything else to keep her talking to me, she turns and walks away.

And never once looks back.

CHAPTER 5

JOCELYN

"Mom, please." I clutch her hands in mine, trying to send her the most pitiful look I can muster. "Please don't make me go. I'm begging you."

We're standing in the middle of my parents' master bedroom, her open suitcase on top of their massive bed. She was packing for the long drive to Oregon when I came into her room and launched into my speech.

The speech about me not wanting to go to Oregon. Just the thought of pretending everything is normal when my entire life is in complete upheaval sends me into a tailspin of anxiety. I can't do it. I can't act like I'm fine, when I'm not.

The expression on my mother's face tells me she's close to cracking. I know that look. I've seen it plenty of times, and it's a good sign. A positive sign. "Your grandparents will be so disappointed."

"No matter what I do, they'll be disappointed in me, Mom. You know this," I remind her, because it's true.

"What about your father?" she asks.

"He doesn't want me there." I let go of her hands and plop down on the edge of the mattress, staring at the floor. "He wants to hide me away for the next six months or whatever and pretend I don't exist."

"That is not true—" she starts, but I send her a measured look and she clamps her lips shut.

We both know it's true. There's no point in her arguing it.

A weary sigh leaves her and she collapses onto the mattress right next to me, slinging her arm around my shoulders and pulling me in for a side hug. "If you stay home, I'll miss not having you around."

Victory makes me want to smile, but I restrain myself. "It's just Thanksgiving, Mom. A totally made-up holiday to celebrate what was really about the slaughtering of indigenous people and how the pilgrims stole their land."

Mom's expression tells me she never quite thought of Thanksgiving like that before. "I like the idea of being thankful for family. That's what I celebrate."

"I know." I exhale loudly. "I just—don't want to pretend to be something I'm not in front of Dad's family."

"They're your family too," she reminds me.

"Of course they are. But still. We're not that close to them, and I'll feel so fake when Grandma asks me what I'm up to and what college I want to attend. I can't tell her the truth. Why put myself through that?" I lean my head against her shoulder and close my eyes, telling myself I won't cry.

It's become my new mantra. It feels like lately I'm either royally pissed off or crying uncontrollably. No in between. I looked it up online and I'm pretty sure it's a pregnancy symptom.

Being pregnant really messes with you.

"You'll be here all alone for almost an entire week, though. I'm not so sure I want you here at the house by yourself," she says, tapping her finger against her pursed lips.

"I'll be fine. I'm almost eighteen." My voice drops. "I'm going to be a mom soon. I think I'm responsible enough."

Mom actually laughs, which surprises me. "That's true, isn't it? But to me, you'll always be my baby girl."

She gives me another side hug before I pull myself from her embrace and stand. I start pacing. "Come on, Mom. Let me stay home."

"Well, I'll have to talk about it with your father," she says.

That's always her standard line. I used to think it was because she couldn't make any decisions without seeking his approval first, but now I realize they're a team. They're in this together. And they like to discuss things before automatically assuming the other will agree to something.

I like that. I respect my parents' relationship, even though I'm not too thrilled with the way my father is treating me since I confessed I was having a baby. He flat out ignores me most of the time. Doesn't ask me very many questions or show much concern. It's like he wants me to disappear.

And that hurts.

I stop in front of her just as she rises to her feet. "Thank you," I tell her, just before I give her a quick hug. "It would be such a relief if I'm able to stay home."

"I know." She pats my back almost awkwardly, and I swear I hear a catch in her voice. "I know."

* * *

T HEY LEFT for Oregon without me.

My younger brother Liam, and my sister Addison were furious, screams of *That's not fair!* resounding throughout the house when our parents made the announcement. Mom took it in stride, giving them a bunch of nonsense about how I'm a senior and I've earned the privilege and blah, blah blah.

Dad seemed almost relieved I wasn't going after all, which pained me, but I concentrated on the fact that, in the end, I got my way. He gave me a big hug before they left for their trip early Sunday morning. Told me that he loved me and that he would miss me.

It felt nice. Normal.

It's already Tuesday, but the day is dragging. While it's been nice having the house to myself and I get to sleep in as long as I want and take all the naps, I'm getting bored. Yesterday afternoon, I got together with Marley at Starbucks and we sat at a table outside, freezing while we sipped our holiday drinks. Mine was decaf since I'm off caffeine. I envied Marley's Pumpkin Spice Frap with an extra shot of espresso.

Then I reminded myself I'm doing what's right for the baby and that made me feel better.

A little, anyway.

Today, though, I'm lonely. I miss my family. I miss my friends. The day stretches on and feels almost endless. Mom called earlier to check on me, but she was distracted. They were getting ready to go to a farm that's close to my grandparents' house, where there was still a pumpkin patch for photo ops and live turkeys roaming free.

Hearing about it made me regret not going. Maybe I should've. It would've been a nice distraction, and I could've had some fun. I also could've focused on family instead of thinking about being alone all the time.

But I can't change my choice. I'm stuck here all by myself until Saturday night.

I'm fixing a grilled cheese for a late lunch when I feel it. A fluttering low in my belly that's like nothing I've ever experienced before. I come to a complete stop, my hand automatically going to the spot where I felt it and I press my palm there, waiting breathlessly.

It happens again. A gentle, rolling feeling that's so faint, I could almost convince myself it didn't happen.

But it did. I think...

It was the baby.

My grilled cheese forgotten, I stand in front of the stove, my hand still pressed to the side of my stomach, holding my breath as I wait for it to happen again. I wait. And I wait. And I wait some more until...

I smell something burning.

"Shit!"

Grabbing a spatula, I flip the sandwich to find the one side completely black and literally smoking. I turn off the burner and scoop up the entire sandwich with the spatula, walking it over to the garbage can and dumping it inside.

Once I've cleaned the pan and put everything away in the dishwasher, I decide to go out for lunch instead. I run a brush through my hair, throw on a hoodie and hop into the car, driving the near fifteen minutes it takes to get into the main part of town.

The streets are bustling. The local supermarket parking lots are full to the brim with pre-Thanksgiving shoppers. Tourists are showing up in droves too, most of them making a stop here to shop or eat before they continue on their way to Yosemite National Park.

I go to Pete's Place because I'm craving chicken strips and fries, but when I spot the extra-long drive-thru line, I park instead, hoping it's not too busy inside. The parking lot is mostly empty, and when I walk in, I see most of the tables are empty save one. There's no one at the counter and I stop at it, staring up at the menu on the wall above the counter, though I already know what I'm going to order.

There's a guy standing behind the counter with his back to me, talking to one of the cooks through the window, and I frown. He looks very familiar...

He turns around and I realize it's Diego.

"Hey." He sounds as surprised as I feel. "Jos. What are you doing here?"

I hate that he calls me by my nickname. I hate even more that I feel no anger upon seeing him. I'm actually glad to see his stupid handsome face.

"I've come to order a late lunch," I tell him, leaning against the counter, suddenly anxious to tell him what happened earlier. How I think I felt the baby move. I even part my lips, ready to confess, but something tells me at the last second I shouldn't.

So I don't.

And maybe I didn't feel the baby. I looked it up, and it's kind of early for me to feel that. Maybe it was just gas.

I don't know.

"Oh. I just—I heard you were going to Oregon." His cheeks flush and I'm dying to know who told him that.

But I don't ask.

"I stayed home. I didn't want to go." I wrinkle my nose.

"Your parents didn't make you go?" He knows what sticklers they are.

I slowly shake my head. "They didn't. Can you believe it?"

I don't tell him the real reason my father is glad I didn't go. Because he's embarrassed by me and my "situation."

"You're here all alone?" He's scowling. "For how long?"

"My family will be back Saturday night," I answer.

"You're spending Thanksgiving alone then?" He lifts his brows.

"Yeah. Well, I might go to Marley's." She offered, but I don't know. I feel like all my friends' parents don't like having me around them anymore. Like what I have might be catching. "It's okay. I've been sleeping in. Taking naps."

God, I sound so boring. This is what my life has become.

His voice lowers. "Still tired?"

I nod. "It's only been a few days since we last talked so… yeah."

"Yeah." He glances over his shoulder real quick before he returns his attention to me. "You ready to order?"

"Yes, I'll have the—"

"Chicken strips and fries, with a cherry Pepsi," he finishes, tapping on the keys of the cash register.

Of course, he knows my order. We used to come here a lot when we were together. "No cherry Pepsi. I've cut back on the caffeine. I'll have a pink lemonade."

"Got it," he says as he totals up the order.

Once I've paid, I ask, "How long have you worked here?"

"A month. Once the dock closed, I needed to find another job. So here I am." He shrugs, looking sheepish as he grabs a Styrofoam cup and fills it with ice. "It kind of sucks."

I start to laugh. "You're used to being outside and having freedom when you work."

Last summer, he worked the boat docks at a local resort while I was a cashier in the restaurant. It's not an easy job. We were constantly busy and I was always on my feet, but I made great money in tips. So did Diego, though he enjoyed his time on the clock mostly by hanging out on the water and working on his tan.

"I've got way more respect for you girls in the fountain now, though," he says, his voice sincere. I wonder if that's actually true. He always made cracks about us girls working at the fountain, as if we were always at his beck and call. It was pretty sexist, but I tried to play it off by telling everyone he was just kidding.

Maybe he wasn't. I still really don't know.

Diego fills my cup with pink lemonade before handing it over to me. "Your food will be ready in a few minutes."

"Thanks." I take the cup from him, our fingers grazing, and a little shiver moves through me.

I ignore the shiver. Instead, I concentrate on the fact that we can have a decent conversation and how—grown up it feels. I'm proud of myself. I'm proud of Diego too. Look at us, being responsible adults.

Next step is for us to talk about the future. And the baby. We haven't yet, but we need to. I need to know. What is he going to do? What sort of role does he want to play in our child's future? Does he want to provide financial support? Does he want custody?

My mother says I shouldn't allow him any custody, but that's messed up. He's the baby's father. He deserves to be a part in our child's life, just as much as I do.

I go sit at a table not too far from the front counter and pretend to scroll through my phone, but I'm secretly watching Diego. The way he concentrates so hard on the register as he rings up another customer. How fast he is, which shouldn't surprise me, considering how fast he is on a football field. He smiles and chats up the customers, a younger couple with kids, and even though he's smiling, I can feel the tension he radiates. Something's bothering him. Something's always bothering him, it seems.

Right now, it's probably me.

It's when I'm actually looking at my phone that he surprises me with his approach, setting a tray with my meal and my drink onto the table I'm sitting at.

"Here you go," he says. "Need anything else?"

I glance up at him, wondering if I'm getting special treatment. I immediately tell myself I'm not. "No thank you. I'm good."

"Enjoy." He doesn't move. Doesn't smile either and I frown, wondering if he has something else to say.

He does.

"Listen, you want to meet up tonight? Maybe?" I part my lips, ready to say no, but he cuts me off. "Don't say no. We need—don't you think we should talk? About everything?"

I swallow hard, my appetite leaving me, replaced by nerves. He's right. We should talk. Wasn't I just thinking that exact same thing? But thinking it versus actually doing it is difficult.

"I don't know…" My voice drifts and I grab a fry, popping it into my mouth. It's hot and salty and has the perfect amount of crunch, and I close my eyes for the briefest moment, enjoying the taste.

When I open my eyes, I find Diego staring at me like he swallowed his tongue. Like he enjoyed watching me eat that fry. "Come on, Jos," he says, his voice hoarse. "I work until five. We can meet after that."

"Where?" Oh, I hate that I asked that. Now I sound like I actually want to do this.

Deep down, despite my anger toward him and the way he utterly, publicly humiliated me with his deceit, I still want to talk to him.

"Maybe…your house?" He raises his brows.

Nope. No way. "How about somewhere more public," I suggest.

The disappointment on his face is telling. What exactly does he think he'll gain, meeting at my house, the two of us all alone?

"Okay, sure," he says weakly. "How about five-fifteen at The Pizza Factory?"

Another favorite place of ours when we were together. Usually it's overrun with people our age, but it's a holiday week and I don't think it'll be too busy.

Or will it…

"That might be *too* public," I tell him.

The door swings open at the exact moment he's about to say something, and I glance over to find the very person I never want to see again, enter Pete's with her best friend. Or latest victim—whatever you want to call her.

It's Cami. Accompanied by Baylee, who's a senior on the cheer team with her.

Diego goes stiff. My appetite swiftly abandons me. Cami glances in our direction, doing a double take when she catches us together. I stare at her, never looking away, my heart pounding in my throat. Her eyes narrow as they rest on me for a brief second before flitting away to settle on Diego.

"Hey baby," she calls to him, accompanied by a flirty smile.

My insides curdle. The fact that she called him *baby* is especially awful, considering our situation.

He practically growls, and I can see both of his hands are clutched into tight fists, his knuckles going white. "What do you want, Cami?"

"Oh I don't know, maybe I want to place an order for food?" She giggles, glancing over at Baylee, who's as white as a sheet. She looks uncomfortable, which makes me feel the tiniest bit better. I've always believed that, deep down, Baylee has a heart.

Unlike Cami.

Diego sends me a look, his dark gaze full of remorse. Regret. If he could say sorry with just his eyes, I know that's what they'd be doing right now. "I gotta go take care of her."

His choice of wording is also awful, and I take them the wrong way, even though I know what he means.

"Go ahead." My tone is hostile, but I don't care. I flick my chin toward the front counter, where Cami and Baylee are currently waiting. "Get back to work."

He hesitates, his entire demeanor saying everything without uttering a single word, and then he leaves me, heading for the counter. I watch as he goes to the register, his expression tight, his eyes wild as he watches Cami.

Cami flirts with him shamelessly, glancing over her shoulder every other second to make sure I'm watching.

I don't look away. I keep watch, my gaze steady, not flinching when Cami leans over and touches Diego's forearm.

He jerks away from her as if her touch burned him.

I thought I'd feel satisfaction at his obvious rejection, but I feel nothing. Nothing at all. I'm numb.

Utterly numb.

It's when they finish up the transaction that I realize I'm already out of my seat, heading for the front doors. My tray of food sits on the table where I left it, and I'm pushing on the door handle, about to walk outside when I hear her voice.

God, why can't she just leave me alone?

Ignoring her, I keep walking, my back straight, my steps determined, my heart…aching. She's calling my name repeatedly, so I finally whirl around, unable to take it anymore.

"What do you want?"

She slows her steps, sauntering toward me as if she doesn't have a care in the world, a little smirk curling her lips. She's gorgeous and she knows it. The only thing that ruins her good looks—besides her toxic personality and wretched soul—are those eyelash extensions that are too long and spidery. They're obviously fake.

And obviously horrible.

"I keep hearing these rumors," she says, coming to a stop in front of me. She's shorter than I am. And skinnier. Especially now. "And I have *such* a hard time believing them."

"Oh, the ones about me being pregnant?" I ask nonchalantly. Her eyes pop wide open at me saying it so bluntly. Why hide it? "They're true."

She laughs, but it sounds nervous. "Bullshit."

I say nothing. Just stare at her.

The laughter dies, and Cami slowly shakes her head. "He told me you were lying."

Anger fills me, making me see red, and I swallow hard, trying to hide it. So they're still talking? Of course they are. "He's an asshole," I bite out.

"Yet you come to Pete's and talk to him." She crosses her arms in front of her, cocking a hip out.

"I had no idea he worked here." Why am I defending myself to this bitch? "And who are you to judge? You're doing the same thing."

"He asked me to come see him." She blinks at me, her eyelashes getting tangled together, I swear to God. "I couldn't resist."

Why is he such a liar? Why did he tell me he's not talking to Cami anymore when clearly, he is?

"What about Wyatt?" I saw the two of them together on the football field last Friday night, all snuggled up and taking pics like they're an actual couple.

"Oh Wyatt." She waves a hand, dismissing him. "He's young. Eager. Fun. Sweet."

A pushover, is basically what she's saying. I cross my arms as well, mimicking her pose. "And why are we talking again?"

Her expression turns stone cold in an instant. "You never did like me."

"You've never really liked me either," I remind her.

"I wanted to." She presses her lips together, as if she wishes she could take that back. "Back in middle school. We hung out in the same friend group."

Sort of. Not really. I never got the sense that we'd be friends. We never had anything in common. Plus, she was a mean girl, and I'm not. "We're wasting our breath," I tell her just as I turn and start toward my car.

I guess being pregnant is making me stand up for myself. It's kind of nice.

Okay, it's really nice. It's actually empowering.

"So that's it? You're just going to walk away from me?" she yells.

"I owe you nothing." I stop at my car, hitting the keyless remote, and open the door. I glance in her direction to find her scowling at me. "You don't owe me anything either."

Her smile returns. "Really. Even though I stole your man?"

Leave it to Cami to say something like that. She's such a nightmare. "You can have him," I tell her, just before I climb into my car and slam the door.

The look on Cami's face as I drive out of the parking lot is priceless. I keep it together for approximately ninety seconds before I promptly burst into tears.

CHAPTER 6

DIEGO

Cami comes back into the restaurant, her cheeks pink, her mouth screwed up in a mini-scowl. She stops at the counter, glaring at me before she asks, "Are you back together with her?"

I glance over my shoulder really quick to make sure no one is listening before I take a step closer, leaning over the counter to whisper, "It's none of your fucking business."

I spring away from her quickly, grateful that I do. Bitch looks like she wants to pop me in the mouth.

"You can't talk to me like that," she says, her voice rising.

Baylee comes over to us, her expression full of worry. "Cami, don't make a scene."

"Shut up," she snaps at her supposed best friend, though her venom is all for me. I can see it in her eyes. "We have unfinished business, Garcia."

"What's done is done." The absolute biggest regret of my life is standing in front of me, reminding me of what a fuck up I am. How I messed everything up with the girl I loved. The rumors spread so damn fast, incinerated by Cami, and there was no way I could control them. People believe what they want to believe.

Even if it's not true.

"I don't think so." She taps her black fingernail against her pursed lips, contemplating me. "You can't just walk away from me."

"I already did," I say through clenched teeth. I don't want to deal with her anymore. Ever. And I hate how she showed up, just as I was having a good conversation with Jocelyn. As usual, Cami fucks everything up.

Well, I fucked it up originally. I have to take responsibility for most of this mess. It's not all Cami's fault.

"Cami, come on," Baylee says, grabbing hold of Cami's arm. "Let's go wait for our food at a table."

Cami glares, letting Baylee drag her away, her gaze never leaving mine. I glare in return, reveling in the anger bubbling inside of me. Wishing I could throw down on this chick, just to give her a taste of her own damn medicine, but I would never. I don't hit women.

Not like my dad.

The second they're at a table, their heads bent close as they furiously whisper, I'm out of there. I push through the swinging door that leads into the kitchen, tearing off my apron as I head for my boss, the owner, Pete. He's standing outside of his office door, watching me as I approach. "I need to take a break," I tell him.

He eyes me up and down, probably feeling the hostility vibrating off of me. "Go for it. I'll have Kristi watch the front."

"Thanks." I ball my red apron in my fist, tunnel vision leading me toward the back door that opens out onto the parking lot. I stand directly out back, at the spot where some of us smoke when we take our break, and I pull out a trashed pack of cigarettes I keep lodged in between two old bricks that make up the siding of the building.

I'm not much of a smoker, but lately, I've been puffing away on cigs while on work breaks, just to take my mind off the bullshit. Can't show up to work high as a motherfucker all the time, so this is the next best thing.

Even though it's gross. And it can kill me.

Fuck it.

Inhaling deeply, I wait for the nicotine to hit, ducking around the corner when I see Cami and Baylee exit the restaurant. Baylee's carrying the bag of food and both drinks, while Cami is ranting on, waving her hands about.

Bitching about me.

"You'd think that asshole would be *thrilled* to see me. Of course, he'd be hanging out with his pregnant ex when we show up." She sounds absolutely disgusted.

"Let it go, Cam. You've got Wyatt now. You and Diego were never going to work," Baylee practically begs.

Baylee's not wrong.

"We could've," Cami says, a sulk in her voice. That's what I hate about her the most. She sulks. She pouts. She practically stomps her feet and has a tantrum, like she's a pissed-off toddler. She's not pleasant to be with, not even sexually. You find that out real quick, because she comes at you strong and hard, acting like she's sweet. Acting like she's interested. It's all smoke and mirrors. The minute she thinks she has you in her claws, her true self comes out to play, and she's not much fun.

This is why guys don't stick around. Jake was the only one who got completely ensnared by her, but I bet he blames that on youth. We were young and she was pretty. I get it.

I get why he wants to have nothing to do with her now. I feel the same exact way.

The girls get into Cami's car, Baylee shuffling the drinks

and food around before she slides inside, and I watch as they drive away. They never spotted me, thank God.

I feel sorry for Baylee. I don't know why she puts up with Cami's shit, but I figure, eventually, she'll be gone too. Everyone abandons Cami. Friends. Boyfriends. Never that bitch of a mother of hers though. Cami refuses to take responsibility for not keeping friends or boyfriends around. She thinks everyone else is in the wrong, and her mother encourages that mindset.

My dad told me once a long time ago that if you think everyone around you is acting like an asshole, then maybe you need to take a step back and look at yourself. Because you're probably the asshole.

It's the most valuable advice he's ever said to me, not that he's given me much.

In Cami's case, she's the asshole. Always. But she never sees it.

What's that like, moving through life as if nothing can touch you? As if you never do wrong? I fuck up left and right, and I know it, even though sometimes—a lot of the time—I don't take responsibility for my actions either.

Shit. Maybe Cami and I are more alike than I thought.

As I suck on my cigarette, my mind shifts to Jocelyn. Seeing her walk into the restaurant alone earlier had been a complete shock. I keep tabs on her, thanks to our mutual friends, and I thought she was going out of town for break.

But she's here. All alone in that big house of hers, with no family around. Is that safe, considering her condition? There's no one to protect her. And if she'd never come in, I would've never known.

Now I know. And I want to be the one to watch over her. She's my responsibility. Her and the baby.

She looked so pretty. Even a little different, but not in a bad way. Her face was fuller, and her hair looked thicker. I did some research and read that your nails and hair grow faster when you're pregnant. Found out some other stuff too. Like she might be able to know what the sex of the baby is soon, though it's probably still too early. If I had my choice, I'd want a boy. A little mini me who I can teach how to catch a football.

Not that I can teach him anything for a while. He'll be too small. And crying all the time. Babies are needy. Helpless. Time consuming. How is Jocelyn going to handle going to college and being a mom? I know she still plans on going to school. I overheard her friend Sam talking about Jocelyn giving up on her San Diego State dream, and how she'll go to Fresno State now.

I feel bad that she's giving up on her dream, but I'm also secretly glad she's sticking around. Like me. I'll more than likely be at Fresno State too, playing football.

Hopefully.

If Coach Callahan caught me smoking right now? He'd have a freakin' coronary. He'd rip the cigarette out of my mouth and stomp all over it, all the while giving me a big ol' guilt ridden speech. Smoking is bad for my lungs. It'll fuck with my running ability and slow me down. But right now, I'm under an enormous amount of stress, and it helps soothe my frayed nerves.

At least for a little while.

Besides the fact that the biggest game of my life is coming up and oh, I'm going to be a daddy here in about five to six months, I also have other concerns. Like my mother.

I still haven't told her about Jocelyn and the baby. And when she finds out? She might try and whip my ass. She could probably do it too. My mama is scary sometimes. This is why I haven't told her yet. And for whatever reason, Mateo still hasn't ratted me out either. Maybe because the bastard is up to no good and dipping into my so-called *secret* cash fund on the regular. I ended up taking a bunch of the money I had in cash to the bank, where I deposited it all into my savings account. I was short about three hundred and I know where it all went.

Into my brother's pockets and up his nose. Or in a vein. I don't even know what he's doing anymore. Why couldn't he stick to weed and that's it?

Fuck that asshole for trying to steal my hard-earned money while he's a lazy ass without a job.

Considering it's almost Thanksgiving, I feel like this is the time where I need to come clean and confess my secret. Mom needs to find out from me before someone else tells her. I can only imagine one of her friends spotting Jocelyn at the grocery store or wherever with a pregnant belly and telling my mom all about it.

Mom isn't stupid. She'd know in an instant the baby was mine. No one else has touched Jocelyn. Just me.

She was mine. Until she wasn't.

I'm running out of time, and I need to make my confession. No matter how difficult it's going to be. I need to man up.

In lots of ways.

In all the ways.

Taking one last puff on my cig, I grind it out in the black plastic ashtray that's left outside and head back into the kitchen, thankful I only have a couple of hours left until I get off work.

And then I can meet Jocelyn at the Pizza Factory.

Will she still meet with me? Or is she all pissed off thanks to the run in with Cami? That bitch knows how to ruin everything.

Like my entire life.

* * *

I show up at the Pizza Factory and wait in the parking lot, scrolling through my phone, ignoring the endless stream of texts from Cami. She started out angry.

Why are you ignoring me?

Who the hell do you think you are?

Fuck you Diego! You're nothing but a cock sucking asshole!

The girl is all class. And she's also an idiot. I can't just stop working and text her back. Though she has no idea what it's like, to actually have to work for a living.

An hour after her initial rant, she tried to sweet talk me.

I miss you.

We were so good together. I know you felt the same way.

Please Diego. I miss you. So much.

Accompanied by a string of red heart emojis.

I hit block, ending that problem once and for all. I block her everywhere, all over social media, unfollowing and blocking and doing all the things I should've done months ago.

Ridding Cami from my life once and for all. Why it took me so long, I don't know. I wasn't thinking straight. When am I ever?

I start to wonder if Cami might be bipolar. Like, seriously. She switches moods so fast, it makes my head spin. And no, I never thought we were good together. We were never officially together in my eyes, so I have no idea what she's talking about.

Sometimes, I also think Cami lives in her own little world. One I definitely don't want to be in.

The clock slips past five-fifteen and I send Jocelyn a text asking if she's coming, but I have no idea if she gets it, since she admitted she blocked me everywhere.

By the time it's five-thirty, I assume I'm being stood up,

and without hesitation, I back out of the parking spot and hit the highway, heading toward the lake.

Toward Jocelyn's neighborhood.

Fifteen minutes later when I turn off the highway, I tell myself I have two options. I can go to Jocelyn's and confront her. Though that's probably not the smartest approach. I'm guessing she's pissed thanks to Cami showing up at my work.

I didn't invite her to Pete's. I can't control where Cami goes or what she does. But I'm sure in Jocelyn's eyes, I'm to blame for it.

My other option is to go see Jake. They stay home for Thanksgiving, and it's one of his family's favorites. His uncle Owen and his family usually spend it with him, and the cousins all hang out together. A couple of years ago I went to their house for Thanksgiving, and it was so much fun. They're like one giant, happy family out of a fucking movie.

I never thought that kind of thing existed. My family always gets together for the various holidays too, but someone always starts an argument. Or someone gets mad. Lots of them drink too much. Eventually, someone cries.

Yeah. Lots of fun.

Choosing my option, I head for the house, telling myself in the end, it'll all be okay. Showing up unannounced, without a call or a warning, is usually no big deal, especially during the holidays. When everyone's hearts are filled with generosity and all that bullshit.

I'll be fine, I tell myself. I'll be totally fine.

Eventually, I pull into the driveway and kill the car's engine, then the lights. I sit in the driveway, my gaze landing on the massive, lit Christmas tree sitting in the front window, the white lights glittering in the dark. It looks homey. Inviting. And it fills my cold-ass heart with longing. Wishing for something I've never had.

Climbing out of the car, I head for the front door, climb the porch steps, and hit the doorbell.

Nothing.

I knock on the door. Rapidly. Three knocks in a row.

Still nothing.

Worry filling me, I glance around, spotting the partially open gate on the side of the house. That's dangerous as fuck. Any asshole can walk straight into their back yard.

Like me.

I make my way around to the back of the house, where I see the kitchen lights are on. There's a lone figure inside, standing at the counter, her long, dark hair in a messy bun. It looks like she's making…

Cookies?

Creeping closer, the sugary, chocolaty scent hits me. Jocelyn is making chocolate chip cookies.

My favorite.

She's got an ice cream scooper thing and she's scooping the dough out of a giant bowl, plopping it on top of the cookie sheet in small round balls. She rubs at her forehead with the side of her hand, since her fingers appear coated in dough, and there's a giant streak of what I think is flour across the front of her sweater.

She's an adorable mess.

I'm so entranced by watching her, I sort of forget I'm not supposed to be there. I come closer to the window. Even closer. Until I'm standing directly in front of it and I can hear her phone is on. Playing an old Spotify playlist that used to drive me up the fucking wall because she listened to those songs on repeat every morning when we sat in her car in the parking lot before class started.

Over and over.

Hearing them now fills me with a nostalgic pain over what I lost.

I was an idiot. A fool.

Jos glances up, as if she can hear my thoughts, and our gazes meet. Lock. She blinks once. Twice, a frown on her face. She grabs a towel off the counter and furiously wipes her hands as she makes her way to the back door. I remain rooted in place, fully prepared for her to tell me to get the fuck out of here.

It's the least I deserve.

CHAPTER 7

JOCELYN

When I got home from the disastrous late lunch at Pete's Place, I immediately knew I needed a distraction, or else I'd go out of my mind running over everything that happened again and again.

So I started making cookies.

Having to concentrate on following the recipe and mixing the ingredients was just the thing I needed to take my mind off my run-in with Cami. The things she said to me. Seeing Diego confused me even more. He's so…nice. He says things that make no sense.

Was he actually ever with Cami? Did they have sex? Everyone said they did.

Everyone.

But he makes it seem like they didn't. She, of course, acts like they're still talking, and maybe they are. It's almost easier to believe the worst of Diego. Believing he did all of those things with Cami gives me permission to hate him. Allows me to keep him at arm's length at all times, so I don't have to deal with him. See his face. Remember everything we once shared.

At one point, our relationship was good. Great. We were —in my eyes—the perfect couple. Yes, Diego is a little rough around the edges, but I felt like I smoothed all of those edges out. I calmed him down. I made him happy.

It happened suddenly, Diego's unhappiness. One day, he was fine, and then the next, he was miserable. At least, that's what it felt like. But maybe I was wrapped up in my own crap and I didn't see the transition. Something was going on in his life that made him angry, and I still to this day don't know what it was.

I'll probably never know.

It's when I'm in the middle of making cookies, absently bobbing my head to the beat of some of my favorite songs while plopping sticky dough on the baking sheet, that I get the feeling that someone is watching me.

Glancing up, I catch Diego standing in my back yard, staring at me through the kitchen window. He's wearing a black beanie on his head and a black sweatshirt, and he looks good in both.

Of course.

Finding him watching me doesn't scare me or freak me out. It's almost as if I expected to see him. Maybe because I didn't show up at the Pizza Factory and that's why it's not a surprise? He's probably pissed.

But as I study his face, see the pain etched into his familiar features, the way his gaze trails after me as I approach, I can tell he's not really angry at all.

He looks downright sad.

I unlock and then open the door, shivering when the brisk cold air hits me. "What are you doing here?"

His expression solemn, he asks, "Can I come in?"

Emotions war within me. I should tell him no, even though my automatic reaction is to say yes. "There's a reason I didn't meet you at the Pizza Factory tonight."

He shoves his hands into the front pocket of his black hoodie. "Let me guess. It has everything to do with Cami."

"She said you asked her to meet you there." When he frowns, I explain further. "At Pete's."

The words linger between us as he studies me, his expression switching from surprise to disgust in a matter of seconds. He makes a dismissive noise. "She would say that."

"So it's true?" My heart sinks. I'd kind of hoped she was lying to me.

"Of course not. We're not together. We were never really together," he says.

I hold up my hand. "Save it. I don't want to hear it."

"Why not? She's one of the main reasons we broke up."

Cami Lockhart was definitely one of the main reasons, but there were other things. His bad attitude for one. How quick he was to anger. We fought a lot. He became so needy, demanding all of my time when I couldn't give it to him. He wanted me at his beck and call, but I was busy. School. Volleyball. My friends. I wasn't going to give up everything for him. I didn't want to lose myself.

Besides, he was busy too. It was difficult, getting our schedules to coincide.

I always figured my unavailability drove him into Cami's arms. The rumors began when I went to Mammoth for a volleyball tournament for the weekend. People whispered about him and Cami flirting at one of Tony's parties. This happened a few times. Until it all blew up in my face during homecoming week, which was a nightmare.

When I didn't make it as a finalist for homecoming queen and Cami did? That was the end. I broke up with him that night, after telling him I was pregnant, though he refused to believe me.

Who does that?

Another shiver steals over me, and I go to close the door. "Let's have this conversation another night."

"No." He steps forward, placing his hand on the door and stopping its progression. "Let me in, Jos. We need to talk. About our future. About our baby."

I'd love to slam the door in his face and tell him to go to hell, but the responsible part of me says I can't. Diego is right.

We need to talk. About our baby.

A deep sigh leaves me as I open the door wider and let him inside.

He walks in as if he belongs here, and I remember the last time he came over. When my parents invited him over for dinner and they ended up making him feel like shit for who he is.

What he is.

He'd been so upset. Almost crying, I swear. I'd tried to comfort him, and he'd looked me straight in the eyes, his expression deadly serious, before he said, "I'll prove to them I'm worthy of you, Jocelyn. I swear to fucking God I will."

Now look. He lived up to their low expectations. My parents knew he'd end up being a great disappointment, and they were right.

"You want a cookie?" I already have one sheet cooked, and it's sitting on top of the stove where I left it to cool. Luckily enough, I didn't put another cookie sheet in the oven before I noticed Diego, or else I probably would've burned them.

"I'll take two if you don't mind," he says.

I busy myself in the kitchen, grabbing the spatula and sliding off two cookies onto a napkin before I bring them to Diego. He's settled in at the kitchen nook table, eyeing the cookies greedily when I hand them to him.

"Thanks," he says, shoving half the cookie in his mouth. His eyes nearly close as he mumbles, "Oh my God, so good."

He always did like chocolate chip cookies. Who doesn't? "You want a glass of milk?"

"Please," he says, cramming the rest of the cookie into his mouth.

I pour him a glass of milk and take it to him, then continue bustling around the kitchen. I place the rest of the already cooked cookies on a plate and then bring the sheet over to the island, where I drop more dough onto it. The timer goes off and I check my cookies, then switch out the sheets and start a new batch.

Diego watches me, and I wonder if he knows I'm trying my best to avoid him. Yes, I know this conversation needs to happen, but no, I don't really want to deal with it right now. I'm scared.

Scared of the unknown. Scared about this baby. I know nothing about being a mom. How am I supposed to do this all by myself? Yes, I'll have my mom's support, but I'm going to be responsible for another human being's *life*.

I'm barely responsible for my own life. I'm kind of a wreck sometimes.

It's when I slide the last cookie sheet of dough into the oven that Diego finally says something.

"Why did you decide to keep it?"

I let the oven door slam shut, turning to face him. "What do you mean?"

"I don't know." He shrugs. "You used that, 'it's my body, I can do what I want' speech on me at one point, and I figured you'd—you know. Get an abortion."

I lean my back against the kitchen counter, remembering when I told him that. He'd been trying to tell me what to do, and I wouldn't have it. "I thought about it. Having an abortion. It probably would've been easier."

He nods, his expression blank.

"But the more I thought about doing it, the more scared I became. And sad. I couldn't just—destroy another human being's life because I'm too young to have a baby. It broke my heart just thinking about it," I explain, knowing I'm not doing a very good job. "I would never judge someone who has to make this kind of decision. It's so difficult. And if their choice is abortion, that's okay. But I couldn't let that be my choice. I couldn't destroy something that we—we made."

It hurt to admit that last part. My voice cracked on those last words, and I know he heard it, but it's the truth.

I couldn't destroy a life we created. Even though our relationship is awful and most likely toxic AF and we shouldn't be together, I couldn't banish this baby to a distant memory of a bad relationship.

Maybe I'm foolish, but that's my choice.

"I guess I get it," he says. "Do you want me to give you money?"

"Can you afford to give me money?"

"Yeah." He shrugs. "Not much, but I want to help."

"I'll take whatever help you can give," I say, my voice soft.

His gaze meets mine. "What about custody?"

"What about it?"

"I want to see him. Want him to get to know me," he says.

My brows shoot up. "Him? What if it's a her?"

"It's a boy," he says with all the confidence in the world. "And we're going to name him Diego Junior."

I burst out laughing. "No, we are not."

"Why not? That's a great name." He actually sounds offended.

"You're being ridiculous. We're not going to name him after you. And for all you know, it could be a girl."

"Nah. It's a boy." He smiles.

I smile too.

His smile fades just as quickly as it appeared. "Hey, I'm sorry Cami showed up at Pete's today. Swear to God, I didn't know she was coming there. And whatever she told you when she followed you out to the parking lot? It was most likely bullshit. She's a liar."

I know she's a liar, but she has this way of making everything that comes out of her mouth sound true. She's manipulative, and of course, she knows just how to get to me.

So does Diego.

When he's mad at me, he turns on the charm for other girls. As if he wants to make me jealous. At first, it didn't bother me. But as time went on, it started to wear on me. Cami is flirtatious too. That's how she entices so many guys, with her flirty, *I want you so bad* ways.

Then they get to know her.

But the two of them together? I'm sure they flirted heavily. They'd probably been dancing around each other for months. The second I became "neglectful," she was on him like white on rice. No girl code for Cami. No caring who she might hurt. It's all about her.

She's one of the most selfish people I know.

"Whatever." I wave a hand, dismissing his apology. I have no idea if he's being real with me right now or not. And I sort of don't care either. Or I tell myself I don't. "I'm sure we can work out a custody agreement once the baby is born."

"When is the due date?"

He doesn't even know. Of course, I've never told him either. "May 26th."

"No shit." He whistles low, as if the date surprised him. "Right before graduation."

"I probably won't get to walk in the ceremony." And that'll break my parents' hearts.

"Sure you will," he says easily. "You'll be fine by then."

"I'll still be fat," I say.

"Good thing we wear those stupid capes and gowns so no one will know what you look like under it," he says.

I start to laugh. "Capes? We're not superheroes, D."

His eyes light up at me calling him that, and I sort of regret it.

Then again, I sort of don't.

"Sure we are. I'm a superhero on the football field, and you're a superhero on the volleyball court," he teases.

This feels familiar. Like when we used to be together. I can't get used to it.

"My volleyball glory days are gone," I remind him. "I'll never play it competitively again."

"Not going to try in college?"

"If I was going to do that, I'd apply to Fresno Pacific. Their team is better." And I'm not good enough to get on their team. It's pretty elite. I don't want to go there anyway. "It's okay. I came to terms with it a while ago."

"And here I am still playing." His expression turns wistful. "We have a real shot."

"Yeah you do."

"You coming to the game?"

I shrug. "I don't know."

"You should."

"Depends on if my friends go." No way am I going alone.

But no way do I want to miss this moment either.

"I'm probably going to end up at Fresno State too, you know," he says conversationally, though his gaze is very, very serious. "Like you."

"Yeah? Maybe we can do baby swaps on campus." I'm teasing, but he's nodding enthusiastically.

"That's a good idea."

I can't help but laugh. "If you say so."

His expression turns somber in an instant. "Hey, I was wondering if I could ask you a favor."

Dread fills me as I tense up. "What is it?"

"It's just that—hear me out, okay? I was wondering if you wanted to come to my house for Thanksgiving?"

"I don't know if that's a good idea..." I start, but he cuts me off.

"I was hoping we could be together when I tell my mom about the baby," he says.

My mouth pops open. "Wait a minute. She doesn't know?"

CHAPTER 8

DIEGO

*J*ocelyn's looking at me like I've lost my damn mind.

"No, I uh." I pause, trying to gauge her reaction, and I can see she's visibly shaken. "I haven't told her yet."

She leaps to her feet, surprisingly fast for being pregnant. Though I guess it's not slowing her down quite yet. "What the hell, Diego? Why are you keeping it from her?"

"I don't know." I shrug. "I just haven't found the right time to tell her yet."

"When were you going to tell her? When I went into labor? Oh my God." She starts pacing the length of the kitchen, back and forth, her face screwed up in concentration as she mutters to herself and shakes her head repeatedly.

I just let her do it. Don't bother stopping her or trying to explain why I waited so long. I don't really have a good answer.

"Are you afraid she's going to be mad at you for getting me pregnant?" Jocelyn finally asks.

Leave it to her to be completely blunt. "No." *Yes.*

"I don't think she'll be mad."

"She'll be furious." My voice is flat. Just like my emotions. Thinking about my mother's reaction sends me into a damn tailspin. This is why I haven't told her. "She'll tell me I'm fucking up my future and I'm flushing my chance at a football scholarship away."

Jocelyn's brows wrinkle. "How is my pregnancy going to affect your chance at a football scholarship? Do they even give those out still?"

"Of course they do."

"My having a baby won't affect that whatsoever."

"I know that. You know that. But my mother will assume that we'll get back together and get married and I'll be distracted by the baby and have to provide for my family, because that's what a man does. He has to step up. She'll expect me to do exactly that, no matter what you want. She won't listen to me, and she sure as hell won't listen to you either." I take a deep breath and exhale shakily. Those were the most words I've said to Jocelyn in a while. She's just watching me, her eyes wide, her lips parted. She looks like she's in pain, and yeah, maybe my words hurt her, but she needed to hear it.

"I don't—want to marry you, Diego. Or even live with you," she says, her voice barely above a whisper. "I don't care what your mother says. She can't force us to do that."

"I won't let her," I say vehemently. "But if you came over for Thanksgiving, we could tell her—together. She'll listen to you, Jos. She respects you. She always has. You tell her how you've got this all figured out, and I'll help wherever I can, and she'll be okay with that answer."

Hopefully.

"I don't have this all figured out," Jos says. "I'm literally taking this day by day. I have no idea exactly what I'm going to do."

"You have a plan for college," I point out.

"Only because my mom said she'd watch the baby for me."

"What about money?"

"My parents will help me. Us." When I frown, she explains, "Me and the baby."

For a second there, I thought she meant me and her.

But that's over. No matter how much I don't want it to be.

"How long is that going to last?"

"Excuse me?"

"Support from your mom. Financial support from your parents. They have their own family to raise. Your brother and sister. And eventually, you'll want out of the house. That'll be a long commute, driving from here all the way into Fresno every single day. You'll want to move down there. Start your own life with you and our son."

Now she's rolling her eyes. "It might be a girl, you know."

I don't think God would be that cruel. Having a baby girl might tear me up inside. I'd have to protect her from all the douchebags like me in the world.

"Whatever it is, you can't stay up here forever," I say. "It'll get harder and harder."

"I'll figure it out," she says with a shrug.

"I can help too, you know."

"You'll have classes and football. You'll be even busier than me."

"I can still help. I want to." The unyielding expression on her face tells me she doesn't believe me. "It's my baby too. I want to be a part of his life."

She plucks a cookie off the cooling rack and starts munching on it, eventually shoving it into her mouth like I did. "Since when did this shit become so complicated?"

"Since the two of us got careless and forgot to use a condom."

We both go quiet and I wonder if she remembers the night it happened.

I do. In that little one room cabin by the lake at Tony's place. I'd been on a high from a game win, and she'd been so pretty that night. So agreeable. The tension between us had dissipated—from negative to downright sexual. We weren't arguing. We were magnetic. And when I slipped inside her without a condom and felt all that tight, wet heat surrounding my dick? Fuck, I couldn't control myself.

Bad decision though. Now look at us.

"If I go to your house for Thanksgiving, you have to tell your mom upfront that we're not back together," Jocelyn says.

I nod, willing to agree to anything to get her to help me make this announcement. I don't want to do it alone.

Does that make me a chicken shit? Yes. But I don't really care.

"Who else will be there?" she asks.

"My aunt and her kids." Including my cousin Marty. He hates me. I guess he should. When he was younger and it was fairly obvious he was gay, though he hadn't come out yet, I pretty much made his life fuckin' miserable. I was a complete dick, showing off for my friends, embarrassed by my gay-acting cousin. I also wanted to impress my brother—that was always my ultimate goal. So I made fun of Marty. And once I got the response I wanted, I bullied his ass pretty much every day.

His mama still doesn't like me very much. Neither does Marty. They hold a grudge against me, and I can't blame them. I've apologized to Marty a few times, but I don't know if he's forgiven me. Or if he ever can.

"Will Marty be there?" Jocelyn asks hopefully. She likes him, and he likes her too. They hang out at school together all the time, which pisses me off, but how can I tell them to stop?

And honestly, it's not that it makes me mad. More like I envy his ability to hang out with my ex while I can only stare at her from afar.

Until today. Tonight. I'm in her house right now, just the two of us. I never felt very welcome here. Her parents didn't approve of me. I figured they thought I was just a stage Jocelyn was going through. The *slumming it with the bad boy* stage. When really, I'm not that much of a bad boy...

Okay, fuck that. I am. I may as well embrace it. I've tried to straighten up this year, but my brother moved back in, setting me on edge. And then the Cami fiasco messed me up. And when my life spiraled out of control, instead of wasting my breath and protesting that everything people said wasn't true, I just went along with it. They wouldn't believe me anyway.

Cami and I fucked behind Jocelyn's back? Yeah. We sure did.

We were hooking up that one night after a game at Tony's house? Uh huh.

Cami rigged it so Jocelyn wouldn't make it into the finals for homecoming queen? So it was easier for us to be paired up? Oh yeah, Cami definitely has that much power at school.

Everyone believes what they want. So what's the point in arguing?

"Yeah, he'll be there. My brother too." The last words I spit out bitterly.

"Oh. I never did get a chance to see him much," she says.

Because I didn't want to bring her around him. I didn't want him to see her. Seeing her makes her even more real in Mateo's eyes, and then he'll try and use her as collateral against me.

I hate my brother. He's the embodiment of our father, and

that is the last person anyone should want to be like. I swore I wouldn't end up like him, yet look at me.

I'm close. Real fucking close.

And it sucks.

"It'll probably be uncomfortable and you're more than welcome to bow out. You don't owe me anything," I explain. "It's just that I…"

Need you.

The words remain unspoken, but it's as if they're floating in the room between us. She knows I need her in this situation. And I know it too.

If I can't have her back, then I can at least remain civil with her. And we can navigate this uncertain future of ours…

Together.

"I don't know." She sounds unsure, and I suppose I can't blame her. "I'm not with you anymore. It might be—weird."

"We're having a baby together," I remind her. "It can't get any weirder than it already is. We're tied together forever, Jos."

Forever.

The realization hits me and nearly sends me toppling over. I'm tied to Jocelyn for the rest of my life. Not just the, *oh she was my first high school love* feeling, where the memories eventually fade and she becomes nothing but a lost photo found in an old box when I clean out my desk or whatever.

No, she is in my life for-fucking-ever. Having a child with her is a permanent tether. I'm not walking away from this baby. And she is sure as shit not going anywhere.

We're in this together.

"Fine." She sighs. "You're right. It can't get any weirder if I show up with you at your house on Thanksgiving."

It could get weirder, but I don't say that. She hasn't been with my family during a holiday. We're a handful.

"If you become uncomfortable or you don't want to deal

with it—us—anymore, I'll take you home. I don't mind." I make the offer because she's doing me a tremendous favor. I can't believe I got her to agree to do it in the first place. She should tell me to fuck off and never bother her again.

Getting along with Jocelyn is easy for me, but I'm not the one who feels as if I was wronged. She is. And maybe someday, when things settle down and there's more distance from the breakup, I can tell her the truth.

If she'll believe me.

"You want another cookie?" She scoops up a couple more and shuffles over to the table where I'm sitting, dropping two cookies on my crumb-covered napkin.

"Thanks," I tell her, wishing she gave me four, but trying not to be too greedy.

We munch on cookies and make small talk about nothing and everything. Until she starts cleaning up around the kitchen and I get up to help her. I wipe off the counters while she loads the dishwasher, and she hands me a container to stash the remaining cookies in, though there aren't many left.

Once we're done, I can tell she's tired. Her eyelids are heavy, and she's moving slower.

"I should go," I say, sliding my hand into the front pocket of my hoodie and jangling my car keys. "Thanks—thanks for everything."

Her smile is faint. A little sleepy. "What do you mean, everything? The cookies?"

"The cookies, yeah for sure. But also for agreeing to come over for Thanksgiving. It means a lot, that you'll be there with me when I tell my mom," I explain.

"Do you really think she'll be upset?" Jocelyn frowns.

"I don't know how she'll feel. But I don't really care." Liar. You care way too much.

"What's done is done."

"I didn't mean to mess up your life, Diego. I hope you

know that," she whispers. "It was never my intention to ruin your life or your chances or whatever. I just—I couldn't stand the thought of not having this baby."

"I know you didn't, Jos." I do. When she first told me, it was all I could focus on. How this is going to affect me. What's going to happen to me. I was a selfish asshole who reacted instantly, instead of thinking things through.

But I've never been one to think things through, so I know she wasn't surprised. That she even tolerates my ass makes me think she has the patience of a saint.

Saint Jocelyn. It fits.

"Whatever happens, it'll be okay." She rubs her hand over her stomach, the first time she's indicated she's actually pregnant since I got here. "She'll be fine."

"You mean he."

Jos rolls her eyes. "Whatever."

"Does it—does it hurt?" When she frowns, I explain further. "Being pregnant. Are you uncomfortable? In pain?"

"I'm not in pain. I'm uncomfortable sometimes, but I'm barely into the second trimester. It's the third trimester when I'll really start being miserable. I'll probably get as big as a house." She sounds grumpy, and it's kind of cute.

"No you won't." I wave a hand at her. She's still thin. I don't see a belly. You'd never know she's pregnant. "Can you —tell?"

She suddenly looks shy. Her cheeks turn rosy pink and she keeps her eyes downcast. "Yeah. You can."

"Can I see?"

Her startled gaze meets mine. "What do you mean?"

"Show me." I point directly at her stomach. "Smooth your hand over your sweater."

Jocelyn stands to the side and places her hand below her breasts, slowly running her hand down the front of her. She has the slightest bump. "It's tiny."

"That could be a cookie baby," I tease, and she sticks her tongue out at me, right before she lifts up the hem of her sweater and shows me her bare stomach. The waistband of her leggings is high, covering her belly button and pretty much her entire stomach. I can see it now.

A tiny baby bump.

"See?" She cups her hand around the swell of her stomach and I'm hit with this unfamiliar sensation that nearly sends me to my knees.

This girl is going to have my baby. She's going to be the mother of my child. I'm going to be her baby daddy.

That is the stupidest saying in the world, but that's who I'll be.

"I see it," I finally say, my throat tight. Full of emotion. "You look good. Carrying my baby."

She smiles, but it doesn't quite meet her eyes and I know I've blown it.

I pushed too hard with that last sentence.

CHAPTER 9

JOCELYN

I'm digging through my closet, trying to find the right thing to wear to Diego's house for Thanksgiving dinner. He's picking me up soon, and I already had an entire outfit planned. My favorite jeans that still fit me, and a rust-colored sweater I found a few weeks ago and begged my mom to buy. Even though she told me Christmas was coming and I could wait until then to get it, I eventually wore her down and she gave it to me.

An early Christmas present, she said, her eyes sad.

I'm tired of the sadness. I need some normalcy in my life. Having Diego around feels…dare I even think it?

Normal.

I slip the sweater on, loving how soft and cozy it is. It feels like a hug, and the color gives off serious fall vibes.

The fact that a sweater feels more like a hug than an actual hug tells me it's been a long time since someone slipped their arms around me and held me close. Mom does, but it's always quick. My friends do, but they spring their arms away from me almost on contact.

Again, I think they believe they could catch what I've got. Hate to break it to them, but pregnancy isn't contagious.

I grab my jeans from where I left them on top of my dresser and shake them out, then pull them on, noticing they fit a little tighter.

Okay, they fit a *lot* tighter. I give them a hard yank over my hips and look down at myself, the way the denim is spread wide, like the zipper can't even bother to come together.

These aren't going to work. They don't fit anymore.

My mother warned me it would happen seemingly overnight. You're living your life and fitting in all your clothes, and then one day, the baby pops and forces you out of your favorite jeans.

I kick them off in frustration and start tearing through my closet, trying to figure out what else I could wear. None of my other jeans fit anymore—those were the last pair holding on, and luckily enough, they were my favorites.

My fun fall vibe is slowly dying.

There are a few skirts hanging in my closet, but I don't think they'll fit either. I'm popping out of everything and it's so freaking annoying. I feel fat. And hungry. I'm hungry all the time, which makes me feel fatter, and that leads to a death spiral of frustration.

Finally giving up, I pull on a boring pair of black leggings —but my absolute best and only pair of Lululemon's—and decide that's as good as it's going to get.

I want to look nice when I see Diego's family, but not like I'm trying too hard. Leggings definitely put me in the not trying so hard category, though I don't want to look like a complete slob either. Earlier, I curled my hair, but not too much. I put on makeup, but not too heavily. I spritzed on perfume, and then immediately regretted it, because the smell almost made me want to gag.

I am so sensitive to scents lately. Fragrant soaps and lotions, body sprays, they all used to be my jam, but now? I have to hold my nose when my little sister comes at me with her Bath and Body Works hand sanitizer-smelling self. Those scents are so strong, they almost make me want to throw up. And speaking of throwing up…

With all that perfume lingering in the fabric, the sweater has to go. At least for a few minutes. I shrug out of it and leave it on the bed, walking around my room in my leggings and bra, hoping the perfume dilutes in the next few minutes while I clean up the mess I just made in my closet.

My phone dings. I go and check it to find a text from Diego.

I'll be at your house in twenty.

I send him a text back, thankful he's not making me drive there by myself. Though I'm at his mercy as to when I can leave. He promised the minute I want to go, he'll take me.

See you soon.

I set my phone on my bedside table and glance at myself in the full-length mirror that's propped against my wall. My gaze drops to my chest. Yes, they're bigger.

I cup my boobs, pushing them together, my eyes going wide. Oh yes. Definitely bigger. And so sensitive. Touching them like I just did sends shivery sensations zinging all over my skin.

Turning to the side, I run my hand over my stomach, much like I did for Diego a couple of nights ago. That moment between us had felt…charged. Intimate. Familiar.

Too familiar.

His dark gaze roaming over me felt like a caress, and I wanted to lean into it. Lean into him.

I caught myself just in time. I can't do that. I don't trust him. Not yet. It's weird, how he's being so nice, and I'm being so agreeable, when only a few weeks ago, we were screaming at each other and I told him I hated him.

Yes, I'm not proud of that. But no, I don't regret it. What he did hurt me so badly, I was blind with sorrow and rage. I wanted to lash out and hurt him.

No idea if my words mattered though. At the time, he was being comforted by Cami. He probably didn't care what I had to say.

Now, I'm being civil, and so is he. I'm trying to do this for the baby, and I assume he's doing the same, but maybe I'm making a mistake. What if I'm leading him on? Leading myself on?

We don't work together. We didn't before. We won't now. But like he said, we're tied together forever. I can't get rid of him, and he can't get rid of me. Having a child with someone is such a momentous step.

It's overwhelming. Especially when you're seventeen and it happened by accident.

Sticking my tongue out at my reflection, I stomp over to my bed and grab the sweater, bringing it to my nose. It stinks of Arianna Grande's latest fragrance, but not as bad as it did a few minutes ago, so I shrug it back on, push up my sleeves and then go to the bathroom so I can check on my hair.

Yet again.

Earlier my family facetimed me, wanting to wish me a happy Thanksgiving. Even my grandparents were there, and they expressed how sad they were that I wasn't able to visit them, but they understood I had a lot of homework to catch up on, and they were proud of me for being so dedicated during my senior year.

I guess that was the lie Dad fed them, so I nodded and smiled in all the right places, playing along with it. Once they were gone and Dad and everyone else left the room so it was just me and Mom talking, she asked me how I was feeling, her voice lowered to the barest whisper.

It made me feel bad. Like I was their dirty little secret.

The doorbell rings and I jerk to attention, realizing I wasted a lot of time thinking when I should've been doing...I don't know. Cleaning my closet? Putting on my sweater? I'm agitated. Nervous. My nerves are shot and we're not even at Diego's house yet.

Seriously, I need to calm down.

I run my fingers through my hair before I head for the front door. I unlock it and swing it open to find Diego standing there with his back to me. He turns around, his gaze running over me like it has so many times before, and I can see the appreciation in his eyes. The interest.

I tell myself to ignore it, but I can't help the tiny shiver of pleasure that steals over me as he continues to stare.

"You're a little early," I tell him, trying to break the spell—hating how breathless I sound.

"Not much traffic on the road. Everyone's already at their destination, I guess," he says, the tiniest smile curling his lips. It fades in an instant. "You look pretty."

"Thanks. You look good too," I automatically say, just like I used to.

Though it's no lie. He does look good. He's wearing black jeans and a white T-shirt, with a black and white flannel thrown over it. He's got the black beanie on his head again, like he did the last time he was here, and it's a good look for him.

"You ready to go?" he asks, running a hand across his tight jaw, his expression suddenly grim.

"Yeah, let me grab my keys and my purse." I go to the kitchen counter where I left my bag earlier and sling it over my shoulder, then make my way back to the front door where Diego waits, never once stepping over the threshold and coming into our house. Just like he used to. As if he could see that invisible line put down by my parents and wouldn't dare cross. I still hate how unwelcomed they always made him feel.

I join him on the porch, pulling the door shut and locking it. Diego heads down the steps and toward his car.

I follow after him, pleased when he opens the passenger side door for me. I slip inside his mom's old Honda while he rounds the front, and I watch him, breathing deep. Breathing in his scent.

Something cold and foreboding washes over me and I have the strangest urge to bolt out of this car and run. This entire moment feels...dangerous. Going with him to his house for Thanksgiving dinner and spending time with his family, as if I belong. Potentially giving him false hope.

I think he still wants to be with me.

Once he climbs into the car and starts the engine, I glance over at him to see a muscle ticking in his jaw, and his lips are thin. He looks serious.

Seriously pissed.

"What's wrong?" I ask once he starts driving.

He gives me a quick glance, keeping his gaze mostly on the road. "Nothing."

This feels familiar. Old Jocelyn would let it go and deal with his shitty mood in silence.

"You're lying," I say. "Tell me what's bothering you."

New Jocelyn calls him out on his shit and demands to know what's up.

Another quick glance from him, this one full of surprise.

"My brother. He's an asshole," he mutters, his voice so low I can barely hear him. "He stayed out last night. Didn't come home until around six in the morning and our mom was freaking the fuck out. She thought he was dead in a ditch, direct quote."

His brother is trouble. I haven't spent much time with Mateo, but I've heard the stories, the rumors. He's lazy. Does drugs. Drinks too much. Messes around with underage girls. Nothing in the total pedophile realm, but he likes them around sixteen, seventeen.

Considering he's nearly twenty-one, that's a little too young. Definitely get arrested young, if he doesn't watch out.

Diego didn't ever want to talk about him or bring me around him. Their relationship was fraught with tension. They physically fought, and often. Sometimes Diego would show up at school with a black eye or a busted lip. He confessed when he was fourteen, his brother broke his nose.

My family isn't prone to violence. I don't understand that kind of behavior at all. Diego has a short fuse and likes to hit things. But never me. I never felt threatened by him. He loves to argue though, and so does his mother. So does Mateo.

His brother is a complete dick.

"Is he all right?" I ask when Diego doesn't volunteer any more information.

"He's fine. He just went on a bender, like usual. He got into a huge screaming match with Mom. Again, like usual. She was all pissed off because she stayed up most of the night worrying about him and now she has to host everyone for the holiday," Diego explains.

"Oh. Maybe I shouldn't—"

"No," he cuts me off. "She wants you there. I told her I was going to pick you up and she practically pissed her pants, she was so happy to hear that you're coming over."

My heart drops. "She'll be disappointed when she finds out we're not together."

"We can't tell her we are, huh?" His words, his tone sound like a joke, but he's not kidding. I think he'd prefer to tell his mother we're actually together. It would make everything easier, and she wouldn't have to worry about Diego as much.

That's one thing I noticed about Diego when we were together. While he can be a jerk, and he always acts like everyone is out to get him, for the most part, he's very protective of his mother. I thought it was because he didn't want to disappoint her. He's the good son in comparison to Mateo.

"No," I say, slowly shaking my head. "I think that would be a mistake."

"We could tell everyone we broke up later, but today, maybe we could pretend to be together." He shrugs, but otherwise, doesn't look at me.

"You've been thinking about this, haven't you?" I ask.

"it's going to suck, telling her she's going to be a grandma and oops, we're not getting back together," he says.

"It sucks worse pretending to be in love with you when we know we won't work out," I say gently.

"Pretending to be in love with me?" He gives me a quick, irritated—*hurt*—look. "You got over me that quick, huh?"

I say nothing. No, I didn't get over him that quick, but there's no way I'm going to say I'm in love with him still when he stomped all over my heart like the careless, thoughtless bastard he can be.

"Maybe this was a mistake," I say after a few minutes of tense silence.

"Jos, I'm sorry." He blows out a harsh breath, slowing down as we come into town. We're only a few minutes away from his house, and I'm starting to become more nervous about hanging out with his family. Especially considering how hostile he's acting toward me. "It's been a bad day, and I'm taking it out on you."

"It's okay," I say, curling my hands in my lap, appreciating his quick apology. So unlike him. "Just—don't put anything on me in front of your family that isn't true, all right? Don't tell anyone we're working on things or trying to get back together. There's no point. We don't have to tell your family we're together, but we don't have to tell them we're not either, you know? Let's just show a united front to your mom, tell her what's going on and that we're going to do what's best for the baby, and I know she'll support us no matter what."

I say that a lot more convincingly than I feel.

"All right. I can do that," he says with a fierce nod.

Oh, I really hope he can.

When we pull up in front of the house, there are already a few people hanging out in the tiny front yard. Kids running after each other, laughing as they play. A group of adults are clustered together under a giant elm, beer bottles clutched in their hands as they talk. When I get out of the car, I realize they're talking about football, and I almost want to laugh at how passionate they all sound, discussing their favorite NFL teams.

"They'll all be at the game tomorrow," Diego tells me as we both start up the walk toward his front door. "They promised me they would."

"That's amazing," I tell him, pleased to hear it. His immediate family is large, and they went to his games all the time, especially when we were younger. But as time went on, I think they became bored, or too wrapped up in their own lives, and they sort of forgot to show up for their own local football star.

"Yeah, it'll be nice to hear them cheering me on. Though the real person who deserves all the accolades is Callahan," he says with a shrug.

So typical. He's all bravado with an audience, boasting about his accomplishments to anyone who would listen. When we're alone, though, he's much more modest. Even a little down on himself. At first I thought he was just looking for sympathy. But after spending time with him, I realized he is actually full of doubt. Not nearly as confident as he would like everyone to believe he is.

His family has expectations they've set upon him. His friends do too. Did he always feel like he couldn't measure up?

"Oh stop," I tell him, sounding irritated, but I don't care. "Today is a day to be grateful, so be thankful for your talents. You have a lot of them."

He stands a little taller at my words, smiling and waving at his aunts and uncles and cousins when they all spot him. There are definitely more people here than he mentioned. "Thanks for the reminder," he murmurs, grabbing my hand and giving it a quick squeeze before he releases it and walks over to his family, letting them all draw him in as they hug him or pat him on the back.

I stand on the walkway where he left me, smiling as I watch him with his family. His eyes are brighter, and his smile is wider. Doesn't seem so forced. A chilly breeze washes over me and I shiver, a little *oh* leaving me when a rush of leaves blow off the tree branches, flying past me. It's a beautiful day. The sky is a bright blue, the air is crisp, and the scent of burning wood lingers in the air. It is definitely fall, and I suddenly feel nostalgic.

I miss my family.

I miss my youth.

My innocence.

Thanksgiving is the kick-off to the Christmas season, and a holiday I looked forward to every year. But it's all different now. I feel older. Like my childhood evaporated completely at this very moment. In a year's time, I'll have a *baby*. He or she will be around six months old.

Half a year already.

Who will the baby look like? Me or Diego? Will she be a good baby? Or will she cry all the time?

I swallow hard, smiling and offering a wave when members of Diego's family turn in my direction all at once and greet me with friendly hellos. Diego is standing in the middle of them, his gaze locking with mine, and he looks so handsome, so carefree, so much like the boy I originally fell in love with, my heart pangs for the boy I lost.

The boy that I will never get back, because he's not like that anymore. This is all just a façade. A trick of the light.

"Hey, who brought the babe?"

The voice is familiar, and I glance over my shoulder to see Mateo standing on the front porch, a beer clutched in his hand and a wobbly grin on his face. He's watching me with those dark eyes of his, the grin fading, replaced by an almost hungry look.

Quickly I look away, trying to ignore the unease that slips over me. But it's there, reminding me there's a reason I never spent much time with Diego's older brother.

I don't like him. I never really have. He's always made me feel…uncomfortable.

"Watch your mouth," Diego's mother says, causing me to look over my shoulder once more. I do just in time to catch her slapping the back of Mateo's head with a dish towel, making him grunt in annoyance. His glare is potent. It's almost like I can feel his anger radiating from his body, and he tosses his head back, bringing the bottle to his lips and draining the beer before he burps.

Loudly.

Some of the guys laugh. His mother glares.

Diego makes his way toward me, coming to stand directly beside me, and it almost feels as if he's trying to protect me. Which is sweet. Maybe he can feel the negative vibes coming from his brother too.

"Jocelyn!" Diego's mom sees me and she makes her way toward me, a giant smile on her face. Rosa Garcia is a pretty woman. Diego looks like her, and so does Mateo, though there's a hardness to him that Diego doesn't have.

Rosa has always treated me with kindness. She accepted me readily, seemed almost relieved that Diego found *such a nice girl.*

That's what she always said about me. That I was such a nice girl.

Not so much anymore, huh Rosa?

CHAPTER 10

DIEGO

If I could, I would beat the shit out of my brother.

He's the nuisance of Thanksgiving. He finally dragged his ass home after partying all night, and I could still smell the alcohol permeating from his skin when he stumbled into the house, waving off Mom when she started yelling. Guess I can't blame him. Who wants to be greeted like that? But he's the dumbass who stayed out and wouldn't answer her calls or texts, making her worry.

He hasn't let up on the drinking all day. It's one beer after another, and Mom won't cut him off. She'll send him dirty looks and call him a disgusting drunk, tell him he's just like his father, but that doesn't do anything.

Her words only make everything worse.

Our father left when I was a kid. I love my mom. We have a good relationship, and when I was a kid? I adored her, practically worshiped the ground she walked on. But she's a nag. She nagged my dad about everything, and he could never catch a break. He started drinking, started staying out at night with his friends or God knows who, and she lit into him every time he came home.

Every. Single. Time.

It got so bad, so volatile between them, he eventually left.

And never bothered coming back.

Mom was devastated, but she stayed strong. She also became angrier. It was her go-to emotion. I tried to stay out of her way, but Mateo thrust his face in hers all the damn time. It's like he wanted her rage. As if he thrived off of it.

Mateo started acting up at a young age. He got caught smoking weed in the boy's bathroom at school when he was in the sixth grade. He and a group of his friends tried to burn down the high school library when they were in the eighth grade.

The arson investigator came to our house and questioned him. They knew he did it. He put on a total innocent act, but the moment the guy left, and Mom caught Mateo laughing about it with his friends, she started hollering at him, "Why are you like this? Why are you such a devil?"

He only laughed in her face and told her she made him that way.

As he got older, it only got worse. Mom never helped matters. When you tell someone they're no good and they're going to end up just like their father, they eventually fulfill that prophecy you set upon them. Mateo did exactly that. He became worthless—it's what mom expected of him, after all. She set all of her hopes and dreams on me instead.

And that turned me into a target. For Mateo.

He tried to hurt me every chance he could get. With words sometimes, though his real weapons were his fists. His feet. Our relationship is abusive. Fucked up. And while I know deep down inside that I could take his ass and tear him apart, I'm scared to. Scared of all those old memories and the words he used to throw at me. Worried Mom will be mad at me for hurting Mateo. It doesn't matter how often Mateo hurt me. We always kept it hidden. I can't even begin to explain why.

The thing that scares me the most? Once I start beating up on Mateo, I might not be able to stop. I've been holding my anger toward him inside of me for years. The moment I let go, it's going to spill out.

All over him.

The moment I returned to the house with Jocelyn, I avoided Mateo as much as possible. It's easy to do, considering how many people are currently crowded in our small house. Cousins and aunts and uncles galore. My grandparents are holding court in the living room, sitting in the recliners and chatting with everyone who comes into the room to sit with them. The TV is on in the background, a football game unfolding on the screen, and I go in there to check the score, and get some breathing room, at least for a little while. Jocelyn is hanging out with Marty, so she'll be all right. They've always been close.

"*Mijo*, come here." My *abuela* crooks a finger at me and I go to her, kneeling down so I'm at her eye level. Her gaze roves over me, her brown eyes twinkling, her lips curled into a smile. "Oh, aren't you handsome."

I smile at her in return. She always says that. To every single one of her male grandchildren. "Thanks, Grandma."

She reaches one of her wrinkled hands toward me and cups my cheek, her gaze locking with mine. "You're a good-looking boy, but you also look so sad, *mijo*. What's bothering you? Is it your brother?"

The old woman acts oblivious most of the time, but she's really as sharp as a tack. "Mateo's fine." My words sound bitter, and I clear my throat, deciding it's best that's all I say, or I'll reveal myself.

Mateo is not fine. He's never fine. He never will be fine.

Her hand drops from my face, her lips twisting into a

frown. "Don't lie to me. He's a walking disaster. Drunk as a skunk and rude."

I press my lips together, trying not to laugh at her obvious disgust. "He's had a rough couple of days."

"He claims he's had a rough life. The boy is spoiled rotten, if you ask me. Running around with degenerates. Doing drugs like they're candy. Drinking all the time. He's your mother's greatest disappointment." She sighs.

I remain quiet.

"*Arbol que nace torcido, jamás su tronco endereza,*" she says, one of her favorite sayings, one she's said to me before.

It means what you do as a child, will shape you as an adult. She's referring to Mateo, of course. And me, as well.

"And then there's you." Her smile makes her whole face glow. "You worried us at first. I was afraid you'd fall onto the same path as your brother."

I did, for a while, especially during middle school. I may hate my brother and hated what he did to me, but I also wanted his approval. And I thought I'd get it if I acted like him.

So I bullied my cousin Marty because he was an easy target. And I talked shit about everyone at school because I hung out with the popular kids and no one said anything to me. And I mouthed off to teachers because they expected me to. I was Mateo Garcia's little brother after all. The bar was set pretty damn low.

Then I met Jake and his famous father, Drew Callahan. And I was blown away. I spent all my free time with Jake, and I wished I had half his confidence. Half his talent. Even when we were in middle school, he could throw a football better than anyone on the high school team, and we were still in youth league. His accuracy was nothing like I've ever seen before. He knew how to aim the ball right at me.

We spent a lot of time together, and we got closer. We

became best friends. Drew Callahan took me under his wing and worked with his son *and* me. He saw something in me, honed in on it and helped me. It was what I needed, what helped me stay on task. When Fable Callahan told me I should concentrate more on school, so I could possibly get into a good college, I listened to her.

It helped that she was a total MILF. Not that I ever said that to Jake.

I still had my moments—I still actually have them. A lot. I'm not perfect. My house is one that's full of rage and resentment, and it's hard to get away from that mindset. Lately, I've had a tougher time escaping it.

"But you've done well, and you make me proud."

I return my focus to my grandmother when I realize she's still speaking to me. She's not angry at all. She's sweet. Stern when she needs to be. It's my grandfather who scared me when I was little. Still kind of does.

"Your grandpa is proud of you too," she continues. "You've accomplished so much. Playing in the league championship game tomorrow. Doing well in school. About to graduate and go off to college. Tall and handsome and such a hard worker. Your mama can't stop bragging about you."

"Grandma." I can actually feel my face heating up.

"What? It's true. You're a good boy." She ruffles my hair like I'm eight, then actually pinches my cheek. I pull away before she can hurt me. Her fingernails are sharp. "Now go get me a glass of wine, please."

With a chuckle I rise to my feet, shaking my head. "You sweet talked me into getting you a drink."

"Perhaps. But everything I said is true. You're a good boy, Diego, and you're going to do good things. Despite what you think," she says.

Her words stay with me as I go to the kitchen to get her a glass of wine as she requested. Will she still be as proud when she finds out Jocelyn is pregnant? Or will she be disappointed in me? Mom will tell her everything—that's her mother. And they'll all talk and worry about me behind my back. Mateo is the colossal fuck-up. He has zero expectations to live up to. I'm the one they pin their hopes and dreams on, and the pressure is enormous.

Meaning when I mess up? I have farther to fall.

I enter the kitchen to find my mom and Aunt Lisa in there, the both of them in front of the open oven, checking out the bird inside.

"Where's the wine?" I ask no one in particular.

They both rise to their feet so quickly, they almost knock heads. "I don't need both of you drinking today," Mom says with narrowed eyes.

I shake my head, hating that she'd automatically go there. "Grandma requested a glass of wine. I said I'd get it for her."

"Oh that woman. She doesn't need any more alcohol either," Mom says with a laugh, her shoulders relaxing. She points toward the counter near the fridge, where I spot an opened bottle. "Pour her some of that. She likes it."

It's when I'm searching for wineglasses that Mom and Aunt Lisa exit the kitchen to go gather up all the leftover appetizer plates in the living room. And it's when I'm pouring a glass of wine for my grandmother that my brother walks into the kitchen so it's just the two of us.

Alone.

"Trying to catch up with me?" He nods toward the glass of red wine in my hand when I turn to face him.

My entire body grows tense, and I do my best to turn my expression into an unyielding mask. A look I've perfected over the years when dealing with Mateo. "It's for Grandma."

He makes a dismissive noise. "Right. You're sneaking Mom's wine, whatever."

I don't bother arguing with him. It would be a never-ending battle. Instead, I don't say a word and make like I'm going to leave, but just as I'm about to pass him, he holds out his hand. Knocking it into my shoulder, keeping me in place.

We're standing face to face, so close I can smell him. Alcohol mixed with sweat. His lids are heavy, his dark brown eyes dull, and I wonder if he recently smoked a joint. Wouldn't put it past him.

"What's up with you and Jocelyn, huh? Why is she here?" he asks, sounding put out.

"Don't worry about it." I jerk out of his hold, but he grabs my arm before I can make my escape, squeezing tight.

"Your girl is fucking hot." Mateo takes a step closer, and I can smell his putrid breath. I wrinkle my nose, disgusted. "What's she see in an asshole like you?"

Anger fills me, and I release a shaky breath, afraid of what I might do if he keeps talking about Jocelyn. All of my protective instincts rise up. "Don't even bring her up, bro. Or—"

"Or what?" He throws his head back and laughs, and the sound is grating. Obnoxious. Just like he is. "You gonna kick my ass? You gonna tell me to stay away from her? Fuck that. I can have her if I want her."

His words are an empty threat. He's just trying to get a rise out of me. When he said shit like that and I was younger, I believed him. I believed he was the better brother. The more charismatic, likable brother. He had a lot of friends in high school. He liked to party, he scored the football team drugs, the girls loved him. He was a good time.

But he was also a huge problem. Teachers hated him. His counselor told him to his face he would amount to nothing if he kept this up. The sheriff deputy came to school and arrested him for drugs on campus twice his senior year.

Twice.

That was the moment I realized he is not the better

brother. And the fact that he hasn't amounted to anything since graduating, just like his counselor predicted, I knew it was true. His friends, the hangers on, the girls, they all disappeared. They went to college or got jobs or both, and became more responsible.

They have nothing in common anymore.

Now he parties with people my age. Fucks around with girls my age—and younger. One day, he's going to get caught.

And he's going to get into huge trouble.

"Just keep her name out of your mouth, okay?" I can hear the anger infuse my words, but can Mateo? Probably not.

He's too wasted.

"Aw, don't get your panties in a wad." He shoves me away from him, the wine sloshing out of the glass and dripping all over the floor. "Mom's gonna kick your ass when she finds out about the mess you just made."

He says things like that, and it's as if we're kids all over again. He'll be the one to tell her, I'm sure. "Tell her I'll clean it up in a minute."

I'm heading for the living room when I hear Mateo call after me, "You're such a kiss ass."

God, I hate him.

I'm sweet to my grandmother when I hand off the wine to her, but otherwise, I'm in a surly mood. Fuck everyone. But especially fuck my brother. And myself for not being man enough to stand up to his ass and tell him where to go.

Straight to hell.

If I can't tell Mateo what to do, how am I ever going to manage this being a dad thing? It's still hard for me to comprehend that I'm going to become someone's father. And that the mother is Jocelyn.

Me. A dad. It's mind-blowing.

After I clean up the mess I made on the kitchen floor—no Mateo in sight, thank God—I go in search of Jocelyn. I find her sitting at a table in the back yard with Marty, their heads bent close together, their expressions serious as they talk. Whatever it is they're saying, they're oblivious to what's going on around them. Kids are screaming, and my uncle Johnny is currently manning the turkey fryer, telling everyone in the nearby vicinity how he prepared the turkey, waving the beer bottle in his hand around as he gestures wildly.

Yes, we're having two turkeys prepared and no, we won't eat all of it.

Ignoring my uncle, I approach the table Jocelyn and Marty are at slowly. Quietly. They're sitting next to each other, their backs to me, and I'm hoping I can catch a snippet of what they're saying. Not that I want to eavesdrop but...

Yeah. Okay, I can admit it. I sort of want to listen in on their conversation.

"...and then Cami follows me out into the parking lot." Jocelyn shakes her head, and I can hear the disgust in her voice. "You should've seen her. God, I hate her so much, chasing after me, calling my name. Telling me that she'd always hoped we'd be friends."

"Since when? Girl has been nothing short of hostile toward you your entire life," Marty says with all the authority of someone who knows what it feels like to be bullied.

By me.

"I know, right? I don't get why she said that. She acted like she wanted to be my friend and then she turns around and makes shitty comments about Diego and how he asked her to come meet her at Pete's," Jos explains.

"He probably did," Marty mutters.

It makes me mad, how he automatically thinks the worst of me, but I guess I should expect it. I've treated him terribly for years. To the point he won't even talk to me, and I don't talk to him either. Our relationship is a big, gaping wound, and I don't know if it can ever be healed. I've apologized before. I should apologize again right now, but Marty will probably think I'm only doing it because Jocelyn is here.

I *want* him to believe me. Apologizing to him in private will definitely be more effective.

"I don't know. I—kind of believe him." She sounds ashamed by her faith in me. What little she has left.

"You shouldn't. He's lied to you nonstop. You know this," Marty says.

See that's the thing. There are lies. And there are half-truths. Most of those lies come from other people. We see what we want to see, and we believe what we want to believe. They already believe I've done the worst, and me trying to defend myself will be pointless. A waste of breath.

So I let them think what they want.

"Has he, though? Cami is a liar too," Jocelyn points out.

"True, but come on. Diego's been flirting with girls since you two got together. There have been rampant rumors about him—messing around behind your back," Marty says.

"Is that all they are? Rumors? Or do people have any proof? Did they see him with another girl? Multiple other girls?" Jos asks.

"We all saw him with Cami, Jocelyn. It was obvious."

"But we didn't see them actually…together? Am I right?"

"They were together," Marty says firmly. "Don't believe otherwise. Don't let him make a fool out of you again."

Despite the negativity coming out of my cousin's mouth, I can't help but feel a spark of hope. Jocelyn is starting to doubt what's been said. What might've happened. She never let me explain myself back then, and I was so fuckin' shocked by her pregnancy confession, I immediately went on the defensive. I acted like a shithead, and she told me to fuck off.

I deserved that.

But I didn't deserve everyone believing the worst in me. Especially when they didn't know the truth.

I start to back away, not wanting to interrupt this particular conversation, when I run right into my brother, who grabs hold of my shoulders from behind and pushes me.

Straight to the ground.

"Watch where you're going fuckface," Mateo bites out.

I land on our scraggly back lawn, a rock digging into my right arm, which took the brunt of the fall. I roll over onto my back with a grunt, staring up at the endless blue sky, my arm throbbing. There are shocked gasps and Mateo's laughing, and the sound of my mother's voice as she screams, *"What did you do to him?"*

She rushes over, Aunt Lisa on her tail, the two of them hovering over me.

"Are you all right?" Lisa asks, offering me her hand.

I take her hand and let her pull me up, embarrassed my brother could knock me down so easily. That he would behave so childishly, and that he did it in front of the rest of the family. And Jocelyn. "I'm all right."

"What happened?" Mom asks me, her tone sharp, her dark eyes blazing with fury when she shoots a look in Mateo's direction.

"I—I must've tripped." It's automatic, how I cover up for my brother. A force of habit. I don't want to admit he shoved me.

It's humiliating.

"Bullshit," Mom spits out, turning toward Mateo. "I saw exactly what you did. You pushed him."

"I did not." Mateo sounds just like he did when he was eleven and he'd trip me. "He fell. He's clumsy."

"The very last thing your brother is, is clumsy." Mom marches right up to Mateo and thrusts her finger in his face, wagging it. "How dare you treat your brother so horribly. All day long, you've disrespected me. Your entire family. I want you to leave."

I follow behind her, touching her shoulder, but she shrugs away from my hand. "Mom, don't make a scene. It's Thanksgiving."

"No. I'm tired of you making excuses for him. See your brother for what he truly is—he's a wreck. I'm tired of dealing with him in my house. Go," she tells Mateo, who's watching her with a nasty smirk on his face. "Pack your things and get out of here. You're not welcome in my home anymore."

Everyone in the back yard has gone completely quiet, even my bigmouthed uncle. Even the kids. Mom and Mateo are having a glaring contest, and she rests her hands on her hips, as if she's settling in, prepared to go nowhere.

"Rosa," Aunt Lisa starts, but Mom cuts her off.

"I don't want to hear it," Mom snaps. "Don't bother defending him. He's a piece of shit. My very own son is a *piece* of *shit*, and I'm done tolerating his ass."

"Is that how you really feel?" Mateo asks from between clenched teeth, his nostrils flaring, the dullness gone from his gaze. He's furious. His body is practically vibrating with rage. "Tell me, Mama. Is that what you really think about me?"

"Yes." She doesn't back down. They're standing toe to toe, neither of them moving. This is where Mateo gets it from. He's stubborn, only because she is too. They both stand their ground, and nothing is ever solved.

Nothing.

"Yes. That is how I really feel," she bites out.

He glances around the back yard, his gaze landing on me for only a moment before it settles just beyond my shoulder. I look back to see Jocelyn and Marty still sitting at the table, both of them frozen as they watch us.

I hate that she's witnessing this moment.

"You tell our lovely mother about your little problem yet?" Mateo asks conversationally, as if he doesn't have a care in the world.

My heart drops into my gut and I part my lips, ready to tell him to shut the hell up, but I'm too late.

"Your precious baby boy got his ex pregnant, and she's going to have the baby. Congrats. You're going to be a grandma," he says.

Mom is gaping at him, swiveling her head toward me.

Fuck.

"Who's the prodigal son now, huh?" Mateo spits on the ground, directly in front of me, before he pushes past us both, heading for the house.

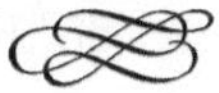

JOCELYN

"Is it true?"

I lift my head to find Rosa Garcia standing directly in front of me, her expression one of concern, though there's lingering anger there too. I can see it in the tightness of her lips, the clenching of her jaw.

But she's not angry at me and Diego. At least, I don't think she is.

Mateo already slammed his way into the house, and Diego is still standing in the middle of the yard, cradling his right elbow with his left hand, his aunt hovering over him, asking him if he's okay and glancing around the yard as if someone else is going to relieve her from her current position.

Diego is in pain. And full of worry. I can see it written all over his face.

Marty nudges me in the ribs, a reminder that Rosa asked me a question, and I slowly nod. What's the point in denying it? It's why I'm here today. "Yes." The word comes out a choked whisper, and I swallow hard. "It's true."

She covers her mouth, her brown eyes wide, and then she

turns toward Diego, waving a hand. "Get over here right now!"

Diego does her bidding, hanging his head as he makes his way over to us, his shoulders slumped. He looks utterly defeated, and my heart—despite everything that's happened between us—breaks for him. His mother is prone to make a scene, and I hope she doesn't do that right now. In front of everyone.

"Marty, if you could please give us some privacy," Rosa says, and Marty immediately shoots up and out of his chair, sending me a sympathetic look as he makes his escape.

I envy him. I envy the rest of the family who scatter away, save for Diego's uncle, who's still manning the turkey fryer.

"Sit," Rosa tells Diego, and again, he does as she commands, falling into the chair Marty just vacated, his head bent, still cradling his elbow. I wish I could ask him if he's okay, but I don't want to say anything right now.

I'd rather let Rosa do all the talking. And I'm sure she has something to say, too.

"You're pregnant?" Rosa asks me, her voice raising into a squeak. "Really?"

I nod, a shuddering breath escaping me. "Really."

"And how far along are you?"

"The baby is due the end of May," I answer.

Rosa rears back, tilting her head, her gaze, her words only for me. "You're already three months along?"

"About," I say with a little shrug.

"You're only telling Diego now?" Her voice is hard, like her eyes.

I part my lips, ready to say something, but I think she knows.

We've been keeping my pregnancy a secret. From her.

Rosa directs her next question toward Diego. "And how long have you known about this?"

"A while." He shrugs, ever the noncommittal answer.

"We didn't know how to tell you," I say quickly, wanting to support him. He's in pain, I can tell. Not just from the fall —I didn't see if Mateo actually pushed him, but I'm sure he did, thanks to Rosa's quick and furious reaction. But the way his brother hurt him on purpose, both physically and with telling their mom about me being pregnant, was beyond messed up.

Like, beyond.

"You two aren't together anymore," Rosa says, narrowing her eyes as she contemplates us. "So what is going to happen to this poor baby once it's born, hmm? Are you going to become a single mother, Jocelyn? Take care of this baby all on your own? And what about school? For the both of you? I'm not in a financial position to offer any help. You're on your own with this one. Diego, you'll need to work, to help support the baby and Jocelyn. You can't go to college anymore. You'll need to be a man and take responsibility for your actions."

I don't like how demanding she's being. That Diego should give up everything he's worked for because I'm pregnant and he has responsibilities.

Why can't we do this together? Why can't we raise a child and work on our goals? Why do we have to give up one thing for another?

"Diego can still go to school," I say, shocking Rosa. I'm sure she fully expects us to agree with her. "He shouldn't have to give up his dream to play football in college because I'm pregnant. We've both applied to Fresno State, and we can make this work."

Saying it like that makes it seem like we planned it. I can feel Diego watching me, even with his head bent, but I keep my attention focused on his mother. If I look at him right now...

I might crumble.

"And how are you two going to afford a baby, if you're both going to college? How exactly are you going to make it work?" Her voice is full of skepticism. She has little faith in us, and I'm not surprised.

They all have little faith in us. My parents included.

"We'll make it work," Diego says fiercely, finally lifting his head, his dark eyes glittering with emotion. I wish I knew what he was feeling right now. What he was thinking. He used to keep himself so bottled up, until he finally exploded. And I can tell, right now, he's so very close to exploding all over the place. "I can work at the resort starting in March. That's when they open. And I'll get more hours at Pete's."

"Babies are expensive. Who's going to watch this little one while you're both in class, or you're on the football field? Babysitters are expensive too, and it's difficult to find one you can trust." She raises a brow, challenging us with every question.

"My mother said she would help," I start, but Rosa scoffs.

"Your mother. I'm sure she would. But if you go to Fresno State, that's so far. And she lives up here. You're going to make that kind of commute every day? That's a huge commitment, Jocelyn. So is a baby. You'll have to learn how to prioritize."

"I know how to prioritize," I say, my voice full of irritation. I'm tired of Rosa acting like we don't know what the hell we're doing. "I'll do what is necessary to take care of my baby." I glance over at Diego to find he's already watching me, and without thought, I rest my hand on his arm, before turning to face Rosa once more. "*Our* baby. We can handle this, Rosa. I know we can."

Rosa sighs and shakes her head, making a tsking noise. "Dreamers, the both of you. I cannot say I'm thrilled you're making me a grandmother, Diego. I'm disappointed. You're too young."

And with those last words, she gets up and leaves the table, heading for the house. Her sister falls into step beside her, the both of them walking quickly inside, the door slamming behind them, making me jump. Diego's uncle Johnny asks them to bring a platter out so he can set the turkey on it, but I don't know if they heard him.

All I can do is focus on Diego, the way he's still holding onto his elbow as if it hurts him.

"Are you okay?" I ask, my voice low.

He lifts his head on a deep inhale, breaking out into a blinding smile. Those smiles are rare, which makes them potent. "Never better. Why do you ask?"

I slowly shake my head. "Did he hurt you?"

"I landed wrong on my arm. My elbow...it throbs, but I'll be okay." He shrugs one shoulder.

He has a game tomorrow night. He has to be okay. "Did he actually push you?"

He hesitates, like he doesn't want to answer, but then he finally says, "Yeah. He did."

"Does he do that sort of thing often? Purposely hurt you?" I steel myself, waiting for his answer.

"Yeah," he croaks.

"Diego." My voice drops and I lean toward him, touching his upper arm. He flinches and pulls away from me, and I'm afraid I might've hurt him. "Are you in that much pain? Should we take you to urgent care?"

"I'm fine. It's just—" He shakes his head, averting his gaze from mine. "Don't act like you care if you don't mean it, Jos."

I frown. "What are you talking about?"

"It's been a fucked-up day, and I'm on edge as it is. If you really don't give a shit about me, yet you were just sitting here acting like we're a united front for my mom, then that sends me mixed signals. And while you seem really concerned right now about my arm and my fucking feelings, I don't know if you're being real. If it's all fake, don't bother. I don't think I can take you being nice to me if you don't mean it."

That's about as real with me as he's been in a long time. The entire day has been rough, and we haven't even had dinner yet. This day has been hard for him, and it's been difficult for me too, but he's the one who's handled the brunt of everything. And while I know I don't want to be with him —at least I don't think I want to be with him—I also know that we need each other. We have to stand strong.

Together.

"I mean it," I say, my voice hushed. "I definitely mean it. I don't know why, but I do. I hate that your brother hurt you, and that your mom has no faith in you. She doesn't have faith in either of us, but we can do this, right? We can make this work."

He studies me for a moment, his gaze roving over my face. I remain quiet, and so does he, until eventually, he slips his arm around my shoulders and pulls me in close. I press my face into his neck, breathing in his familiar scent, and a wave of comfort washes over me.

It feels good, to have him hold me like this. To know he's going to be there for me, no matter what.

"We can make it work," he says, his voice rough.

A glimmer of faith lights up in my chest at his words. That he believes we can do this is…staggering. He wants to be with me. He wants to do right for me. Sometimes, I wondered if he didn't care anymore.

Scratch that. Not sometimes. All the time.

But maybe I was wrong.

* * *

"UNCLE JOHNNY, YOUR TURKEY IS AMAZING," Diego says, as he loads up his plate for round two.

I'm still on my first. It's delicious, but I'm still tense after everything that happened. Diego acts like it just rolls off his back, and I wonder if that's because he's used to it.

Probably.

Johnny beams with pride at Diego's words, picking up a giant turkey leg and biting into it. "I did a damn good job. Better than your regular ol' turkey from the oven, Rosa."

"Whatever," Rosa says good-naturedly. Her cheeks are flushed and I think she's about three glasses in on the wine. Meaning she's feeling pretty good. "My turkey is delicious. Don't you dare knock it."

"Let's do a cook off at Christmas!" Johnny roars, making people laugh.

Things calmed down once Mateo left. I heard he sulked and kicked things in his room. Tore apart his bed, even pulling his mattress off the frame. He yanked all the drawers out of his dresser, dumping whatever contents he wasn't taking with him onto the floor. Came snarling out of his bedroom when he was done, carrying two duffel bags and a backpack slung over his shoulder. This all happened when we were still outside, talking to Rosa. He was leaving when she went back into the house, and I guess they got into another screaming match. One that got so bad, Aunt Lisa threatened to call 9-1-1.

Just another fun Thanksgiving with Diego's family. Now they all act like what happened earlier was no big deal. The argument and Mateo's outburst are long forgotten. Even our pregnancy confession is not mentioned. Rosa made conversation with me throughout the meal, at one point offering to give me the family recipe for her stuffing when I told her how delicious it is. Diego's grandma keeps watching me, her gaze sharp, knowing. I wonder if she has us figured out.

I'm going to do my best to avoid her for the rest of the evening.

I help clear plates, along with Uncle Johnny and Marty. We rinse dishes and stack them in the dishwasher while Diego's mom and aunt clean up the kitchen. Various family members are crowded into the living room, watching the football game, and Diego is in there with them. I thought I wanted to go home right after dinner, but I'm feeling pretty comfortable and don't want to rush out of here right after I ate. Plus, Diego seems relaxed, and I assume that's because his brother isn't around.

When we were together, he never told me how bad their relationship was. I knew he didn't like him, but I didn't realize it was so fraught with tension. I also knew Mateo used to beat him up, but I thought it was just kid stuff. Typical older brother razzing younger brother type behavior.

Now I realize Mateo has a terrible mean streak. And it runs long and wide.

I'm taking various pies and other desserts out of the refrigerator at Rosa's request, when I can feel someone's presence looming behind me. I turn with the Costco pumpkin pie clutched in both hands, dread socking me right in the solar plexus when I see who it is.

Diego's grandmother, watching me with her hawk-like gaze.

"How are you feeling?" She raises a thin brow.

I shut the fridge door with a kick of my foot and set the pumpkin pie on the nearby kitchen counter. "I'm so full from dinner. But I still want pumpkin pie. How about you?"

"I'm not talking about dinner, dear." Now both brows are shooting up. "Diego's been keeping secrets."

She must've talked to her daughter. It's only natural Rosa

would tell her. "Are you talking about what I think you're talking about?"

"Oh, that you're pregnant with my first great grandchild? Yes." She crosses her arms, the expectant look on her face reminding me of Rosa. "That's why I want to know—how are you *feeling*?"

I need to be honest with her. There's no use in playing like this isn't happening. We both know it is. "I'm feeling… good. Tired."

"Are you eating right? Plenty of fresh fruits and vegetables? Drinking lots of milk?"

She sounds so much like a grandma right now, I sort of want to laugh. Or cry. "Yes." I hate milk. But I can eat my weight in cheese. "I'm taking prenatal vitamins every day."

"Good. I could tell you were pregnant, you know." Diego's grandma appears very pleased with herself.

My mouth drops open in shock and I immediately snap it shut. "How?"

"Your face is rounder. Your hair is thicker. You've got a glow about you. It's all classic signs of pregnancy." She sighs, shaking her head, and I realize I'm just shaking in general. I don't know why this woman intimidates me so much. I should be more scared of Rosa. But I know what to expect from Diego's mom, while this woman…I don't know her at all. "You're a lovely girl. A smart girl. And while I certainly didn't expect—*this* from you two, I have a feeling you can make this work. You're not only smart, you're also strong. How else would you be able to put up with Diego for all this time?"

Now I do laugh, because it's true. "Diego was—a lot."

"He's not like his brother though, thank goodness. He has a heart. It hasn't been completely destroyed yet." Her shrewd gaze meets mine. "Was he beside himself when you broke up with him?"

I wonder if she knows all the details. Does Rosa? "He—cheated on me. I had to break up with him."

His grandmother frowns. "Cheated on you? Diego? If you said Mateo, I'd believe it without hesitation. You wouldn't have to convince me. But Diego? I can't imagine it."

"He flirted with other girls throughout our entire relationship. It was a—problem between us." I hated it. He'd always reassure me he wasn't interested in anyone else, but it was hard for me to believe him when I kept hearing the rumors.

"Flirting and cheating are two very different things," she says. "You two are so young, and his life hasn't been easy. I'm not making excuses for him. I know what type of person Diego is. He wants approval from everyone. All of us. Even his brother, who treats him like garbage. This is why he's done bad things. Why he bullied his own cousin. Why he allowed Mateo to lead him down the wrong path for a period of time. He wanted his big brother's love, and he thought doing what Mateo did would earn him that love."

"So cheating on me was a way for him to gain Mateo's approval?" It sounds far-fetched.

"No. Of course not. Are you absolutely sure he cheated on you?"

No. I'm not sure. But I don't answer her. I shrug my shoulders instead.

"Ah, so it's like that." She takes a step closer and grips my shoulders in her hands, forcing me to meet her gaze. "Make sure you know why you're keeping him at a distance. You might be doing it for the wrong reasons."

Tears spring to my eyes and I try to blink them away. "I don't know what to think. I'm so confused about... everything."

"Pregnancy hormones are the worst, aren't they dear?" She pulls me in for a big hug, and I cling to her, closing my eyes. It feels good to talk to someone who's not so judgmental or full of doubt. My mother is worried all the time. Dad acts like it's not happening. Diego's mom clearly doesn't believe we can handle it.

But his grandmother is talking to me as if I actually have a brain in my head, and it feels good.

"He wants to help you," she murmurs into my hair. "This baby could be just the thing that forces him to grow up."

I slowly pull out of her embrace, the tears flowing freely now. "I don't want him to feel obligated. Or forced."

"Do you want to be with him?" she asks me point blank.

"I don't know," is my honest answer.

"*Para cada olla hay su tapadera,*" she mumurs and I frown at her in confusion. "It means, for every pot, there is its own lid."

I smile through the tears. "Are you saying I'm the pot and Diego is my lid?"

She shrugs. "Maybe."

Maybe not.

"Tune out what everyone is telling you, including yourself, and listen to your heart." She rests her hand lightly against my chest. "Focus on what it's telling you. Very rarely do our hearts steer us wrong."

I could argue with that, but I don't feel like it.

Instead, I let her take me into her arms again, and I cry. For all the things I don't know, or understand.

I cry even more, knowing what I have to do.

CHAPTER 12

DIEGO

Once the football game blaring on the big screen was over, I couldn't hustle Jocelyn out of my house fast enough. Mom was giving us a suspicious look, and the last thing I wanted to do was have another conversation like the one we had in the back yard earlier, after Mateo, the asshole, shoved me to the ground and then got kicked out of the house.

I don't think it's fully hit me yet, that he's gone. Oh, he's not *gone* gone. He'll definitely be back. He always comes back when he needs money or food. But I won't have to deal with him fighting with mom in the kitchen daily, and that'll be a nice change. He won't be sneaking into my room and stealing my shit either, though I doubt he gave up his house key, so he can still walk back in here whenever he wants.

That makes me uneasy, considering how pissed off he must be at all of us, but I'll worry about it tomorrow. Or maybe not tomorrow, since we have our game. I'll worry about it over the weekend.

I'm driving Jocelyn home, and she's quiet. I don't bother trying to make conversation, because what's the point? It could get weird, especially because I don't know what she's thinking. I'd rather keep this good feeling going tonight. Jos and I are getting along. I'm relieved Mom knows about the baby, even though she's not happy about it.

I'll deal with that later.

I don't need to think about the bad stuff. Like how my shoulder and elbow still ache thanks to Mateo. Or how Mom thinks I should abandon my college dreams and man up.

I forget all about that stuff and try to remain positive.

I did notice that Jocelyn looked like she'd been crying earlier, when she helped my grandma bring out the dessert plates. Her face was flushed and her eyes were puffy and I wanted to ask her if she was okay, but I didn't want to call attention to her in front of everyone else, so I kept my mouth shut.

And maybe it's a mistake to ask her about it now, but... fuck it.

"Were you crying earlier? When you were with my grandma in the kitchen?"

"Yes," she answers straight away.

I like how real we're being with each other lately. When we were together, especially near the end, it always felt like we were being evasive and playing games.

We weren't happy, and we were lashing out at each other. It sucked.

I don't miss that. At all.

"Why? Did she say something to upset you?" That's completely unlike my grandmother, but hey, I don't know.

"No, she was brutally honest. And I needed to hear some of those things she said." I can feel Jocelyn's gaze on me, and I glance over at her quickly, before returning my attention to the road. "You've kept a lot of secrets from me, Diego."

"Like what?" Her words sound like an accusation. And I don't know exactly what she's talking about.

"Your brother and how awful he was." She pauses and I remain quiet, so she keeps talking. "I had no idea he was so mean to you."

"It wasn't your problem."

"But I wanted to know your problems. That's the point of being in a relationship. We support each other, no matter what." A sigh escapes her. "Were you afraid to tell me? Or did you just think I didn't deserve to know?"

She sounds so damn disappointed in me, in us, it makes my chest ache. And not in a good way. "I didn't know how to tell you."

"That is such a bullshit answer," she says bitterly.

"I was scared to tell you, okay?" The words blast out of my mouth, and I sound like a dick, but it's too late now. "It's humiliating, having to admit your brother is borderline abusive toward you, and has been pretty much your entire life."

I'm breathing heavily, like I just ran the length of the football field twice, and I tell myself to calm the fuck down.

"Borderline abusive?" she asks, and for the quickest moment, I'm afraid she's going to tell me I had no reason to feel that way. Or that I'm a weak ass for not being strong enough to stand up to my brother. "There's no *borderline* about it, Diego. He is *incredibly* abusive toward you, and I can't believe your mother never saw it."

"We hid it pretty well," I start, but she talks over me.

"Don't you dare defend her. I know you love your mother and you two are close, but she did you wrong with your brother. She never tried to protect you. Not once."

Now Jocelyn sounds ferocious. On my behalf.

"She didn't know," I say after a few moments of terse silence. "Like I said, we hid it from her. I always made up some excuse for why I had a black eye or whatever. And she always believed me."

"She had to know what was going on. Deep down, she *had* to. It's fairly obvious how awful your brother is toward you. I think your mom was just in a serious state of denial." I glance over at Jocelyn to see she's scowling. "I refuse to be that way with my child. My children. I want my eyes open at all times. I'm not going to hide my head in the sand."

I should defend my mother. I always have. I've always defended Mateo too, but it's so damn exhausting, making excuses for both of them all the time. And maybe Jocelyn is right. Maybe Mom did me wrong and I should be pissed at her right now.

"It was hard for her, being a single mom," I finally say.

"There you go, defending her again. And I'm going to be a single mom. I'm sure it's really tough, but I think I'm up for the challenge," she says.

"You don't have to be a single mom," I tell her.

She's quiet. Again, I can feel her gaze on me.

"I'll help you," I add.

"I'll take your help, but that's it," she says firmly.

My heart cracks, letting all the anger and resentment flood back inside, and it fuels me. "You don't want me."

"Don't put your abandonment issues on me, Diego. This has nothing to do with what your dad did to you and your family. Or what your brother is currently doing to you. Don't forget what *you* did to *me*," she says, her voice rising.

"And what exactly did I do to you anyway? Huh? Tell me!" I'm yelling now. Gripping the steering wheel, mentally telling myself to calm the fuck down.

"You cheated on me! You fucked Cami Lockhart behind my back, and didn't bother breaking up with me before you did it! Remember? Or did you so conveniently forget?" She's screaming too, and I realize almost too late that I'm about to pass the turnoff to her neighborhood.

I jerk the steering wheel to the right, my tires squealing as

I turn onto the road. The motion sends the car swaying, and Jocelyn tips over, slamming the right side of her body into the door when the car swerves wildly.

"Diego, oh my God!" She's glaring at me now. "You could've killed me!"

"I had it under control," I mutter, righting the car completely.

"No, you didn't. You could've. Killed. Me. And the baby," she says, her voice shaky as she reaches out and grabs the handle above her head. "It's like you don't even give a shit about us."

"I'm sorry, *Jesus*," I snap at her, pulling over immediately. I hit the brakes hard, the car skidding to a stop. I throw the gear into park and turn to look at her. She's already watching me, her eyes wide and unblinking, and I recognize that look anywhere.

She's ready for a fight.

Great. So am I.

"Like I don't even give a shit? Did you really just say that?" I ask her. "I care way too much about what you think about me, and what's going to happen to you and the baby. And me. He's my baby too, you know."

"She," Jocelyn corrects. "It's a she."

Why does that even matter? "How do you know?"

"I can feel it," she says with a little shrug.

I cover my face with my hands for a couple of seconds, telling myself I can do this. I can handle this. But Jocelyn is also being fucking ridiculous.

"Oh, so you're psychic now, and you know what you're having? Plus, I need to know—were you going to push me straight out of your life and never let me see the baby if I hadn't tried to talk to you a few weeks ago? I think you were. Is that coming from your mom? I'm sure she hates that you're pregnant with my baby and wants to keep me away from you forever," I say.

"It has nothing to do with you," she murmurs, and I start to laugh.

"Nothing to do with me? Your parents have hated me since day one. They've looked for any and every excuse to keep us apart, though that probably made you want to see me even more. Slumming with the bad boy. Fucking around on the side, never letting Mommy and Daddy know what a bad girl you actually are. And now you're pregnant with my baby. I bet they're beside themselves with horror."

Her eyes fill with tears. "You don't know what you're talking about."

"I know exactly what I'm talking about. You're ashamed of the fact that you're going to have *my* baby," I throw at her.

"No, I'm ashamed of the fact that I was so stupid to get pregnant when you were having sex with Cami behind my back the entire time! You made a fool of me and now everyone at school thinks I'm stupid!" she screams.

"I never had sex with Cami!"

We both go silent. Our breathing is ragged. We're panting. I'm pressed against the driver's side door, and she's doing the same on her side. As if we need that distance. And what I just said is sitting in the space between us, damn near overwhelming us both.

"I don't believe you," she finally says, her voice small.

I laugh, though I'm not amused. "Of course you don't."

"You had sex with her. Everyone told me you did."

"You got any photographic proof? Someone send you the used condom? Get those DNA test results back yet?"

"Shut up."

"I'm being serious. Did anyone give you proof that I actually stuck my dick in Cami's pussy, because I didn't, Jos. The only pussy I've been in is yours, and we've definitely got proof of that now," I say vehemently.

"Don't lie to me. I'm tired of you always lying to me." She is full-blown crying, the tears streaming down her face freely, her shoulders shaking. "You were with her. Maybe you didn't have actual sex with Cami, but—"

"I never bothered denying the rumors because you assumed the worst, just like everyone else does about me. So what was the point in denying it? You believe I fucked Cami, and so does everyone else. Cami played up the rumor because her favorite thing in life is causing drama, and being in the middle of it. Besides, I was hurt. I wanted to make you jealous, and hurt you too. You were pulling away from me, and I didn't know what else to do, or where I went wrong."

"You were too much for me." She puts her fingers to her mouth the moment the words are out, as if she didn't mean to say it.

But she did.

"What do you mean, too much?"

"You were so needy. You always talked about how much you needed me, and you wanted to spend all of your time with me, but I was busy. I had things to do, just like you. Volleyball took up so much of my time, and I had so much homework," she explains.

"Volleyball took up all of your time," I spit out. I was jealous of her devotion to the sport, and her team.

When we were together, I wanted her to be that devoted to me.

"Just like football takes up all of *your* time," she points out. "I'm just as dedicated as you, Diego. And I understood that."

"You're saying I wasn't understanding." I was a suck-ass boyfriend is what she's really saying.

"I'm saying you put a lot on me and I didn't think I could handle it! You had all of these expectations. You wanted a serious relationship and I did too, so we fell in love. Once we had sex, everything shifted. You wanted me *all* the time, and it felt like that's *all* you wanted. You didn't just want to hang out or get something to eat, or go out with our friends. You wanted to get me alone and get me naked. And then you wanted to always let me know how much you needed me. It was—overwhelming. You were overwhelming. It became too much. I couldn't handle it. I couldn't handle you." She hangs her head back against the seat, closes her eyes, and cries.

I watch her, her words playing over and over inside my head. Yeah, of course once we had sex, that's all I wanted. I'm a fucking teenager. It's normal. And maybe I was a little too needy, but fuck. I loved her. I still love her, despite everything that's happened.

"Please, just take me home," she says, after a few minutes of her crying, and I still haven't spoken. "I'm tired. I want to go home and go to bed."

Without another word, I put the car into drive and pull back onto the road, taking it slow as I make my way back to her house. We're quiet the rest of the way there, my mind running over everything she said. Everything I said. If we'd had this exact conversation a few months ago, I would've been pissed.

Not now though. It hurts to know I overwhelmed her, that maybe my neediness drove her away, but I'm glad she was honest with me tonight. I think that's something our relationship lacked near the end.

Honesty.

When I pull into her driveway, I put my car in park and glance over at her. She's sniffling, accompanied by little hiccupping breaths, and I feel like absolute shit that I upset her so badly. I don't know how to make her feel better either. I'm at a complete loss when it comes to this girl.

So instead of trying to find comforting words that she'll think mean nothing, I tell her how I'm really feeling.

"Thank you again for coming with me today. It helped having you there," I say, which is the truth. I don't think I could've gotten through the day without her.

"Thank you for having me." Her hands are curled in her lap and her head is bent, her dark hair falling, covering her face so I can't really see her. "I had fun."

I want to laugh. *Fun?* She's out of her mind. "It was a shitshow."

"It wasn't so bad."

"Jos." She glances up, her gaze meeting mine. "It was awful."

Her lips curl into the faintest smile. "It was pretty bad."

"A nightmare," I add.

"It was fun hanging out with Marty. He gave great commentary about your family." Now she looks like she wants to laugh.

"I'm sure he did." Marty is funny. When we were kids, he cracked me up. Now, he doesn't even talk to me. "He hates me."

"No, he doesn't hate you. He's just—wary of you."

"I need to apologize to him. Again," I say, meaning every word.

"Yeah, you do. I think he would like that." She goes silent and so do I. "Does your arm hurt?"

"A little," I admit. "I'll take something when I get home."

"You going to be able to play tomorrow night?" she asks.

I make a dismissive noise. "Of course."

She finally laughs, and the sound just—does something to me. Twists me up inside. Makes me want to immediately make her do it again. "I should never doubt you when it comes to football."

"You should never doubt me when it comes to a lot of things, Jos," I say, my voice quiet.

She releases a shivery breath, tilting her head down again before she lifts it, staring at the dark house in front of us. "Will you walk me inside? Look around in all the rooms for me before you go?"

"Why?" I ask incredulously.

"Just—I want to make sure no one is inside. Hiding." She shrugs. "It's scary, staying here all alone night after night."

I fucking hate the fact that she's staying in this big house all alone for a week. Her parents are messed up, leaving her by herself while they're in Oregon having a good time. Why didn't she go with them? And why didn't they decide to stay home with her? "You want me to check it out and make sure everything's safe?"

She nods, looking like a little girl.

A girl who's pregnant with my baby.

Life is fucking crazy, man. It constantly throws curve balls at you, and I guess all that matters in the end is how you handle them.

My dad ran. He couldn't handle the curve ball that was my mother. My brother can't deal with life in general. It's one giant curve ball and he's constantly getting hit, but mostly it's because he asks for it. My mother faces her curve balls with anger every single time, never trying to stop and figure out that maybe she should handle each situation differently.

Now it's up to me. I can decide how I'm supposed to handle this curve ball that has become my life.

"I'll walk you inside," I say to Jocelyn and I can tell she's relieved.

"Thank you," she whispers.

I study her face, suddenly overwhelmed with the urge to kiss her. It's been a long time. Too long. I miss her so damn much, and spending time with her like this, even when we're yelling at each other, it's like I'm savoring every minute.

This evening is pretty much done, which means we'll go back to avoiding each other. Having formal, awkward conversations about the future of our baby. Someday, after the baby's born, we'll be meeting each other at the park, or in the Von's Supermarket parking lot or wherever, exchanging the baby so I can have my weekend visits. Eventually the baby will get old enough and not want to be with me. He'll cry for his mama when she hands him over, and she'll have to blink back tears when she kisses his head and tells him it's going to be okay.

And that's going to suck. So fucking bad. We could've done this together. But I fucked it all up.

Royally.

CHAPTER 13

JOCELYN

It's weird, having Diego prowling around my house so late at night, with no one else around. He walks into every single room, flicking on lights, scaring my mom's cat. I can hear him open closet doors, yelling into the silence, "*Hola!*" and it makes me giggle.

Diego has a silly side, but he doesn't show it very often, not even to me. He's just so serious all the time, and I'm sure it's exhausting. It feels like he's always waiting for the other shoe to drop. Like everyone's out to get him or trick him.

After seeing his brother and the way he treats Diego, I realize it's mostly Mateo's fault. That's why Diego acts that way. His brother is lurking in the shadows, ready to get him.

Constantly.

I wait for Diego in the kitchen, pouring myself a glass of cold water and taking a long drink to calm my frazzled nerves at having him in my house, especially after everything we said to each other.

The very specific thing he said.

That he never had sex with Cami.

God, I want to believe him, but it's so hard. What if he's

lying to get on my good side? It would be a smart move on his part, and a dumb move on mine to buy what he says without question.

Besides, why would so many people say he was cheating when he never was? There's always a nugget of truth in a rumor. It's why rumors get started. And why would Cami agree and actually help spread that rumor, if it wasn't even true? Does she not care how she looks?

Maybe in her eyes, she looks like a winner. She stole Diego from me. Look who's on top now.

Yet I wouldn't consider us a top tier couple on campus. At least, I never thought of us that way. Did I pay attention to who were the most popular couples at school? Yes. Did I think I was one of them? Not necessarily. It's not a status I sought out. That was more Diego's style. He always worried about what other people thought about him, especially his friends.

I sort of get it now, why he felt that way. Acts that way. His family situation is worse than I ever imagined. I'd be insecure and needy too, if I had to deal with a big brother who treated me so terribly. And a mother who pretends it isn't happening. She stepped up today, but was that only because there were so many witnesses?

I don't know.

Diego isn't the only one who worries about what people think of it. I do too. Especially now.

I'm the pregnant girl. That's who I'll be when we graduate high school. That's how they'll remember me ten years from now, when we go to our high school reunion.

Oh yeah, Jocelyn Douglas. The girl who got pregnant by Diego Garcia during our senior year.

And while I don't like being thought of that way and wish I could change it, I have accepted it.

Somewhat.

Not like I have a choice.

"It's all clear," Diego announces as he enters the kitchen. He stops, leaning against the kitchen island, his gaze contemplative as he studies me. "No one's in the house. Just you and that huge cat."

"His name is Kirby," I tell him.

"Kirby is a giant fluff ball," Diego says.

"Yeah, he is." I smile fondly, thinking about that silly cat. He acts like he hates me most of the time, yet he's been sleeping with me every night while my parents are gone, snuggled up against my feet, making me too warm. I think he misses my mom.

I miss her too.

My eyes sting and I stand up straighter, pushing the emotion aside. I can't cry like a little girl over missing my mama. I need to act like the responsible adult I'm about to become.

"You good?" Diego asks quietly.

I nod, sniffing. I blink hard, my vision blurred by unshed tears. "I'm fine," I say, my voice breaking, just before I start to cry.

Yet again.

I cover my mouth and turn away from him, my shoulders shaking as my tears turn into full-blown sobs. Today was—a lot. I think I held up pretty well, but of course, I have to completely break down in front of Diego.

"Jos—" he starts, but I lift my hand, waving him away.

"I-it's o-okay. R-really. I'm j-just—it's b-been a l-long day." I'm a sniffling, shuddery inhaling mess, and I don't know if he can understand me, but I sort of wish he would leave.

So I can cry alone.

I press my hand against the cold granite counter, gripping it tight as I continue to cry. The tears flow down my cheeks, and I'm sure I look a mess. But I don't care. I'm beyond caring now when it comes to this boy. Man. Father of our unborn child.

His scent reaches me first, just before he settles his big hands on my shoulders. He gives them a squeeze, his fingers brushing against the bare skin of my neck and it's like I can't help myself.

Turning into him, I slip my arms around his torso and hold on tight, crying into his shirt. I close my eyes and breathe deep, inhaling his comforting smell, and his arms come around my waist. He presses his cheek on top of my head, whispering words of comfort into my hair. Things I can't even hear, since I'm sobbing so loud, but it's such a typical Diego gesture. He's a whisperer when we're in the midst of an intimate moment, always full of gentle encouragements and compliments.

I try my best to calm my shaking shoulders, the near hysterical breathing. It takes me a few minutes, but I finally manage it, and when I start to quiet, I can actually hear what he's saying.

"You're going to be the best damn mom, Jos. I know you are. You've got this. You're so strong."

Sniffing loudly, I open my eyes and tip my head back, meeting his intense brown gaze. "You really believe that?"

Oh, the doubt rings true in my voice, and it hurts. I hate how insecure I feel right now. My entire life has been turned upside down, and I really haven't talked about it with anyone. My pregnancy makes everyone uncomfortable. Even Diego, at first.

"I definitely believe it," he says, as serious as I've ever seen him. "Do you really believe me?"

I frown. "What do you mean?"

"What I told you earlier." He hesitates. "About Cami." Another hesitation. "Do you believe me?"

I want to, but it's so difficult to change my mind after clinging to what are supposed lies all this time.

Is he actually telling the truth? Am I the one in the wrong in this situation? If that's the case, I feel like an absolute asshole.

"It's true," he whispers when I still haven't said anything. "I know it's hard for you to wrap your head around, since that's what you've been told, and yeah, I said some fucked-up things around that time. I did some fucked up things too. I can't deny that Cami and I hung out after we broke up."

I part my lips, ready to drop some reminders, but he forges on.

"And before we broke up too. We did. She was showing me attention and you weren't around and it was a shitty thing for me to do. I know it was, and I'm sorry. I'm stupid. And selfish."

I don't argue with him. Everything he's saying is accurate.

"But I never actually did anything with Cami Lockhart, Jos."

"Really?" I hear the hope in my voice, and there's the tiniest part of me that's whispering, *don't be a sucker. Don't fall for his lies yet again.*

I shove that voice into the farthest corner of my brain and tell it to shut up.

"Really. I swear on our baby's life, I didn't do anything with her," he says fiercely.

We remain silent, staring at each other. The refrigerator kicks on, the steady hum filling the room and it kicks me out of the spell Diego is weaving with his words and the way he looks at me.

As if I'm the only thing that matters to him.

"You going to be okay here all alone?" he asks.

I nod, trying to pull myself out of his arms. "I'll be fine."

"You sure?"

"You trying to scare me?" I ask him.

"Never." He smiles. "You're strong. I don't doubt you've got this handled."

This time I pull myself all the way out of his arms, straightening the hem of my sweater before I run a hand through my mussed hair. "I'm sure I look terrible."

"You're beautiful," he murmurs.

"I'm fat." Uh oh, pity party for one.

"Not even."

I smooth my hand over my stomach and turn to the side. "See? Look at the bump. I swear to God, it got bigger overnight."

His eyes widen and he reaches his hand out, pausing right in front of my stomach. "Can I touch you?"

I carefully lift my sweater up, showing off the bump covered by my high waisted leggings. "Sure," I tell him.

He shifts closer to me and settles his hand on top of my stomach, spreading his fingers wide, running his palm up and down very, very slowly. "You're definitely bigger. Even from a few days ago."

"I know," I say morosely.

His gaze lifts to mine. "It's just the baby. You don't look bad."

"I'll probably be as big as a house by the time this is over." I sound like a pouty child, but I can't help it. I hate how fat I feel right now.

"Isn't that normal though?" He presses his hand against my stomach a little more firmly, rubbing my belly. "There's a baby in here, Jos."

"I know, D."

He cracks a smile. "Have you felt him kick yet?"

I bite my lower lip, remembering what drove me to Pete's Place a few days ago. "Yes, I think so."

"You think so?" He raises a brow.

"I don't know. It's hard to describe, but yes. I think I felt the baby. Just this light fluttering. It was—it was cool." I smile at him in return as we both stand in the middle of my kitchen, his hand on my stomach as we talk about our baby.

Tonight, everything feels real. This is happening.

"I wish I was there and could've felt it too," he admits, as he continues caressing my belly. "Come on little guy, kick me. Show me what you got."

"It could be a girl," I remind him, pretending that his hand on my body isn't affecting me whatsoever.

But it is. His touch—feels good. I can't deny it. I've missed being with him. Having him hug me. Kiss me. I miss human contact, specifically from my boyfriend. Ex-boyfriend.

Father of our future child.

"Think she'll like football?" Diego asks, his gaze still on my stomach as he runs his hand over it.

"Maybe." I shrug.

"I guess he's not going to kick right now." He looks so disappointed.

"Someday you'll feel it. I have six more months of this, you know," I remind him, trying to make a joke and lighten the moment.

But it doesn't work. He's still stroking me, his heavy-lidded gaze on my face, his lips parted. I know that look.

It's the same look he gets right before he's about to kiss me.

"I miss you so damn bad, Jos. I miss this." He licks his lips, hunger in his eyes when they connect with mine. "I miss us."

I part my lips, ready to answer him, tell him that I miss us too, but the moment I start to speak, his mouth lands on mine.

And I don't stop him. I let him kiss me. His mouth is slow. Searching. Questioning. He doesn't push. He doesn't over-whelm. He barely moves, and I don't really move either. I'm too caught up in savoring the sensation of his mouth on mine, how he tilts his head, breaking the kiss for only a moment before his lips return once again.

He breathes my name just before he deepens the kiss, his hand lifting away from my stomach and circling around my nape, his fingers threading through my hair. It's the only place he's touching me, and my hands remain at my sides, my entire body leaning toward his as he slides his tongue against mine. Something deep within me awakens, and pleasure hums through my blood as I shift closer, his warmth drawing me in.

I rest my hands on his chest. His other arm wraps around my waist, yanking me into his lean, hard body.

He feels good. Too good. My brain short circuits and I curl my arms around his neck, my fingers buried in his thick hair, a moan escaping me when he slides one large hand down to my butt.

"I've missed you so fucking much," he whispers in between kisses. "Is this really happening?"

"Stop talking," I tell him because I'm scared words could ruin this moment. They've ruined so many moments between us before, and I don't think I could take it.

I don't want to think about the past, or the future.

I just want to feel.

He does what I ask, remaining quiet, concentrating on kissing me instead. We stand in my kitchen for what feels like hours, kissing and kissing. He kisses my neck. His hand returns to my stomach and he strokes me there, his fingers trailing lower, making me throb. My entire body is tingling, I feel strung tight, and the need for him to touch me between my thighs is almost overwhelming.

In the many articles and YouTube videos I've watched about pregnancy, they mention an increased sex drive a lot, especially in the second trimester, which I'm just starting. I get it now.

I'm horny.

Oh God, I kind of hate that word, but I so am.

It's when he starts sucking and nibbling on my neck, his hands wandering, that I can't take it anymore. I grab his hand just before it lands on my boob and pull away from his seeking mouth. He's frowning, his lips swollen, his brows furrowed, his hair mussed.

"What's wrong?" he asks, and I can tell he's steeling himself for me to reject him.

I interlace our fingers together. "Come with me," I say, tugging on his hand and pulling him out of the kitchen.

He follows behind me, our steps eager as we make our way to my bedroom. I push open the partially closed door, and I turn to face him, his hands coming up to cup my cheeks as he kisses me with everything he's got.

Urgency fills us the moment we enter the room. My skin itches as I try to shrug out of my sweater, and he helps me, his eyes widening when they see my chest, my barely constrained breasts. I'm growing out of this bra. I guess I'll need to buy new ones.

It'll be worth it, just remembering that appreciative gleam in his eyes as he continues to study me.

"You're changing," he says, running his finger along my cleavage.

"In lots of ways," I tell him as I reach for the hem of his shirt, trying to pull it off of him.

He sheds his shirt quickly, and I do the same. We haven't spoken about what we're going to do, but we know.

We know.

CHAPTER 14

DIEGO

I've got Jocelyn spread out on her bed as a feast just for me. She's only wearing a bra and panties, and my dick is straining against the front of my jeans, eager to get inside her.

But I take my time. She complained in the car all I wanted from her was sex, and I can admit she wasn't wrong. It's true. Once I had a taste of her, once we finally did it, it was all I wanted to do. I thought she felt the same way. She was always just as eager to kiss me, to touch me, to yank my shirt off or pull my jeans down. It was good. The sex between us was always so damn good.

That we're here in this moment right now blows my mind.

I rise from the bed and toe off my shoes before I get rid of my jeans. Now I'm just in my boxer briefs and when I glance over at Jocelyn, I find she's checking me out, her greedy gaze roaming over me like she can't wait for more.

I stand a little straighter. Puff out my chest. I study her just as thoroughly as she looks at me.

"You miss me?" I ask, my voice rough.

She nods, reaching behind her and undoing the clasp on her bra. She rids herself of it quickly, as if it just caught fire. "Come here," she whispers.

I go to her, falling on top of her, careful not to crush her. She hooks her legs around my waist the moment our mouths meet, clinging to me. Her heels dig into my ass, pressing my lower body against hers, and I thrust against her nice and slow, showing her exactly what she does to me.

Jocelyn moans, arching beneath me, and I lift up, reaching between us. I stroke the front of her damp panties, then sneak a finger inside.

She's soaked.

"Oh my God, don't stop," she says when I hesitate, my finger still beneath her panties. "Touch me."

I begin to stroke her, slowly at first, but I quickly increase the pace. She lifts her hips, her breaths coming in frantic pants, her eyes squeezed shut. I watch in utter fascination as she chases my fingers, chases that orgasm I'm about to give her, and within seconds, she's a shuddering, gasping mess.

A beautiful mess.

It usually takes a little longer for her to come, so I'm surprised. It's like she was primed and ready. And normally after she comes, she gets a little sleepy. A little lazy. That's why in the past I didn't like going down on her before we had sex. She'd try to cop out of it, which I'm going to be honest here—sometimes pissed me off.

Not this time though. She's wide awake and eager for more. I lift away from her as she sheds her panties, kicking them off onto the floor. She's reaching for me, her hand going to the front of my black boxer briefs, stroking me, making me sink my teeth into my bottom lip so hard, it fucking hurts.

"I want you," she tells me, her voice firm, her eyes a little wild when they meet mine. "Hurry."

I practically rip off my underwear, fumbling around like an idiot. Jocelyn throws her head back and laughs. She actually laughs.

"You're so cute," she tells me when I return to her. She wraps her hands around my shoulders and pulls me to her, so we're skin to skin, our lips connecting in a long, tongue filled kiss. She never hesitates, her hands everywhere, grabbing hold of my cock, stroking me, squeezing me tightly. It's been a while since I've been with her, and I'm already close.

Just like she was earlier.

And I'm not about to come all over her stomach right now.

"I need a condom," I tell her, and that really makes her laugh. Right in my face.

"Diego." She clasps hold of my cheeks with her hands, forcing me to stare into her sparkling eyes. "I'm pregnant. You don't need a condom. Unless you've been with someone else since I've been with you."

I swallow hard, trying not to get lost in how beautiful she is in this moment. How carefree. Was she ever like this when we were together? I don't think so.

Has the pregnancy already changed her?

Maybe.

"I haven't been with anyone else," I say, my voice solemn.

She smiles and stretches beneath me. "Then what are you waiting for?"

"I won't hurt you right?" When she frowns, I continue. "Having sex right now won't hurt the baby, will it?"

"No, she's safe."

"He," I correct.

She rolls her eyes. "It's a girl. I know it."

"We probably shouldn't talk about him right now." I lift up, grabbing hold of my dick right at the base, and start dragging the head through her folds. Damn, she feels good. Too good. It's been a long time. I think she's enjoying it too, from the way she spreads her legs wider, her eyes sliding closed as a murmur of pleasure falls from her lips. "We might traumatize him for life."

"She won't be too terribly traumatized," Jocelyn says, a little hitch in her breath when I enter her with just the tip. Ha, just like old times. "This is how we got her, after all."

"What do you mean?" I slip farther in, gritting my teeth at the hot sensation of her pussy gripping me. Fuck, I could probably come right now, but I breathe deep and tell myself to get my shit under control. I refuse to be a two-pump chump.

"You begging to have sex without a condom. That's how we got to this point," she reminds me.

Shame washes over me and I press my forehead to hers, poised above her, dying to sink deep inside but needing to say this first. "Do you hate me for it?"

"For what?"

"For getting you pregnant. I fucked up, Jos." I swallow hard and close my eyes. This moment feels so damn serious, and I don't know why I'm having an attack of conscience right before we actually do it, but here I am.

"It's not *all* your fault. I'm just as responsible as you are," she says softly, her fingers stroking my cheek. "I don't blame you."

"I'll do right by you." I push inside her, inch by inch, and her body welcomes me until I'm sunk deep. As deep as I can get.

That's what it feels like, with Jocelyn. I'm in so deep, I can't get out. And I don't want to.

"I know," she whispers, and when I open my eyes, I see the tears shining there.

I kiss them away.

"I swear to God, I won't fuck up again," I say fiercely. "I promise."

We don't say anything else. There's no need. Soon enough, we're lost in each other, and it's so damn good. Better than it's ever been. And since no one is around, and we're not cramped up in the back seat of a car, we take our time, and then we do it again.

And again.

And again.

*   *   *

I PULL up in front of my house just after six in the morning. I didn't want to leave Jocelyn. She was warm and snuggly, and her blankets are thick and soft. I could've slept there for days. And besides, she's all alone in that big house. How could I go?

But I needed to get home before my mom woke up, and she told me I should go, reassuring me she'd be safe. She walked me to the front door and kissed me before I left. Murmuring promises of coming to the game tonight.

I'm going to keep her to that promise. I need her there. She'll be my good luck charm.

I drove home in a daze, reliving the moments in my head, grinning like a damn fool the entire time. I feel on top of the world. Being with Jocelyn is like an adrenaline rush. I'm pumped and ready to play. We're going to win that game tonight.

Nothing—and no one—can stop me.

Climbing out of the car, I'm careful not to slam the door. My mom has extra strong hearing, and I don't want her to know exactly what time I got home. I texted her at some point during the night, letting her know I went to Jake's. His entire family is there, and it's plausible that we'd hang out together. Even though that fucker Eli Bennett was there, since he's dating Jake's little sister, Ava.

Don't know what she sees in that asshole, but whatever.

I don't even notice Mateo as I walk around the side of the house, prepared to sneak in through the back door. A low whistle comes from the back yard, and when I glance up, I see Mateo sitting in one of the chairs that got left out from yesterday, wearing a hoodie with a bulky jacket over it, one of our old sleeping bags draped over his shoulders.

Dread fills me at seeing him, and I stay put, not wanting to approach him. "What are you doing here?"

"So welcoming," he quips, sounding pissed. And tired. Dawn is coming, there's faint light in the sky, so I can just make out his features. I bet he's drunk. High. Whatever. "Where've you been?"

"Jake's." No way am I telling him the truth.

"Yeah right. Please don't tell me you were with your baby mama." I do my best to keep my expression neutral, but I hate how he has me all figured out. "It's like you can't break the habit. Already dipping your dick in the same ol' pussy again."

I'm quiet. What's the point in saying anything?

Mateo shakes his head. "Didn't you learn your lesson the first time?"

Anger fills me and I clench my hands into fists. My rational side is telling me I should ignore him.

My impatient, sick of my brother's shit, side is telling me I should knock him to the ground for saying all that shit about Jocelyn.

"You not saying anything is confirmation. The chick owns you, man. And I don't even get why. Don't settle for one pussy for the rest of your life when you could have all the girls you could ever want. You're not even eighteen, and now you're going to be a dad." He sits up straighter, throwing his arms out wide. "If you actually get a chance to go to college, and you play ball there? You'll have to shake them off of you, and you better take advantage of every single one. I'll take your leftovers."

He laughs and laughs, like what he said was so fucking funny.

"Did you sleep out here?" I ask, my voice tight.

"Went and partied for a while. Realized I had nowhere to crash, so yeah. I came back." He tugs the sleeping bag back around his shoulders. I'm sure he about froze his ass off out here. It's cold as fuck and only going to get colder. "I'm leaving tomorrow though. I'll stick around for your game, and the party afterward, but then I'm gone. Mom will be pissed. I won't call her. Fuck that bitch."

"Don't talk about her like that. Don't talk about Jocelyn like you just did either," I snap, my patience thin. I'm tired as fuck, and I need to go to bed, get some sleep for a few hours before we have practice for tonight's game.

I don't want him here for the game. Or the party.

I want him gone.

"Whatever," he mutters, rising to his feet and letting the sleeping bag hit the ground. "Why should I even go to the game and support your ungrateful ass? You've never liked me. You always thought you were too good for me."

My mouth drops open, and my anger is momentarily forgotten. I'm too in shock over what he just said. "Are you serious right now? *You* don't like *me*! You never have. You've treated me like absolute shit since pretty much the day I was born. I'm the nuisance who won't leave you alone. Who brings you down in front of your friends. The one you pick on and torment. You've abused me ever since I can remember. I never thought I was too good for you. I wanted to be just like you."

I'm breathing heavy when I finish my little speech, and

Mateo just glares at me in return. Nothing to say as usual. My feelings don't matter to him.

They never have.

And if he actually believes the bullshit he just said, then I'll never get through to him.

"Such bullshit," Mateo mutters, shaking his head.

My voice rises. "No, you're bullshit," I tell him, pointing a finger in his direction. "You can't keep a job. You steal money from me and mom to buy your drugs, and you fuck around with every chick you meet. Even better if they're not legal."

"You can't judge me," Mateo snarls and I just laugh.

"Too late. I'm judging the fuck out of you. You're a loser. I bet someday, you'll end up in jail."

Mateo charges in my direction, a ferocious yell emanating from him. I dodge out of the way at the last minute, fast on my feet thanks to muscle memory, like I'm out on the football field. He falls onto the ground with a grunt, rolling over on his back and clutching his shoulder.

Reminding me of what he did to me yesterday.

"That fucking hurt," he howls.

"You did it to yourself," I tell him, feeling smug.

He struggles to his feet, wincing in pain, his movements sloppy. "I hate you."

"Feeling's mutual."

"I could kick your ass right now," he threatens.

"Go ahead." I approach him fast, practically thrusting my face in his. "Try me."

We glare at each other, our faces so close I can see how bloodshot his eyes are. His skin is pale. His breath is stale. He looks terrible. And my brother is a good-looking guy. When he turns on the charm, everyone loves him.

He is slowly but surely losing all of that charm.

"You want to go?" he asks, lifting his brows.

"Nothing would give me more pleasure than smashing your face in," I tell him, meaning every damn word.

"Let's go then." Mateo's moves are hesitant and slow. I don't think he really wants to do this. He knows I can take him on and fuck him up. I've been waiting for this moment for what feels like forever. Finding the courage to finally destroy my brother has been a wish of mine for a long time. I always worried over what our mom would think, but I'm to the point where I don't care. I refuse to let him disrespect me, or our mother, or Jocelyn. He's a piece of shit.

Someone needs to put him in his place.

"I'll even let you throw the first punch," I say tauntingly.

"Aren't you a generous fuck?" Mateo lunges, swinging his fist, and I duck out of the way at the last second, and sock him right in the stomach.

Sending him crumpling to the ground.

That was too easy, but I had the advantage. I may not have gotten much sleep, but he's the one who stayed out all night in our back yard. He's probably hungover and still high. He's definitely not firing on all cylinders.

"Wanna try again?" I ask him, kicking him in the back, not putting all my effort into it, trying my best to ignore the guilt that floods me at hurting him.

He hurts me all the time. He's hurt me for years. I have physical and emotional scars all over me thanks to my asshole big brother, and here I am, feeling guilty.

Fuck that. He doesn't deserve my guilt or my concern. I've put up with him for years. Basically my entire life, he's made a living hell. I'm tired of taking his abuse.

He deserves to hurt, just as much as I have.

Mateo wraps his arm around my calf and yanks me to the ground. Bad move, considering when I land, my foot connects with his face, knocking him right in the jaw, which only further enrages him. He comes for me, struggling to pin me to the ground, and I fight back with everything I have, until I'm the one who's sitting on top of him, locking his hands above his head.

"Get off me, dickhead!" He won't stop moving, but he's slow. Tired.

Defeated.

"What in the world is going on?" Mom's voice rings across the back yard and we both glance up to find her standing on the porch in her robe, fury in her eyes as she takes us in. "Diego, get off your brother right now!"

I do as she says automatically, leaping to my feet. Mateo takes advantage and kicks at me, almost making connection with my knee.

I kick him directly in the ass in return. And damn, that felt good. The fucker deserves this. He's lucky I haven't totally unleashed on him yet.

"Mateo!" Mom runs out into the yard, stepping in between us. "Don't you dare hurt your brother! He has the most important game of his life to play tonight!"

"Always defending his precious ass, when he's the one who just fucking kicked me!" Mateo roars.

"I've had enough of the violence between you two. And didn't I ask you to leave?" Mom asks Mateo. "What are you doing here?"

He struggles to his feet, wiping his backside off as he glares at me. "I had nowhere else to go."

"You'll need to find somewhere else. I don't want you here."

"You're really going to kick me out? Choose him over me?" Mateo points at me, his hand trembling.

"I'm not choosing him over you. You wore out your welcome a long time ago, Mateo. Until you can get your act together and act like a responsible adult, you're not allowed to come into my house," Mom says, crossing her arms. "Now go, before you make me call the cops."

"Call the cops? Are you fucking serious right now?"

I see something unfamiliar flicker in Mateo's gaze and it dawns on me quickly.

It's fear. He's scared. He knows Mom wouldn't hesitate to call the cops on him. The last thing Mateo wants is police attention. He's shady as hell, and is harboring all sorts of secrets.

"You're going to let her do this. Let her throw me away like trash." He says this to me, and I slowly shake my head.

"You brought this on yourself," I tell him, my voice grim.

He glares at us then grabs the discarded backpack on the ground and hitches the strap over his shoulder. I thought he took a couple of duffel bags when he left, but I'm not going to ask about them.

I just want him gone.

"You're gonna pay for this," Mateo says, his voice low and full of menace. "You can't just tell me to fuck off and expect to never have to deal with me again."

"Do not threaten me," Mom says, marching right up to him and thrusting her finger in his face. "You do anything to me, you touch anything I own or one hair on my head, I will have your pitiful ass tossed into a jail cell. Mark my words."

His gaze shifts to me, and it's full of pure evil. "Watch your back," he says before he leaves the yard.

Icy cold dread slithers down my spine as I watch him go. Mom is trying to reassure me, saying he can't touch me, but I don't know.

He's more powerful than she thinks.

CHAPTER 15

JOCELYN

I am in full-blown Badger gear. I have my navy sweatshirt on with a giant white badger strutting his stuff in the center. I'm wearing a blue and white fleece headband I bought at the student store my freshman year and never really wore much. I got together with Sam before the game and we painted our faces with navy and white stripes, and Sam even drew a badger paw on my cheek.

I considered painting Diego's number on the other cheek, but I chickened out. It's not like we're officially together again, though it feels like we are. What we shared last night was—magical. There's no other word for it. He texted me earlier, letting me know he had a run in with his brother when he got home and it got heated. I immediately facetimed him, and he reassured me everything is okay. His brother is gone for good, but I heard the hesitancy in his voice when he said that.

Mateo will probably be back, but I don't want to worry Diego. He has other things to concentrate on right now.

Like this game.

We're playing at home, which is amazing. This is the first

time in our high school's history we've had home team advantage for the playoff finals. Our football coach—and former NFL quarterback—has been interviewed everywhere. Even on a couple of national networks, including ESPN. Jake, his son, has been right beside him for every interview. In one of them, they spoke to other members of the team and how pumped they were for this game, including Caleb and Diego.

He sent me the newsclip earlier via text, claiming he was a superstar, followed by a bunch of star emojis. Near the end of our relationship, his bragging felt like that—bragging. Cocky. Annoying. Everything he did then was annoying to me. We were both unhappy, and our relationship was in a bad place.

Now I think his arrogance is kind of cute.

I'm sitting up in the stands with Sam and Marley, and Hannah and Sophie joined us as well. Ava Callahan showed up with her boyfriend, Eli Bennett, who's the quarterback for our rival high school's team. Her best friend Ellie is with her, and also a guy named Jackson Rivers, who I've never met, though I've heard about him. He goes to school with Eli and also plays football. He throws huge parties all the time, more often than Tony, and almost always out at the lake. I guess he can also play the guitar, which is a reason that all the girls love him.

Meeting him, I find Jackson is definitely super cute and very charming. Not necessarily my type, with the longish blond hair and sad boy emo vibes, but I can see the appeal. Ellie watches him as if he walks on water. Eli keeps slapping him on the back of the head, which in turn enrages Jackson, but he's always left defenseless thanks to Ava sitting in between the two of them and Eli using her as a wall.

It's kind of funny, but also a little annoying, only because I want to focus on the game, not their antics.

The team we're playing is from a high school down in the valley, and they're good. They were state champions a couple of years ago, a title we've never held. If we win tonight, we go on to state.—

This game is a huge deal. And I'm nervous as shit about it.

"Want to go to the snack shack and get some pizza?" Sam asks me about halfway through the first quarter.

I shake my head, never taking my gaze off the field. "No way. I feel sick."

"Aww. Baby issues?"

"No, I'm just nervous," I say with a little shrug.

"You're nervous? Why?" Ava suddenly asks. She's sitting directly behind me, and she leans forward, our faces extra close. "I thought you two broke up."

"I still want the team to win. It's important to your brother, and Jake's my friend. A lot of the guys on the team are," I say, my cheeks growing hot. Which I'm sure is obvious, considering it's freaking freezing out here.

"Uh huh." Ava smiles, her gaze never straying from mine, and I look away first. She's the most perceptive of the Callahans, I swear. Her brother is a moody bastard most of the time. I don't really know her older sister, Autumn, that well. And her little brother is a tank, with a funny sense of humor. He's in the same class as my sister Addy. "You two are back together, aren't you?"

Well, she just knocked me for a loop. How did she figure that out?

"Shh," I tell her, glancing around, grateful no one is listening to us. "Not really. Sort of. Maybe. I don't know."

"Ahhh. I have no room to judge. Look at me and Eli." Ava laughs, nudging me with her elbow. The early days of their relationship were fraught with drama. "This is so great! I love this! I mean, I know Diego is a lot, and there are all those Cami issues—"

I reach out and press my gloved hand against Ava's mouth, silencing her. "Don't say her name. *Please.*"

We both simultaneously glance down at the sideline where Cami stands in her usual spot, front and center. The team is in the middle of a cheer, something about defense stop that play, and I watch her as disgust rolls through me. Her smile is bright, her movements sharp, her voice so loud I can hear her above everyone else on the cheer team. She's a good cheerleader, I have to begrudgingly give her that.

That's as kind as I can be when it comes to Cami. I can't stand her.

"God, I hate her," Ava says when I drop my hand away from her face, and I can't help the laughter that sneaks past my lips. Ava hates her almost as much as I do. Maybe more. "She's the worst human being on the planet."

"She's a liar," I agree. "Spreading rumors that aren't true all the time."

"Remember what she did to Hannah and Jake?" Ava asks me, tilting her head toward her brother's girlfriend, who's sitting only a few inches away from us. "She tried to break them up. Made it look like she was sneaking around with Jake, just to hurt Hannah. And she said some pretty shitty things to me too, about Eli."

"Fuck that chick," Eli pipes up, his words laced with venom. He hooks his arm around Ava's neck and kisses her forehead. She leans into him with a big smile on her face, and I can tell she loves the attention he lavishes on her. It makes me the slightest bit jealous. "Like she stands a chance against *my* warrior princess."

Ava grins, looking very pleased with herself. She is a warrior princess, considering she socked Cami right in the face during cheer practice, after Cami said something extra shitty about Eli—who she's also been with. That chick has been with so many guys, it doesn't matter if the rumors are true or false.

She's got a reputation, and no one wants to deal with her anymore.

"Hey, I heard Wyatt dumped her," Sophie says, her eyes wide when she tells us. She's Tony's girlfriend. Very quiet and shy, yet a competitive dancer who has no problem performing on stage in front of all sorts of people. A bit of a contradiction who I wish I knew better. I like her. She's smart, and really nice, but we've never been close. "The day before Thanksgiving they got into a huge fight, and he said he was done with her shit. He told Tony all about it."

"Oh wow." Ava slowly shakes her head. "I still can't believe they were together."

"He's such a stupid ass, getting with Cami in the first place," Eli says, practically growling.

Ava laughs. "Eli doesn't like him. He thinks Wyatt is always trying to make moves on me."

"It's because he's actually made moves on you." Eli scowls.

A roar from the away crowd sounds and I return my attention to the field, disappointment filling me as I watch the opposing team score a touchdown. My heart sinks and I gnaw on my lower lip. We only got a field goal when we had the ball, so they're already leading.

We can't let this team gain control. If they constantly one up us every time they have the ball, we're screwed.

Doomed.

"This is intense," Sam says, and I smile at her, though it's weak. "You going to be able to stand watching this? I'm a bundle of nerves and I have nothing at stake."

"I don't have anything at stake either, but I'm so nervous." My gaze snags on Diego as he jogs out onto the field, right beside Jake, Tony and Caleb following just behind them. "I don't want them to lose."

"Is it that you don't want *Diego* to lose?" I'm about to protest, but my best friend is sending me a pointed look. "I sort of overheard your conversation with Ava just now."

A big sigh leaves me. "I don't know what's going on between us. We spent Thanksgiving together yesterday, and it felt like old times, you know?"

"He cheated on you, Jocelyn. Don't forget that. He cheated on you, he rubbed it in your face, flaunting Cami everywhere he went, and he said really shitty things to you. He accused you of lying about being pregnant." Sam's voice shoots up.

Reaching out, I pat her leg. "Shh. I don't want everyone to hear you."

"Sorry. It's just, he works me up. He was *so* awful to you, and you swore you would never get back together with him. Yet here you are, spending time with him and acting like you two are still in love."

I remain quiet. Maybe I am still in love with him. And what's so wrong with that? I suppose I look really stupid, falling for whatever he's saying, but I want to believe him. He was so sincere when he told me he's never been with Cami, and he's right. There's no proof he's been with her. Just a lot of rumors and hearsay. And yes, he said shitty things to me, about me, but I know Diego lashes out when he's feeling defensive or upset.

Am I making excuses for him?

Maybe.

Yes, okay. I am.

"He's the father of my unborn child," I finally say, my gaze still on the field. "I want us to get along, for the baby's sake."

What a crock of shit. What happened last night when we got back to my house had nothing to do with getting along for the baby's sake, and everything to do with me wanting to be with him. Me wanting him, period.

And the night had been amazing. I want more. I'm hoping

for more tonight, after the game. Though he might be tired and not in the mood.

A little smile curls my lips. He's always full of adrenaline after a game, especially when they win. I have fond memories of a few of those nights he unleashed that adrenaline rush all over me.

Like the night we conceived the baby growing inside of me. Just before everything went to total shit.

"I just don't want him to hurt you again, like he did last time," Sam says, her voice cautious, as if she's prepared for me to argue with her. "You were devastated, Jocelyn. I didn't know if you would be able to actually pick up the pieces of your life and go on."

"I did eventually, didn't I?" I raise my brow, and Sam just slowly shakes her head. The disappointment on her face is clear. She can't believe I'm doing this.

Well, guess what sis? I can't either.

"Yeah, with our help," Sam says. "I don't want him to do it to you again. Because—I hate to say this, Jocelyn, you know I do—but he's going to. He's going to do or say something, and it's going to send you straight over the edge, and you'll be back where you started with this entire mess. Pissed at Diego and feeling all alone."

I ignore her, focusing my attention on the game, watching as Jake throws the ball and Diego catches it. My heart's in my throat the entire time he runs down the field, someone from the other team chasing after him. Getting closer to him, until he lunges for Diego and tackles him to the ground.

The entire crowd cheers for Diego and he leaps to his feet, saying something to the guy who just tackled him before he struts off the field. So much attitude. I'm attracted to it. I'm attracted to him.

I still love him.

But is loving him enough?

Or will what Sam just predicted come true and I'll end up hurt and alone all over again?

"I'll support you no matter what you do. Marley will too," Sam says, interrupting my thoughts. "Just—be careful with him, Jocelyn. He's selfish. He says all the right things, but deep down, he only cares about himself."

"That's not true," I say automatically. "He cares about me. He cares about the baby, too."

"Okay." The doubt in Sam's voice rings clear, and I angle my body away from hers, mad at her for voicing her concerns.

For making me doubt my feelings for Diego. For making me feel cautious.

And for ruining my good mood.

CHAPTER 16

DIEGO

Two minutes left. The scoreboard reads 45-38.

We're leading, but barely. They currently have the ball. If they score a touchdown and get the extra point, they'll tie us. They complete a two-point conversion, and they'll be up by one. Almost every time we have the ball, we drive it down the field, and eventually score. Our only mistake was that field goal we got at the beginning of the first quarter, instead of a touchdown. During the third quarter, all they could manage was a field goal.

Our defensive line has held them well, but they're fuckin' good. It's a high scoring game, lots of back and forth, lots of shit-talking out on the field. I just cursed out the asshole who took me down earlier, and he just smiled at me and told me he was going to fuck me up and good when the game was over.

Yeah, tonight the rivalry is pretty fucking strong between us. Nothing like what we've got going on with the Mustangs, who are our biggest high school rival, but we both want this win tonight. So we're out for blood.

I've got streaks of it all over my uniform. Both from my

own injuries and others. I've already cut my lip and there's a scrape on my jaw. Pretty sure my ribs are gonna be all bruised up before this night is over, and I'll be moving slow, but not right now.

I can't afford to be slow.

I'm playing like I'm at war, locked in a battle where no one is going to get out alive. I know my teammates feel the same as I do. The tension is high. There's not a lot of chatter or jokes tonight, not like usual. Not even from Caleb, who is the most light-hearted motherfucker on our team.

Our coach is wound so damn tight, I think his head is going to explode. Jake's little brother Beck is on the sidelines, screaming at us like a miniature copy of his dad, and any other night, I would've found this hilarious.

But not tonight. Tonight I wish I could tell Beck to shut the fuck up. I wish I could tell everyone to shut the fuck up. I need to concentrate.

I glance toward the stands, spotting Jocelyn immediately. She's already watching me, and I smile at her, which she returns. I found her in the crowd before the Star-Spangled Banner finished playing, and I've been looking at her every chance I get. She's my good luck charm, and so far, she's bringing me all the good vibes.

I need more. Just for those remaining minutes on the clock. They're ticking by. We're less than two minutes to go, and our defense is holding them, which is fucking amazing. Our defense has played like a bunch of superstars, and I cup my hands around my mouth, cheering for them.

Then I remember how distracted I am by everyone yelling for me tonight, and I shut the hell up.

I saw Mom in the crowd earlier, sitting with Aunt Lisa. They both waved at me, and I waved back, playing it cool. Secretly fucking thrilled they showed up. Spotted my grandparents too, which blew my mind. A few of my cousins, and Uncle Johnny of course.

Didn't see my brother at all, and I'm fine with that. I really don't want that asshole around. He'll ruin everything.

"They're not going to score," Jake suddenly murmurs, his gaze never straying from the field. "We're holding them."

"Fuck yeah," I say and we smile at each other, then immediately scowl.

We don't want to jinx ourselves.

"Looks like this might not be the last night we play together after all," Jake says with a grin.

I smile back, but it's forced. I'm not one to swim in my feelings, but it makes me sad, thinking this could be the last official game I play with Jake. If we go on to the state game next week, that's one more chance. One more game full of possible catches made by me, with amazing passes thrown by him.

The melancholy hits me swift and hard. This growing-up shit sucks, man. I'm ready to get the hell out of high school, but I'm also going to miss this so bad. The community coming out to support us. Seeing our friends, hell even our enemies in the stands, cheering us on. Having the teachers tell us *good job on the game Friday night* when we return to school Monday morning.

They treat us like gods on campus, and I'm a top dog. I've been a top dog since we started school in August. Even with all the bullshit between Jocelyn and me, and then Cami and me—and Jocelyn, I still never toppled from my spot in the popular hierarchy.

Jos always said I worried about that shit too much, and she's probably right.

I'm starting to realize she's right about a lot of things.

"Hey." I glance up to see Coach Callahan approaching us, a thunderous expression on his face. "You two. Listen up.

You're about to get back out onto the field, and this is your chance to cement the win. Remember what we discussed earlier in the locker room?"

Jake and I both nod, remaining quiet.

Drew Callahan shifts his gaze from Jake to me, then back to Jake again. "Do it. Try it. Make this shit happen, and put this game on lock."

Jake and I share a look before he says, "Love it when you pick up our slang, Dad."

"Can't help it. I'm around you little motherfuckers practically seven days a week." Coach actually chuckles before he leaves us, striding swiftly away, back over to the rest of the coaching team and Beck.

"Did my dad actually *laugh* just now?" Jake shakes his head, amazement filling his voice. "He must be feeling pretty confident."

Our attention quickly returns to the game. The other team is about to try and kick a field goal, so we watch, all the breath leaving my lungs when they get into position and the kicker sends the ball flying. He's gotta kick it pretty far at thirty-five yards, and I watch the ball arch into the air, just before it falls short of the goal post.

It's no good.

"Fuck yeah," Jake says, and we both shove our helmets on top of our heads, running out onto the field.

It's go time.

We get into position, and I remember all the other times Jake and I have been in this exact place during the last quarter of an intense game. How many times we've made that last play, clenched that final touchdown, and won it all.

If all goes as planned, we're about to make that magic happen yet again.

I glance up at the sky for a moment, spotting only a single star in the otherwise pitch-black night. It's cold as fuck out here, and I didn't think I'd find any stars since a storm is rolling in, but it's like this one is shining down, just for me. Guiding me.

I wish on it like I'm five, asking for strength. I glance one more time in Jocelyn's direction, and she presses her index finger against her lips, kissing it before she points her finger at me.

I feel that simple gesture zap me in the chest, sinking into my heart. My girl's got me in her sights. I can do no wrong.

I downright refuse to do wrong.

Jake makes the call, and then we're running. I slip away from the asshole who's been tailing my ass all night, losing him somehow, and I turn, the ball landing in my hands at the exact moment I knew it would.

Tucking the ball under my arm, I haul ass and tear down the field. I feel as if I'm not even touching the ground, I'm so fucking fast. I can hear the announcer counting off yard gains, encouraging me to keep going. As I run, I can hear two guys coming after me, their heavy pants, the thud of their feet as they draw closer. One of them calls me a mother-fucker, and I just laugh.

I actually laugh.

"Go Diego, go!" Tony yells, an old saying they used to throw at me when we were on the JV team. I hated it back then, since it referred to the cartoons on Nickelodeon, with Dora the Explorer and her cousin Diego, who eventually got his own show, *Go, Diego, Go!* It embarrassed me, and some-times I would even get into arguments over them calling me that.

Stupid right? What's the big deal? God, I used to be a real asshole.

What am I saying? I am still an asshole.

But I want to be better.

I cross into the end zone just before I'm tackled. I can

hear the announcer's enthusiasm as he screams *touchdown*. The roar of the crowd. The joyous cries of my teammates. I fall to the ground, my foot already over the line, the ball still lodged firmly under my arm. I scored the touchdown.

I actually made it.

My teammates on the field run toward me, all of them yelling and cheering. The clock comes to a stop, but there's less than thirty seconds left. They can't score two touchdowns in that amount of time.

We just won.

We.

Won.

The crowd goes nuts. Everyone is losing their minds, including us. Coach has to round us up and calm us down so we can get on the field and make the extra point. We get back into position, our kicker sending the ball sailing over the goal post with ease. The other team gets into position, but it's game over for them. People in the stands are counting down the clock, their voices ringing louder and louder, and all of us on the sidelines are facing them, waving our arms. Encouraging them. The buzzer sounds, the announcer yells, "And the Badgers take it!"

And then we explode all over again.

It's mass chaos after that. The other team slinks off the field, and I'm so fucking grateful that isn't us right now. It could've been. They totally could've beat our asses. They were a worthy opponent.

But we were better.

The next few minutes pass in a blur. Lots of congratulations. I lost my helmet somewhere, but I don't care. I get plenty of hugs and slaps on the back from my teammates. Jake actually tells me he loves me, and I tell him I love him too. I get choked up. I feel tears streaming down my face, and

I don't even bother trying to hide them. Caleb is crying too. We're a bunch of pussies.

Pussies who won a league championship, but hey.

It's only when I spot Jocelyn coming onto the field that everything comes to a stop. I can see nothing or no one else but her as she approaches me, a giant grin on her face. She's flanked by the other girlfriends of my friends on the team. Hannah. Sophie. Ava is with her too, and so is fucking Eli Bennett.

I hear him call out, "Good game, motherfuckers!"

I flip him the bird.

Jocelyn laughs and pulls away from them, running over to me, and I scoop her up in my arms, twirling her around as she gazes down at me, her hands braced on my shoulders. Her smile is huge. Mine matches, and my heart starts to race. Even harder than it was because we won.

The look my girl is giving me right now…it's everything I've wanted, I've craved since I lost her.

But now she's back.

I come to a stop and slowly slide her down the length of my body, until her feet touch the ground. And then I bend down and kiss her, for all the world to see.

Let them see. I don't give a shit. I just won.

When we break apart, Jocelyn's cheeks are flushed, and her eyes sparkle. I touch her cheek, glancing around, and of course, the first person I spot watching us is Cami. Her expression is full of disgust, and she mouths the words, "Fuck you," right at me before she turns her back on me with a flounce.

Bye, bitch.

"I knew you would win," Jocelyn tells me smugly, drawing my attention back to her.

"You did? Thank God you had all the confidence, because

I sure as hell didn't," I tell her, kissing her again, because I can't help myself.

"You liar. You've been strutting all over this field all night long," she teases, her sky blue eyes sparkling. "You played like you already won it."

"No way." I'm frowning, but she's nodding yes. "I didn't even realize it."

"I'm so happy for you." Her voice lowers. "Proud of you too, D. You did it."

"Yeah, I did, didn't I?" I look around yet again, feeling like I'm king of the entire mountain. On top of the world.

"Hey, good game, cuz."

I whirl around to see Marty standing there, his hand out for a congratulatory shake. I take his hand and we perform a complicated handshake we made up years ago, when we were little kids. It comes together so naturally, like we've never hated each other, that I actually start to laugh.

"Thanks, Marty," I tell him with a smile. "It means a lot, coming from you."

"Yeah. I've seen the light lately," Marty says, his gaze shifting to Jocelyn, who's standing right beside me. "She's told me a few things."

My smile fades and I take a step closer to Marty, my voice lowering. "It might not mean as much, considering I'm saying this in front of Jos, but you have to know how shitty I feel over how I've treated you through the years."

"I know." Marty nods, his smile a little sad. "You haven't said boo to me since we got into high school. I figured it was all instigated by Mateo."

"I had a hand in it too." My friends thought it was hilarious, me bullying Marty when we were in middle school. Middle school is the fucking worst, let me tell you.

I can only imagine how Marty felt about that time.

"Yeah, and you've apologized to me already."

"I mean it," I say, taking his hand and yanking him close to me. "I've missed you."

"I've missed you too, you cocky fucker." Marty gives me a quick hug, and I swear to God, all feels right in my world at this very moment. "You played great tonight."

"You coming to Tony's party?" I ask, moving away from him and wrapping my arm around Jocelyn's shoulder. "You should."

"Maybe. I don't know." Marty shrugs. "We'll see."

I look beyond Marty's shoulder and spot my mother and the rest of our family in the distance, standing on the sidelines, waiting for me, I guess, and I wave at them. They all wave in return, and I know I have to go over and talk to them, but I freeze when I spot Mateo lingering behind the group, his expression hard, his smile grim.

Despite the win, despite everything, the dread creeps back in. That familiar, shitty feeling I always have when I deal with my brother.

What the hell is he doing here?

We make eye contact, and Mateo aims his finger at me like he's pointing a gun. He lifts it in the air, like he just shot me, and then he blows on his index finger, his smile growing.

Then he turns and walks away.

"I'll see you guys later, okay?" Marty slaps my shoulder, oblivious to what just happened, before he runs off.

"Where's he going?" I ask, glancing over my shoulder.

"His boyfriend plays in the band, remember? He's probably going to talk to him," Jocelyn answers.

Unease slips down my spine when I see Mateo still standing there with my family, his gaze locked on the both of us. I grab hold of Jocelyn's hand a little too tightly. "Let's go say hi to my family."

I practically drag her across the field and she comes to a

stop. I turn to her with a questioning gaze. "Are you okay?" she asks. "You look a little pale."

It felt like Mateo just walked over my grave or some shit, which is stupid, but I can't help the spooked-out sensation that's currently sunk its claws into me. He's out to get me, and now I feel like I have to be on watch for the rest of the night, looking for the threat.

Because that's what he is. A deadly threat to my well-being.

"I'm fine," I tell Jocelyn, forcing a giant grin. "I just—this is a lot right now."

That's not a lie. It's a little overwhelming, what just happened. There are local reporters everywhere, and I see a crew fast approaching me. I know they want to do an interview. They have before.

"Don't worry about a thing," Jocelyn encourages with a gentle smile. "Enjoy it, Diego. This is an important night."

I know what she's saying is true, but it's hard to fight the wariness that's settled over me like a dark cloud, following me everywhere I go. Slowly but surely eating away at my good mood. I can feel Mateo's presence on the field, in the stands. Even though I don't see him, I can sense he's still here, and I wonder if he's lying in wait.

I wonder if he's trying his damnedest to take away every last bit of happiness I have. Look how well he's doing it already, considering I can't even see him.

Just knowing he's here has that much of an effect on me. I hate him.

Pretty sure he hates me too.

CHAPTER 17

JOCELYN

Long after the game and the interviews and all the congratulations, Diego and I finally arrive together at Tony Sorrento's house. Before we left the high school, I tried to convince Sam to come with us, but she backed out, claiming she was tired. I don't really believe her. I think it has more to do with her obvious disapproval of me being back together with Diego.

Though it's not like we're official or anything.

I know Samantha is watching out for my best interests, and I appreciate that. I really do. But what I do is my business. I don't need her approval to get back together with him. Besides, he's the father of my baby. Don't people want us back together?

We can actually be a little family if we are. And that fills my heart with all sorts of warm fuzzies.

"I'm tired," Diego tells me as we head up the sidewalk leading to Tony's front porch. We're hand in hand, and this feels familiar, yet new. He's not perfect, and neither am I, but I feel like I understand him so much better than I did even a few days ago, thanks to our talks. And spending time with his family. Seeing what his life is *really* like.

"I bet. You played hard," I tell him, giving his hand a squeeze.

"It has more to do with the fact that someone kept me up pretty late last night." He smirks.

I blush.

"You weren't complaining last night," I tease him.

His eyes somehow grow even darker as he yanks me to him, wrapping his arm around my waist and dropping a kiss onto my upturned lips. "Neither were you," he murmurs.

I shove at his chest, and he takes a couple of stumbling steps back, laughing. My heart soars at seeing the joy on his handsome face, and I want to capture this moment. Bottle it up and save it forever, so I never forget what it feels like.

Watching Diego and the rest of the team play magnificently. The pure happiness that emanated from them when they won. How the community roared their approval and gave them a standing ovation when the team performed their end-of-game ritual of standing in front of the stands with their helmets in their hands, simultaneously yelling, "Thank you!"

It was a moment to remember, and I'm not ashamed to say I cried.

"You ready for the onslaught?" I ask Diego as we walk up the porch steps.

"What do you mean?" he asks with a frown.

Reaching forward, I open the door. The second people spot Diego as we enter, everyone's on him as if he's the hometown hero, which he totally is, right behind Jake.

There are a lot of people milling about inside Tony's house, but I know the party is actually happening outside in the back yard, like always. I let go of Diego's hand when he's mobbed by the various well-wishers, and I make my way through the kitchen and out the backdoor, waving at people I know. Hugging some of them, including Ava, who told me she just got there with her boyfriend only a few minutes ago.

Once I leave Ava and Eli, I see Tony standing alone, close to the house, with a beer clutched in his hand and a satisfied expression on his face as he surveys everyone out back.

"Jos." He tips the beer bottle in my direction when he spots me. "Glad you could make it, babe."

Ha. He just called me babe. I think he might already be drunk.

"I always appreciate a party at Sorrento's," I tease him, knocking my shoulder into his upper arm. He's not as tall as Jake or Diego, but he's lean and muscular, with harsh features offset by a full mouth and warm brown eyes. He's definitely attractive, but also very intense. He and the sweetly shy Sophie don't quite match up as a couple in my eyes, but they seem to work.

And speaking of sweet Sophie…

"Where's your girlfriend?" I ask, glancing around for her blonde head.

"She couldn't make it to the party. She has a dance comp that starts pretty early tomorrow," he says before he takes a swig of beer.

"Are you going to watch her compete?"

"She never wants me there," he says with a shrug. "She's worried about being embarrassed, and what I might think."

"Why would she be embarrassed if you watch her?" I've seen her dance. There are YouTube videos out there of her at various dance comps over the years, and somehow I stumbled upon them recently. She's a beautiful, graceful dancer.

"I don't know. She's shy." Another shrug. Another drink from his beer, this time he drains it. "I think we might break up."

His announcement startles me and I scoot closer to him,

lowering my voice so no one will overhear. "Why would you say that?"

"It hasn't been the same, not since Halloween. I don't know what happened. She's busy. I think her parents hate me. They hate my entire family." He sends me a dark look, and I see the pain that flashes in his eyes.

I know nothing about Tony's family. They're downright mysterious. Never around. I don't even know if he has brothers or sisters. I've never gone to school with any of them. I think he's an only child, but maybe he's the youngest? I honestly don't know. He moved here when we were in elementary school. Fifth grade, I think. Or was it sixth?

"They wouldn't encourage her to break up with you, would they?" I ask him.

"I don't know. Weirder things have happened, am I right?" He raises a dark brow at me and I can feel my cheeks heat up the slightest bit. "How you feeling by the way? I hear Diego brought you with him. You two back together?"

Ignoring his question, I say, "Wow, word travels fast. We literally just got here." I cast my gaze around the back yard, at the many, many people out here. It's freezing cold tonight, and Tony has a few patio heaters going, but not enough to take the chill off unless you're standing right next to one. Lots of people are wearing thick coats and hats, clutching their drinks with gloved hands.

People will do anything to party.

"You two are the talk of the night. That and the win of course, which we all expected anyway, but didn't want to say. Didn't want to curse ourselves." Tony laughs. "Even though I felt it in my bones we would win, I still can't believe it happened."

"It was amazing. Well-deserved," I say. "You going to play football in college?"

"I don't know." Yet another nonchalant shrug. It's like it's his signature move. "I'm decent, but I'm no Diego Garcia. And I'm definitely not a Jake Callahan."

"Who is?"

"He's in a league of his own," Tony agrees, his gaze going to where Jake is sitting nearby on an outdoor couch, his girlfriend slung under his arm as he talks to the group surrounding them. A king and his court. "He'll go on to do something with himself."

"Diego wants to do something with himself too," I say. Tony glances over at me. "With football. He wants to play in college. Desperately."

"I know. He used to talk about it all the time, until recently." Tony hesitates before forging on. "What about the baby though? And you?"

I love that Tony doesn't pretend it's not happening. He just confronts our situation head on. "I'm not going to stop Diego from going to college. He wants to go to Fresno State. So do I. I just hope we both get in there."

"You're going to Fresno State together? As in *together* together?"

I laugh. He sounds like a middle schooler talking rumors right now. "Well we didn't plan it *together* together. It's more that our recent plans just happened to coincide."

"How handy for you both." Another quick hesitation. "And are you two actually together now?"

"I don't know what we are, but we're not mad at each other anymore." The back door opens and I watch as Diego walks through it, people trailing behind him, all of them clamoring for his attention, including a few girls. Underclassmen. I tamp the flare of jealousy down, telling myself none of those girls matter to him. They're going to follow him everywhere tonight. He's wearing that invisible crown too, just like Jake.

The moment he spots me, he makes his way over to us,

and a shiver of delight courses through me. The jealousy is gone, just like that, when I see the intimate smile he flashes in my direction. That smile belongs to me.

He doesn't care about anyone else here tonight. Just me.

"I'm glad you two are trying to work it out for the baby," Tony says.

"It's not just for the baby," I tell him, just before Diego grabs me, pulls me to him, and presses his mouth to mine in a long, glorious kiss.

Everyone starts making *oooh* noises and I push him away, blushing. He laughs. Pulls me back in and kisses me again.

"Just in case you didn't know," he yells as he holds me close, causing pretty much everyone in the back yard to quiet down. "Jocelyn and I, we're back together."

There's a smattering of applause, as if we're on a stage and putting on a performance. There are a few people who are watching us with skeptical expressions, and I even catch a couple of eye rolls. They've seen this before. They've seen *us* like this before.

And they figure we're not going to last.

Hopefully, we're going to prove them wrong.

"Good luck!" someone yells, and I see a flash of rage cross Diego's face for the quickest second, before he smooths it over and plasters on a fake smile.

"Hey, say that to my face!" he calls out, his tone deceptively friendly. I take a step away from him, shifting closer to Tony.

I don't want to see Diego turn confrontational tonight, but sometimes it's like he can't help himself.

A low murmur starts within the cluster of people, and then the crowd parts, and out walks Diego's brother. He looks a lot better than the last time I saw him, which was only a little over twenty-four hours ago. He's dressed in jeans and a black hoodie, his dark hair combed back, his face clean-shaven. He appears alert. Almost handsome. Diego and his brother actually look a lot alike.

"Well, here I am," Mateo says when he comes to a stop directly in front of Diego, "saying it to your face. Good luck, you dumb fuck." Mateo laughs, glancing around. "Look at me. I'm a poet."

Diego's hands clench into fists at his sides, and he exhales loudly, but otherwise, doesn't say a word.

"Nothing to say, huh? Maybe because you know I'm speaking the truth? This is all such bullshit, Diego, and you know it. They're all celebrating your ass, but the real hero of tonight's game is Callahan. That guy is fucking *untouchable*," Mateo says.

The crowd is now silent. They all want to hear this, witness the Garcia brothers put on a show, and my heart is literally breaking for Diego. This is a public humiliation that no one deserves.

"You're just the lucky asshole who can catch his throws. I mean, fuck. Who couldn't? His accuracy his unprecedented. He'll go on to the NFL for sure, especially being a prodigy and all. It pays having Drew Callahan as your father. And what are you going to do? Play for Fresno Community College for a season or two? Pray you don't get hurt and maybe they'll accept your ass as a Bulldog when you transfer to Fresno State? If you can manage to stay in college long enough." Mateo taunts.

Someone coughs, but otherwise, no one says a word.

"You're just jealous," Diego throws at him, his voice just as taunting as his brother's. "Jealous you didn't amount to anything. Jealous you're a coked-out loser. Jealous no one likes your ass and you have to resort to hanging out with *my* friends, who only tolerate you because you're my big brother and you can score us alcohol and weed and whatever other drugs people want. That's the *only* reason, Mateo. The only reason they want you around. No one gives a shit about you, not even me."

"Fuck you," Mateo bites out, taking a step forward, his chest brushing against Diego's. "You're only feeling brave because your friends are here. If we were alone, you wouldn't say a goddamned word."

Worry slams into me and I turn toward Tony.

"Who invited him?" I ask. "Are you going to stop this?"

"Everyone's welcome. I don't block anyone from walking through my door," he says to me.

"Maybe you should," I retort.

Tony makes his way over to the brothers, trying to step in between them. They don't budge from their positions, making it tough to intervene. "Why don't you two break it up, okay? I don't want any fights going down at my house. This is a night of celebration."

"Fuck you and your celebration," Mateo says to Tony, his gaze never leaving Diego's.

The glower on Tony's face is unmistakable. When he's mad, no one wants to mess with him. "This is my house, asshole. I can do and say whatever the hell I want. And I want you to get your ass out of here."

"Oh, so I'm good enough to provide some liquor and bring you some coke, but now I can go fuck off?" Mateo shakes his head, his entire body practically vibrating hostility. "You're an ungrateful son of a bitch, you know that?"

"I didn't ask you to bring me shit," Tony says through gritted teeth. "I didn't even know you were going to show up."

"Hey!"

We all turn to find Jake Callahan and Eli Bennett making their way toward us, Jackson Rivers and Caleb walking behind them. I take another step back, bumping into someone, and relief fills me when I see it's Hannah.

She slings her arm around my shoulders and steers me away from the group of boys who are all now standing in a circle, studying each other with unrestrained contempt. The tension is thick. The testosterone is palpable. They're looking for a fight, and I'm sure Mateo is eager to deliver.

One wrong move on his part, and they'll destroy him.

"You should do as Tony asked and leave," Jake says, stopping directly in front of Mateo, subtly nudging Diego to the side. Eli is standing beside Jake. Caleb and Jackson stand on the other side of Diego and Mateo, so the two brothers are surrounded. "We don't want any trouble, Mateo."

Mateo practically growls as he whips his head around, glaring at all of them. "Stupid young motherfuckers, thinking the world owes you one. Just wait. You're all going to get yours." He points at Diego. "Especially you. I'm not done with you."

"You keep saying that," Diego taunts, grabbing hold of his brother's wrist and shoving Mateo's hand out of his face. "Yet nothing ever happens."

"Oh, it's coming. When you least expect it." Mateo glances over his shoulder, our gazes connecting. I recoil at the pure evil I see emanating from his pitch-black eyes. "Watch out, little mama. I'm coming for you too."

That was the wrong thing for Mateo to say. One second he's still on his feet, looking pleased with himself for threatening me.

The next, he's on the ground, Diego on top of him, his arm rising up as if in slow motion, just before he lowers it swiftly, his fist connecting with Mateo's face.

People start screaming as they all scatter. Diego won't stop swinging. The rest of the guys swoop down, trying to get Diego off of his brother, but it's difficult. Diego resists. Mateo won't stop howling, blood streaming from his nose, and he's cursing nonstop. Finally, Caleb and Jake lift Diego off of his brother, and Jackson and Eli jerk Mateo up onto his feet. He shakes them off, sending them both dirty looks before he spits blood onto the grass, and his lips curl into a snarl.

His nose is swollen and bleeding, and his eyes appear as if they're about to swell too. There's a cut at the corner of his mouth, and he keeps spitting out blood. Seeing him so battered, I sort of feel bad for him, but then again, I don't.

He asked for this.

I thought Diego was angry all the time. His older brother takes it to a whole new level.

"Get out of here," Tony tells him, grabbing Mateo by the arm and dragging him toward the side of the house. "You need to go party somewhere else. You're causing too much trouble."

"Fucking hate all of you," Mateo yells as Tony leads him away. "I hope you all go to hell! Fuck you, Diego! And fuck your little bitch too!"

Diego rushes over to me the moment his brother disappears from view, wrapping me up in his arms and whispering, *I'm sorry* over and over again.

I cling to him, grateful everyone leaves us alone. I can hear people come back out into the yard. Hear conversations resume. There's even music playing. They're not going to let a little fight between brothers ruin their night.

Hopefully no one is paying attention to us, but that's probably wishful thinking. I'm sure many of them are.

"Let's go inside," I suggest, just in case.

He grabs hold of my shaking hand and we head into the house. I glance down at our linked hands, sucking in a sharp breath when I see his scraped-up knuckles. I take him for a quick detour, pulling him into a nearby bathroom, and close the door, locking us away from everyone else.

"Let me see your hand." I bring our connected hands

closer to the light, shaking my head when I see the scrapes and swelling on his knuckles and fingers. "Is this from the fight? Or the game?"

"The fight. I hit him as hard as I could," Diego says tightly. "And I don't regret it either, so don't bother giving me a speech."

I ignore the anger in his voice. I know it's not aimed at me. He's still fired up over his brother.

"You could've done serious damage to him. And to yourself," I say. "And you can't take any of it back."

"I don't give a shit, Jos. I hate his fucking guts. He's out to get me, on some sort of revenge kick I don't understand." Diego's troubled gaze meets mine. "And he sure as shit can't threaten you. Did you hear what that asshole said? I couldn't let him get away with it."

"I'm not worried about him," I start, ready to dismiss the entire thing, but Diego cuts me off.

"You should worry about him. Don't take what he says lightly. He's dead serious. He hates me, and that makes him hate you too. He knows how much you mean to me, and that you're pregnant with my baby. *Fuck.*" Diego turns to face the mirror, thrusting both hands into his hair and tugging on it in frustration. "I hate him so goddamn much."

"Maybe we should call the cops," I suggest.

He watches me in the mirror. "They won't do shit. What can they do? Wag their fingers at him and tell him to stop? Making threats isn't breaking the law."

"But beating someone up is," I remind him, my voice quiet.

He turns to face me, dropping his arms to his sides. "You're saying I shouldn't have done it?"

"I'm saying you shouldn't have gotten so out of control," I correct gently.

Diego scoops me up his arms, our gazes never straying

from each other's. He's so close, I can feel his rapidly beating heart. See the frantic emotion filling his gaze as he studies me. "He threatens you, I can't be held responsible for what I might do to him. I can handle him. You can't. And if you haven't figured it out by now, let me tell you what's going on. You're everything to me, Jos. Every precious, single thing that matters to me is you, and the baby you're carrying. My baby."

"Our baby," I say with a little smile.

His smile is faint, and it's a relief to see it. "Right. *Our* baby. You're pregnant with my child. I don't know what I'd do if he messed with you. If he—hurt you. And the baby."

Those last words are practically choked out.

"He's not going to hurt me." I reach out and push a few strands of dark hair away from Diego's forehead. "He doesn't scare me."

"He should. He should scare the shit out of you." Diego's voice wavers. "I know he scares the shit out of me."

"You have everyone here supporting you," I remind him, as I continue stroking his thick, soft hair. "Including me. He can't hurt you."

"I'm sure he's pissed I beat his face in. The public humiliation has probably sent him straight over the edge." Diego smiles grimly when I settle my hand on his cheek. "It actually felt good, hurting him. Does that make me a bad person?"

"No, it makes you human. He's hurt you for so long, it's natural to want to hurt him back." I rise up on my tiptoes and press my mouth to his. "But you can't keep hitting your brother every time you see him, Diego."

"He's hurt me in some way or another for years. With his words. With his fists. With his kicks. Throwing shit at me. Pinching me when we were little and sitting in the backseat of my parents' car. When my dad was still around." Diego slowly shakes his head. "He hates me so damn much, and for what? Because I was born?"

I kiss him again, not wanting to hear the pain in his voice anymore. I decide to say the words that have been building in me since he spent the night at my house.

"I love you," I whisper against his mouth. "I love you so much. And I love our baby. Cut your brother off. Don't see him anymore. Don't talk to him. Do this for yourself. For your sanity. And for our future."

"You're right. I know you're right." He gathers me up in his arms and holds me close. "I love you too, Jos. So damn much, it hurts. I'm so sorry for everything I've done to you. I'm an idiot."

I hold him close as he repeatedly apologizes. I try to give him comfort.

And can only hope what I offer him is enough.

CHAPTER 18

DIEGO

I sleep in because I can—plus I'm exhausted from everything that happened last night. I grab my phone off the nightstand as usual, checking my notifications. The Snapchat text notification came sometime in the middle of the night. And it's from…

Cami.

Of all people.

I unblocked her ass yesterday because I was curious—so sue me. Once I heard Wyatt telling everyone in the locker room that he dumped her, I wanted to see if she posted a bunch of sad girl shit, videos of her crying or whatever, or if she got all, *I'm an independent woman who doesn't need a man,* which is another tactic she uses.

Instead, she posted nothing, which I found odd. I checked and forgot about her so quickly, I also forgot to block her again, which means she was able to send me that text.

I almost don't want to open it.

Yet I do, and it's a provocative photo of her. Pouty, parted lips. Big doe eyes. Thin white tank top on with plenty of skin and cleavage on display. With the caption, *I miss you*, on the photo.

I screenshot the photo and send it to Jake.

Do you miss this shit?

My friend responds seconds later.

Jake: **Not at all. Why would you screenshot it? She knows you did. She got the notification.**

Me: **Like I give a damn if she knows what I do. I didn't even respond.**

And he never responds to me either. I forget all about it when my mother busts into my room seconds later, her expression fiery as she stares me down.

"You put your hands on Mateo," she says.

I sit up, worry filling me. "Is he here?"

"No, he sent me photos of his face and told me you were responsible for the damage. You broke his nose." She marches into my room and settles on the edge of my mattress. "You can't go around punching your brother whenever you feel like it, Diego. It's not right, putting hands on your family."

I start to laugh. Like, hysterically laugh. My throat is scratchy from all the talking and yelling last night, and my body aches from the game and the fight. Oh, and the sex Jocelyn and I had when I took her back home after Tony's party.

It was a big night. I'm fucking exhausted. And of course, Mateo is trying to get me in trouble with Mom. Love how he turns it around and makes me look like the bad guy.

Unbelievable.

"This is not a laughing matter," Mom huffs.

"Oh, I know," I say in between chuckles. "It's not funny at all, how you totally didn't see what was happening in your own home."

"What are you implying, hmm?" She crosses her arms, that stubborn expression on her face that I know so well.

"The fact that Mateo's been torturing me since pretty much the day I was born."

She shakes her head. "That is not true."

"It is. He's been hurting me since I can remember, and you always would blow me off when I came to you and told you about it. Or you were too wrapped up in your own problems with Dad, or Mateo, to ever really listen to me."

Mom presses her lips together, her gaze hostile. "Are you saying this is my fault? What Mateo did to you?"

Realization dawns, like a slow awakening. Or when your foot falls asleep. That prickly feeling is crawling all over my skin.

The way she said that, makes me think...

She always knew.

She always knew what Mateo was doing to me, and she never did anything to stop it.

"So you did know." It's not a question.

Her brows draw down together. "What are you talking about?"

"Have you known what Mateo's been doing to me all these years?"

She starts to say no. I can tell by the way her lips are formed, but I cut her off.

"Don't lie to me, Mom. Tell me." Leaning forward, I grab hold of her shoulders, and she drops her arms to her side. "Did. You. *Know?*"

Her entire body seems to sag, and I wonder if I wasn't holding her up, if she might collapse onto the floor. "I had my suspicions," she admits.

My hands spring away from her, as if touching her is poisoning me. "Get out."

She rears back. "What did you just say to me?"

"Get out of my room," I bite out. "I don't want to look at you right now."

Mom leaps to her feet, pointing at me. "This is my house. You can't tell me what to do."

"Why didn't you do anything to stop it, huh? Why didn't you make him stop?" I'm yelling, and she hates it when I yell, but I don't even care. It's all we know in this house. Yelling. Screaming. Accusations. Anger. Pain.

What kind of mother is she, to let her one son hurt her other one? What the fuck is wrong with my family?

"I only just figured it out!" She throws her hands in the air. "I kept telling myself Mateo would never harm you."

"I told you what he did to me when I was five," I remind her. "I kept telling you, every time he did something, and you would just brush me off. You'd give Mateo some lame ass speech, and then he'd *really* do something awful to me for being a snitch. And because you never stopped it, I eventually stopped telling you."

Her eyes widen the slightest bit, but then she seems to just—brush off what I say. Typical. "It was kid stuff. You can't keep beating each other up. He's an adult now. You're close to being one yourself. Next thing you know, the police are involved, and then you both end up with a record."

I turn my back on her. All she cares about is appearances. What people think of her. Of us as a family. We're already a mess. She doesn't want us looking any messier.

Too late. We're a fucking disaster.

"Just—leave me alone," I mutter, bending my head, which is suddenly too heavy with all my thoughts.

She knew, yet she never did anything about it. Until Thanksgiving, and even then, that came too late.

That's her problem. She's always too late.

"I kicked your brother out of the house," she tells my back. "I don't know what else you want from me. He's a lot to handle, you know this. And I'm sure he'll be back. He can't stay away."

"Because he has no other option. He can't go anywhere else." I feel stuck too, and this is the last place I want to be. "Kicking him out is pointless anyway. He'll be back. And you'll take him back, because you want to believe what he says so damn bad, you'll ignore all the obvious signs that he's a liar and a thief."

"It's not that I believe what he says—"

"Bullshit." I turn to glare at her. "You fall for his words every single time. He knows how to manipulate you, and you make it so damn easy. He's got you wrapped around his little finger. Too bad you can't see what a piece of shit your oldest son really is."

"Don't you say that." Her voice trembles.

"It's fucking true."

"And don't you curse at me either. I won't stand for it."

I start laughing all over again. "You won't stand for me cursing, yet you stand for your beloved son being violent toward your other son. Got it. Your priorities are really messed up, Mom."

She gapes at me. It's not easy to stun my mom speechless, but looks like I managed it. "You don't understand," she finally sputters.

"Understand what? That Mateo is an asshole and he has you completely under his thumb? That no matter what I do or say, you won't care, because you have your truth, and I have mine?" She says nothing, so I forge on. "I'm going to be a father in like, six months. By the time I graduate high school, I should be a dad. When Jos and I came to you on Thanksgiving, we were looking for your support. But you weren't willing to give it to us. You fed us a bunch of negativity and then went about your business, like what we told you didn't matter."

She's trembling. Indignant. Strangely silent.

"Besides, you'd rather support your adult son who can't find a job and would rather drink and smoke weed all day," I tack on, because it's fucking true.

"You like to drink and smoke weed too," she tosses at me.

"I didn't touch anything last night at Tony's party, and I had every opportunity," I tell her, though I'm not sure why. To prove to her that I'm better than she thinks I am?

That she thinks so lowly of me in the first place is painful.

"And why should I support you getting your ex-girlfriend pregnant? You're not even out of high school yet! You got yourself into this mess," she reminds me. "You'll have to figure out how to get yourself out of it."

"Gee, thanks for the support, Mom." I flop onto my side on the mattress, my back to her. "You can go."

She's quiet for a moment, and I can tell she wants to say something so badly, but she doesn't.

Instead, she leaves my room, the slamming door making me jump. I curl my body into a ball, wrap my arms around my bent knees and close my eyes.

Fuck this.

Fuck everyone.

* * *

"What's up with you calling a meeting or whatever?" Caleb asks me when he enters Tony's house.

After about an hour of wallowing in self-pity, I texted Tony and asked if I could come over. When he said yes, I texted Caleb and asked him to meet us there, and then I texted Jake.

We're all four sitting in Tony's living room, and they're watching me with expectant gazes, since I'm the one who wanted to talk.

"I'm moving out of my mom's house," I announce to them.

They all send each other a look. Caleb says something first.

"Right now?"

I nod. The idea took flight before my mom even walked out of my bedroom. "I can't live there anymore. Mateo is an asshole and he's coming for me. He will always come for me. I don't feel safe there. It doesn't matter if she kicked him out. He'll be back."

"Where do you want to live?" Caleb asks.

"I guess I can get an apartment here, ride out the rest of the school year, and then I'll move to Fresno," I explain, though I'm not one hundred percent sure how I'll qualify for a rental agreement. I have money for a deposit, but do I have enough? Plus, it would wipe out my savings, moving somewhere on my own. "Well, I'll work at the resort starting this spring and through the summer, then I'll move to Fresno for school. I'll need the money."

I'll need as much money as I can get.

"You're really going to try and live on your own?" Tony asks. "Will you be able to afford it?"

"Maybe Jocelyn will move in with me and we can split the rent." They all start to protest and I hold up my hand, silencing them. "We're going to have to move in together eventually. We're having a baby soon."

"Uh, have you talked to her about this?" Jake asks.

"Not yet. Wanted to run it by you guys first. Get your input on how to handle it." I explain to them what happened between my mom and me earlier. They already know about my feelings toward Mateo. What Mateo's done to me over the years, though they don't know too many details.

I never could bring myself to share everything with them.

"I don't know if it's a good idea," Jake says when I finish, and I can tell he's choosing his words very carefully. We're both hot-headed, and have gotten into plenty of arguments in the past.

We always come back around for each other, though.

"It's going to be expensive," Tony says in agreement. "Even up here, rent isn't cheap. You'll have to work full-time, plus go to school. That'll be rough."

"Does Jocelyn even want to live with you? Are you two back together for real?" Caleb asks.

"Yes." Not that we've said anything to each other to make it official, but come on. We said we loved each other last night. We've had sex two nights in a row. That's telling me we're back together. "I want to do right by her, and the baby."

"I'm glad you want to step up and take care of your responsibilities," Jake says. "But you might be—I don't know —stepping up too fast?"

"I just want the fuck out of that house." I start pacing. Caleb and Jake are sitting on the couch, and Tony's in a recliner. I'm the one who's full of too much energy that I can't settle down. "I can't stay there anymore. My mom doesn't give a shit about me, or the baby. She doesn't want to help us. She may have kicked Mateo out of the house on Thanksgiving, but he'll weasel his way back in, just like usual. And she knew."

"She knew what?" Tony asks.

I come to a stop in the middle of Tony's giant ass living room. "She knew Mateo's been torturing me all these years, and she never once did anything to stop it. She *knew*. She basically admitted that to me earlier."

They're all silent. They probably feel sorry for me. I appreciate that they care, but this isn't a Diego pity party.

I need to put a plan into action and get my ass out of that house once and for all.

"That's fucked up," Jake finally says, and I can see the pain and sympathy etched on his face. Man, I love this guy. "I'm sorry, D."

"Yeah, I'm sorry too," I practically spit out. "That's why I want to leave. I can't live with her. She doesn't give a shit about me. She never really has."

"Maybe she's scared of Mateo too," Tony says. "Have you ever seen him get violent with her?"

"No. They mostly just scream at each other," I say with a shrug. She doesn't act scared of him. She's always in his face.

"There could be more there, that she doesn't want to admit to you," he says.

"Whatever. It's not my problem," I say, glancing around at all of them. "I need to find another job."

"You should just move in here," Tony suggests casually.

I frown. "Are you serious?"

"My mother is never home. Dad is long gone. They wouldn't even realize you're staying here," he says. "Move in with me."

It's not a bad idea, but…

"I couldn't."

"Actually, maybe you could," Jake says. "And if Tony's offering, you should. If you don't feel safe in your own damn home, then get out of there. Live with Tony and save your money so you and Jocelyn can get a place when the baby comes. Don't bother renting something here. You do that, and you might never leave this town."

Jake's right. We find an apartment or a duplex in the area and settle in with the baby—we might not make it to college. We could end up putting it on hold, and then not going altogether. And I don't want to risk that. Not for myself, or for Jocelyn.

We have plans.

Dreams.

And they're too big for this town.

"If you don't want to live with Tony, you can move in with us. We have plenty of room," Jake continues.

Aw man. My friend is trying to make me fucking cry right now, swear to God. I'm already on edge as it is, thanks to that conversation with my mom. And what happened last night. Over Thanksgiving. It's been an emotionally-charged past few days.

"I'd offer you to move in with me, but we don't have a lot of room at my house," Caleb says, and I know he means it. Yes, Caleb is a player with the girls at school, and most people don't take him very seriously, but he has a good heart buried deep down inside.

"I know, man. Thanks," I tell him before I glance over at Jake. "And thanks to you too. I know your family would take me in without hesitation."

"They would. They've done it before," he says, referring to Ash Davis, his older sister Autumn's boyfriend. Ash had a shit home life too. Worse than mine. We grew up in the same neighborhood, but he used to live in that shitty apartment complex that's full of drug dealers and losers.

Pretty sure Mateo hangs out around there quite often.

Luckily enough, Ash Davis turned his life completely around, and he's the starting, star quarterback at Fresno State. He's going to be a senior when I'm a freshman, and if I get in, and I'm lucky enough to ever catch a ball thrown by Davis, it'll make my fucking season.

Most likely I'll warm the bench for most of my freshman year, but a man can dream.

"Move in with me," Tony says again. "It sucks being in this house all alone. Even the cat avoids me."

"You have a cat?" Tony and his family don't strike me as the type to have pets.

"Yeah. She was my mom's. But she loves me now because

I'm the only one who feeds her twice a day. Otherwise, she steers clear of my ass." Tony shakes his head.

We all chuckle, and it somewhat eases the tension I brought into the room. The tension in me that's slowly dissipating, thanks to Tony's offer.

"Are you sure?" I ask him, not wanting to overstep or assume. This is a big deal. Tony and I are friends, but we've never been close. He's pretty quiet and keeps a lot of things bottled up.

I'm the one who's loud and obnoxious and says shit I don't always mean. Tony chooses his words carefully. I could probably learn a thing or two from him.

"Positive, bro. Move in. You can take one of our many guest bedrooms. Move in tonight. If you hate living there that much, then get the hell out while you can," he says.

Relief punches me square in the chest, and I collapse in a nearby chair, feeling grateful for every single one of these motherfuckers sitting in this room. "You guys are the best. Seriously. I know I've been kind of shitty this year—"

"Kind of?" Jake interrupts, both eyebrows shooting up.

"Fuck off," I say good-naturedly. "But seriously. It's been hard. Shit keeps happening. Some of it, I've asked for, and some of it, I can't control. I'm glad you guys didn't totally turn your backs on me, even if I deserved it."

"We knew you were going through a rough patch," Tony says, his voice low, his expression sincere. "And we get it."

"We got you," Caleb adds. "We've always got you."

I can't help but grin as I swing my attention to Tony yet again. "You really won't mind if I move my shit in this afternoon?"

"Not at all, brother. We can be bachelors together," Tony says with a laugh.

"But what about your mom?"

"She's on some two-month-long European vacation, no

joke. She left last week. She won't even be here for Christmas," Tony explains, his expression completely neutral. As if the fact his mother doesn't even want to spend the holidays with him doesn't bother him at all.

My family makes me insane, but at least they rally around each other when it counts. Sometimes. Tony's parents have straight up abandoned his ass.

And that's all sorts of fucked up.

I will never do that to my future child. My future son—I know Jocelyn's having a boy. I can feel it in my bones. I will teach my child kindness. And I refuse to allow toxic behavior in my household.

If that means I will never allow Mateo to see my child ever, then I'm okay with that.

More than okay.

CHAPTER 19

JOCELYN

"Check out my room." Diego flips his camera and shows me the cavernous bedroom that he's now occupying in Tony Sorrento's house. "What do you think?"

"It's big."

"That's what she said." He cracks himself up, and I smile too. He facetimed me a few minutes ago, letting me know he just arrived at Tony's house and that he brought most of his stuff with him.

I can't believe he's moving in with Tony, but I guess it makes sense. Diego explained earlier that he got in a huge blowout with his mom, and he can't go back there. He doesn't trust her. He trusts no one, he said.

Except for me.

And of course, that admission brought back all of those old feelings. The pressure he used to put on me when he said I was his whole world. I love him, but when someone says nothing else matters but you? It's a little intimidating.

At least, it is to me.

"Ha ha." He flips the camera back around just in time to catch me rolling my eyes at him, which makes him chuckle more. "How'd it go with your mom? How'd she react to you moving out?"

"She didn't even care." He makes a dismissive noise, shaking his head. "Told me if I moved out, this is it. She won't let me move back in. I know she's full of shit, since I'm sure Mateo is already staying there at this very moment. I thought I saw him lurking around in the back yard when I was moving my stuff out, but maybe not."

My heart hurts for his relationship with his family. It's so much worse than I ever realized. "She's just upset. I'm sure she feels like everything's falling apart."

"She's always upset. She wouldn't even let me take any furniture. Not that I need it. This room is totally furnished and the stuff is better than mine. Though I guess when we move in together, I'll have to start completely over and find new furniture for us."

I'm frowning. "When we *move in* together?"

"Well, yeah. When we go to college. We should move in together, to raise the baby, right?" He raises a brow.

"Oh." That wasn't part of my plan. I haven't even considered moving in with Diego. Everything feels very new and fragile between us still.

Now he's frowning. "That wasn't part of your plan?"

"I guess I never thought about it." When we broke up, I just assumed I was doing this on my own. Single mama Jocelyn.

I'm still in single mama Jocelyn mode.

"Well, I'm going to help you," he says firmly. "And I want us to move in together. Eventually, we can get married."

Oh. Shit. *Married?*

I decide to ignore that little bomb.

"I might be able to get affordable housing through the school." I was planning on doing some housing research this weekend.

"Yeah? That would be amazing. Whatever deal you can find, we need it," he says as he collapses on the bed. "Damn, this mattress is firm. Swear to God, I've had the same mattress since I was born."

"My family is coming home tonight," I mention, wanting to change the subject. Mom texted me extra early this morning, before I was even awake, letting me know they left Grandma and Grandpa's house. It's such a long drive, so I know they won't arrive until late.

"Yeah? That kind of sucks, though I'm glad you won't be there alone anymore. I have to work later, or else I'd come over." He smiles, and it's full of wicked promise, reminding me of what we did last night.

Somehow, the sex is better between us. And I think it's because of the surge of hormones I'm dealing with. It's like I crave him all the time, and I'm not shy about it either.

"I remember you telling me you had to work," I say, forming my mouth into an exaggerated pout. "I guess we'll have to wait and see each other Monday at school."

"What about tomorrow?"

"I have to write an English paper tomorrow." Ugh. This is what I get for procrastinating until the last minute. "And I have to finish my college applications. They're due on the 30th."

"I submitted mine already. Mrs. Chavez helped me." That's one of the counselors at school.

"That must be a relief," I say. "I wish she helped me."

"She's cool. Always watching out for me. I need someone to. My mom definitely doesn't give a shit." The last sentence is filled with extra disgust.

"Your mom does give a shit," I say, not sure how I should approach this. I've thought about his family situation a lot, and I'm trying to be more forgiving toward his mom. It can't be easy, dealing with her sons, and the constant struggle between them. "It's just—I think she's torn between the two of you. You and Mateo."

"Whatever. She'll always take his side."

"She didn't on Thanksgiving," I remind him.

"Only because it was so damn obvious what he did to me. The motherfucker pushed me in front of everyone," he says, as if I wasn't there and didn't witness it.

I only saw the end of it. We both looked over our shoulders at the same time, Marty and I both gasping at the malicious look on Mateo's face, his hands still up in the pushing motion. The pure satisfaction that filled his gaze when Diego tumbled to the ground. It had been awful.

And Diego's been dealing with that sort of behavior for *years*.

"You going to curse like that in front of the baby?" I ask him, raising my brows, my lips curved into the faintest smile.

I'm trying to lighten this conversation. We don't need to rehash what Mateo did to him.

"Yeah." Diego shrugs, his expression defiant. "My son won't mind."

"So when he tells the doctor *fuck you* when she tries to give him a shot, you'll be cool with it?" I'm totally teasing now.

"If he's gonna stand up for himself that young, hell yeah I'm cool with it." He laughs, and so do I.

"We should watch what we say. My brother and sister were total parrots when they were little. They repeated every bad word my parents ever said." It's like they knew they were taboo words, too.

"Don't worry. I'll watch my mouth. I know how to when needed." A sigh escapes him. "I have to get ready to go to work."

"Okay. I'll let you go." I smile. "I'm happy for you."

"I'm happy too. I needed to get out of there. Tony's cool.

Cooler than I ever thought." Diego laughs. "This house is badass. And now I'm practically your neighbor."

"Yeah you are." I tilt my head to the side. "I'll miss you tonight."

"I'll miss you too. I always miss you. I'll text you later, when I'm off work, okay?"

"Okay. Bye." I wave at him.

"Love you. Bye." He ends the call before I can tell him I love him back, but that's all right. He knows I love him.

Inspired by Diego already having his college applications turned in, I decide to work on mine. My mom told me I could apply to three schools considering the application fees, though we both know I'm going nowhere else but Fresno State. On a whim, I decide to try for a couple of others. Just to make myself feel better. I need better odds. What if I don't get into Fresno State, yet I get into San Jose? Or Chico?

I can't stand the thought of not getting into my only real option, so I push it straight out of my brain. I don't really have a choice. If I don't get in, then it's community college for me, and I can handle that too. It's just…I want the full college experience. I have since I started high school.

How is that even going to happen, considering you'll be a mom by the time the fall semester starts?

I guess I won't join a sorority. None of them would want me anyway. Maybe I could play volleyball for Fresno State after all, but I don't know if I'm good enough for the team. And it would take up a lot of my time, time I won't have, considering I'll be a mother by then.

Diego saying he wants us to move in together freaked me out. I had no plans on moving anywhere my freshman year in college. The entire reason I planned on staying here is because of my mother. I need her to help watch the baby, which she said she'll do. But that's with me still living at home and driving down to Fresno to go to school.

How am I going to be able to make that work? Fresno is kind of far. At least an hour one way. I'll be commuting two hours round trip for what? A couple of classes a day? Maybe I can schedule all of my classes on Tuesday and Thursday, and then I won't have to go to school Monday, Wednesday and Friday.

But I can't control the schedule completely since it's all based on class availability, and I doubt it would work out so easily for me being a freshman. This is going to be difficult. It would've been difficult even without the baby.

A sigh escapes me and my shoulders slump in defeat. Maybe I should go to the community college here. The campus is small, and they don't have a lot of classes to offer, but I could definitely make it work. I could enroll in a few general ed classes while I take care of an infant. Once the baby gets older, then I could transfer to another college. Maybe even my dream college...

There I go again, imagining my future without Diego in it. I got so used to that, it's hard to shift gears and change plans. I should be thrilled he wants to be a part of the baby's life. That he wants to be a part of *my* life. I love him. I really do. And I know he loves me too.

But can we really make this work?

Instead of letting my thoughts continue to spiral out of control like I just did, I decide to take a shower. Blow dry my hair. Curl it. I'm avoiding my laptop, when I know I should finish my college applications, or at the very least, start working on my essay that's due in English at midnight on Monday. He's the only teacher who gave us an assignment over break, and I sort of hate him for it.

Once I finish curling my hair, I decide to put on a little mascara. Some lip gloss. As I stare at myself in the mirror, I realize I look good. My face is fuller, but it doesn't look...bad. My skin is clear. Despite all the stress and worry I've dealt with,

I haven't had a zit in weeks. Now that things have gotten better between Diego and I, I don't look so pale and sickly either.

In fact, I look pretty damn good.

I head out to the living room with my phone and start taking photos beside the Christmas tree. I take a bunch of selfies, hating almost all of them, until I finally take one where everything looks good. It's my favorite angle, and my smile, my hair, the tree lights glowing in the background, I like it.

It's a total keeper. Instagram worthy.

Opening Instagram, I work on my caption and post a couple of photos, leading with the best one, and ending with a funny one with my eyes closed and my mouth twisted into a weird smile.

Ready for the season! All good things come to those who wait. #itsmytime

I make the post, then share the image in my stories too, because what the hell. I want everyone to know I'm not afraid of who I am or what's happened to me. So I'm pregnant. So what? I'm still a senior in high school, and I don't believe my world is coming to an end due to this pregnancy.

Immediately I get lots of likes and comments. They make me smile.

SAM: **Gorgeous girl!**

Marley: **Hottie**

Hannah: **You are soo pretty**

Jake: **Lookin' good, J.**

Sophie: **Your hair! I love it**

Caleb: **Damn woman**

Ava: **I want to be you!**

Eli: **Hot AF. Don't let my GF see this comment**

Ava: **Too late! Saw it!**

I CRACK UP. This was just the mood booster I needed.

Setting my phone aside, I go back to the CSU college application and finish it within minutes. All that procrastination, when really, it was pretty easy. I decide to tackle the English assignment next. I've only written the first paragraph when I see I got a notification from Instagram.

Cami_Lockhart has sent you a message!

Dread fills me. I shouldn't open it. She's probably saying something shitty and I don't need to let her words get into my head. She's the absolute worst. Mean. Like a snake.

I open my DMs anyway, like the weakling that I am.

You're an idiot.

That's all it says.

Me: **Didn't ask for your opinion, but hey thanks.**

She responds almost immediately.

Cami: **I was with him.**

Me: **Who?**

Cami: **Diego. After he left your house.**

What? When?

Cami: **Last night. I messaged him about it this morning and he took a screenshot of my Snap. See?**

She sends me an image of her activity on her phone, and yes, it says *Diego Garcia screenshot your snap.*

Oh. My. God. Why would he *do* that?

Did he really go see her last night? After he was with me? He did bail pretty fast. I told him I wanted him to stay, but he said he couldn't.

Me: **I don't believe you.**

Cami: **Of course you don't. You don't believe shit, even when it's happening right in front of your face. Why**

would you get back together with Diego anyway? He cheated on you. With me.

She sends another image, one from the homecoming game. We had barely broken up at that time. And she somehow convinced him to take photos together out on the field. Diego is standing next to Cami, and she looks perfectly adorable in her cheer uniform, snuggled up close to his side. His expression is grim. His eyes, flat.

He doesn't look happy. I see it now. Back then, all I could see was the two of them together, and in a way, I suppose Cami is right.

I was blinded by it.

Me: **It doesn't matter anymore. We're having a baby.**

Cami: **Because you're the fool who believes everything he says. Look. This happened LAST NIGHT!!**

Another image comes through. It's dark, partially in shadow, but I can tell it's two people kissing. He's not wearing a shirt. Neither is she. I recognize Cami's profile. I can't see his face, but his hair is dark. Black.

Like Diego's.

Cami: **I snuck him into my room and we fucked all night. He even said having sex with you sucks since you're pregnant and fat now.**

Rage makes my blood run hot. I don't believe Diego would ever say that. He doesn't think I'm fat. I'm barely showing. That all came from Cami.

But that image. It's…

Incriminating.

I zoom in on it as best I can, trying to make out the guy's face. I can't see it, not really. Just the barest line of his jaw, which is similar to Diego's. He's got on track pants, and they remind me of a pair Diego owns.

All the boys in our class wear pants like that, especially the football players. This means nothing.

Me: **Quit messaging me. We have nothing to talk about.**

Cami: **You need to know who you're dealing with.**

Me: **Oh I know. You're a total snake.**

Cami: **I'm not talking about me, stupid. I'm talking about DIEGO. He doesn't give AF about you. He will always come back to me. And once you have the baby? Forget it. You two are done.**

Her words hurt because that's my biggest fear. Getting back together with Diego, only to have him abandon me once the baby comes. Or worse, before I have the baby, when I'm fat and miserable and completely vulnerable and dependent on him. I've never told him this, because I knew he'd get defensive.

It's like Cami is inside my brain, sifting through all my secrets and insecurities. It's disconcerting.

Another image pops up. Very similar to the other one, where I can't make out the guy's face. I can definitely tell it's Cami though. She is literally smiling for the camera, as if she's got her arm stretched out and is taking a selfie of the two of them. His face is pressed against her neck. His dark hair a mess with her hand clutching the back of his head, as if she's holding him to her. His shirt is still on, and it looks like the same hoodie Diego had on last night.

My heart drops. No. I don't believe this. He wouldn't do that. Leave my bed and go to hers. He's not that heartless, is he?

He's hurting, I know that. Feeling a little lost, thanks to his family falling apart. But he wouldn't go from me to her, would he? He doesn't like her. He told me that. I don't understand why she's still trying to insert herself into the middle of our relationship. I just...

I don't know what to do.

One thing I know is that I shouldn't engage with her anymore. The tears start as I go into my settings and block

Cami. Not sure why I didn't do this sooner. She brings bad vibes into my life, even when she's not personally attacking me.

I toss my phone onto my bedside table and close my laptop, my English assignment forgotten. Rolling over, I press my face into my pillow and I cry.

* * *

My FAMILY finally gets home around nine. They're exhausted. My dad heads to their bedroom to take a shower. My brother and sister go straight to bed. Mom comes to talk to me in my room, and when she sees my face, she knows something is up.

I don't bother trying to hide it. I tell her everything, without going into too much detail. About me and Diego. About going to his house for Thanksgiving. Going to the game and that they won. She's smiling at first over the win, though confusion clouds her gaze, and I know she's not thrilled with the idea of me being with Diego, but I know she also wants me happy.

Then I get into the bad stuff. Diego's horrible brother. The fight last night between them. Cami's messages. The incriminating photos. I even tell her about our confrontation at Pete's Place.

"I don't know if she's telling the truth or not," I practically wail as I throw myself into my pillows, grateful they muffle my sobs. "I hate this."

She lets me cry for a few minutes as she gently rubs my back. I'm a torn-up mess over this, and it feels like nothing's changed. I let Diego back into my life, and here I am. Upset and crying. People are lying to me and I don't know who to trust.

"Do you want me to be honest with you?" Mom finally

asks.

Uh oh. When she asks, it's usually because she's going to drop some brutal truth bombs on me. But I need the truth.

"Please," I tell her with a sniff.

"It's obvious to me you still don't trust Diego. And with good reason. What he did to you, cut you to your very soul." Her expression is solemn. "Cheating on someone is such a disrespectful gesture toward the one you supposedly love. If he did it once, he could do it again."

"But he said none of it was true, Mom! He may have hung out with her after he was *accused* of cheating on me, but they never actually did anything." I'm defending him, and I'm sure she thinks I'm pitiful.

"That he allowed you to believe that they were together is almost as bad as them actually being together in the first place," Mom points out.

I start to cry harder. "What are you saying?"

"I'm saying that this boy is going to bring you nothing but heartache and pain, Jocelyn, and you don't deserve that, especially not now. You gave him everything, and look what he's done to you. He doesn't care about you, not really. He only cares about himself. You two have fallen into roles with each other, and it's like he can't help but hurt you. And I hate that too. I hate seeing you so broken up over him. It's not good for you, to get so upset. And it's not good for the baby."

I sit up, trying to suck up my tears and stop crying. I don't want to do anything to hurt the baby. That would break my heart if I did. "I'll try and get my emotions under control."

"It's hard, considering you're pregnant, and your emotions are all over the place." Her smile is gentle as she reaches out and pulls me in for a hug. "I love you, Jocelyn. I don't like seeing you in pain. And you have to realize...this boy. He brings you nothing but pain."

"Are you forcing me to break up with him?" My shoulders

shake and I cling to her. The sobbing is back. God, I'm so tired of crying all the time.

"I'm not forcing you to do anything. But you need to take care of yourself and the baby. He doesn't seem to make you feel very good about yourself, or your decisions."

"H-he's b-been s-so n-nice l-lately." I'm stuttering. The sobbing is affecting the way I talk, which is something I used to deal with when I was a little girl. Sometimes I would get so worked up when I cried, I could barely breathe.

"I'm sure he has. It's just enough for you to let your defenses down, and then he hurts you all over again." She pulls away from me slightly, her hands gripping my shoulders. "Maybe you shouldn't do this to yourself right now. Have you considered—taking a break? From Diego?"

I shake my head furiously. "We just got back together!"

"And look at you. You're crying uncontrollably." Mom's lips tighten. "Just like before."

I know she's watching out for me. And maybe she's right. Maybe Diego and I do need to take a break. Even if what happened with Cami isn't necessarily true, the fact that she's still so fixated on him, on *us*, means she will always be there.

Trying to make my life miserable.

Can I take that? Is she really part of the package now? God, I don't know. She enrages me and sends me into a pit of despair, all at the same time.

I hate her. I hate even more that Diego was ever tempted by her in the first place. He's weak. When it comes to girls and attention, he's very weak. I blame his family life. He's always felt rejected. Abandoned. Beat up. Alone. When someone showers attention on him, he soaks it up like a sponge. Cami gave him what he thought he needed at the time.

After all, that's what I did, before we became a couple. I flirted with him. Showered him with attention, believing deep down I probably had no chance. But something told me I should try, so I did.

He responded quickly, and I was thrilled. He was one of the cutest boys in our class, and one of the best football players. And he wanted to be with me.

It was heady stuff.

Now look at us. We're a complete mess. My mom is right. We shouldn't be together.

I need to end it.

Now.

CHAPTER 20

DIEGO

*J*ocelyn: I can't be with you. It's too much, dealing with all the drama and the heartache you put me through. I know we were good together once, and it felt good these last couple of days, being with you again. They felt like old times. But we're not the same people anymore. Drama follows you everywhere you go. Some of it, you can't help, like with your family. But some of it happens because of the choices you've made, and I don't think it's fair that I have to deal with the repercussions. I'm sure if I were to let you talk to me, you'd deny it all, and tell me it's all untrue, and maybe some of it is, but I can't keep this up. The up and down roller coaster ride that is our relationship. I'm getting off the ride, Diego. I have to, for my health, and for the baby's. I still want you to be a part of our child's life, but right now, I need distance. I don't want to see you anymore. I can't. It hurts too much. There will always be a part of me that loves you, and that will never die, but I am done. You should let me go too. Or go be with Cami, if that's who you really want. You don't have to lie to me or keep that from me. It's okay if she's your choice. I don't like it, but I can deal with it. Just...we have to keep our distance from each other, and live our lives on our own. Once the baby comes, I'll let you know, and we can make custody arrangements then. And don't bother trying to call or text, or Snap me or whatever. I've blocked you everywhere. This is for the best. For my sanity, and my health. Thank you for respecting my wishes. Not sure exactly when, but I'll be in touch.

YEAH, this is what greets me when I get off work from Pete's. It was an extra busy night for some reason. Pete explained to me at the beginning of my shift that everyone goes out to dinner after eating nonstop turkey for two days, and I guess he was right. We were slammed. Big groups, mostly families, came in to eat their weight in hamburgers, chicken strips and fries. I was exhausted by the time I got into my car and checked my notifications on my phone, only to find this long ass *I'm dumping you* text from Jocelyn.

Seriously, what the fuck?

She doesn't even give me a chance to argue, or ask her what the hell she's talking about. She brings up Cami like I want to be with her. Uh, no. Where did she get that idea? Haven't I told her enough that I don't want to be with Cami?

What hurts the most? How she said I'm nothing but drama and she can't have it in her life.

Talk about a slam.

I punch the edge of the steering wheel, cursing as loud as I can before I punch it again. Then again. Still in park, I gun the engine of my car, revving it up before I peel out of the parking lot, driving with barely restrained rage all the way up the mountain, until I find myself not at Tony's house as I originally planned, but in front of Jocelyn's.

Instinct brought me here. I don't even remember the majority of the drive. I'm breathing raggedly, as if I just ran a race, and I glare at her beautiful house, the tall Christmas tree blinking merrily in the front window.

Nice. Normal. That's what her house looks like. She's perfectly fine, snuggled up in bed, considering the light in her bedroom window is off, while I'm out here all alone. My head spinning. My world thrown completely off-kilter.

There's more light coming from the living room besides the tree, which makes me think someone is still up. Maybe Jocelyn? Her parents' car is parked in the driveway, so I know they're home.

It doesn't matter. I put the car in park, shut off the engine and climb out, ready to go to Jocelyn's bedroom window and throw rocks at it. To get her to come outside and talk to me like a fucking adult, damn it.

The moment I step foot on the lawn, their front door springs open as if someone was lying in wait, and my heart drops before it starts to speed up.

But it's not Jocelyn.

It's her mom standing on the front porch. Glaring at me, pure hatred shining from her eyes.

"What are you doing here?" she whisper hisses, pulling the door shut behind her. She's in a thick black sweatshirt and gray sweatpants covered in little white stars. She looks ready for bed.

I really don't give a damn.

"I need to see Jocelyn." I don't bother whispering. I want Jos to hear me. She needs to say all that shit in the text to my face.

"She's sleeping. No thanks to you." Her mother's face twists into a scowl.

"What the hell did I do?" Last Jocelyn and I talked, everything was cool. We were good. I don't understand.

Why does this always happen to me?

"She can't trust you. You've given her no reason to trust you, and it's not good for her health, to be so upset all the time. She needs to watch out for the baby." She crosses her arms. "You should leave."

"I'm not leaving until I talk to Jocelyn." I can be just as stubborn as this woman is. Probably more so.

"She doesn't want to talk to you. Didn't you get her text?"

I rear back a little. So she knows about the text? My brain goes into overdrive. "Did *you* send it?"

"No, of course not. She made that decision all on her own." She drops her arms to her side and takes a step forward. "Aren't you tired of hurting her all the time? Or do you get some sort of sick thrill out of making my daughter cry?"

"I don't even understand why she's crying! *What did I do?*" I'm yelling. It's my go to when I'm angry. I throw my hands up in the air, frustration filling me when the woman remains silent.

I wish I could read her mind.

What I really wish I could do is see Jocelyn.

"Talk to Cami Lockhart. Oh wait, I think you already do that enough." The annoyance on her face is clear. Somehow, she thinks I'm still seeing Cami.

I guess that means Jocelyn believes that too. But *why?* How much do I have to say and prove to her that I'm not with Cami? I never really was.

I mean, fuck. I sort of was, but my heart wasn't in it. We hung out. We went on a few dates. Yes, I kissed her. We messed around a little, but nothing serious. No D or V involved.

Besides, I missed Jos so damn bad after she broke up with me. I just followed along with what Cami wanted because I didn't know what else to do. Stupid on my part. I don't make great decisions.

Understatement. I fuck up most of the time.

But I swear to God, now I want to do right by Jocelyn and our baby. I love her. I love our unborn child too.

Clearly, she doesn't love me in the same way.

"You must really hate me," I say to Jocelyn's mother.

Her lips tighten. "I hate what you've done to my daughter."

"I never meant to hurt her," I start, but her laughter cuts me off.

"Please. That's all you do. Hurt her. Make her cry. Stress her out." Her laughter stops as quickly as it started. "Can't you see? You two need a break from each other. She has to focus on herself and the baby. You need to learn how to clean up your act and be a man. You're about to become a father soon. Act like one."

With that she turns, heading for the door.

"What if I don't leave?" I call out to her.

She glances over her shoulder, her expression pinched. "I'll call 9-1-1 and have a deputy escort you off my property. It's your choice."

Seconds later, the door slams. The living room light shuts off, as does the tree. She's gone to her bedroom.

Leaving me alone.

I stare at Jocelyn's dark window for a few minutes longer, jingling my keys in my jeans pocket. I could still go to her, but what's the use? She's given up on me. So has everyone else—except my friends. My teammates. *They* haven't given up on me. They're the only ones who've told me I got this. That I can do this.

An idea strikes me, and I go to my car, quickly sliding into the driver's seat and starting the engine. Without thought I head to the Callahans' house, needing to talk to someone. Anyone.

Really? I need to talk to my coach.

Fable answers the door, her expression full of surprise. "Jake's up in his room," she tells me as she opens the front door wider, letting me in despite the lateness and me showing up unannounced.

I enter the house, watching as she shuts the door. "Um, I don't want to talk to Jake. Is uh…Drew around?"

I rarely call him Drew. When I first met him, I was so intimidated. He was Mr. Callahan, the NFL superstar. Once he started helping coach our league team, he just became coach, though he told me when I was at his house I didn't need to call him that all the time. He's a good guy. Like the father figure I never had, but desperately needed.

"Drew is definitely around." Her face is a mask of pleasantness. I'm sure I shocked her again by not wanting to see my best friend. "He's watching TV. Come on."

I follow her as she leads me through the house to the family room, which is where the family usually hangs out at night. Drew is sitting on the couch, completely relaxed, his gaze on the big screen.

"We have company," Fable calls, a faint smile on her face when Drew glances toward us, doing a doubletake when he spots me standing beside his wife.

"Diego. What's up?" Drew rises to his full height—he's got me beat by about five inches or so—and he holds his hand out as he walks toward me. I take his hand and give it a quick shake, trying to fight the nervousness that's buzzing through my veins.

But it's no use. I'm anxious as shit.

"I was hoping you might have a few minutes so we could talk in, uh, private?" I send a quick glance in his wife's direction, and she turns away at the last second, as if she's not paying attention to us.

I know he'll end up telling her everything once I leave, but right now, I can't talk about my problems with Jocelyn—and Cami—in front of her. I'll feel like a complete asshole the entire time, and I'd probably clam up.

"Sure, let's go to my office," Drew says easily.

He leads the way and I follow him to his office. He turns on the lights as I walk inside, and once we're both in the room, he shuts the door and settles into the chair behind his desk.

I sit in one of the chairs opposite his desk, exhaling loudly.

"Everything okay?" Drew asks.

"No." I shake my head. "My world has gone to shit."

Again.

I proceed to tell him everything. He knew about Jocelyn and I breaking up before, and the pregnancy. He also knew about me getting with Cami—and I tell him how it wasn't as big of a deal as everyone thought it was. That Cami played the entire situation up, and I didn't stop her. How she's still playing it up, interfering with my relationship with Jocelyn now.

I don't leave many details out. I even tell him that Jocelyn and I had sex again. I thought we were good. I thought we were back together.

"I was wrong," I admit, handing him my phone so he can read the text Jocelyn sent me. "I went over to her house," I say as he reads it. "But her mom basically kicked me out of there. Said she'd call 9-1-1 if I didn't leave."

Drew slowly shakes his head, his lips pressed together as he continues reading the text. "You fucked this up pretty good, didn't you?"

"*I* fucked it up?" The words explode out of me and I leap

to my feet so I can start pacing. I can't sit still for a second longer. "How did I mess this up? It wasn't my fault what just happened. Cami said something to Jocelyn, but I don't know what. I tried texting the both of them, but they're ignoring me."

Frustration rips through me and I run my hands through my hair, tugging on the ends. I want to punch a wall. Someone's face. Maybe even my own.

"You want my advice?" Drew says, setting my phone down on his desk.

"Please." I sound desperate. I am desperate. I just want to make everything right. I want my girl back. I want my life to be normal. This situation feels so completely out of my control, and for once in my life, I want to fix it.

But it's like I can't.

"Respect her wishes, and leave her alone."

I stop pacing, gaping at him. "Seriously?"

He nods, his expression grim. "You keep coming at her, you're going to drive her away. Leave her alone. Give her some space. Give her some peace. That's all she wants. She's dealing with a lot."

"So am I," I interject.

He levels me with a look, and I feel like an asshole for what I said. "Not as much as she is. She's the one who's having the baby, and this is a huge responsibility. I'm sure it feels like it's all on her."

"It doesn't have to be all on her." I slap my hand against my chest. "I want to help her."

"I know you do, but I think the best thing you can do to help her right now is…leave her be. The both of you need to work on yourselves," Drew says. "At least for a little while."

"But I might never get her back." I sound whiny, and I stop myself, clearing my throat. I need to be a man. I can't show any weakness.

"You're right," Drew says softly. "You might not."

My eyes sting and I rub at them, recognizing what's happening, but refusing to let it. "Fuck that. She can't just reject me."

"She can, and she is. Listen, she's just trying to protect herself. All this drama isn't good for either of you. So do what she's doing, and focus on yourself. Work on yourself. She'll be doing the same. Maybe some time apart is just what you two need. You'll get through the rest of your senior year, and when you can, try and recognize where you went wrong," Drew explains, his tone kind. Downright gentle.

Like he knows what I'm going through, and he's not judging me for it.

My vision gets blurry and I collapse on the nearby loveseat, resting my hands on my face as I lean back. "I had her," I say against my palms, my voice muffled. I squeeze my eyes closed as tight as possible, but it's no use. A few tears leak out. "I had her, and I lost her. Again. I'm so fucking stupid."

My heart feels like it's completely deflated. My life...it's over.

I've ruined everything.

"Sometimes we have to walk away from the one we love the most, to heal ourselves," he says.

That sounds like some profound bullshit, but I say nothing.

"I did that." He pauses for only a moment. "With my wife. I walked away from her, when she was the best thing that ever happened to me."

I drop my hands from my face, blinking back the tears. "Why'd you do it?"

"I was a fucked up mess." He smiles ruefully. "And I got scared."

"How'd you get back together?"

"We ran into each other randomly a couple of months later. That's when it hit me. I was meant to be with her. She was the one who fought me then. My wife is a fighter. She doesn't back down from a challenge, ever." He shakes his head. "I almost ruined everything. But now look at us."

Giant house. Great careers. Four kids. "Life is good for you guys."

"Life is fucking excellent, but when I was in college, it was terrible. Until I met her." He ducks his head, looking pleased. "Now, I'm a lucky son of a bitch."

I want to be him. I want to be that lucky. But I don't know if it's ever going to happen for us like it did for them.

"You're tied to Jocelyn forever, through your unborn child. Give her the time she's requesting. Respect her needs, and let her have some distance. She might realize she misses you," he says.

She might also realize she doesn't need me at all.

"Sure. Okay." I nod, but this is going to be tough.

Am I up for the challenge?

It hits me quick, like a bolt of lightning.

Yes.

But I can change. I know I can. I'll do my damnedest to prove to her that I'm a better man. That I can be there for her, no matter what. I can take care of her and our unborn child.

I'll prove it to them all.

CHAPTER 21

JOCELYN

*N*ine months later...

"OKAY," I say to myself as I slowly close the door behind me, tempted to sag against it in relief. Instead I stand up a little straighter and head out to the living room, where my guests await me. "She's finally asleep."

"So bummed. I was hoping I could cuddle her for a little longer." Ava Callahan is sitting in my living room, accompanied by her best friend, Ellie. They come over a lot since Eli is going to Fresno State. Jackson Rivers is here too, but he's been rather...elusive lately.

To the point that he got suspended from the football team for a couple of weeks. So ridiculous. He's too mysterious for his own good sometimes.

"She needs to nap. She gets really cranky if she doesn't." I wouldn't mind a nap either, but I appreciate the company too. Plus, they mentioned going to grab dinner later, where they'd pick it up at the Bulldog Grill and bring it back to the apartment so I wouldn't have to take the baby anywhere.

I'm already hungry for a tri-tip sandwich and fries.

"So uh, Jocelyn. Will you go with us to the game tomorrow?" Ava asks out of nowhere, an eager expression on her pretty face.

I collapse in a nearby chair, taken aback for a moment. "I have no one to watch the baby."

"What about your mom? I thought she was helping you," Ellie suggests.

"She is, but weekends aren't part of our deal," I tell them. And I don't feel right in asking for the extra support either. I already need her too much.

My mother has been a saint throughout this entire year. Supporting me unconditionally with everything I do. Eventually my dad came around too, which was such a relief. I'd been holding onto a lot of resentment with how he treated me. His job keeps him busy and he can't devote as much time to me and the baby as he'd like. And Mom is pretty readily available, thanks to support from Dad.

After winter break, I switched to online for most of my classes. It was easier for me to stay at home and not worry about people talking behind my back while I was at school. It also helped me not have to see Diego all the time.

Once I wasn't on campus on a regular basis, I rarely saw him. Only fleeting glimpses in a car or at a store. I'd duck and hide like a coward, but I wasn't ready to see him.

I got accepted into Fresno State in March. I also got into Chico State, but my parents shut that option down before I could even discuss it with them.

Not like I wanted to go there. I knew that was unrealistic. Though she initially told me I could, Mom wasn't thrilled I wasted the application fee on the other two colleges, and I felt bad, but I had to give myself better odds. If you apply to only one school and can't even get into it, then what was the point? I would've felt like a loser.

In May, I received a lot of money in community awards, and I went up on stage with my giant belly, accepting every single one of them with a smile on my face. I also earned a few other scholarships thanks to my SAT scores. It helped that I played up my being an expectant teen mom who wasn't letting anything get in her way to get that prized bachelor's degree in the essays I had to write as part of the application process.

It took me a while, a lot of finagling and convincing my parents it was the right thing for me to do, but I finally secured off-campus housing that's actually very close to campus by the end of May. Two days later, I gave birth to my sweet baby…

Girl.

Take that, Diego Garcia. No son to throw footballs with. Though nothing's stopping him from tossing the ball to his daughter, that's for sure.

I walked in our graduation ceremony twelve days after having the baby. My mom cradled her in her arms the entire time. Mom told me Rosa Garcia approached her when the ceremony was finished, asking to hold the baby. Mom reluctantly let her. Rosa stared at the baby's face for long, unspoken minutes, displeasure slowly dawning as she drank in my precious baby girl's features.

"She looks like Jocelyn," she announced, pushing the baby back into my mother's arms before she flounced off.

I'm really glad I wasn't there to witness it.

My mother comes down to Fresno every Tuesday and Thursday to watch the baby while I'm in class. Next semester, she'll be enrolled in the childcare program they offer on-campus. I had to get on a wait list, and luckily my turn came quick. Mom prefers being with her right now anyway, and I don't think she's that thrilled the baby will be in a childcare program, but I need to eventually do this on my own.

It all came together so easily, I had to take my opportunities where I could, and somehow, everything fell into place.

Even ending my so-called relationship with Diego.

I had to cut him off, and while it hurt, and I continued to cry nonstop for weeks after it happened, eventually I realized my mother was right. I needed the break. I couldn't be around him.

He upset me too much.

It doesn't matter anymore whether what Cami said was true or not. Eventually, word got out that it wasn't Diego who she was with that night. Here's the shocking part—

It was Mateo.

I couldn't believe it, yet...I could. And while I feel bad for putting the blame on Diego, I also know I couldn't help it. It was a wake-up call.

I didn't trust him. I wasn't over it. And I was going to do damage to my mental health and to my baby if I didn't cut him off.

I'm sure Diego was pissed I could give up on him so easily, but I had to protect myself, my health, and the baby's.

Oh, and my heart.

He needed to grow up, and so did I. Is he doing better? I think so. Do we talk a lot? Not really. Not at all. He picks up Gabriella from my mom and drops the baby off to her too. That's the arrangement Mom suggested, and I went along with it. So did Diego. They're the ones who make the baby exchange, but lately...I've been curious.

Like I want to see him. Talk to him for a little bit. Mom says he's good with the baby. Responsible. He only takes her a few days here and there. His schedule is completely filled up, thanks to football and school, but he told my mom once the season is over, he wants the baby more.

I guess that's fine.

He's also given me money. We don't have a formal custody or child support agreement, and Mom says I really need to put something together. She wants me to go to the county courthouse, but I don't have time. I can worry about that later.

There's too much going on right now, and I'm trying to balance…everything.

It's hard.

Mom also says Diego doesn't ask about me. So I doubt he wants to talk to me either. Which is also fine. I'd rather live in a bubble and pretend everything's settled between us.

"You should ask your mom if she'd watch her Saturday night, so you can go to the first home game of the season," Ava suggests, her soft voice pulling me from my overloaded thoughts. "It'll be fun. Your first game as a college student. I can't wait to watch Eli play."

"He's not going to play," Ellie reminds her. "Ash Davis is the quarterback. He'll get all the glory."

"He might toss a ball back and forth with Ash before the game," Ava says with a shrug. "That should be enough."

"I don't know if I should go…" My voice trails off. "I have homework. And my mom already does so much for me and the baby. Why would she willingly give up her Saturday to watch Gigi yet again? She probably wants a break."

That's what I've started calling the baby--Gigi. She is Gabriella Garcia after all. Yes, I gave her Diego's last name. It was the right thing to do, and he thanked me profusely when I told him the day after I delivered her. I hear he loves his daughter with everything he's got, which is reassuring. He was so dead set on having a boy, I figured he'd be disappointed.

"Aw, Gigi? Is that her new nickname?" Ava rests her hand against her chest, her green eyes extra big. "I love it so much."

She's been a good friend to me during this new life of mine. Sam and Marley ended up going away to college, and while I'm thrilled for them, I miss them terribly, though we talk pretty much every weekend. Ava is still in high school, and so is Ellie. When they're not at school, they're always wanting to hang out with me. Which I love and appreciate.

I'm desperate for company beyond my mother and the baby. I don't get out much. I go to class, I come home, I'm with the baby or my mom, I'm doing homework. Rinse. Repeat. Over and over again. Ava and Ellie brighten my day with their constant chatter and gossip from home. I'm not really meeting anyone on campus, because I barely make conversation with my classmates, and they're the only other people I see on a consistent basis. I see others I know from high school and I always stop and talk to them, but it's not the same.

I'm too busy, too focused, too in my head. Plus, they ask me about the baby with an almost anxious tone. No one ever mentions Diego, though. It's like they know that's a big no-no.

"Are you going to ask your mom if she'll watch her?" Ellie asks, gently nudging me.

"I don't know." I lean back heavily in the chair I'm sitting in, staring up at the ceiling. "The game will run late. I doubt she'll want to stay here overnight."

"Have her take the baby up to her house," Ellie suggests.

"She does have a bassinet for her." I tap my index finger against my pursed lips. "I mean, the worse she can say is no, right?"

"Oh my God, yes. Do it," Ava says. "Ask her."

I pull my phone out of my pocket and send a quick text to my mother, explaining what I need from her, and telling her she doesn't have to say yes. It's not that important to me. It would be nice to feel normal and go to a football game without a baby sitting in one of those slings strapped to the front of me, like I go everywhere else with Gigi.

And while yes it would be fun to go to a Bulldogs game, I don't want Diego to get his hopes up if he sees me there. Not that he will. The stadium is huge, not like a football game at home. It's not like I'll seek him out either. I'm figuring he probably won't get much game time, considering he's only a freshman. Besides, I'm not going to this game to see him, I tell myself firmly.

Even though it might be a tiny lie.

I send the text to my mom and chat with the girls, laughing when Ava tells yet another funny Eli story. The guy keeps her constantly entertained, and I love that they're still going strong despite her being in high school and he's here in college. I wasn't sure if they would last.

Guess their relationship is stronger than mine and Diego's. Though that probably isn't a fair comparison.

Can't help but feel like I failed though.

My phone dings and I check the text from my mother. I'm in complete shock. I glance up to find Ava and Ellie watching me expectantly. "She said she'll watch her."

"Oh my God, I *knew* she'd say yes. Yay!" Ava leaps to her feet and starts jumping around like a maniac. Ellie whoops and hollers. I keep shushing them, but it's no use.

I hear the baby start to wail.

Ava's eyes are huge when she comes to a stop in the center of my tiny living room. "Oh crap, I did that."

"Yeah, you did," I say wryly as I stand. "I'll go get her."

"Can I do it? I want to hold her," Ava says.

I barely nod and she's already busting into my room, eager to pick up Gabriella. I live in a one-bedroom apartment. It was the cheapest rent I could find this close to campus, and the baby is small enough that she doesn't need her own room yet. My parents are helping me with rent and college expenses, which is a huge blessing. I appreciate everything they do for me, and how supportive they are. But I want to do this on my own.

Eventually, I'll have to get a place with two bedrooms, and that's stressful to think about, considering it costs money I don't really have.

But we'll cross that bridge when we get to it.

Seconds later Ava emerges from the bedroom holding a sleepy, tight fisted Gigi. Fat tears cling to the corner of her eyes and the little huffing breaths she takes make her glossy lower lip tremble.

She is so stinking cute. And I don't know what Rosa was thinking. This child looks more and more like her father with every day that passes.

"Poor little baby wants to join the party," Ava croons, pressing her lips to Gigi's downy soft black hair. "Don't you Gigi?"

Ava's bouncing the baby in her arms, but the second Gigi spots me, the lip starts to quiver in earnest, and then the tears begin to fall. I reach for her and Ava hands her over. I cuddle Gigi close, pressing my nose into her sweet-smelling hair, and breathe deep.

I love this girl, so much. I didn't know I could love someone this fiercely. She means everything to me. I would do anything to make her life better, and that means improving mine as well by going to college and getting an education, and then eventually I'll be able to provide for her.

My problem? I don't know what to do with my life.

I started Fresno State with my major undeclared. I'm in all general education classes currently, so it doesn't really matter if I know what my major is or not. But next semester I'd like to take some courses that might go toward my major.

I just need to figure out what that is first.

"So you're going to the game with us," Ava states once I have Gigi settled and eating. I'm still breast feeding, though not as much as I was in the beginning. Mom bought me a pump so I do that too. It's weird, you know? If you would've told me a year ago that I'd be breast feeding a baby and hanging out with seniors in high school while I'm going to Fresno State, I would've either laughed in your face or cried buckets of tears.

Funny how life throws you for a complete loop, and you just have to go with it.

"I am going to the game with you," I tell them both.

Ellie breaks out into a smile and Ava does a little shimmy.

And I'm immediately suspicious.

They're acting like they have something planned, and I don't know what it could be. Well, I sort of know, and I hope that's not what they're thinking.

"You're not going to try and get Diego and I to talk, are you?" I send them both a suspicious glare.

They share a look before they shake their heads in unison, their expressions both completely innocent. "Of course not," Ava says. "You've told us plenty of times already that you're not ready to see him yet."

Stupid right? He's the father of my child. The last time I actually saw him was when I gave birth to Gabriella. He was at the hospital the entire time I was in labor, Tony sitting with him in the visitors' lounge, until finally, my mother went out and got him and he was able to witness Gabriella being pushed into the world.

He cried when he first held her. He thanked me for giving him a daughter with tears shining in his dark eyes, his expression full of wonder and disbelief. He held Gabriella as if she was the most precious, fragile thing he's ever seen. Witnessing him staring at his daughter's face as if he couldn't believe she was his, broke my heart. I resolved within myself that I couldn't see him again for a while. He would completely break me. Wear me down, and somehow convince me we could still be good together.

I need to prove to myself I can stand on my own two feet first before I consider anyone else.

"And we're respecting your wishes," Ellie adds.

I smile at them both. "Thank you. But I still don't trust either of you."

Ava bursts out laughing. "Fine. There's a guy on the team that Eli thinks would be perfect for you."

My mouth drops open. "Your boyfriend is trying to set me up with someone?"

"Yes," Ava agrees. "He is. He thinks this guy is a gem, as he said. Straight-up guy. Nice. Polite."

"Everyone's polite compared to Eli," I mutter.

"True." Ava grins. "But seriously. He's twenty, so he's a little older, and he has a twin brother who also happens to be a father of a newborn. So he's all into babies. Meaning he won't bat an eyelash when he finds out about Gigi."

"There's being cool with being an uncle, and then there's freaking out when the girl you might be interested in is actually a single mother." I slowly shake my head. "I appreciate you guys—especially Eli—looking out for me, but I'm not interested."

"We're not asking you to marry him," Ellie says teasingly. "Eli wants to introduce you to him after the game. That's it. Nothing more."

"Where at?" I ask warily. I don't want Diego around when this happens.

"There's a party after the game. Not sure where. Maybe a frat house? I don't know." Ava shrugs, and I wonder if she's telling the truth.

I contemplate them both. They still got the innocent

thing going on, which is a huge crock of shit, but whatever. And while I am not ready to date, it might be fun to flirt with a guy for a few minutes.

"Fine," I say with an exaggerated sigh. "I'll let Eli introduce him to me."

"It'll be great," Ava says, Ellie nodding in agreement. "Just the change of scenery you need, I just know it."

I hope Ava's right. Lord knows I need a change of scenery right now. I also need to go out with people my own age and have a little fun. I sort of knew what I was getting into with this whole going to college and being a mom thing, but it's hard work. Maybe I do need to let off a little steam.

Sounds like going to a football game and meeting a cute guy is the exact thing I need.

CHAPTER 22

DIEGO

Sitting on the bench through the majority of your first at home college football game sucks major ass.

I'm not used to it. At all. Throughout my youth league days, I was on the field constantly. To the point that other parents complained I got too much game time.

I can't help it if I was damn good, even back then.

I played my ass off on the junior varsity football team my freshman year in high school, wanting to prove to the coaching staff that I had what it takes. When playoffs started and the JV team's season was over, coach pulled me up to the varsity team. I was the only freshman to go up. Not even Jake went. Callahan wanted to keep his son on the JV team because we were undefeated that season. The first time in Badger history.

And also, we had Ash Davis as our varsity quarterback. He's damn good. He's my current quarterback now, and he's only gotten better. A senior literally on top of his game. He throws as good as Jake and has a way about him that makes it look so damn easy. His mood is different than Jake's too. He's lighter. Friendlier. Doesn't get as stressed out. He's having fun out on the field, and it all seems to come to him naturally.

I'm envious of his carefree attitude, but I don't hate him for it. Old me would think he was a major dick. New me realizes he's been doing this for years, and he's allowed to be confident. While I'm on the sidelines dying for a chance.

Sitting on the bench for the majority of the game next to Eli Bennett also sucks major ass.

Can't believe this guy is going to Fresno State, and is on my team. He and Ash are buddy buddy thanks to the family connection—they're both dating a Callahan sister. Those first few hot and intense days at practice, his confidence rubbed me the wrong way.

Not that I ever felt great about Eli. He said such shitty things about us and our football team throughout our high school years, since he was the quarterback for our biggest rival. As we practice together, I can grudgingly admit he's good. He's trying to be my friend, and I throw up a wall every single time. My allegiance is to Jake, and Jake hates Eli.

Well, that's not true. They've learned to get along. Jake's even admitted to me that he doesn't mind Eli anymore, and that's huge.

Maybe I should be nicer to Eli too. Though it'll be hard to break my habit of treating him like utter garbage.

He's currently wound up tight and obviously furious he doesn't get any field time. He had to know this going in, though I can definitely relate to his frustration. His being third string to Ash Davis means he's pretty much benched all season. The only chance he'll get to play is when the score is so high, there's no chance the other team can win. Then they'll unleash the rookies and we'll look like chumps compared to the rest of them.

"Feels like we're starting all over again," Eli mutters to no one in particular.

Glancing up, I realize he's talking to me. But I don't respond. I just scowl at him instead.

I used to hate this guy. He was a bragging, arrogant, swinging dick who couldn't keep his mouth shut to save his life.

And now this big swinging dick is dating my best friend Jake's little sister and Jake hangs out with the guy—voluntarily.

"We *are* starting over again," I tell him. irritably. "And you've got a long haul in front of you."

"Third string is bullshit," Eli spits out. "Have you seen the way that other dude throws? He sucks."

The second-string quarterback is great. Eli is just frustrated and jealous. "If you're so damn good, why didn't another college recruit your ass so you could be the starting QB?"

"I didn't want to go anywhere else," he admits, swinging his head to look in the other direction. "I wanted to stay here."

For Ava. His girlfriend.

I'm just as pussy-whipped as he is, but the girl who's got me wrapped around her finger weighs about fifteen pounds or so, has the same brown eyes as mine and will someday call me daddy.

My heart swells just thinking about Gabriella. She's so beautiful. And sweet. Even when she cries. Even when she craps all over herself and me. She's also kind of disgusting. She spits up curdled milk. She farts—loudly. She's peed on me. She cries and cries, getting snot all over my shoulder, inconsolable.

I love her fiercely.

Too bad her mama wants nothing to do with me.

"You goin' to the party tonight?" Eli asks, knocking me out of my baby-induced thoughts.

"What party?"

"Chavez is hosting a bash at his fraternity." Miguel Chavez is a senior defensive lineman and one of Ash's closest friends. "Said we're all invited. Even the freshmen."

"Are you going?"

"Hell yeah, I am. My girl will be there too," he says.

It amazes me that they're still together, considering she's still in high school. "I don't know if I'll go."

"Gotta watch the baby?" Eli raises his brows.

Everyone else talking about my baby is a bit of a sore subject to me at times. He knows about Gabriella thanks to Ava and Jocelyn being such good friends. "No, I don't have to watch my child."

Eli rears back at my vicious tone. "Whoa, simmer down, compadre. We're on the same team now. No need for hostility."

I glare at him, my annoyance over my situation between Jocelyn and I more than anything else. "You're irritating as fuck sometimes, you know that?"

"Yeah, actually I do." He laughs, not looking offended by my insult at all. "But I've decided I can't keep fighting it. I am what I am."

I say nothing. What's the point? He's embraced his personality. At least he's self-aware.

"What's it like, anyway? Being a dad at eighteen?" Eli asks me, like he wants to make conversation with me.

"I would imagine it's like being a dad, whatever your age is," I say. "It's a huge responsibility."

"I'm guessing it's a little different for an eighteen-year-old going to college being a dad, versus a guy who's married with a career and a house," Eli says, sounding completely logical. "Your kid is cute, I'll give her that. She must take after her mama."

Jealousy rises within me. I don't like hearing any guy talk

about Jocelyn. Even Eli, who is very happy with Ava. "Gabriella actually looks a lot like me."

"She's got your brown eyes, but otherwise, Gigi looks like Jocelyn," he says.

Is he really arguing with me about who my baby looks likes? God, this guy. I can't—

Wait a minute.

"What did you call her?" I ask.

"Jocelyn?" Eli's brows shoot up. "Uh...I called her Jocelyn."

"No. Gabriella."

"Oh yeah. Gigi. Jocelyn came up with it. For Gabriella Garcia. Cute, right? Ava told me about the nickname." He's frowning so hard, I bet it hurts. "Don't you call her that too?"

No, and God damnit, I should know the nickname the mother of my child gave our daughter before this guy.

"It's cute," I bite out, hating how jealous—no, *envious*—I feel. "Our daughter is pretty cute, so it fits."

"She is. You may be a jerk sometimes, but you make adorable babies. Though man, I wouldn't want a baby right now. That sounds kind of like a nightmare. I'm an attention whore. So are babies. We'd be in constant competition." He throws up his hands when I shoot daggers at him with my eyes. "No offense, seriously. You gotta admit it's not every-one's dream when they're eighteen."

"It wasn't my dream either," I mutter. But I wouldn't take it back.

"You should definitely go to that party. Let off a little steam," Eli suggests, circling back to our original topic. "You're tense as fuck, Garcia."

"So are you," I remind him.

"I hate not being part of the action." Eli shrugs. "What's your excuse?"

My life. But I don't say the words out loud.

Instead, I turn my attention back to the game.

And sulk.

* * *

I LIVE off campus in a three-bedroom apartment with Caleb and Tony. Tony has the master bedroom so he pays the most —and his rich ass can afford it. The rent at this place is pricey, but I needed my own room for when I have the baby, which isn't very often considering my schedule. But once football season is over, I want to split our time up fifty-fifty, so I can have Gabriella more.

It sucks how Jocelyn still doesn't really want to see me or talk to me, but I'm respecting her wishes, though I'm to the point that I think she's being kind of immature.

Rough doesn't even begin to describe how I felt when she sent me that shitty text saying she was cutting me off. And cut me off she did. I was iced out of her life completely, and at first, I was furious about it. So angry, no one would hardly talk to me for days, scared I'd bite their head off.

Eventually, I realized she had a point. Together, we *were* borderline toxic. She was right—I was too needy. My family dynamics messed with my head and I put a lot of expectations on Jocelyn when we were together. I also made some bad choices—lots of bad choices. Flirting with other girls when Jocelyn wasn't around, craving that constant attention from females, whether it was good or bad? Not smart.

Not healthy.

I eventually found out through other sources—thank you Hannah, Jake's girlfriend—that Cami sent Jocelyn photos that were supposedly of the two of us, and that's why Jocelyn cut me off. She felt like she had no choice. Cami inserted herself into our relationship, making it even more toxic. The bitch doesn't know when to stop. I don't understand her obsession with me.

Or her obsession with Jocelyn.

Then I found out who Cami was messing around with—Mateo. Seriously. He said he was coming for me, that he would do us in, and look. He made good on his promise, the asshole. He aimed his finger at me like it was a gun, and he shot a giant hole right through my relationship with Jocelyn.

God, I hate him.

Don't know why Cami felt the need to lie to Jocelyn and say we got together that weekend, but I'm guessing it was thanks to Mateo's influence. What they did is all kinds of fucked up, and they fucked *me* royally. Whatever she said, it all went straight into Jocelyn's head, and sent her plunging into a downward spiral. That's on me. If I'd denied everything Cami said from the beginning, Jocelyn would've seen me in a different light.

Despite my anger toward Cami and Mateo, and how they interfered with my relationship, I take responsibility for everything. The hurt I caused Jocelyn can't really be forgiven.

Everything that's happened between Jocelyn and me has pretty much been my fault. I see how I'm to blame. I was an immature, irresponsible kid who said shitty things and was completely selfish, but I'm not that same person anymore.

I've grown up.

Thank God for Tony. Getting out of my mother's house helped tremendously. Talk about toxic. Spending time away from her and Mateo and the constant arguing cleared my head. Made me realize that life doesn't have to be locked in a constant battle. Mom treats everything like a war she needs to fight. Mateo handles life as if he has to squash it like a bug, yet he's the one who ends up squashed. I haven't seen him in months, which is a good thing because right after I found out he messed around with Cami, I probably would've destroyed him.

I hear he's back home yet again. No job. No life. No nothing.

Figures.

Once I get home after the game, I realize I'm pretty fucking tired. Do I really want to go to that party? Not particularly. Caleb is already there. He rushed in the fall and is now part of the same fraternity Chavez is in. I don't know where Caleb came up with the money, but I do know he worked his ass off over the summer at one of the restaurants on the lake. Started out as a busboy, used his charm on everyone and quickly became a waiter, making lots of money in tips by flirting with all the women. It didn't matter the age. Young or old, pretty or hideous, he flirted, he winked, he smiled, he complimented. They practically stuffed dollar bills down his pants, they were so excited by his attention.

The guy knows how to work women like no other. I'm sure the frat life will be perfect for him.

I'm about to enter my bedroom when Tony's door swings open and he's standing in the doorway, contemplating me. He's on the football team too, but coach suspended him and Jackson Rivers for not showing up to practice for almost a week. I don't know what's up Tony's ass, and I don't ask him.

He's been single and grumpy as fuck over it since winter break last year. Sophie broke up with him. He never told us why. He doesn't talk about her at all. It's like his heart formed into steel and nothing can penetrate it.

"Where you going?" I ask him, noticing that he's fairly dressed up in jeans and a black button-down shirt. As in, he's not wearing shorts and a T-shirt, which is his usual attire.

"To Chavez's party." He raises a single brow. "You going?"

I shake my head. "I'm beat."

"You didn't play."

"Still tired." I shrugged. "Had to listen to Bennett run his mouth for the last half. That's exhausting."

Tony actually grins, though it doesn't quite reach his eyes. "That guy is irritating."

"Tell me all about it. He'll be there, if that deters you from going," I say as a warning.

"He'll be with Ava all night. I'm not worried." Tony takes a step forward, invading my personal space. "You should go. Might do you some good."

"Do me some good, how?" I push open my door and walk inside my tiny bedroom. There's a queen bed in there, a small dresser, and a little bed for Gabriella. A bassinet, is what Jocelyn's mom calls it. In the back of my old Toyota sits a car seat. Look at me, all domesticated and shit.

"When was the last time you did something just for you?" Tony asks as he follows me into my bedroom.

"I do something for me all the damn time. I go to school. I play football." And somehow Jocelyn allows it, instead of demanding I take the baby more. Her mom is helping us out tremendously. I owe that woman a lot. She's also seemed to come around in her opinion about me. I don't feel her hostility aimed at me anymore.

I kind of think she's impressed by me stepping up. She probably thought I'd end up a deadbeat dad who didn't want anything to do with his baby.

Yeah. No. I love my little girl too much to ever let her go.

"That's all stuff to further yourself. When was the last time you had a beer and relaxed? Talked to a pretty girl?" Tony presses.

"Probably the last time you did," I say pointedly. He's just as closed off as me. He doesn't date. He doesn't seem to have any fun. He disappears sometimes, and I don't know where he goes. I don't ask either.

He's always been quiet and mysterious, but now he's even more so.

"That's why I'm going to the party right now." He flicks his chin at me. "You should join me."

"Nah."

"Diego."

"Tony," I say in an equally firm voice. "Not interested."

"There's free booze."

"That won't tempt me." Though it used to.

"Every drug of your choice."

"Don't do that anymore either." Gotta stay clean for my baby girl.

Tony's shoulders sag a little. "When did you become so good?"

"When my baby girl came screaming into the world," I say truthfully.

Most important moment of my life. I was so grateful Jocelyn let me be in the delivery room with her before she started to push. I'd been frantic in the waiting room, wishing I knew what was going on, hating how she kept me in the dark when all I wanted was to be in there with her. Holding her hand and reassuring her everything was going to be all right.

I got my wish. I watched my child come into this world a squalling, red wrinkly mess of wiggling flesh. She was beautiful. I held her in my hands, and she was so tiny. So fragile. Her mother watched us, tears shining in her eyes, beautiful even after she spent the last hour in hard labor, pushing with all her might. It scared me.

Giving birth is a miracle. It's also stressful AF. And I'm not the one who had to do all the work.

That night was as close as we've gotten since she cut me off. Once I cut the umbilical cord, I went to Jocelyn and handed her the baby. I held her as she held our daughter. I forgot all about wanting a son.

I had everything I could ever want, right there in my arms. And then Jocelyn slipped out of them, pasting a wan smile on her face. Reminding me that I might be the father of her child, but I wasn't allowed in her world anymore.

And that broke my fucking heart.

"Be my sober driver then," Tony says, slapping me on the back as I drop my duffel on the edge of my bed. "You shower in the locker room?" When I nod my answer, Tony continues. "Get changed. We're going to that party. I'm not taking no for an answer."

CHAPTER 23

JOCELYN

It feels weird, being at a party. Despite knowing Gigi is with my mom, and she reassured me countless times that I needed to get out and have a little fun, I still feel guilty. And oddly enough, alone. When I'm out and about, I'm used to having the baby with me.

Right now, I feel like I'm untethered. Floating like a wayward balloon through the swarms of people filling the giant two-story house, smiling and nodding at anyone I make eye contact with, though I know none of them.

Our high school was small. I knew everyone in my class. Practically everyone on campus. There's an intimacy in a small school that is both wonderful and awful, all at once. All the faces are familiar, some of them even comforting. Everyone knows your business. Nothing or no one new and exciting ever appears to change the dynamic.

Here, it's a whole new world, filled with tons of people. To the point that I'm feeling a little claustrophobic.

I also had to go home real quick and use the breast pump my parents bought for me. My boobs were leaking since Gigi isn't around to feed, and I thought about backing out of going to the party. Even if I do meet a new guy, what am I supposed to tell him?

Hey sorry, gotta get home so I can breastfeed my baby. My nipples are leaking milk and that's kind of gross, you know?

Yeah. That's a little weird.

"Come on, let's go outside," Ellie says as she takes my hand and leads me through the living room.

"Have you been here before?" I yell at her. I rode over to the frat house with Ava and Ellie, and Eli was outside waiting for Ava when we walked up. They already took off together.

Ah. Young love.

"No." Ellie shakes her head and stops, giving me time to catch up so I'm standing right beside her. "But there's got to be a back yard around here somewhere, right?"

"Right," I say with a laugh, though it feels forced, so I stop.

I'm uncomfortable, when I really don't want to be. It's stifling hot in this house, with so many bodies crammed inside. It was a not-so-cool ninety-five degrees today, and the game was borderline insufferable, even though it went long into the evening. September in Fresno is miserable. Home is only an hour away, but it's at the three-thousand-foot level and we get cool mountain breezes every night.

I think of home. How Gigi is with my family right now, safe and protected, and sleeping in a cool house. While her mom is out at a party, about to meet a guy her friends want to set her up with.

The guilt is immense, and I try to shove it aside, but it's difficult.

Finally we make our way outside. Ellie grabs a beer for herself and one for me, but I refuse it, and find a water instead. I'm still breastfeeding, so I don't consume alcohol and severely limit my caffeine. I had a Coke once, right before I breastfed the baby, and I paid the price.

That little wiggler stayed up for hours.

"See any cute guys?" Ellie asks me as she glances around the back yard, which is most definitely filled with lots of cute guys. Not that I care.

"Not really," I say. "Not any that interest me."

"Wait until you meet Kevin." That's the guy they want to introduce me to. "He's really cute."

"I'm sure," I say before I take a sip of my water.

"No, seriously. He's awesome. I met him last week. We all went to dinner together."

Ava and Ellie are spending a lot of time in Fresno, with Eli here now. The drive isn't that far from my hometown, but still. How do they get any time to do their homework?

Geez, I sound like a mother, even in my thoughts.

"Why don't you get with him then?" I ask genuinely. If this guy is so great, why is she not interested? They're hyping him up so much, I'm worried meeting him is going to be a total let down.

"But we're setting you up with him." Ellie frowns, her brows drawing together.

"Which is great. I appreciate it. But I'm really not interested. I'm not ready for a relationship yet. I'm still trying to figure my entire life out," I explain. "With school and the baby and living on my own, it's been…"

"A lot?" Ellie provides for me.

"Yeah." I smile faintly. "That."

"Are you still not over Diego?" she asks quietly.

I would never admit this to Ava, because she might tell Jake, and Jake would then tell Diego. Even though Jake is down at USC and crazy busy, he and Diego still talk constantly. At least, that's what I hear, and it makes sense. They're best friends.

Distance won't change that.

"Kind of," I admit. "Though please keep this between us."

"Sure. Of course," Ellie says, nodding repeatedly. "I'm sure it's hard, considering you have a baby with him now, and you see him all the time."

"I don't see him though," I remind her. "Not really."

"Oh. Right. Well…do you miss him?"

Yes. I miss him. It's so stupid, but I do. I miss his smile and his laugh. Our long talks. The way he made me feel like I could do anything in the world that I wanted. I miss the tender way he would talk to me, though those moments were rare.

Has he changed since Gabriella came into his life? Is he the man I saw in the delivery room? The one who was so supportive and sweet, who held his baby for the first time and unashamedly cried?

I want that version of Diego, but I don't know if it was a fleeting thing.

"I do miss him," I finally admit. "But I don't miss the horrible way he made me feel."

"I hear he's changed," Ellie says. "I don't want to say too much because I know it bothers you, but he's matured. A lot."

I actually want her to say more. I want to fall to my knees and beg her for any bits of information she might have about Diego, but I keep myself restrained and my expression neutral. "Having a baby is a huge responsibility."

"You've changed too," Ellie says and now I'm frowning.

"How?"

"Having a baby is a huge responsibility," she repeats to me with a grin. "You're a mom now, Jocelyn. It's mellowed you out."

"And also stressed me out," I add wryly, making her giggle.

I change the subject and we talk about the game. I tell her about my classes and she tells me what's going on at the high school. Wyatt is now the star on campus, best-looking boy in the senior class. Without the boys from my class there to overshadow him, according to Ellie, all the girls want him.

"Even though he was with Cami?" I can't believe I just said her name out loud. I don't really think about her anymore. I used to. I devoted a lot of energy toward that girl, all for nothing. She even used to haunt my dreams.

No longer. Last I heard, she went to Chico State—dodged that bullet—and is already out partying constantly and hooking up with guys. How do I know this? Various friends of mine see her constant Snapchat stories showcasing her partying ways.

She is all class, that girl.

"Honestly, I think being with Cami gave him more cred. That he got with a girl a year older than him, and then he dumped her on his terms." Ellie laughs. "He only did it for the sex, I'm sure of it."

"Gross," I say with a little shiver. I figure you have to be pretty desperate to want to have sex with Cami Lockhart.

Though she's beautiful. And popular. If you don't know any better—like Wyatt—when a hot girl like Cami, who's more experienced and the captain of the cheer team starts flirting with you, you respond.

They always find out too late that her soul is a black pit of despair.

Eventually Ava and Eli find us—God knows where they went or what they were doing—and they've got someone with them.

The first thing I notice is how tall he is. Well over six feet. And broad. His shoulders are like mountains. His smile is big and his skin is dark and his brown eyes sparkle when they meet mine.

"Jocelyn, this is Kevin," Eli says, sounding very pleased with himself. "The guy Ava was telling you about."

"Hi," I say, offering Kevin my hand.

He takes it, his engulfing mine, and gives it a quick shake. "Nice to meet you."

"So formal," Eli teases and Kevin sends him a look.

"It's called being polite," Kevin says as he drops my hand.

"He doesn't know the meaning of the word," I say, leaning into Kevin as if I'm telling him a big secret, though my voice doesn't drop at all.

"Hey, I'm offended," Eli protests. "I know how to be polite when it's necessary."

"Sure you do," Kevin says easily, his eyes crinkling when he smiles.

He's cute. If he can tolerate Eli Bennett, that also means he's patient.

We form a circle and start talking. Kevin is standing right next to me, and his big body radiates heat. The scent of his cologne lingers in the air between us and I take the occasional discreet sniff. When I glance over at him, I catch him checking me out every once in a while, and it makes my cheeks grow warm. His interest is obvious, and I'm sort of reveling in it.

Okay, there's no sort of about this. I *am* reveling in it. It feels good, to have a man's attention, after feeling like nothing but a baby machine for the last year.

Which is wild in itself, that it's been nearly a year since I discovered I was pregnant. Time goes by so fast. Gigi has already changed so much. I wonder if she's sleeping right now. Or keeping Mom up—

"Eli told me you have a little girl."

I shake myself out of my thoughts at hearing Kevin's soft voice talking directly to me. I turn to look at him, appreciating the interest in his gaze even more now. I guess having a baby doesn't deter him. "He told you that? And you didn't run screaming from him?"

"Yeah. He did tell me." Kevin chuckles. "And no, I didn't run screaming. How old is she?"

"Almost four months." I smile just thinking about her.

"My nephew is two months old. My twin brother's wife is a saint, she is so good with him. That motherly instinct is just natural, huh," he says.

I think of Diego's mother, and how much motherly instinct she lacks. "Most of the time."

"The baby's father in your life?" Kevin asks curiously.

Oh. Guess Eli didn't tell him that part. "Yes. Somewhat. He sees the baby when he can." I hesitate only for a moment, deciding I need to be truthful. "He's on your team."

Kevin frowns. "He is?"

"Diego Garcia. He's a freshman."

"Ahh." He nods, rocking back on his heels. "Yeah. I know who you're talking about. Never really talk to him, though. Seems like a decent dude. Quiet. Keeps to himself."

I frown. That sounds nothing like the Diego I know.

"You two aren't—together are you? Maybe Eli got it wrong," Kevin says.

"No, we're not together. It just—it didn't work out. But that's okay. He's a great dad, and we're doing the best we can," I say.

"I admire you for doing this." When I look at him in confusion, he goes on. "Having a baby at your age. Going to school. Being responsible and having a decent relationship with the father of your child. That takes balls."

I laugh. "I don't know if I have balls."

He chuckles. "You know what I mean." His expression turns serious. "It's a lot, what you're doing. I'm two years older, and I don't know if I could handle it."

"You'd be surprised what you can do when you're put into a certain situation," I tell him.

"True. We adjust as we go, right? Life doesn't ever turn

out exactly as we planned," he says with a faint smile. He has a nice one.

He's kind. Talking to him is easy. I get the sense he's still interested, despite the baby talk and the fact that the father of my baby is on his football team. That didn't faze him at all. This guy is almost unreal.

But there's no spark on my part. He's attractive, but I'm not attracted.

We keep talking, until Kevin excuses himself to go grab another beer. The moment he's gone, my friends and Eli all turn to me with expectant gazes.

"What do you think?" Ava asks, her voice hushed.

"I love that guy," Eli says. "He's been cool to me since the first day of practice."

"He's nice," I say, and leave it at that.

Ellie rolls her eyes. "Oh, come on. That's not enough. Do you *like* him?"

"I don't know yet." And that's the truth. I don't know him well enough. We just met. And it's not like I'm going to let a stranger into my life easily. I have someone else to think about now. Not just me.

I'm not ready for a relationship either. They should realize this. My guard is up. I don't think I'm interested in Kevin like that, though I'm not going to say anything. I'd rather keep the fun evening going, and let them know my real feelings later.

But they're all still looking at me as if they're waiting for me to say something else, and impatience gets to me.

"Guys, seriously. I don't know how to feel about him." I send them all an exasperated look. "He seems like a great guy, but you know I'm not ready for a relationship."

"We get it," Ava says with a nod. "And we're not trying to put pressure on you, I swear. But...it's okay to flirt. To have a guy pay attention to you. When was the last time you had that?"

Since Thanksgiving weekend last year and that turned into a complete shitshow.

"A long time," I confess.

"Just have a little fun," Ava says, smiling her encouragement. "Chat up Kevin for the night. Have a beer or two. I'm driving, so you can drink up if you want."

"I'm still breastfeeding," I start and Ava shakes her head.

"Not tonight, you aren't. You won't go get Gigi until the morning, right? It should be out of your system by then?" Ava lifts her brows in question.

This is such an odd subject for us to be talking about. We're too young for this.

Yet here I am, a teenage mom.

"I don't know." I bite my lower lip.

"If you drink, you might get your baby drunk. That could be kinda funny," Eli suggests. Ava elbows him in the ribs. "Ow, what? I was just making a joke."

"It's not funny." Ava scowls before turning a sunshiny smile on me. "You're right. You probably shouldn't. And I won't push, because that's not cool. But try and relax and have fun. Out of everyone I know, you deserve it the most."

I almost want to cry, Ava's being so understanding. Reaching out, I snag her hand in mine and give it a squeeze. "Thank you."

"Anything for you," she tells me, squeezing my hand in return.

Kevin suddenly reappears, a red solo cup in hand, a pleasant smile on his face. "Hey. Whatcha guys talking about?"

"Beer. And you," Ava says truthfully.

"Hope it's all good stuff, whatever you're saying about

me." He turns that smile on me, and I can't help but grin in return. "They filling your head with lies or what?"

"Not at all," I say, shaking my head. "They're all a part of your fan club."

"I didn't realize I had a fan club. Awesome. I'll have to send them some autographed swag." He chuckles, and I do too.

All while the three stooges watch us with smug expressions on their faces. Like they knew we'd make a great match.

I appreciate their wanting to look out for me, but this probably isn't going to happen.

We end up finding a couple of chairs, and Kevin and I sit together, talking easily for at least an hour. Maybe longer. I don't know. Time passes by quickly chatting with him, and it feels good to have a conversation that has nothing to do with my past, or where I'm from, or what happened to me. He asks me lots of questions, but nothing too personal, and I do the same. We're getting to know each other, and we're keeping it pretty light.

I desperately need light.

Kevin seems very thoughtful. I appreciate the way he listens when I speak. His quick wittedness. He's funny. Self-depreciating. He laughs a lot, and it comes easy to him. He's not wound up or tense or angry.

Meaning, he's nothing like Diego.

People start to leave the party and we're still talking. He tells me about growing up in Paso Robles, which is not too far from the coast, and how he wanted to play pro basketball so bad when he was a kid.

"Then why didn't you?" I ask when he pauses in the middle of our conversation. "You seem tall enough."

"I got the height, but I don't got the skills." He laughs. "I'm a better defensive lineman. I'm fast. I can block. I'm not as fast on a basketball court. I lose control of the ball all the damn time. Pissed my coaches off to no end."

There's more laughter, and I'm sort of in shock. Diego would never act this way. I'm starting to realize not everyone is like Diego.

I mean, I knew this. Of course I did. But I was so caught up in him, I didn't really see anyone else.

"You're a really good football player though…" My voice trails off, because I don't actually know what kind of football player he is. "That's what I hear, at least."

"You didn't see me on the field tonight?" His brows shoot up in question.

"I'm sure I did, I just didn't know it." I feel bad, but I'm not going to lie.

"You'll have to come to another game and watch me sometime. If you're interested," he adds with a sly smile.

"I might be." I mean, probably not, but maybe? What can it hurt?

"You might be, huh? Hey, that's better than a flat-out no," he says.

I rise to my feet. "I need to use the bathroom. And look for my friends. We should probably go soon." I check the time on my phone, shocked to see how late it is. "I'll be right back."

"No worries," Kevin calls after me as I head for the house.

I send Ava a quick text, asking where she's at. She responds quickly, thank God.

Ava: **In the car with Eli.**

I wrinkle my nose as I walk into the house. Did I interrupt something?

Me: **What about Ellie?**

Ava: **She's with us too. We were just talking.**

Ah. I figured she was messing around with Eli if they were alone in the car…

Me: **I'm going to use the bathroom and then maybe we should go?**

Ava: **Sounds good.**

I turn down a narrow dark hallway, spotting an open doorway with light shining from within. I can see a mirror on the wall, a shadow of someone at the sink washing their hands, and I assume it's a bathroom. I speed up my steps, filled with the urgent need to pee.

The door opens fully, a tall male body filling the doorway, his frame backlit so I can't make out his features at first.

Until I can.

And realize too late that it's Diego.

CHAPTER 24

DIEGO

I blink repeatedly as I watch Jocelyn, figuring she'd disappear because I have to be hallucinating. No way would she be at a frat party. She should be home with our daughter right now.

Christ, and doesn't that make me sound like a misogynistic asshole? I'm more fully evolved than that, aren't I?

"Jos." I clear my throat, taking a step toward her.

She takes a step back without saying a word, her eyes wide with shock.

Guess she's just as surprised as I am.

"What are you doing here?" I ask her.

I take her in, and I like what I see. Swear to God, she's thinner than before she was pregnant, though her tits are bigger, thanks to her feeding Gabriella, I'm guessing. She's got on jeans that cling to her hips and thighs almost lovingly and she's wearing a red Bulldogs T-shirt, looking like every other girl here at this party tonight upon first glance.

But she's just not every other girl. This is *my* girl. The one I let slip through my fingers, and she looks better than ever.

"Uh, I'm here for the party," she tells me, tilting her head to the side. "What are you doing here?"

"I was invited." I shrug.

"Same."

We don't budge. We don't say anything else either. I used the bathroom real quick and was planning on going in search of Tony so we can get the hell out of here. Caleb disappeared a while ago, and I figure he's with a girl, like always. Tony and I have wandered around the house and yard together, talking to a variety of people, including girls, but I'm not interested.

The only one I'm interested in is standing directly in front of me and completely unattainable.

"I need to use the bathroom," she says and I snap to attention, getting out of her way so she can walk inside the room. "Thanks. It was nice seeing you."

I watch as she enters the bathroom, and slowly closes the door, flashing me a quick smile before she disappears.

That's it? *It was nice seeing you?* That's all she can say?

I lean against the wall and wait for her, quickly texting Tony that I'm almost ready to go. He says I can take my time, and I plan on it. I have a few things I need to say to Jocelyn first.

And it's going to be more than it was nice seeing you.

She takes what seems like forever and finally the door opens. She stops when she sees me standing in the spot she left me, and her full lips curve into a frown.

"Were you waiting for me?" she asks incredulously.

"Of course I was." I push away from the wall and approach her. "We haven't seen each other in months. Not since you had the baby. You think I'm going to be satisfied with a, *it was nice seeing you,* and walk away?"

"I'd kind of hoped so," she mutters, shaking her head.

Fuck, that hurts. I rub at my chest and look away, releasing a ragged exhale. "We should talk."

"What about?"

I return my gaze to hers. "Gabriella."

"What about her? She's doing great. She smiles all the time, and I think I made her laugh—"

"She's beautiful. She's amazing. I'm completely in love with her, and I wish I could see her more," I say, interrupting her. I wish I could see Jocelyn more too, but I don't say that. "Where is she tonight?"

Jocelyn stands a little straighter, her expression turning defensive. I know that look. I recognize it well. "With my mother."

"Cool." I nod, feeling like an idiot. "Did you come to the game?"

"Yes."

"I didn't play."

"I didn't think you would."

Damn, that hurts too. She's brutal tonight. "You look good."

"Thank you."

"I was hoping maybe we could go somewhere and talk." I am completely winging it. I don't know what I could gain out of going somewhere and talking to Jocelyn right now, but I'm saying this because I don't want her to walk away from me. I want to stare at her face for a little while. Spend time with her.

"Right now?" She frowns. "I was just about to go home."

"We could go back to your place," I suggest hopefully.

"I don't think so. Not tonight. I'm pretty tired."

"Can I pick up Gabriella from you tomorrow? Maybe we could talk then."

She studies me for a moment, her big blue eyes so beautiful, I feel like I could drown in them. "I don't know if it's a good idea for us to talk right now."

Frustration ripples through me, making me want to say something angry. Say something I'll regret. "We haven't really talked in months."

"I know," she says quietly. "Have you missed me?"

"Fuck yes," I answer without hesitation.

"See, that's the problem. I'm not so sure if I feel the same way," she admits, her voice quiet.

I go silent, her words punching me deep. Jabbing me right in the heart. Tearing me to shreds.

"We've gone through a lot, you and me. And I don't want to see us fall back into our old habits, if we were to start—spending time together again," she continues.

She's right. I know she is. But—

"I've changed," I say vehemently. "I can prove it to you."

"You don't have to prove anything to me, Diego. You just need to be—responsible. You've been great with Gabriella," she says, and I stand up a little taller, proud she'd say such a thing. "My mother tells me how good you are with her."

"She's easy to love, considering she's ours." And that is one hundred percent the truth. I couldn't love that little girl more, and what makes her extra special?

The fact that Jocelyn and I made her. She belongs to us, and no one else.

"She is pretty easy to love," Jocelyn says with a fond smile, as if she's thinking about the baby right now. "I have to go."

"Can I text you?" I ask as she's about to pass me by.

She stops, and she's so close, I could lean down and kiss her easily. The urge to do so is strong, but I restrain myself.

"I unblocked you a long time ago," she admits. "You can text me whenever you want."

I had no idea. "I never tried because I didn't want to make you mad."

A sigh escapes her. "We're long past that, don't you think?"

"I don't know what we are, or what we're over. It all feels so damn fresh, Jos. I still lo—"

She slaps her hand against my mouth, stopping me from telling her how I feel. "Don't say something you don't mean."

I try to send her an imploring look, but it's as if she's thrown up an impenetrable wall, one I can't tear down no matter how hard I try. I wish she would believe me. I wish we could forget everything that happened between us and start fresh.

But we can't. There are a lot of old wounds and fresh pain that still scar us both. I might never be able to convince her we could work. I'm willing to try though.

Will she be willing to listen?

Jocelyn drops her hand from my face, watching me with those giant blue eyes. "We can't get back together."

I part my lips to protest and she raises her hand, pointing her finger directly in my face.

"Let me finish." She drops her hand, and I remain quiet. "But I'm willing to listen to what you have to say. You're Gigi's father. It would be nice if we could get along. So she can see that we genuinely care about each other, and respect each other, too. I don't want her to see anything like what you grew up with."

I wince, though I know she's right. My family is all sorts of fucked up, and I don't want my little girl exposed to any of that.

"Can we talk tomorrow?" I ask.

"Maybe," she hedges. "I'll text you first, okay?" Without warning, she pulls me into a hug, and I hold her close for a heartbeat. Two. Her lush, warm body molds to mine, and I press my face into her fragrant hair, breathing in its scent.

And then she's gone, shaking herself a little bit, as if she has to shake me off too.

"Bye," she says softly.

"Bye," I tell her, waiting a few moments, until I hear the backdoor close.

I'm in hot pursuit of her in seconds. I move through the house and slip out the backdoor, my head whipping left, then right, trying to find her. The place has really cleared out, there's not many people left, and I spot her easily.

Talking to Kevin Nelson, one of the defensive linemen on our team. He's a junior, with the same easygoing attitude as Asher Davis's that I admire so damn much. She's standing awfully close to him, and he's watching her with obvious interest.

I clutch my hands into fists, wishing I could smash his face in. He could take me easily though. It wouldn't be a fair fight, and I know it.

When he pulls her in for a hug and holds her a little too long, I see red. Vivid blood red. I feel like the fucking Incredible Hulk, ready to smash heads together just to watch them break, and I'm incredulous as I watch her slowly withdraw from his embrace, a warm smile curving her lips as she wiggles her fingers at him in a flirtatious goodbye wave. She turns on her heel and heads for the side of the house with the gate that leads out into the front yard, and she spots me. Catches me staring.

Her expression is cool as we continue to stare at each other and she looks away first, never saying a word as she walks by. Never offering me up a cute little wave either.

Fuck. I have competition.

My gaze goes back to Kevin, watching him with undisguised disgust as he polishes off his drink in his cup and then starts gathering up all the discarded cups near him. I almost groan in disbelief. This guy is a do-gooder. Who goes around and cleans up before the party's even over?

Fucking Kevin, that's who.

"There you are." I turn at hearing Tony's voice. His eyelids are heavy and he appears half-baked. Great. "Ready to go? Did you drink anything?"

"I sipped on a beer when we first got here." My heart wasn't in it and I left it on a table somewhere.

Hopefully Kevin picks it up and throws it away for me.

"Good. You're the designated driver." He dangles his car keys in front of me and I swipe them from his fingers. "I'm about a million shades of fucked-up."

"Clearly."

"Who were you glaring at?" I frown at him. "Just now? You were sending someone the thousand-yard stare, your hands all bunched into fists. Looked like you wanted to kick some major ass."

"You know Kevin?" I wave a hand in his general direction.

"Sort of. Not really. I don't talk to the defensive line much. And besides, I'm suspended," Tony reminds me.

"Right." Still don't understand why he doesn't give a damn, but whatever. "Yeah. Well, I think he's hot for Jocelyn."

"Get the fuck out of here." Tony flicks his head toward the house. "Let's go."

I tell him what I witnessed as we cut through the house and leave through the front door. I explain my conversation with Jocelyn by the bathroom, and how she went outside to say goodbye to Kevin. She gave me a hug, and then she gave him one too.

It's like that hug she gave me didn't really matter. She likes Kevin.

Not me.

"You think she's into him?" I ask when we're settled into

Tony's fine ass Mercedes. This car is powerful, and he's only let me drive it once.

Looks like tonight is my lucky night to drive it again.

"I don't know what to think, but she probably doesn't like you very much right now," Tony says, his head lolling against the seat.

Ouch. Why the hell is everyone being so damn brutal tonight? "You really think so?"

"I don't know. I think your girl is confused. You treated her like shit for a long time, D. And you can't deny it. She had to cut you off, to make you miss what you took advantage of," Tony explains.

"I took advantage of her?" That sounds shitty.

"Yeah, you did. She forgave you endlessly. And you just kept doing what you do. She finally had to tell you *no, you can't hurt me anymore,* and then blocked your ass everywhere, and it worked," Tony explains.

"I didn't mean to." Half the time, I didn't know I was doing it. I was so wrapped up in my own bullshit, I didn't realize how I was hurting her.

And that sucks. I'm a dick. I know this, but it's like my eyes were finally being pried open and realizing that *yes, asshole. You're a complete dick.*

"You think she's over me?" I ask, my voice quiet as I pull out onto the street. I tell myself to remain calm. I don't need to wreck Tony's car just because I'm mad that I ruined the one good thing I ever had.

"She might be over you. But she's got a constant reminder of you named Gabriella Garcia." Tony grins. "She's hella cute, too."

"She is," I agree. "So is her mom."

"Jocelyn's looking good."

"I know."

"She looks…happy."

And I'm not the one who made her happy—I haven't been a real part of her life in months. Throughout the last part of our relationship, I made her miserable. No wonder she cut me off. She did it for her own mental health.

Being away from her helped me too, though. I can admit it. Not having her around allowed me to focus on myself. I learned quickly I needed to stay away from my mother. Tony had a hand in that as well.

"If you two don't get back together, you still have to stand by her and support your child together," Tony says.

"I can do that," I say, nodding.

"Can you though?" His gaze is on mine, and he won't look away. It's as if he's trying to force me to be honest with myself. "Or are you always going to want her back?"

"I'm in love with her," I admit. "Of course, I want her back."

"Then shoot your shot. Give it one more try, and if she tells you no, respect her wishes, and let her go."

That sounds a hell of a lot easier when it's coming out of his mouth.

"I'll try," I mutter, already feeling like a failure.

"Don't get down on yourself," Tony says, scolding me like I'm his child and he's giving me a pep talk. "Show her that you've manned up. Prove to her that you're a better person now, thanks to becoming a father."

"I *am* a better person."

"You've realized your worth," Tony says.

"I have?"

He laughs. "Yes, asshole, you have. You're not just Mateo's little brother who gets beat up all the time. You're not just that Garcia kid who comes from the shit neighborhood, who knows how to catch a ball. You're Diego fucking Garcia. The one who graduated high school and got into Fresno State, and who's playing on their football team. The *man* who's a

father now, and has taken on the responsibility with everything you've got. You're a dad. You're in school. You're doing
what's right. You're a fucking catch, man. She'd be stupid to
let you go."

"You're right." I keep nodding my head, tapping my
fingers against the steering wheel as I drive down the street
toward our apartment. "I've changed. I'm a man now."

"Prove it to her," Tony roars, like a challenge.

"I will," I yell back, pumping my fist in the air.

I will.

CHAPTER 25

JOCELYN

I went to my parents' house late Sunday morning only to find Gigi just went down for a nap after my dad fed her. Mom made me French toast and bacon, and we sat and chatted at the table in the breakfast nook. I told her about the game, and the party I went to after.

There is no point in hiding anything from my mother anymore. She knows all my dirty little secrets, and supports me anyway.

I even tell her about running into Diego inside the house, and how eager he was to get me to spend time with him.

"He's changed," is all my mother says before she takes a swig of her coffee.

I keep eating my breakfast, even though my appetite leaves me after mentioning Diego. Not because I can't stand him and he makes me sick. More like thinking about him makes me…nervous.

And the tiniest bit excited.

Does this make me a fool? Yes, most likely. But I can't help the way I feel.

"What do you mean?" I ask, dropping my fork on the edge of my plate.

"He always had this—energy coming from him near the end of your relationship. It was angry. Defensive. Downright hostile sometimes." She sets her cup down, her gaze meeting mine. "I worried for you when you two were together. He was sweet to you at first, but then he just seemed…so arrogant. Always expecting you to wait for him, wait *on* him. Be the good little girlfriend and do what he wanted you to do."

I'm in shock. "Mom. Why didn't you ever tell me you felt like this?"

"Because you would've told me to mind my own business and want to be with him even more." She sends me a shrewd look. "I'm not dumb. I was a teenage girl too, you know."

I want to hear about her relationships with boys in high school, but later. "He did treat me like that sometimes. Eventually I ignored him when he did that." And he sought attention from other girls.

Just flirting though. Of all people to confirm this, it was Caleb. We have a math class together this semester, and we sit by each other. I adore Caleb, I always have. He may be a complete manwhore, but he's also nice. And he's always been sweet to me.

One day before class started, he mentioned Diego, and I had to ask. About the past. He reassured me that there was nothing going on between Cami and Diego before we broke up. He couldn't confirm or deny that fact after we split, and I don't want to know.

Again, does that make me a fool?

Oh yes.

"He doesn't have that open hostility anymore," Mom says, pulling me from my thoughts. "He's much more relaxed. Even with the baby, which I thought would make him nervous. He's so good with her. She goes to him easily, always cooing and making noises at him." She smiles. "It's rather sweet."

My heart feels like it's swelled to three times its size. "She loves him?"

"Almost as much as she loves me." Mom throws her head back and laughs, and I do too. "Yes, she loves him. She is a very well-loved baby. We were all fighting over who got to cuddle with her last night."

"Thank you for taking care of her for me." I reach across the table and settle my hand on hers. "And just for…everything. I couldn't do this without you."

"I actually think you could." She smiles, but it's tremulous, and she's blinking rapidly, as if holding back tears. "You're so strong, Jocelyn. I'm so proud of you."

"Aw, Mom." Now I'm crying too, and we're both sitting at the table, blubbering like babies, when my father walks in, holding the actual baby in the family in his arms. He stops short when he sees us, wearing that look men get when they don't know what to do with a crying woman.

"Should I leave?" he asks as he starts to back up.

"No, we're just being sentimental," Mom tells him as I rise to my feet, dashing the tears away quickly before I scoop Gigi out of his arms. She comes to me willingly, her little head bobbing, her feet kicking. I hold her close, kiss her cheek, and fall back into my chair.

"Thank you, Dad, for watching Gigi overnight," I tell him with a smile, so grateful he's come around.

"It was worth showing my granddaughter my favorite movie of all time." He raises his brows. "Worth every minute of her crying at two in the morning."

"What movie did you watch?" I ask.

"*Point Break*," Mom says, rolling her eyes.

"I should've known," I say with a laugh.

"Keanu Reeves and Patrick Swayze together? A true masterpiece," he says with the utmost sincerity.

If you grew up in my house, you've seen *Point Break* multiple times. He loves the movie that much.

We chat for a while longer, until I tell them I have to get back to my place so I can get a start on my homework. On the drive home, Gigi falls back asleep. I listen to my new favorite Spotify playlist, not one depressing song on that list either, thank you very much, and I sing along with Ariana to "Thank You, Next."

I know the song is old, but it was my anthem when Diego and I first broke up, and it's kind of been my anthem the entire time we've been apart. It's empowering. Her lyrics touch me deep, and while I can't deny I still have feelings for Diego, I should probably tell him he doesn't stand a chance.

It would be better for my health, and my sanity, if I continued keeping him at an arm's distance. Seeing him last night threw me for a loop. Hugging him had been a test. Would I feel something? Want him?

The moment his arms came around me, it was like my body sighed in relief. I relaxed against him. Clung to him too long. His scent, his warmth, his everything felt familiar.

Right.

So right, I pulled out of his arms when I realized it, regret filling me. I wasn't near as ready to take that test as I thought I was.

I went to Kevin and did the same thing. What would it feel like to hug him? He's solid as a rock and radiates heat like a furnace. He smells really good too. It was…nice. Pleasant.

But being in his arms didn't rock my world. I didn't want to cling to him, though I held onto him for a few seconds longer than necessary, just to see.

Nothing happened. No spark. No pull.

I'm going to have to tell my friends I'm not interested in him, not like that. I'm sure he'll be okay. There are a lot of girls on campus who are probably dying for a chance to get with him. He could have anyone he wants.

By the time I'm back inside my apartment with the various equipment a baby needs, and the actual baby, I realize I have three texts waiting for me.

One from my mother.

Let me know you made it home safely! Love you.

One from Kevin.

Hey. WYD?

And one from Diego.

I know you said you wanted to text me first, but I couldn't wait.

I put Gigi in her vibrating chair thing she loves so much and answer my mother first.

I'm home! And we're safe. Love you too.

Then Kevin.

Nothing much. WBU?

And then Diego.

Is everything okay?

Mom sends me a couple of heart emojis in response. Kevin doesn't respond. Diego texts almost as fast as my mother.

Diego: **I just miss our daughter.**

I smile. There were times I wondered if Diego had a heart. I now realize that he doesn't—Gigi owns it.

Diego: **Can I come over and pick her up?**

Me: **Sure. What time?**

This will be the first time we don't use my mom as the go to between us. Meaning, this is kind of a big deal.

Diego: **Give me the address and I can be there in less than thirty.**

Me: **Okay.**

I send him my address before I think better of it, and immediately go in search of something to change into. I just threw on some old leggings and a T-shirt before I went and picked up Gigi. Now I want to look…nice.

Which is dumb, I know, but I can't help it.

I slip on a pair of jeans and a cute flowery print top that makes my waist look skinny. I've lost all the baby weight and more. I'm always on the go, or breastfeeding a baby, and the pounds just melted off. Mom said the same thing happened to her when she had each of us, so I guess I inherited her genes.

Thank goodness.

I run a brush through my hair to fluff it up and then add a little mascara. That's it. I don't want to look like I'm trying too hard. I always look like this, you know?

Ha. Yeah right.

Gigi starts whimpering and I go out into the living room to check on her. She spots me, and her eyes well up with tears. Clearly, something's bothering her.

"What's wrong, baby?" I croon as I undo the belt and pull her out of the chair. I hold her close to me, her little face pressed into my neck as I thread my fingers through her soft hair. "You hungry?"

I do not want to be breastfeeding her in front of Diego. Stupid, I know, but that feels too intimate. Too early.

I start pacing the living room, trying to comfort Gigi, who's having a little fit. She's making these weird half-crying, half-fussy noises, and I keep shushing her, bouncing her in my arms, hoping she'll be on her best behavior when her daddy shows up.

I come to a stop in the middle of the room, absorbing that word. *Daddy.* It sounds so sweet. Diego is her daddy and I'm her mommy.

Just thinking it almost makes me want to cry.

God, hormones are the worst.

I keep up the pacing, noticing that Gigi seems to be even more rattled. I wonder if I'm giving off nervous vibes. I am a little keyed up over Diego coming over. Maybe she can sense it. She's actually very perceptive to my moods.

The doorbell rings, and I rush to answer it, unlocking and then throwing open the door…

At the same time Gigi throws up all over the front of me.

"Oh shit. Someone's excited to see me," Diego says as he rushes into my apartment.

I glance down at myself, the baby spit up covering my cute shirt, my exposed chest. Oh God, I think it's even on my neck. In my hair. Gross. "Uhhh…"

"Let me take her." He plucks Gigi out of my arms, and I glance up just in time to see her beam at her father as if he's the best thing she's ever seen, kicking her little legs in excitement.

I kind of can't help but think he's the best thing I've ever seen too. He looks good. When does he not? Black T-shirt that clings to his wide chest. Jeans that mold to his thick thighs. He's letting his hair grow out a little longer, so it flops over his forehead in this adorably appealing way.

While I stand in front of him with vomit all over me. Nice.

"I'm going to go clean myself up," I tell him, waving a hand at myself.

"Go. I've got this. I'll clean her up too. Won't I, sunshine? Yes, daddy's gonna clean you up, and then we're gonna talk to mommy, aren't we?" He grabs her little hand, and she curls her tiny fingers around his.

Ugh. Too cute. I need to focus on vomit, not how sweet Diego is with our daughter.

I lock myself away in the bathroom and peel the wet with baby spit up shirt off and rinse it out in the sink. It comes out easily. I then grab a clean washcloth and dampen it before I add some foaming soap. I scrub at my neck and chest. Wipe it out of my hair before I twist it up into a ponytail, giving up on the cute vibe I had going on.

That moment came and went.

It's only when I'm hanging my wet shirt over the shower curtain rod that I realize I'll have to walk out of the bathroom with my bra and jeans on because I forgot to bring another shirt to change into.

Meaning I'm an idiot.

I contemplate asking him to find me a shirt in my closet, but that's asking too much. Besides, he's taking care of the baby.

Guess I'll have to walk out there in just the bra. A nursing bra too, so not like it's anything sexy. And not like he hasn't seen me in one before. We did make a baby together, after all.

Taking a deep breath, I throw the door open and dash out of the bathroom, heading straight for my bedroom, which is literally only a few feet away. "Give me just a minute," I call, my gaze somehow finding his.

He's sitting on the coach, one arm wrapped around Gigi as she tugs on his hair. He's watching me, heat flaring in his brown eyes as they race over me, drinking me in.

My skin warms and I look away, slamming the door hard, my heart pumping.

Well. That didn't go as I originally planned.

I find another shirt—not one as cute as the previous shirt, but it'll have to do—and slip it on. Spritz myself with body spray, so I don't smell like sour milk, and then walk back out into the living room with a smile plastered on my face.

"There's Mommy. Wave hi." He grabs her little arm and makes it wave at me. Gigi makes a gurgling noise in greeting.

"Hey baby." I go to the couch and sit next to them, realizing too late that we're sitting so close, our knees bump into each other. "Guess you feel better now that you threw up, huh?"

"She seems good. I found a new outfit for her in the diaper bag," Diego says. "Plus I changed her diaper."

He says this not in a way to get credit, which a lot of men do. They talk about their children as if they're doing mom a favor for watching them or dressing them, or getting them ready for school. Isn't that their responsibility too?

No, Diego states it matter-of-factly, and I'm just damn grateful he helped in any capacity.

"Thank you," I murmur, my greedy gaze eating him up. I know I should stop, but it's like I can't help it. "She seem okay?"

"She's perfect." He grabs her fist and brings it to his mouth, kissing it. "She's all better now."

"I'm sure," I say as I sag against the couch with a sigh. "I bet it was the drive from my parents' house. She slept through most of it, but sometimes she gets so hot and sweaty in her car seat, and my dad fed her again right before we left."

"She gets car sick?" Diego asks.

"Maybe." I shrug. "Who knows? Sometimes she barfs for no reason. She's a baby."

"That's what they do," he agrees, staring at her face for a while before he turns his gaze on me. "She's the most beautiful baby on the planet, yet my mother never wants to see her. I reach out, text her. Call her. Try to meet up with her, but she's always too busy. I've finally quit trying."

"I'm so sorry," I murmur. "And here I thought my parents would be the difficult ones."

"Keeping it real right now, but I thought the same thing. I figured Mom would embrace the baby news. She's all about family, or so she says." He shakes his head. "Ever since Thanksgiving, she hasn't behaved the same. She's mad at me for moving out, but I had to do it. Mateo's living with her again."

"Of course he is." This doesn't come as a surprise.

"Still hanging out with high school kids. Getting high with the guys. Messing around with the girls." Diego scowls, but it's not as angry as it used to be. His face evens out quickly, and he once again appears completely neutral, and at ease.

"He's going to get in trouble someday," I say, shaking my head. "He lives too close to the edge."

"I know." He tilts his head down, staring at nothing. "I hate that my mom won't see the baby. Makes me feel like shit, if I'm being honest."

My heart breaks for him. The push and pull between him and his mother and brother has to be exhausting. I don't know how he does it. "She'll come around," I say, hoping I'm telling the truth. "Eventually."

"I hope so." He breathes deep and smiles. "I like your place. You actually live pretty close to me. Which uh, I kind of knew."

"How'd you know?" I ask with a frown.

"Once you told me you unblocked me, I might've stalked you a little bit. And saw you on Snap Map." He makes a face. "Don't be mad."

"I'm not mad," I say with a little laugh and it's true. I'm not. At least he's being honest. "I didn't even think to do that to you."

"You've been a little busy."

"True."

"And I'm currently a little obsessed," he adds.

"With who?"

"You."

Oh.

He doesn't look away. Doesn't even bat an eyelash. I stare

back at him, caught up in the spell he's putting me under. Until Gigi starts patting his cheek, smacking it harder and harder and we both seem to jolt.

"Ow." He grabs her hand and playfully growls at her. "Stop hurting Daddy."

"She's on a rampage," I tease. "Puking on Mommy. Beating up Daddy."

He smiles. I smile too.

This feels way too easy. I should have my guard up. He'll do or say something and ruin it all.

So I sit there, suddenly awkward as I try to remember all the shitty things he's done to me in the past. Hanging on to those bad memories are only bad for me, but I need them right now, to build up my resolve. To remind myself there's a reason why we're not together anymore.

And he's to blame for it.

It's almost as if he realizes I've thrown the wall up and he's doing his damnedest to tear it down, piece by tiny piece. He plays with Gigi. Makes me explain how I came up with the nickname for her. Starts calling her Gigi as well, and when he croons the name to her in his deep voice, she bounces in his arms, overly responsive, like he just gave her a shot of adrenaline.

I can relate.

He makes no move to leave and I don't ask him to. My homework is momentarily forgotten. Diego offers to order a pizza for dinner and I agree without hesitation. He seems pleased by this, and I'm tempted to say he shouldn't look at us hanging out together as a sign, but I say nothing.

Because I'm looking at us hanging out together as a sign, even though I shouldn't do it either.

It's all very cozy and domesticated, and once the pizza arrives, I'm pulling down plates from the cabinet while Diego ambles over to my tiny kitchen table after putting Gigi in her vibrating chair when I hear my phone ding with a notification. It's sitting on the table where I left it.

"Can you check who's sending me a text?" I ask Diego, hoping it's not my mom.

He checks the phone, and I glance over just in time to see the grim expression on his face when he answers, "Kevin."

Oh. Oh shit. I forgot Kevin texted me earlier and I responded. It took him a couple of hours to return my text.

"You like him?" Diego asks.

Even though he doesn't sound angry or hostile, I can't help but feel the tiniest bit defensive. "He's nice."

"He seems like a good guy."

That's all he says. His lips are tight. His shoulders are too. But otherwise, he remains quiet.

And this is so unlike Diego, the Diego I know, I'm shocked.

"My friends were trying to set me up with him last night," I admit.

Diego frowns. The pizza box sitting on the table between us is momentarily forgotten. "Who?"

"Ava. Ellie. Eli."

"Fucking Bennett," Diego mutters, shooting me a quick look. "Sorry. That guy is so annoying."

"He kind of is, but he's harmless." I smile.

Diego doesn't smile back. He looks...hurt.

Confused.

"Are you interested in Kevin? I'm sure he's interested in you. You're gorgeous. Smart. Strong." Diego flips the lid open on the pizza box. "How many pieces you want?"

His quick change of subject startles me and I automatically answer, "Two."

He doles them out, slaps three pieces on his plate, shuts the lid and starts eating. That's it. No more talking about Kevin.

I discreetly check my phone, reading the short text from Kevin.

At a party. You should come over.

Yeah. No. I can't.

Me: **I can't. But thanks for the invite.**

Kevin: **Some other time then.**

I gnaw on my lower lip, wondering how I should answer him.

I decide to be honest.

Me: **Probably not. I'm really busy right now with school and the baby.**

He doesn't respond. I probably made him mad. I know my friends said he's a good guy, and I'm sure he is. But he's not really looking for a girl with a baby. He's probably just looking to hook up.

And I can't blame him.

"I'm not interested in him," I say a few minutes later, trying to interrupt the heavy silence that seems to have taken over the apartment.

Diego frowns, his mouth still full. He chews and chews, swallowing before he says, "Interested in who?"

"You are such a faker." I ball up my napkin and throw it at his face, nailing him right in the cheek. "Kevin."

The tension melts away from him and he slowly smiles. "Good."

That's all he says.

Good.

And I can't help but smile at him in return, laughing when he throws his crumpled napkin at me and misses.

CHAPTER 26

DIEGO

It's been over a month, and Jocelyn and I have come to some sort of truce. An unspoken agreement.

I don't know what to call it, but we're getting along. Spending time together. A lot of time together, as much as we can fit in considering we both have busy schedules. We claim we're doing it for the baby, we actually say it out loud and often, and maybe that's true on her part, but I don't know.

I'm spending time with Jocelyn just so I can. So I can soak up her energy and her laugh and her smiles. Watching her with our baby makes my heart want to burst. I look forward to our easy conversations, our daily texts, our playing with the baby on the floor as we encourage Gigi to have tummy time and all those other things babies should be doing as they grow.

We're acting like a couple, but we don't do all of the couple-y things.

We don't really touch.

We don't hug.

We definitely don't kiss.

And we're most definitely not having sex.

It's killing me. K-I-L-L-I-N-G me.

I want to beg for her forgiveness, once and for all, and tell her how much I love her, but I don't. I remain quiet instead and enjoy the fact that she's willingly spending time with me. Most of her free time, it seems. That's major, right?

My friends don't know what to think. They hear rumors about all sorts of guys being into Jocelyn. Why wouldn't they be? She's beautiful. She's sweet. She's funny. She's smart. Caleb has English with her, and he says all sorts of dudes flirt with her on the daily, which drives me out of my mind.

Makes me crazier that one of my best friends has a class with her and I don't. How'd he get so lucky?

Those dudes may flirt with her, and Jocelyn is polite to them, but she gives off a vibe that says, *not available*. That's pretty much what Caleb told me. Yet when I say nothing is going on between us beyond platonic friendship, Caleb is baffled.

"Why haven't you tried to hit that again?" he asks me, as we're sitting inside the Bulldog Grill and stuffing ourselves with tri-tip sandwiches and fries. We're here for lunch in between classes, and as usual, the place is packed.

"It's not like I can just make a move on her and hope she responds," I say after I take a sip of my soda.

"Please. You put a baby in her. You can definitely make a fuckin' move," Caleb says.

Tony is with us, quietly eating his sandwich, and he sends Caleb a measured look. "In Jocelyn's eyes, he fucked her over royally. He has to earn back her trust first. Not that you'd know anything about that, considering you don't stick around long enough with any girl that trust is ever an issue."

"True that." Caleb grins, not insulted in the least. "Why

stick around and settle in, when I can sample all the hot babes who want me?"

My friend is fucking ridiculous, but he's also highly entertaining.

"Wait until you fall in love," I tell him. "Then you're completely fucked."

"Love is for pussies," he says seriously, tossing a fry at me. "You won't catch me doing that. Not for a long time. If ever."

"You going to be a player for the rest of your life? Be one of those sleazy old men trying to pick up young girls?" I'm teasing him, but I'm also trying to show him that being alone might not be the best choice.

"I'm only eighteen, motherfuckers. Of course, I want to be single. I'll get married when I'm forty." He grins. "I've got twenty-two years to go."

"What the fuck ever," I say with a groan, wondering if I'm being ridiculous.

Caleb has a point. We're only eighteen. Jocelyn and I aren't at war anymore, but do I really want to be with her for...*ever*? Marry her?

My chest tightens just thinking about it. At one point I thought I was, but I'm not ready for marriage. That seems so final, and our relationship is still so fragile. Uncertain. But I want to commit to her. I'm in love with her.

I am. I know it.

"Our boy here is ready to pull the trigger now," Tony says.

I glance up to find him already watching me. "It's not like I want to marry her."

"You may as well, since you have a baby with her," Caleb points out.

"I don't even think she wants to marry me," I say.

"What do you want to do then?" Tony asks, his voice quiet despite the noisy restaurant.

"I want to be with her. I want to see if we can actually make this work. It's working so far."

"Maybe because you haven't had sex with her. You two could end up being better off as friends," Tony says.

"You can't be friends with a woman," Caleb says with a finality that is completely unlike him.

We both send him a curious look. "Explain," Tony says.

"It's hard to be friends with someone of the opposite sex. You always start imagining boning them, you know? Like, what does she look like naked? What does she look like with her lips wrapped around my—"

"We get it," Tony interrupts, and I start laughing. "You don't look at women as human beings, you look at them as potential holes for you to fill."

"Hey, that's an insult," Caleb says, sounding vaguely hurt.

"I'm calling it like I see it." Tony returns his attention to me. "You should tell Jocelyn how you feel."

"Now?" I rub my suddenly aching chest. "It might be too soon."

"It's time. You two are past that sort of thing. You have a kid together. Your lives are forever entwined. If you want to know if she actually wants to be with you, you should flat-out ask her. Tell her how you feel," Tony explains.

"What if she tells me no?"

Tony raises a brow. "What if she does? What will you do?"

Fling myself off a mountain. Drown myself in a river. Crash my car into a brick building.

But then I think of Gigi. Her big brown eyes and toothless smile. The way she reaches for me, like I'm her favorite person. Her scent. Her warm little body snuggled up close to mine.

Yeah, I wouldn't do any of those things. I need to be here for my daughter. I'd move on and get over my intense feelings for a woman who doesn't love me back. I'd live my life, let Jocelyn go, and raise my daughter with her. We could co-parent.

Eventually. Hopefully, my feelings would fade.

"I'd move on," I finally say.

"Right. Because you've turned into a responsible adult, unlike us." Tony waves his hand at himself and Caleb. "That's why you should continue being a responsible adult, and tell Jocelyn how you feel. She either feels the same way, or she doesn't. There's no point in prolonging this. You should go to her."

Should I though? Really?

"Yeah, you should," Caleb says, echoing Tony. "I like Jocelyn. She's a cool chick."

That's major praise from Caleb. "I thought you can't be friends with women."

"I can be friends with my bros' women. Jocelyn and I, we get along. When you two were together, she was good for you. She seems good for you now," Caleb explains.

"Nah, the way Diego is now has nothing to do with Jocelyn, and everything to do with himself. He's realized he's a decent human being," Tony says.

How the hell did my friends become so perceptive? "I manned up," I say.

"Fuck yeah, you did," Tony agrees.

Once we finish our lunch, and we're in Tony's car headed back to campus, I decide to get something off my chest.

"Before I go to Jocelyn, there's one more thing I need to take care of," I say.

"What's that?" Caleb asks from the backseat.

"I need to talk to my mom." I don't want to, but it's necessary. We've been avoiding each other for months. Pretty much ever since I moved out, and that was almost a year ago.

She's only seen Gigi once, when she was a newborn. I haven't seen my brother in what feels like forever.

Which I'm cool with. I don't miss that guy. At all.

But I miss my mom. I ran into my aunt Lisa a few weeks ago at Target, and she told me she was worried about her. She was with her son Marty, and I told him for about the tenth time how sorry I am for what I did to him when we were younger.

"I forgive you," he said with a faint smile. "You don't have to keep apologizing."

His saying that lifted a weight off my shoulders. I was tired of being seen as the bully. The runner-up to my brother, who is the ultimate bully.

I'm not like that. Not anymore.

"You should go talk to her," Tony says. "But if she slings a bunch of insults at you and accuses you of anything, walk out. You don't need to take her shit."

Says the guy who took his parents ignoring him for years. Who still does.

"She'll put the blame on me for something," I admit. "It's just her way."

"And this is why you stay away from her. But if you feel the need to go try and mend that broken fence, go for it. Just know that it could all come crumbling down, especially if Mateo's there," Tony says.

"I want to bring Gigi with me. She needs to know her granddaughter." It kills me that she doesn't want to see her.

What the fuck did I do to my mother to make her hate me and my kid so much?

It sucks.

And I'm gonna call her out on it.

Even if it might break my heart when I find out the reason.

* * *

I TAKE Gigi with me on a Sunday afternoon to my hometown. I never come up here anymore. What's the point? I guess I could go visit the Callahans, but they try their best to come to as many games as possible so I see them there, though their son Beck's football schedule can interfere.

Besides, I've been too damn busy. Between school, football and Gabriella, I don't have much time for anything or anyone else.

But here I am today, giving my mother yet another chance to do right by me and her granddaughter.

I texted Mom right before we left, letting her know I was going to stop by, and she said okay. That she was home and we were welcome to come over, which surprised me. I figured she'd deny me, and I even considered driving up unannounced, but it would've been a wasted trip if she wasn't home, or worse, Mateo was there.

She told me he wasn't, without me even having to ask. That's how well she knows me.

I pull up in front of the tiny house and park my car. Grab Gigi's diaper bag, slinging it over my shoulder as I go to pull out her car seat. Once we're situated—a baby has a lot of gear —I carry her up the front walk. Before I even get a chance to knock on the door, it's thrown open and Mom is standing there with a giant smile on her face.

"I'm so glad you're here," she says right before she kneels down, staring at Gigi. "Who is this adorable chunk of love?"

I can't help the tight fist of anguish that's wrapped around my heart at my mom's behavior. Where was all her welcoming a few months ago, when Gigi was born? Why is she gushing over her now?

What the hell is going on?

"Come on, come inside." Mom rises to her feet and holds the door open wider, letting us in.

I enter the house, glancing around in hopes of spotting

any evidence of Mateo. The place is immaculate. It doesn't look as rumpled and cluttered as usual. There's a candle burning on a nearby table, making the normally stale house smell nice.

It looks nice too. Cleaner. Brighter. Curtains are open when they usually aren't.

"You want something to drink?" Mom asks, wringing her hands together as her gaze meets mine quickly before it drops to Gigi. "Anything to eat?"

"I'm good, Mom." I glance around, taking everything in yet again. "You cleaned up some."

"Oh, I cleaned up a lot." She laughs, and it sounds a little forced. I think she's nervous, which is surprising. "Once your brother moved out for good, I decided I needed to freshen this place up."

I'm immediately skeptical. "When did he move out?"

I fully expect her to say two days ago.

"A month ago," she answers.

My jaw drops. "And he hasn't been back?"

"Oh, he tried. At first he did, at least. But I refused. Called the cops on him, twice. He's not wanted here. Not anymore. I'm tired of putting up with him. What he did to me...I can never forgive him for it." The sadness washes over her. It's as if I literally watch it happen, and I'm speechless. What is she talking about?

"Let's sit down. Can I—may I hold the baby?" she asks.

"Of course." I take Gigi out of her car seat and hand her over to my mother after she's settled in her favorite chair. She takes her and cuddles her close.

"Oh, she's so beautiful. Oh my goodness." She holds her up above her, Gigi's legs dangling. She starts kicking, smiling at my mother and Mom doesn't hold back from smiling at her in return. "Look at her! She's so big. I missed so much already."

"Only a few months, Mom," I say before I sit on the couch. "You can catch up. Make up for it."

"Can I, though?" Mom glances over at me, still holding Gigi aloft. "You haven't called or texted me for a long time."

"Same goes for you," I throw back at her.

"I thought you were mad at me."

I was. "I thought you hated me."

"Diego. I could never hate you. I was just trying to—protect you. I don't know, it sounds so ridiculous, but I was. I didn't want you to come around to the house, especially with your baby. Not while Mateo was still here. He probably would've done something aw-awful to her." Mom holds Gigi so close to her, it's as if she's trying to absorb her.

And Gigi doesn't like it. She starts to struggle, a little whine escaping her. I'm about to shoot off the couch and rescue my baby, but Mom relaxes her hold, cradling Gigi in her arms instead as she stares at her pretty little face.

"She is the most beautiful, precious thing. I hear you're a good dad," Mom says.

"From who?" I ask incredulously.

She laughs. "Word gets around. Our town is small, and though you never come back here anymore, people still talk."

I find it hard to believe people still care what's going on with my life, but okay.

"I ran into Jocelyn's mother at the grocery store a couple of weeks ago. I tried to pretend I didn't see her, but she marched right up to me and asked when I was going to go see my grandbaby. Oh, she was mad, that woman. I didn't know she had it in her," Mom explains.

Well, damn. I didn't either. "What did you tell her?"

"I couldn't say anything at first, she wouldn't stop talking, she was so fired up. When she finally went silent, I told her I was only doing what I thought was best for you and Gabriella." Mom sighs. "She said I was full of horse shit."

I want to laugh. I almost do.

"I lived in denial all these years, Diego, and I'm sorry. I know Mateo was abusive toward you. He was abusive toward me too. I always believed I was strong enough. I could take his constant defiance. When he was younger, he was completely out of my control, and I didn't know how to handle him. I did the best I could. It didn't help. At all."

I remain silent. These are the words I've longed to hear for years, and I didn't even have to ask for them.

"I told myself it wasn't that bad. I knew you two argued. That you fought, but I didn't realize how much—damage he did to you. I think if he was given the chance, and knew he could get away with it, he could possibly kill you," she admits, just before she drops her head in shame.

I flinch at her words, but again, not surprising. I agree with her. There was a hint of conscience buried deep inside Mateo, and it somehow always stopped him from taking it too far.

Though he always pushed his limits.

"He confessed it all to me, you know. Right after you moved out. Told me you left because you couldn't handle him, and how he was only trying to make you tough enough for the world. The things he said to me..." Her voice drifts and she sucks in a quivering breath. "Broke my heart for you and disgusted me. He's a despicable human, and he's my *son*. My oldest son. Despite it all, I love him."

Despite it all, a part of me still loves Mateo too. Even after everything that's happened between us.

"I get it," I tell her, my voice tight.

"Maybe you do, maybe you don't. I suppose you do, since you're a father now." She smiles down at Gigi before lifting her gaze to mine. "I didn't want him to hurt your child. That's why I didn't want to see you. Why I pushed you and Jocelyn away from me. I know it might sound like an excuse, but I was trying to protect you from your brother. And now that he's gone, and I know he's not coming back, I want to see you more. Both of you. All of you. Are you and Jocelyn together?"

"I don't know what we are," I admit truthfully, but I don't want to talk about me and Jocelyn. "Where's Mateo, Mom?"

"Oh, he moved. Far away." She's been so vague.

Too vague.

"I just heard he was still hanging around here, doing drugs and hanging out with kids from the high school." I like how I sound as if I'm above them, when I was a student there not even a year ago.

But that feels like forever ago. My life has changed completely since the birth of my daughter.

"He was, up until a month ago. An old friend of his from high school asked him to move to Colorado and help him run a weed farm." Mom makes an irritated face. "He jumped at the chance."

I start to laugh. "Figures."

She laughs too, and even Gigi giggles, copying us. It's her new thing.

"He could come back," Mom says once our laughter dies. "Knowing him, he eventually will. But I'll refuse to let him move back in. He's pushed me too far. All of us, really. He doesn't deserve our forgiveness."

Her eyes are shiny with tears, and they tug at my heart. I've always been close to her. This last year has been extra tough without her, but I told myself it was for the best. I felt like she abandoned me when I needed her the most, and it forced me to grow up. I don't think that was ever her intention, but maybe our being apart for a while was a good thing.

Just like my being apart from Jocelyn was a good thing too.

"Do you forgive me, Diego? For what I've done to you?

And what I haven't done? I was just so scared. Confused. And torn. I didn't know what to think. Didn't understand why my two sons hated each other so much." She's full-blown crying now, clutching Gigi to her as if she's never going to let her go.

"I forgive you," I say quietly, letting her cry it out. "I put a lot of blame on you for not seeing it. I thought you were purposely ignoring all the signs."

"I was." That she agrees so readily is startling. "I'll admit it. I couldn't face what my family had become, and that it was my fault. Your father abandoned us, and I let my hatred for him almost destroy me. Mateo continuously hurt you, and I did nothing. He turned his wrath on me, and that's when I had to make it stop. I truly believed he might kill me in my sleep. I couldn't live like that."

Her words ease my pain, as does her apology, but I'm still resentful. I probably will be for a while.

We continue talking, and it feels good, spending time with my mother. Watching her with my child warms my heart. And while I said I forgive her, and I do mean it, it's going to take a long time for me to be able to trust her again. To want to spend a lot of time with her.

I'm not going to deprive my mother the opportunity to get to know her granddaughter, but she's going to have to work for it. She has a lot to prove to me.

And I'm open to whatever it is she has to say.

CHAPTER 27

JOCELYN

I haven't seen Diego in over a week and I…

Miss him.

He's had a couple of away games, two Saturdays in a row. We had midterms, which were hard and ate up a lot of my time, and he complained about the same thing. We've chatted via text. I send him lots of photos of Gigi, and he worries over her forgetting what he looks like while he's gone. I could be mad at him for not being around. I could cry it's unfair and demand he pick up his daughter so I can get a break, but I don't.

I know he hates being away from her. And from me too.

It's weird, how easy things are between us. We hang out together, like we're actually a couple, but nothing goes on. No touching, no kissing, nothing. It's not that I don't want to. It's just I'm afraid to make the first move.

What if he rejects me?

Though he told me more than once when we first started talking again that he was still in love with me. Or if he didn't say it outright, he implied it. And while that makes me feel good, gives me a little ego boost, I'm still unsure about…

Everything.

He spent time with his mother recently and took Gigi with him, which made me happy. Rosa deserves to get to know her granddaughter. I want my baby girl to know she's loved by all sides of her family. I guess Lisa and her gang went over to the house when Diego and Gigi were there, and they all went nuts over the baby, which I think is the sweetest thing.

Diego needs his family. Maybe not his brother, but he loves his mom. He told me a few things about her and Mateo, and how Mateo was physically abusive toward her, and that's what made her push him out of the house, but I thought it was a little too late for that. He might forgive her, but I'm still going to hold onto my grudge for a while longer. She didn't protect Diego well enough throughout the years. I know they're both her sons, but she should've known better. She should've done more.

Maybe that's me being judgmental. Oh well. I'll get over it.

Eventually.

I'm putting Gigi down for the night when I hear a notification from my phone on the bedside table. Gigi fusses a little bit and I smooth my hand over the top of her head, stroking her dark hair. It's getting long. A little wild. I put headbands on her, but she always tries to tug them off.

Little brat.

Thankfully she doesn't fully wake up and I sprint over to my phone, immediately shutting the sound off before I check who the text is from.

Diego: **I'm outside your apartment. Can I come up?**

Oh. This is unexpected. And honestly? A pleasant surprise. My stomach pings with what feels like a thousand butterflies fluttering inside.

Me: **Sure.**

Within minutes I can hear his familiar footsteps running up the stairwell and then there's a soft rap at the door. I go to it immediately, not pretending to play coy or feeling the need to make sure I look pretty enough for him.

I am who I am, and currently that's me in a navy blue Fresno State T-shirt my dad gave me that's like two sizes too big and a pair of threadbare black leggings. My hair is in a sloppy top knot and I'm not wearing a bra, since I got out of the shower recently. My face is clean too, and I was about to go to bed.

He's seen me at my worst, and he's seen me at my best, and he still hasn't left. I feel no need to try and impress him anymore.

I swing open the door to find a very attractive, slightly windblown Diego on my doorstep. He smiles when our gazes meet, and I open the door wider for him so he can walk inside.

"If you're here to see Gigi, I'm sorry, I just put her down," I tell him as I shut and lock the door.

"I'm not here to see Gigi, though I do miss my favorite girl." I turn to face him and find he's staring at me almost… hungrily. "I'm here to see you. My other favorite girl."

"Oh." My smile fades. So does his. Now he seems very, very serious. "Is everything okay?"

"Everything's pretty great. Hopefully." He rubs at the back of his neck, glancing around the room, almost as if he doesn't want to look at me. I wonder if he's…nervous?

What is going on?

"What do you mean, hopefully?" I ask.

"I mean, I hope you respond to what I'm about to say to you positively."

My stomach drops to my toes. I don't like surprise announcements. "Diego, you're scaring me."

"Good, because you scare me too. So damn much." He

takes a step forward just as I step back, my butt hitting the door. "I've missed you."

His stark admission, accompanied by his hungry gaze, makes my mouth go dry. "I-I've missed you too."

"It's been torture, these last few weeks," he admits.

I frown. Torture spending time with me?

"Being with you, and not being able to touch you. I always held myself back. I didn't want to scare you or have you reject me." His lips tilt up in this little half smile. "I don't know if my heart could take it again."

I part my lips, ready to speak, but he keeps talking.

"But I've held back long enough. Being away from you this last week has really shown me how big a part you play in my life, and how I don't ever want to lose it. Lose *you*." He crowds me, his body invading my space as he braces his hands on the door just above me. "You feel it too, right?"

My entire body starts to shake at his nearness. He's so close. I can feel his warmth radiating toward me, and I want to reach out. Touch his chest. Smooth his riotous hair away from his forehead. Pull him in close and feel his body press right next to mine.

I do none of those things. I just stare at him as if I'm frozen.

"You're leaving me hanging here, Jos." Oh, he sounds so nervous. "Do you need to hear me say I'm sorry again? Do you want me to beg for your forgiveness, for what I did to you? And to Gigi? I will. I'll apologize every single day for the rest of my life if it means I can spend my life with you."

I give in to my impulses and reach out, settling my hand in center of his chest. His heart pounds beneath my palm, and I smile at him.

But I still don't say a word.

"You're killing me," he whispers. "I want you so fucking bad. Do you know how beautiful you are right now?"

See? I don't need to pretty myself up for him. He wants me as I am.

"I'm in love with you. I've never stopped loving you, and seeing you with our daughter makes me so fucking happy, Jos. You're so strong. Nothing stops you. Not even my stupid ass."

I smile. Run my hand up his chest so I can cup his shoulder. "Keep talking."

He smiles in return, and I see a flicker of relief in his dark eyes. "You're a good mom. You're doing it all, and I feel like half the time I'm barely keeping my head above water."

"You're a good dad," I tell him. "Though I wasn't sure if you had it in you."

There's pain on his face, and I know I wounded him, but we're being completely honest right now. "It sounds like an excuse, but I didn't have a good example growing up. My family is messed up. But we're trying. You taught me a lot. How to be more patient. And kind."

"You had some of that in you already," I tell him, because I believe it. "You would just get caught up in what you believed Mateo expected from you. What your friends thought you should do. The persona you put on at school."

"Mateo did expect me to be a miniature copy of him. I thought I had no choice, and when I was younger, I really didn't. It was either act like an asshole, or get my ass beat." He shakes his head, his jaw tight, his mouth grim.

I trace my fingers along his jaw, trying to ease the tension. "This could end up being a big mistake. Us. Together. Trying it yet again."

"No way," he says firmly. "We've been through too much already and look at us. We're still standing. Here together. I'm not going anywhere, Jos, unless you tell me to leave. I want to be a part of your life. I love you. I want to take care of you and our daughter. We're in this together."

Tears start falling from my eyes and I don't bother trying to stop them. "You really love me?"

"Fuck yes, I'm in love with you. You and Gigi are the best thing that's ever happened to me. I know I've hurt you so much already, but I swear to God I will never hurt you again," he says fiercely, reaching out to wipe the streaming tears away from my cheeks. "We're going to make it, you and me. And Gigi. We belong together. You and Gabriella are mine forever, Jos."

All those old feelings, the worry over him being too needy, too much, start to fade away. He sounds so grounded and mature. Unlike the Diego of old, who would constantly tell me how much he needed me and I was his lifeline.

Those declarations scared me. Suffocated me. I loved him then, and wanted to be his girlfriend, but he expected too much from me.

"Do you mean that?" I ask, my voice low.

"Yes." He suddenly falls to one knee in front of me, grabbing my hands and holding them tight. I stare at him, dumbfounded. "I'm so fucking sorry, Jocelyn. I need your forgiveness. I was an idiot. I didn't know what I was doing, or what I wanted. I was so caught up in my own bullshit, I didn't see what I was doing to you. How much I was hurting you. You should hate me for what I did. How I used Cami, and never denied the rumors. I just let them be said and deep down, I wanted to encourage them. They put some excitement in my otherwise shit life, you know?"

Damn, the truth hurts. And I really don't want to dwell on our past right now. "I don't want to talk about this."

"We need to," he says, squeezing my hands. "Let me just get this out. I fucked up. I know I did. I hurt you, and at the time, I didn't give a shit. I was hurting all the damn time, and I thought that was normal. Lashing out was my deflection. My defense. It wasn't right. Everything I said and did to you, and to others, it wasn't right. I was wrong. I need to apologize to so many people, and I'm sure most of them won't forgive me, but I'm sorry for everything I did and said to hurt you. That's not who I am anymore. I'm not that guy. I'm different. I swear, I am."

I'm still crying, but they're tears of happiness. These are the words I longed to hear. Not just his apology, but his admittance of what he did wrong. My tears run down my face freely, dripping onto the front of my shirt, and the anguish on Diego's face at seeing them is obvious.

He rises to his feet, his brows lowered. "Please don't cry. Your tears are killing me."

"I'm sorry. I can't help it. I think I'm still hormonal." I huff out a weak laugh as I rest my hand on his chest once more, gathering the fabric of his T-shirt and pulling him closer. "I know you're different, Diego. You've changed."

He braces both hands on the door now, just above my head, his body angled toward mine. I run my hands down his sides, resting them at his hips, and I slip my fingers beneath the hem of his T-shirt to touch warm, firm skin. "For the better, I hope."

"Oh definitely." I nod. Smile. Let my hands roam up his back, as far as I can touch, before they're sliding back down again. "I'm not the same girl I was either, you know."

"I know. I love this version of you even more," he says.

"We're going to keep changing. We're still young," I remind him.

"We can grow and change together." He tilts his head to the side, his lips parting when I run both of my hands across his stomach. I can feel the muscles beneath my fingertips quiver, and I know he wants more. I want more too. "So you can touch me, but I can't touch you?"

"I never said you couldn't touch me," I whisper, my voice, my words an invitation.

He takes it, pushing into me so I'm flat against the door, his body flush with mine. He's hot and hard and I gasp when he grabs hold of me, lifting me up so I have no choice but to wrap my legs around his waist. "You want this?"

That he asks instead of just taking makes my heart soar. We've come a long way, Diego and me.

"I want *you*," I whisper, wanting him to know it's not just this.

It's him.

His mouth settles on mine. Warm and sweet and familiar, yet different. He doesn't push his tongue into my mouth, he doesn't push at all. He just kisses me, his lips meeting mine again and again, coaxing me. Drugging me. Pulling me under his spell. I go willingly, wanting more, chasing after his mouth when he pulls away. I can sense his smile, his happiness, and then his mouth returns to mine, his tongue licking at my lower lip, retreating when I try to slide my tongue against his.

He's a tease, and that's a word I would never use to describe this man kissing me now.

And that's another thing. He's not a boy anymore. He's definitely a man. We may be young and still have a lot of growing up to do, but he's come so far, and matured so much. I love this new and improved version of him.

I love the new and improved version of me too.

We kiss for what feels like hours. Staying pressed up against the door. Ignoring the notifications coming from both of our phones. The air between us becomes heated. Charged with energy and hormones. He's hard beneath his jeans, and I'm grinding against him, the friction sending sparks across my skin. I wrap my arms around his neck and tug on his hair, needing something, anything to relieve the ache inside me.

"Should I go?" he asks at one point, and I know he's joking, but I still overreact.

I pull his hair harder, making him yelp. "Absolutely not."

"You want to take this somewhere else then?" His mouth slides down my neck, hot and wet. I throw my head back, giving him better access, hissing when he uses his teeth to nibble on my sensitive skin. "Or should I fuck you against the door?"

Everything inside of me goes hot and loose at his words. I wouldn't mind if we had sex against the door but…

"I'm nervous," I admit.

He slowly pulls away, his eyes heavy-lidded, his mouth swollen from our kisses. "It's because of me, huh. You still don't trust me."

"That's not it," I say, shaking my head. "It's just—I haven't had sex since I had the baby."

He looks pleased with this confession. "Good to know."

"It's taken me a while to—recover down there," I continue, needing to be completely honest.

He frowns. "Are you okay?"

"I'm fine. I'm just—I'm a little nervous. About you. Being…" I swallow hard and tell myself to get over saying the words. We're adults now. People who share a child. "Inside me. It might hurt."

"Oh." He smiles. Leans in to drop a kiss on my jaw. "I'll be gentle," he whispers, sending shivers down my spine.

"I'm sure you will be." I rest my hands on his shoulders, tilting my head back.

"I'll kiss you everywhere. For as long as it takes." His mouth is on mine, hot and sweet, languid yet urgent. "Until you're wet for me."

"Pretty sure I already am," I admit.

He groans into my neck. "It's been so long."

"I know."

"I haven't been with anyone else. Not since Thanksgiving, with you," he confesses.

I'm shocked. I pushed him away completely. Didn't talk to him at all, and he had his chance to be with whoever he wanted. I couldn't be angry at him for it either, since I cut him off.

Yet he was with no one. And that's shocking.

"Really?" I ask.

He lifts away from me, his dark eyes sincere. "Really. You're the only one I ever want."

I shove him away from me, and he looks adorably confused. Until I take his hand and tell him, "Come on."

I lead him down the short hallway and into my bedroom. Hold my finger against my lips, tilting my head in the crib's direction and Diego nods in understanding. We switched out from the bassinet to the crib only a couple of weeks ago. He helped me put it together, and while it got a little complicated and he cursed a lot, it was still fun.

And emotional. Putting together Gigi's crib felt like a moment.

Like now. This is a moment. Of us coming together, after being apart for far too long. We had to get to know each other again. Be respectful of each other. And it was worth it. Worth every moment of longing and anger and sadness and happiness and frustration.

"I don't know if I can be quiet with you," he whispers as he yanks me into his arms.

"You'll have to." I reach for the hem of his shirt and yank it up. He withdraws from me, and gets rid of it quickly, tossing it onto the floor. I let my eyes roam all over his sculpted chest, the dark hairs curling in the center of it are new. He had a few when we were last together, but not a lot.

He looks that much more manly, and it's hot.

Without a word he pulls me back into his arms and my

hands wander all over him, testing him. Teasing him. He slips his hands under my shirt, and when he cups my bare breasts, he smiles. "No bra."

"I'm feeling reckless." It's a risk, going braless while breastfeeding. I would've put a bra on before I went to bed, just so I can contain them. I'm still a milk producing machine, and my breasts—my nipples in particular—are really sensitive.

He thumbs one and I wince. "Maybe...not so much of that."

"They're bigger, you know," he murmurs, cupping them in both of his hands.

"They should be," I tell him. "They're full of milk."

He pulls away the slightest bit, frowning. "Should I leave them alone?"

I can't help but start to laugh, resting my fingers over my lips to contain the sound. We've trained Gigi to sleep despite the everyday—or every night—noise, but I don't want to risk waking her up.

"Maybe you should. But just for now." Smiling, I rise up on my tiptoes and brush my mouth against his. "We can do plenty of other stuff."

He takes advantage of my position, sliding his hands down to my butt and gripping it in his hands. "We're going to do plenty of stuff. All the stuff."

His words are full of promise, as is the glow in his eyes. All the love he feels for me is shining from them, and my chest tightens. I don't know how we got so lucky to be given this chance. I can't even call it a second chance. Maybe it's the third? Fourth?

I don't know, but I'm not questioning it. Diego is here, in my bedroom, shirtless and staring at me as if he wants to eat me up.

And there's nowhere else I'd rather be.

CHAPTER 28

DIEGO

ocelyn is naked and spread out on the bed. I was smart for once in my life and brought a couple of condoms with me. And I plan on wearing them from the very start, too.

We're not about to go down this road again—not yet, at least.

I get rid of my shoes and jeans and underwear in a matter of minutes. Seconds even. I grab one of the condoms I stashed in the back pocket of my jeans and roll it on with shaky hands. I'm nervous. Excited. Overwhelmed.

I truly believed I wouldn't have this chance, yet here I am. The woman I love lying on a bed, naked and waiting for me.

"Diego." She whispers my name and I glance up to find her watching me, her eyes full of heat. She's positively glowing right now. Her lush, curvy body on full display. She's thinner than she was before she got pregnant, but Jocelyn was never what I'd call skinny. She has an athletic body, one that was lean with muscle in her volleyball playing days.

Now she looks a little softer. Her breasts are fuller. Her stomach isn't as flat.

She's gorgeous.

"What, babe?" I start to stroke myself, putting on a bit of a show, because she's always loved that.

Her gaze becomes hungrier, stirring something low in my gut. "You're teasing me."

"You love it."

"I do." Her expression becomes solemn. "I love you, Diego. I love you so much."

Her admission fills me with relief. She hadn't said it yet, though I believed that she did. I needed to hear the words. Don't we all?

"I love you too." I join her on the bed, climbing on top of her. She spreads her legs for me, letting me settle in between them, and I lock my eyes with her, pushing the hair out of her eyes. "So fucking much."

She smiles, arching her body beneath mine. "Show me."

Greedy, demanding Jocelyn is hot. I rise up and stroke her body with my fingers, skimming them across her breasts, her stomach. Between her legs. She spreads her thighs wider, telling me what she wants without saying a word and when I sink my fingers into her scorching hot flesh, I find that she's soaked.

She lifts her hips, not so subtly making my fingers slip. I stroke and tease, circling her clit, slipping my finger inside of her, nice and slow. I don't want to hurt her. She said she's worried and I'm not going to push. I want her ready for me.

I decide to do something about that.

My mouth follows the path my fingers took. Across her chest, her breasts. Down her stomach, lingering on the spots where she feels softer than before. She's beautiful. She'll always be beautiful to me. She gave birth to my child with this body, and that's a fucking miracle.

A soft moan escapes her when my mouth finds her pussy. I nuzzle her. Lick her. Tease her, savoring her taste. How responsive she is. I keep it light at first, not wanting to go too fast, but she grabs the back of my head and basically pushes my face into her.

I laugh, the sound muffled. I can't help it. She giggles too. Though it all stops when I draw her clit between my lips and suck it, my tongue flicking. A single *oh* falls from her lips when I slip a finger inside of her. Then another. I pump them in and out, slow at first, my tongue and mouth working her over. She moves with me, her hips shifting. Lifting. Her clit contracting beneath my lips. Her inner walls squeeze around my fingers.

She's close. I want to send her straight over the edge.

Her breathing is ragged and I can tell she's close by the way her thighs tense up. I know for a fact I can make this girl's toes curl when she comes. I've seen it happen before.

It's kind of cute. Good for the ego, that's for sure.

"Oh-ooh God. Don't stop. Right there." She grabs my head and holds me in place. I don't let up. I keep licking and sucking and fucking her with my fingers. Within seconds, she shatters beneath me, a keening wail coming from her as her entire body convulses with her orgasm.

It's only when she lets go of my hair that I can hear Gigi whimpering from her crib.

Damn.

I rise up on my elbows, still positioned between Jocelyn's legs, lifting my brows. "You woke the baby."

My erection is throbbing, eager to get inside her, but looks like we're going to be interrupted.

"Sorry. Couldn't help myself. You just gave me an amazing orgasm," she throws back at me with a grin. She's flushed and sweaty and beautiful.

"You don't sound sorry at all."

"I'm not." She gently pushes me out of the way and gets

up, walking over to the crib as naked as can be and pulling our daughter out of it. "You okay, sweetie? Are you hungry?"

I get rid of the condom in the nearby trash can and then watch in fascination as Jocelyn brings the baby back into bed with us, pulling the covers up to her lap. Gigi is clad in just a simple pink onesie and a diaper, fussing and waving her arms around as she works herself up into a cry. I readjust my position on the bed so I'm lying beside them both.

"You going to feed her?" I ask.

"Yes." Jocelyn smiles down at the baby. I don't think I've ever seen her look so happy as she does at this very moment.

"I've never seen you do that," I admit.

"I know. I was also kind of—shy about it." She sends me a look.

"I want to watch."

She laughs. "You sound like a creeper."

"Do you think I'm creepy?" God, I hope not.

"No, you're just curious. It's perfectly normal." She holds the baby to her, and Gigi's head bobs as she goes in search of Jocelyn's nipple. Jocelyn guides her, and she latches on quick, beginning to eat in earnest. I can hear her greedy little mouth sucking, and watching the two of them in the dark, Jocelyn tousled and flushed from her earlier orgasm as she feeds our daughter, it does something to me.

Makes my chest feel like it could crack wide open and my heart and blood and everything else would spill right out of me.

These two girls, they own me. They've got me on lock.

"Sorry you didn't get your turn," she tells me after a few minutes.

"Yet," I say, sounding like an arrogant ass and making Jocelyn laugh.

I lean in close, running my hand over the back of Gigi's

silky head. She opens her eyes, blinking once. Twice. It's like she realizes it's me. She lets go of Jocelyn's nipple with a popping noise, her eyes wide as she stares up at me.

Then she smiles. And I smile back.

"She knows it's you," Jocelyn whispers. "It's your daddy, isn't it? Your daddy is sharing mommy's bed, and I don't think I'm going to let him leave it for a long time. What do you think about that, huh?"

I know she's talking to Gabriella, but I decide to answer. "I'm cool with it."

Jocelyn smirks at me. "I bet you are."

I can't help but smile back.

Gigi stays up for a while, nursing and then taking a break. Nursing and then taking another break to smile and coo and flirt with me. To the point that Jocelyn accuses her of playing around and goes to set her in her crib.

She immediately starts to wail.

"Bring her to me," I say, making grabby hands for my daughter.

Jocelyn is still naked, and I can't help but give her a quick scan before I take the baby from her. "Perv," she utters, making me chuckle.

I hold Gigi to my chest, her face in mine. She drools on me. Bobs her head and nearly smashes my chin with it. She is a flailing, excitable mess and Jocelyn is a little beside herself.

"It's so late. I don't know why she won't go back to sleep."

"It's okay," I tell her. "If you're tired, go to bed. I'll hang out with Gigi for a while."

"Are you sure? I am kind of sleepy."

She'd always get sleepy after we had sex. I thought sometimes she was faking it, but I think she legit gets tired after she comes.

Kind of weird, but whatever.

My boner is long gone. I'm all about taking care of my

daughter now, and relieving Jocelyn. I decide to slide out of bed, and Jocelyn giggles sleepily. I glance over my shoulder, and she's lying on her side, the covers pulled up around her.

"What's so funny?" I ask her.

"You're naked."

"So are you."

"Do you think we're scarring her?"

"She doesn't even know we're naked. I just want her to know she's loved," I explain as I lean in and press a sloppy kiss to Gigi's cheek.

"Aw, that's the sweetest thing you could ever say." Jocelyn's pretty blue eyes are huge as she watches us. "You two look cute together."

"I should probably put on something. Here." I lay Gigi beside her on the bed. "Let me slip on my underwear."

I pull on my boxer briefs, Jocelyn blatantly watching me. We have nothing to hide now. I've bared all to her, physically and emotionally, and there's no going back. I feel the same about her. We're in this.

Together.

"Where are you two going?" she asks with a yawn when I pick Gigi up from where I left her on the bed.

"To the living room. We can hang out for a little while. Maybe I'll tire her out." Leaning down, I drop a kiss on her head. "Go to sleep, mama."

"Love you," she whispers right before I exit the bedroom. "Love you both."

"I love you too," I tell her, trying to keep my shit together.

I don't want to break down and bawl like a baby but...

I could.

* * *

Approximately ninety minutes later, I'm slipping back into Jocelyn's bed, my discarded boxer briefs on the floor, a sleeping Gigi in her crib. I scoot closer to Jocelyn, pulling her into my arms, spooning her. She wiggles against me, her ass pressing against my dick and just like that, I'm hard.

"Mmm, where's Gigi?" she asks.

I push her hair away from her neck and start kissing her there, thankful I brought a couple of condoms with me. There's one on the bedside table where I left it, ready for me to grab. Gotta make sure Jocelyn is in the mood first though. "Sleeping in her crib," I answer.

"How long was she up?"

"Over an hour." I slip my arms around her, cupping her breasts, gently brushing her hard nipples. "She was wide awake."

"What a little jerk." There's a smile in her voice when she says it, so I know she's just teasing.

"She's the cutest little jerk I know. Likes to pull hair though. That's not cool." I keep touching her, my hands sliding lower, until my fingers are between her legs, sliding into her wet heat.

Jocelyn melts into me, leaning her head back with a sigh.

"Interrupts us at the worst moments too, so mama better keep her mouth shut. No moaning or groaning for you," I tease her, smiling against her nape.

"I'll try my best," she whispers, shifting against me. "You feel so good."

"So do you."

"I've missed you so much."

"It's only been ninety minutes, tops."

"No, I mean these last few months. Practically an entire year." She turns so she's facing me, winding her arms around my neck. "You don't know how happy I am right now."

"You can feel how happy I am." I thrust my cock against her, giving her an idea.

A happy little moan escapes her just before she kisses me. It's a sloppy, dirty kiss. Full of tongue and low moans, and wandering hands. I roll her over so I'm on top of her, reaching out to grab the condom, and within seconds, I have it on, ready to thrust inside her.

Jocelyn braces her hands against my shoulders, stopping me. I hang my head to look at her. "What?"

"Gentle, remember? I'm a little nervous." She makes a cute worried face, her delicate brows furrowed, her lips formed into a pout.

I reach between us, gripping the base of my cock and dragging it up and down through her drenched folds. "I think you're going to be okay. But I'll go easy. Just relax."

"Okay." She nods, and it's like I can feel her tense up beneath me.

To cure that, I kiss her until my jaw aches. Slowly but surely pushing my cock inside her welcoming body, inch by inch. I'm impatient, eager to start pumping fast, but I take my time. Make sure she's okay. That she's ready for me.

And she is. She so is. As if she were made for me. Eventually we start to move together, finding our rhythm, the bed squeaking, but not too loud.

Not loud enough to wake up our sleeping beauty, thank God.

In the past, I always rushed through it. Eager to get to the end. Impatient when Jocelyn would tell me she needed more. More time, more foreplay, more everything. Now that she's already come, and I have to be gentle with her, I realize how good it is, to take it slow. To enjoy the ride.

Literally.

I explore her skin with my mouth. I focus on the way her heels dig into my ass when she wraps her legs around my waist. I listen to her shallow breaths, the whispery sighs, the low moans. Our skin grows damp from sweat, and the scent of sex lingers in the air.

Never really noticed any of this before, and that's a damn shame, because all of this is pretty fuckin' awesome.

Too soon I'm close. Like one firm thrust away from coming. That familiar tingling starts at the base of my spine, moving into my balls and I grunt, reaching between us and toying with her clit with slippery fingers.

"I'm gonna come," I warn her and she nods eagerly, her tits bouncing.

"I'm close too," she admits between panting breaths.

"I don't want to be gentle." I'm asking for permission without saying it.

"I'm okay," she reassures me.

I rise up on my knees and grab hold of her waist, thrusting in earnest. Glancing down, I watch my cock enter her body. In and out, in and out, and I throw my head back when I push in deep, so deep, I can feel her inner walls squeeze around my dick.

Wrenching the orgasm right out of me.

I come with her name falling from my lips, and I can feel her quivering beneath me as another orgasm washes over her. My entire body is vibrating, and when I collapse on top of her, completely exhausted, I feel her arms come around me, her hands on my back, her nails skimming my skin.

Making me shiver.

"That felt like a long time coming," she whispers a few seconds later.

"Literally," I say, making her laugh.

"Will you stay the night?"

"You don't even have to ask." I lift away from her so I can stare at her pretty face. Her eyes are open, and they are sparkling. She's glowing. Smiling. Absently touching my hair, my temple, my cheek.

"I love you," she whispers.

"I never stopped loving you," I admit.

"We're going to make this work, aren't we?" she asks with a grin.

"Fuck yeah, we are," I say vehemently, making her laugh.

"Fuck yeah, we are," she repeats.

Right before she kisses me.

EPILOGUE

JOCELYN

I'm at a Bulldogs playoff game on a cold Saturday night, sitting in the suite reserved for players' family and close friends. Somehow, word got out that Diego is a father, and despite his not playing much this season, the coach offered me and a couple of my friends tickets to sit in the suite and watch the game.

Of course, I didn't say no.

I've got Gigi in my arms, wrapped up in a blanket and clad in a fuzzy gray and white sleeper that has a hood with ears on it. With the hood on, she looks like a koala bear. Ava and Ellie came with me, and Ava's excited because we're winning by a landslide and Eli is actually running out onto the field. He was able to keep his number one jersey, and Ava is currently wearing a #1 pendant on the thin gold chain around her neck.

Swear to God, Eli Bennett has the biggest ego I've ever seen, but he embraces it wholeheartedly, and isn't ashamed of it either. Ava seems to love it. Whatever works for them. They're totally adorable together.

And then there's poor Ellie, who would do anything for

Jackson Rivers, despite how much he ignores her. The guy is a complete idiot. He's either blind to her adoration, or he doesn't give a shit.

I'm hoping for the former.

Caleb is going through every girl on campus he can find, discarding them like Kleenex once he's done. He just smiles and puts on the charm, and they all forgive him.

I get it. He's very charming. I adore him. And surprisingly enough, he's very good with Gigi. He holds her every chance he gets, and she slaps his face and smiles at him the entire time.

Even my daughter has fallen under his spell. I like the fact that she hits him though. That's the kind of girl he needs. One who thinks he's amazing, yet won't take his shit.

"Oh my God, Diego's going out there too!" Ava grips my arm, bouncing in her seat.

I glance toward the field to see Diego running out there, and the offense forms into a huddle. My stomach starts bouncing and I regret the giant plate of nachos I ate earlier.

Seriously hope I don't throw up.

"I can't believe they're playing," Ava says. "Eli's been waiting for this since the first day of practice."

"So has Diego," I admit.

They haven't got much field time, and it makes the two of them go out of their mind with frustration. They understand why, but they don't like it. The first-string team is mostly seniors, with a few juniors thrown in here and there, including the one and only Kevin. I tell Diego this means he'll get his chance sooner than he thinks, he just has to prove himself once he gets the chance.

Looks like tonight is his chance.

Oh and Kevin? He's become friends with Diego. He's also found a really sweet girl named Mari and they've started dating. Kevin even suggested to Diego we should double date sometime.

Diego and I agreed. Why not? I was never interested in Kevin, not like that. He's a nice guy.

And I love that Diego isn't jealous of him.

Ellie takes Gigi and walks her around the suite while Ava and I concentrate on the game. Eli throws one play out of bounds. The next one, a tight end catches it and runs for a few yards. There's a first down. A near interception that has the entire stadium expressing their disappointment loudly.

Ava makes a face. "If he threw an interception, he'd beat himself up for the rest of the night."

I'm sure he would.

Finally, the stars align. Eli's arm is poised, and he throws the ball. Diego is running. Running and running, glancing over his shoulder, his hands coming together, ready to catch. The ball falls into his open palms and he tucks it under his arm, sprinting toward the end zone.

"Holy shit!" I scream, jumping up and down. Ava is right there with me, clutching my arm, screaming excitedly. Other people in the suite are also yelling their encouragement, some of them laughing at us, but I don't care.

I'm too excited for Diego and this play.

He crosses over the end zone just in time. He's tackled, brought to the ground, but the referees have their arms above their heads, signaling for a touchdown.

And Diego made it.

"Oh my God, did you see that?" Ava turns to face me, hauling me in for a tight hug. She's rocking me back and forth and we're both laughing, blubbering like idiots. When I finally pull away, I see that she has tears shining in her eyes and surprisingly…

So do I.

"Why are you crying?" I ask, wiping away the tears from my cheeks.

"I'm just so happy for Eli. He's been wanting this moment for so long." She sniffs loudly. Rubs her knuckles beneath her eyes. "Why are you crying?"

"Diego has been waiting for this moment too." He's wanted it so bad. He just wants to prove himself to someone, and while they were already going to win no matter what, it must feel good to put a score on the board. To know they were responsible for it.

"Well, they did it," Ava says, smiling. "And they did it together. Who knew this would happen?"

I sort of sensed it would. It makes sense. Eli is Diego's quarterback now, and I know it bothers him, because he's not the biggest fan of Bennett, but he told me he would be professional no matter what, and put his personal feelings aside.

Diego has made such tremendous gains in so many ways. He has a relationship with his mother again. The three of us go over to her house for dinner. Or we'll go to my parents' house for dinner, too. My mother loves him. My dad is still a little skeptical, but a lot better than he was.

We're all getting along for the most part, especially Diego and I. I sometimes want to pinch myself, I'm so surprised that we've been able to make this work. I never thought we could. I thought we were done. Destroyed.

Guess I was wrong.

And I've never been happier to admit my mistake in my life.

Diego

. . .

I AM ON A HIGH, and it cannot be contained. I'm grinning from ear to ear, slapping hands as they're offered to me in the locker room. We won. We knew we were going to win, so that was a given.

But Eli and I went out onto the field and made the magic happen. The magic I only thought occurred between Jake and me. The magic I thought was maybe a fluke. Maybe it was only because Jake was so damn good, and I was the lucky bastard he threw the ball to.

I don't believe that anymore. I am part of the magic, and it looks like Eli Bennett and I are a good fit.

Never thought I'd say this, but that asshole can throw the ball pretty fuckin' far. And he's decently accurate. He's no Jake Callahan or Ash Davis, but he'll do.

"Good job tonight," Ash tells me as I approach him. "I remember you in high school. You were good then. You're even better now."

I beam, basking in his praise. "Thanks man. You're fucking amazing."

Ash laughs. "You should come over for Thanksgiving at the Callahans and play football with us. Talk about fucking amazing. Drew plays, and so does his brother-in-law, Owen Maguire."

I've heard about these legendary football games on Thanksgiving, and have always wanted to play, but never wanted to intrude or invite myself. "That sounds awesome."

"It is awesome. Talk to Jake. I'm sure he'd love for you to be there. Bennett will be there too. It'll be his second one." Ash grins as Eli joins our conversation. "Held your own tonight, didn't you?"

"Fuck yeah, I did." They slap hands in an easy bro shake

before Eli turns his attention on me. "Garcia. You can run as fast as a motherfucker. I didn't know you had it in you."

"That's because you were too busy running your mouth to pay attention to what we were actually doing on the field," I tell him, smiling. "Kidding man. You made it easy for me to catch that ball."

"Yeah, well I had nothing to do with you running it in, so good job."

It's just one big dick stroke right now, and I'm eagerly participating. It feels good, being on top. Knowing that you contributed. After sitting on the sidelines for practically the entire season, to be given a chance and to make something of it…

I'm on top of the world.

We wrap it up in the locker room and then I'm walking out, flanked by Eli and Caleb. Tony bolted the second the game was over, so I have no idea where he's at. Not sure where Jackson is either. He might be with Tony.

Whatever.

"So does this mean we're friends now?" Eli asks me and Caleb.

"I don't know if I would call us friends," I start, though I'm just giving him shit.

"Come on, Big D. Lighten the fuck up," Caleb says, slapping me on the back and making me nearly trip. "Eli's not so bad."

"It's good ol' Big D who's the nightmare." Eli shakes his head, laughing. "What a fuckin' great nickname. I'm actually jealous."

"It's not always the greatest nickname. Sometimes I am a complete dick." Not so much anymore now though.

And the reason for that is standing about thirty feet in front of us. My two girls are waiting, both of them appearing happy to see me.

Jocelyn's smiling from ear to ear as I make my approach, and Gigi is bouncing in her arms, as if she's ready to launch herself right at me. She's wearing the cutest fuzzy suit that makes her look like a little bear, and she's reaching for me, her tiny hands opening and closing when I take her from Jocelyn.

"Hey," I tell her, wrapping my arm around Jocelyn's waist as I pull her in close, Gigi clutched in my other arm as I hold her tight. "Sorry to make you wait."

"You did so good tonight," Jocelyn says, rising up to press a kiss to my cheek. "I'm so proud of you."

"Thanks baby." I drop a kiss on her forehead before we both turn our attention to Gigi. "How's this little girl holding up?"

"I think she's tired." She reaches out and brushes her thumb against Gabriella's cheek. "You had fun tonight watching Daddy play though, didn't you?"

Gigi bounces and gurgles in answer.

I get that familiar tight feeling in my chest, the one that tells me my heart is ready to make its escape. I tell it to settle the hell down, it's not going anywhere. I've got everything I need, right here, both of my girls in my arms.

I'm the luckiest son of a bitch alive.

And I know it.

* * *

The next book in the Callahans series is Making Her Mine, featuring the baby of the family, Beck Callahan!

* * *

Check out Tony Sorrento's story in The Freshman, the first book in College Years series! Keep reading for a sneak peek!

THE FRESHMAN

CHAPTER ONE

Tony

There's a pretty girl staring at me.

I pretend I don't notice, keeping my head down, my focus on the phone clutched in my hands. I'm absently scrolling through Instagram, bored out of my skull while stuck in the waiting area at the Range Rover dealership in San Francisco, dreading the upcoming visit with my dad. My parents divorced when I was twelve, and Dad up and disappeared, moving to San Francisco so he could be closer to his business.

And his then new mistress.

That mistress eventually turned into his second wife, she gave birth to twin girls almost two years ago, and Dad forgot all about me. Until I turned eighteen and he decided he wanted to take me under his wing and turn me into his new protégé. I've resisted as much as I can, but it's tough. He's persistent.

I haven't met my stepmom or my half-sisters yet, but that's all happening today.

Good times.

Not really looking forward to meeting the new fam, but I was coming here anyway to get my car serviced. My father knew—I'm guessing the dealership informed him of the recall issue, and now here I am.

Yes, my father basically abandoned me, but he still gets me a new car once a year, which means this is my third car since I turned sixteen. Fucking ridiculous, right? He's a rich bastard and he spoils the hell out of me with materialistic things and plenty of cash, as if that might make up for his constant neglect over the last six years.

But anyway.

Fuck thinking about my dad. I'd rather focus on the girl.

As sly as possible, I slowly glance up, my gaze meeting hers for the quickest second before she dips her head, a tiny smile curving her lush pink lips. I look away, too, gazing through the window at the bright blue sky outside. Not a cloud in sight. It's still pretty early in the day. I rolled out of bed first thing in the morning and hopped in the car, driving straight here, cursing at the traffic the entire drive.

I'd never want to live in the Bay Area, I know that for certain. I'm used to our small town and the fresh mountain air. The complete lack of traffic. How everyone knows everyone else—

Wait. That's not such a great thing. When everyone knows each other, they're all up in your business. Like when your parents get a divorce. Or you and your girl break up seemingly out of nowhere.

That part sucks.

My gaze, once again, slides to the girl, like I can't help myself. She's sitting in an overstuffed chair across from me. Her teeth are sunk into her plump lower lip, her brows furrowed as she concentrates on whatever is happening on her phone. There's a white Chanel bag sitting by her side. Golden Goose shoes on her feet. They're scuffed and kind of dirty, which is what they're supposed to look like, despite costing around five hundred bucks.

I don't get the appeal.

That I know these things is telling. Mom isn't around much, but when she is, she's got the jumbo Chanel, the multiple pairs of Golden Goose—she's trying to appear youthful, she says—and she's always dripping in Van Cleef jewelry. Mom is a self-proclaimed designer brand whore, and she stands out like a sore thumb in our small town during the winter months. In the summer when all the tourists descend, she fits right in. Mostly.

I check the pretty girl's wrist and yep, she's got a Van Cleef bracelet clasped around it. Of course she does.

This girl is from money. My mother would probably love her.

I check her out in bits and pieces. Long, tanned legs. Black shorts that ride up, showing off her sleek thighs. A plain white T-shirt that probably costs hundreds of dollars. A bunch of delicate gold chains around her neck, some unadorned, others with tiny charms and pendants. One is a string of scattered stars.

This girl is trendy AF.

I can tell she's still staring at her phone, occasionally tapping at it as if she's sending an urgent text, and I keep my gaze away from her face on purpose. I'm not ready to look at it again. Not yet. What if I'm wrong? What if she's not as hot as I first thought? Not like anything's going to happen anyway. She's some rich girl who probably lives in Pacific Heights or Nob Hill. For all I know she could be my dad's neighbor. She's probably a spoiled brat who'll make my life a living hell just for trying to talk to her.

Forget it.

I shift in my seat, holding back the sigh that wants to escape as I return my attention to Instagram.

"Car trouble?"

Her sweet voice makes my head jerk up to find she's already watching me, her blue eyes wide and questioning. I wasn't mistaken in my first assessment of her.

She's hot AF. I can't even tell you which feature of hers is the most prominent or is the prettiest. She's just flat-out gorgeous everywhere I look. I stare at her for a moment, caught up in the shape of her lips before I realize I need to stop looking like a dumb shit and actually say something.

"No. Brought it in to fix a recall issue and get my back windows tinted," I tell her, tilting my head to the side as I contemplate her. She watches me just as boldly, not backing down, not looking away or giggling or being overly coy and flirtatious. Seemingly nothing manufactured or phony about her, which I appreciate. I figured she *would* be phony, with her trendy clothes and expensive accessories.

Girls can't be trusted. They'll stomp all over your heart if you give it to them, and then walk away like you never mattered. Happened to me before. It's happened to me practically my entire life, and not just with girls. My ex-girlfriend left me because dance was more important to her than me. I try to show interest in other girls, but they all blow me off.

Then there's my family. Dad left me because new pussy was more important. Mom left me every week when I was in high school, out looking for someone new. Something better.

Better than her old life and her son.

"How about you?" I ask when she hasn't responded.

"The recall issue." She shifts her legs, uncrossing and then recrossing them, and my gaze drops, taking them in yet again. They're long and slender and conjure up all sorts of dirty thoughts. I wonder how tall she is. "My father wanted to buy me a new one but I've only had this one for six months. I thought that was a bit—excessive."

"Sounds like we might share the same father." Mine had

mentioned something similar to me when I let him know about the recall notice. I told him that was ridiculous. I've only had the car for a couple of months.

Her brows shoot up. "I certainly hope not."

Huh. Is she flirting with me? I've been off girls since midway through senior year in high school so maybe I'm out of touch. Well, not *totally* off girls. I hooked up with a couple of Italian hotties when I went to Europe over the summer. I accompanied my mom to visit her family who still lives over there. My cousin Sergio would take me out every night, and we'd get blindingly drunk. I'd kissed a pretty Italian girl. I kissed quite a few. Felt them up. On the rare occasion, I'd even get a blow job.

I had a good time in Europe. The best part? No expectations, no strings attached. Plus, I'd never see them again.

"I don't have any long-lost siblings," she continues. "Though I wouldn't put it past my father if some turned up."

She smiles. I smile too.

"What's your name?" I ask her, because fuck it. If I can flirt with a girl at the Range Rover dealership to pass the time, I may as well go all in.

"Hayden." She tucks a strand of blonde hair behind her ear. I'm a sucker for a blonde. Always have been. "What's yours?"

"Tony." I offer up a closed-lipped smile.

She does the same.

"Well, Tony, are you in college?"

I nod. Squirm in my seat a little. This girl will lose interest when she finds out where I go. She probably attends Stanford. Or Berkeley. She's probably smart as hell and a complete overachiever. "Yeah. You?"

A little laugh escapes her, and it's a sweet, tinkling sound. "Yes. Where do you go?"

May as well be upfront. Again, this is all happening at a

dealership in a city I don't live in. I've got nothing to lose. "Fresno State."

Her mouth pops open. "No way," she breathes, sitting up straighter, her hand going to her chest. "I do too!"

"You do not." I chuckle, shaking my head. She has to be playing me.

"I so do! They have a great liberal arts program. I want to be a teacher, much to my father's dismay." She laughs again, a little louder this time, but I see the hurt that flashes in her eyes.

She hates that her father is disappointed in her future career choice. I feel this. I really do.

"What about you? Why are you going to Fresno State?" she asks.

"I grew up near there." I shrug. "A lot of my friends chose Fresno State, so I did too." Not the greatest answer, but it's the truth.

I knew I wanted to go to college, but I never really wanted to go somewhere far, and I had no idea what I wanted to major in. I finally found my core group of friends in high school, so why would I want to leave that? Completely immature thought process, but fuck it. I like my comfort, and currently, I find comfort in my friends.

Family dumps you. Girls do too. Friends don't. Bros stick by you no matter what.

Thankfully, a few of my friends got into Fresno State, like I did. And I've made new friends too.

"What's your major?" Hayden asks, pulling me from my thoughts.

"Business." It was the most neutral major that appealed to me, and what do you know, it made my father happy when he found out. Not that I particularly want to, but eventually, I'm sure I'll be working alongside my father, cutting ruthless business deals and buying up real estate all over the Bay Area.

That's why I need to focus on having fun in college now, because all the fun is going to evaporate from my life in approximately four years. You're only in college once. I need to make the best of it.

"Do you know what you want to be when you grow up?" Her eyes are dancing when she asks the question, and I like how direct she is. How confident she seems.

This girl seems like she has her shit together. No "poor little rich girl" vibes coming from her.

"Not sure yet," I say with another shrug, slouching in my chair. Trying for nonchalance. Like it's no big deal that I'm having a conversation with the hottest girl I've met in a long ass time.

"Are you from around here then? No, wait, you said you grew up near Fresno." She frowns. "They have a small Range Rover dealer there. Why are you here?"

"Their service department is booked out for weeks, and I didn't want to wait any longer on the tinted windows." Dad bought me the Range Rover as a belated graduation gift, bestowing it upon me right before I started college. Considering the gorgeous and very expensive vehicle ends up sitting in a parking lot most of the time, baking under the hot sun, I quickly decided I needed all the windows tinted to help keep the inside cool.

"Ah, that makes sense. And while it's here, may as well get the recall work done, right?" I nod. She smiles. "I'm visiting my dad for the weekend. He wanted family time, as he calls it. His girlfriend is only seven years older than I am."

Hayden rolls her eyes and I can't help but laugh.

"My stepmom is thirty," I tell her with a chuckle.

"I don't understand why they always trade in for a newer

model," she says. "Though my mom eventually did the same thing."

"My mom swears she'll never get married again. Says my father turned her against love," I say, hating the flash of sympathy I see reflected in Hayden's gaze.

Maybe I said too much.

"Love is for pussies," she says with confidence. An older woman sitting nearby shoots her a dirty look and the smile teasing the corners of Hayden's mouth makes me smile in return. She probably enjoyed shocking that old lady. "It's true and you know it."

"It is true." My ex-girlfriend Sophie stomped all over my heart and left it a bleeding mess right before she left our high school for good and went to a performing arts school up in the mountains near San Diego. Last I heard, she was in the dance program at USC, where my best friend Jake goes. He actually ran into her recently and called to tell me all about it.

Made me feel like shit, but I had to pretend his seeing Sophie didn't bother me. It sucks when you realize people always eventually leave you. Hell, in a way Jake did too, though of course he left to go play football for USC, and I don't blame him. We got a lot closer senior year and now he's gone. I've learned a lesson from all of this, one I'll never forget.

Everyone leaves.

"So you're spending your Saturday here at the dealer, huh?" she asks.

It's a bye week at home, so no football game tonight. Not like I'd get a chance to play anyway. I rarely do. "Yeah. Hasn't been too bad though."

She grins. I grin back.

"What are you doing afterwards?"

My smile fades. "I have a get-together thing my dad wants me to attend tonight."

That is the last thing I want to do. Especially now, when I have a much more interesting prospect sitting in front of me.

Her smile disappears too, replaced with a frown. "Yeah, you know, I have something too."

This hot girl was going to ask me out. I could feel it. And that gives me the confidence to ask, "Can I get your number? Maybe we can get together sometime in Fresno."

Can't believe I never noticed her on campus before, though I guess it's not a surprise. It's a huge campus. We all sort of seem to take the same general ed classes at the same time, though, but maybe her schedule is totally different because of her major.

"Sounds good." She lifts her phone and starts tapping. "Why don't you give me your number first."

I rattle it off and she types it in her phone, my phone buzzing immediately with her simple response of *hi*. "I'll text you for real early next week."

I smile. "I'll hold you to it."

"Oh I will." Her eyes are sparkling.

I could stare at her all damn day.

We make small talk for a few minutes more, until one of the service advisers enters the waiting room and approaches her, letting her know her car is ready. She rises to her feet, slinging her Chanel bag over her shoulder, and she stops by my chair. The service adviser waits for her nearby, his impatience obvious.

"It was nice meeting you, Tony." She touches me on the shoulder, very lightly.

I feel that touch sink all the way to my balls.

"Nice meeting you too, Hayden," I say, my voice even. I sound normal. I bet I even look normal.

Inside, I'm anything but. This girl is hot. Interesting. Confident. For the first time in a while, I'm intrigued.

I want more.

ACKNOWLEDGMENTS

First, a big HUGE thank you to Jan for making this book happen. We owe it all to her - I had zero plans to give Diego and Jocelyn a book. Diego was the villain in Falling For Her. He was AWFUL. Mad at the world and everyone else in it. No way did I want to redeem that guy.

But Jan pushed for it. She mentioned a Diego book in my **reader group** and people said they actually wanted it. I was shocked. And intrigued. Maybe I should write their book after all…

So I did. And here it is. I'll be honest - I went into writing this with mixed feelings about Diego, but when I finished, I loved him. I still love him, and Jocelyn and their little family. I love ALL the characters in this book, and in the entire Callahan series. I'm so excited a spinoff series is happening, featuring the rest of the characters in this series (Tony's book is next!). I hope you're excited too.

As usual, I want to thank all the people at Valentine PR - Nina, Casie, Megan and Daisy especially. I want to give a shout out to my reader group for their never-ending enthusiasm. And I want to thank all the readers, reviewers, and bloggers for taking a chance on my books. I appreciate you all more than you'll ever know.

It would mean everything to me if you could take a few moments and leave an honest review for **Fighting For You.** Thank you.

THE PLAYERS

Playing Hard to Get

Playing by The Rules

Playing to Win

WEDDED BLISS (LANCASTER)

The Reluctant Bride

The Ruthless Groom

The Reckless Union

The Arranged Marriage boxset

COLLEGE YEARS

The Freshman

The Sophomore

The Junior

The Senior

DATING SERIES

Save The Date

Fake Date

Holidate

Hate to Date You

Rate A Date

Wedding Date

Blind Date

Never Let You Go

THE RULES SERIES

Fair Game

In The Dark

Slow Play

Safe Bet

THE FOWLER SISTERS SERIES

Owning Violet

Stealing Rose

Taming Lily

REVERIE SERIES

His Reverie

Her Destiny

BILLIONAIRE BACHELORS CLUB SERIES

Crave

Torn

Savor

Intoxicated

ONE WEEK GIRLFRIEND SERIES

One Week Girlfriend

Second Chance Boyfriend

Three Broken Promises

Drew + Fable Forever

Four Years Later

Five Days Until You

A Drew + Fable Christmas

STANDALONE YA TITLES

Daring The Bad Boy

Saving It

Pretty Dead Girls

ABOUT THE AUTHOR

Monica Murphy is a New York Times, USA Today and international bestselling author. Her books have been translated in almost a dozen languages and have sold millions of copies worldwide. Both a traditionally published and independently published author, she writes young adult and new adult romance, as well as contemporary romance.

facebook.com/MonicaMurphyAuthor

instagram.com/monicamurphyauthor

bookbub.com/profile/monica-murphy

goodreads.com/monicamurphyauthor

amazon.com/Monica-Murphy/e/B00AVPYIGG

pinterest.com/msmonicamurphy

tiktok.com/@monicamurphyauthor